THE BOTTICELLI AFFAIR

TRACI L. SLATTON

parvati
press

This book is a work of fiction. Names, characters, places and incidents are either the product of the author's imagination or are used fictitiously. Any resemblance to actual persons, living or dead, or to actual events or locales is entirely coincidental.

The Botticelli Affair

Cover designed by Blacksheep Design-UK
http://www.blacksheet-uk.com

Cover art:
Copyright © Getty - 108150195 - Main Image; 83515123 - Picture Frame
Copyright © SuperStock - 1746-3233 - Botticelli Painting

Published by Parvati Press
http://www.parvatipress.com

Digital design by Telemachus Press, LLC
http://www.telemachuspress.com

Visit the author website:
http://www.tracilslatton.com

ISBN 978-1-935670-86-5 (eBook)
ISBN 978-0-9890232-3-8 (Paperback)

Version 2011.07.20

Printed in the United States of America
10 9 8 7 6 5 4 3 2 1

Books by Traci L. Slatton

Immortal

The Botticelli Affair

Fallen

Cold Light

Far Shore

The Love of My (Other) Life

Dancing in the Tabernacle (poetry)

Piercing Time & Space

El Inmortal

Caido

The Art of Life (with Sabin Howard)

To

Sweet Naomi Hendel, the Number 1 fan of all things vampire

and to

Julia Howard
Jessica Hendel
Madeleine Howard
and
Sabin Howard

Of whom I am a fan

PROLOGUE

Evening was voluptuous, filled to bursting with good and evil, for the one who listened.

Let's take him during the night, get his daughter to find it for us!

Their proposal was a whispered chord, a call through the ether to others of their kind. They could link minds this way, after feeding as a group, which let them join consciousnesses and broadcast a message. Feasting together made them powerful, heightened their senses. Would they know he was there, Bolingbroke wondered, standing in the shadows, listening? He who no longer was like them, but also was not unlike them?

John Bolingbroke no longer knew what, exactly, he was. He used to be just like *them*, the coven he now watched. In fact, he was only half different from them. He still possessed all the same seething dark passions. He still experienced blood lust in all its tender ferocity. His senses still took in a welter of information that no human could possibly understand. Nor did he age. He looked exactly as he had in July, 1483, more than five hundred years ago, when he was last human.

But Bolingbroke no longer had to feed on a living vein. Nor was he required to avoid the sun. He had a heartbeat, he had yearnings for love, his chest burned not just with desire but also with loss and anguish, just as humans felt. But he was no longer human, just as he was no longer vampire.

Fifty years ago, a whimsical god granted him half a soul and bestowed upon him unruly, inescapable powers. Bolingbroke had a capacity to astral-project out of his body, a capacity that neither humans nor vampires possessed. He could see the protean umbra of spirit infusing and spilling around living things. And he could overhear vampires' world-spanning telepathic calls. Bolingbroke was changed. He was gifted and tormented. He was alone. His exquisite clairvoyance showed him how different he was from all others. Now, spying on the coven to which he had once belonged, he wondered if his half-soul would expose him to them. If it did, would they kill him? Could they?

No, they would not discover him. The cool damp basement stone of the Metropolitan Museum of Art shielded him from their perception. The hum and patter of hundreds of humans overhead also helped. All those living, pulsing heartbeats were far more interesting to vampires than a halfling—half-undead, half-alive—with no coven or station of his own. John Bolingbroke was on his own, the ultimate outsider.

He preferred it that way. He liked freedom.

The vampires were gathered in a circle at the center of the cavernous space. They were a coven, eleven, and an elder coven at that. Vampires formed and re-formed themselves into groups, according to their shifting whims, but certain covens stuck, even when individual members had intertwined into dozens of other side alliances. This coven was old, powerful, and vicious. Bolingbroke distrusted them. He watched them both because he didn't know what they would do to him if they discovered his differentness, and because he had promised humans that he would spy for them. Bolingbroke kept his promises. That was a matter of honor, and honor was his existence.

Bolingbroke liked humans. For the first hundred years, he did what every vampire does: used, ravished, and carelessly murdered humans for their delicious hot wetness. Then it all changed. Bolingbroke remembered the exact moment when the value of humanity broke across his cold undead mind: December 25, 1652, in the church of Santa Maria della Vittoria in Rome. He had followed a young prostitute into the church. She had stumbled in from the cold, stealing a moment for a Christmas prayer between customers. Bolingbroke wasn't able to feed on her in church, of course. The sanctity of the space almost paralyzed him. He intended to follow her back out to the Tiber's cold auspices, where he would feast on her. Why not? She held her life in such little esteem that she would sell herself into the most degrading acts. Bolingbroke offered her an escape from that, an exit during which she would redeem herself by nourishing him.

First he stared at her silky black hair swinging over her shoulders under a white mantello, her cloak. Then his eyes turned toward the altar.

But it wasn't an altar he saw. It was Bernini's masterpiece: the ecstasy of St. Teresa. Teresa's beautiful face was thrown back in bliss conjoined with pain, a look that Bolingbroke knew well: that shattering moment when the supernatural intrudes on earthly flesh, when earth and not-of-this-earth meet. Bolingbroke had seen it on the faces of his entrees as he drained the jugular. His preternatural sucking elicited a tremor of agonized pleasure through a human's circulatory system. That tremor rippled through the fascia, through muscles and nerves and deep into the spinal cord. Bolingbroke never understood it, the ecstasy of being pierced. He recognized it, though. And here it was on this exquisite marble face.

How was it possible for a mere human to know this expression? And to know it so intimately, so precisely?

How was it possible for a mere human to render this expression in lifeless stone?

What kind of mastery was this, that a vampire could not begin to attain? Because a vampire could create this image in flesh for only a moment or two, while Bernini had created it for as long as stone endured.

Bernini, that weak human, was victorious.

In comparison, the immortality of vampires was emptied of its meaning.

Struck with wonder, Bolingbroke staggered back. He asked himself what his time on Earth meant. He found himself sitting on a pew, staring. He could not look away from the cherub with his arrow pointed into Teresa's core. The prostitute left the church. Mass rose and fell. The sacred liturgy enervated vampires, and Bolingbroke was weakened, but he could not leave. He kept staring, staring, would have wept if he could have. But vampires did not have tears.

That was the moment that inspired his appreciation for the frail beings who did not know that they were not alone upon the earth, but were stalked by stronger, remorseless predators. Predators who were physically stronger but devoid of true mastery. True mastery entailed creativity, the power to make art that could give the viewer an experience of revealed truth. Bolingbroke, from the moment he laid eyes on St. Teresa's ecstatic face, hungered for that power, that mastery. It fired his quest to return to human, a quest which had come to partial fruition, and a total dead end, fifty years ago....

Now, in the present, underneath the Metropolitan Museum of Art, they heedlessly tossed an object to the side. It landed near Bolingbroke. The sick earth scent and flailing limbs identified the object as a dead human. A woman: young, pretty. She was pale now, her lovely face still twisted in rapture. This old coven—Intihuaca, the leader, was an Inca from Pre-Columbian Mexico—had drained her. They had shared her blood so they could participate in a telepathic call.

This planning made Bolingbroke even more uneasy; vampires were coordinating around the world. That meant danger.

Let's kill him now!

This call came from a distant coven, and Bolingbroke heard it as if he were still a vampire. He didn't need to feast with the others. He could simply receive the message.

Wait, it is not time to act on our plan.... The call was answered by Intihuaca, whose great age and cunning were respected by vampires around the world.

"Perhaps he'll have the painting soon, and we can proceed?" whispered the youngest vampire, a small female with a mass of raven hair. She was birthed in the last century, but had already maneuvered her way into this powerful coven. She was sly, covetous, relentless, remorseless, cold to the suffering of other creatures: all the qualities Bolingbroke hated most in vampires. And in himself, when he'd been one. She had taken his place, in fact. She was welcome to it, but she bore watching. He recalled her name: Kadja.

Intihuaca grunted. "He may have come to an impasse. That's the reason for the call. But the pieces are not in place to make the time ripe for our plan."

"You're right. We shouldn't take him too soon, as bitter a blow as it would be to his group." The female smiled. "He may yet obtain the painting. Let's take his daughter."

"We wait and watch, and gather information." Intihuaca shrugged. "We could use her as incentive. Though he has severed relations, so perhaps he doesn't care anymore."

"He cares. Fathers always do. Human fathers." The female chuckled softly. "Laila Cambridge matters to her father. He will protect her at all costs. I say we take her now."

Bolingbroke stilled his indrawn breath. He knew the woman they meant, Laila Cambridge.

Intihuaca considered. "Not yet. We watch her; we know where she is. She also knows the world wherein we seek the painting. If he fails, she will succeed."

Bolingbroke had watched Laila for the last decade. Initially, her work had brought her to his attention. Her clever way with a paintbrush reminded him of an old friend, Michelangelo Buonnaroti. Bolingbroke had admired Laila's work, back when she was painting. Now he respected her determination to make something new of herself, something better. He identified with the impulse.

He had also worked with Laila's father, admired the man's passion to protect his kind. And through him, Bolingbroke had come to know Laila as a young woman of substance and character. He'd promised Robert he'd protect Laila.

The question was, could he keep that promise, if the coven wanted to use her?

Chapter 1

I SAT IN MY FAVORITE BAR ON West 23rd Street and Tenth Avenue, checking out the hottie as he walked in and seated himself near me. I'd come here to look over my books and think about my dissertation. At least, that's what I told myself—though lately I'd been wondering whether I just came here to drink. Columbia University had good places to look at books and this bar was located far from them.

And then in strode Tall, Dark and Good-Looking, and the angles of his face fascinated me. I forgot the book on the counter.

He noticed it, though. I have to give him credit, he seemed to notice the paintings before he fixed on my tall-with-lots-of-red-hair-and-boobs thing. Good man.

"Botticelli? You're a painter?" he asked.

"Not anymore," I said. And wouldn't it solve some problems if I still were? "The Botticelli book is for research. I'm getting my doctorate in art history."

"Impressive. The book's in Italian, you speak the language?" he asked.

"Where are you from?" I responded. A blunt non-sequitur, but it changed the subject.

"Italy, originally." His eyes crinkled at the corners as if he were trying not to smile at my suave confrontational style.

"That's not an Italian accent." With diplomat parents, I had traveled the world. Picked up a bunch of languages along the way, too. It was useful for an art history doctoral student to have that kind of fluency, though it had been useful in my former profession, too.

"I've passed through many other places since then," he said, tilting his head in a way that smoothed the craggy edges of his features and gave him an aristocratic bearing. It also made him look familiar.

"Do I know you?"

"Not yet." He smiled, and I decided he was way too good-looking in a high-cheekboned, rough-hewn, barbarian way for me to let any chemistry progress. No more handsome men for me. "What's your interest in Botticelli?"

"I'm writing about him," I said, then grimaced. I was blocked, had been for months, and it was derailing my career as an art history professor. A career I was convinced would redeem me of my past sins. If anything could. "Trying to." I sipped my drink and looked at him out of the corner of my eye. Wavy dark hair cut close to his head, broad shoulders held very erect, and, if I was guesstimating right, about four inches taller than me. He was *way* hot. I knew I shouldn't go down this road, but I took off the horn rims I wear around to discourage random interest. The flame-haired, bosomy thing I've got going, silly as it is, tends to act like an advertisement even when it isn't. I inquired hopefully, "You like Renaissance art?"

"I prefer the modern painters. I'm partial to de Kooning, the raw expression of the artist's individual character, not masked by technique." He smiled.

"Not masked by technique? It could use some masking. That stuff's ugly crap!" I cried. Usually I'm more tactful when someone mentions their preference for twentieth century art. I mumble something sympathetic and then try to sell them a canvas stuck in the back of my closet that looks like a Richard Diebenkorn, from the early period, when he was still aping Bonnard. Only an expert with the finest eye could tell them apart.

"You don't approve of the primal energy, the savagely applied pigments, the underlying shiver and delicious terror of sexual compulsion?" he asked. He was looking at my mouth. I felt myself flushing. He saw the color and smiled, the kind of lazy, knowing grin a man gives a woman when he's lying on his back in bed. All my worries faded and I found myself entirely in the moment, and far more stimulated than a few ounces of bourbon could explain.

"I approve of primal energy and sexual compulsion." My voice was husky. What a strange, stimulating conversation! He wasn't just gorgeous, he was interesting—a rare treat in a guy.

He looked away. "Aren't you already struggling with one compulsion?" "What?" Had I missed something? "The compulsion to paint. Isn't that why you don't paint anymore?" "Why I don't paint anymore?" I repeated. "What are you talking about?" How could he possibly know about my dark past?

"You said you don't paint anymore. Is that perhaps because you wish to recreate of yourself something better, something purer?" His deep voice turned cool, dismissive. I found my hand resting on his arm before I quite knew what I was doing. Hard and muscular, a pleasure to touch. I didn't want to keep touching him, but I couldn't stop myself. Hadn't I sworn off beautiful men? My hand, that slut, wasn't listening to my good sense. It stroked his arm.

Weren't vows made to be broken? Some, anyway.

"What do you know about why I quit painting?" I murmured.

"Your tone was one of regret; your eyes and mouth drooped with longing. I've seen your affect in addicts who have given up their addiction only after a struggle, when someone has been hurt. Your decision to quit painting must have had something to do with an error, perhaps a lapse in self-restraint."

"The error of the material world, a lust for beauty." I grinned, then wiped my other hand across my eyes. So now I was wrestling with myself. With the temptation that was always there. Some part of me longed to use the secret skill, the ability I'd once worked at so long and so hard and with such fierce pride. But people had gotten hurt because of my skill, and that wasn't the woman I wanted to be. So then I had worked just as hard to give her up. Looking away, I felt both a wash of loss and a shiver of pride.

"But aren't we all trying to break free of the siren song of the material realm? The *Bhagavad Gita* says, 'The wise man looks with equal detachment at a lump of dirt, a rock, or a piece of pure gold.'"

"I don't have that kind of detachment," I whispered. "I enjoy the siren song. I'm so drawn in by beauty. I don't think I'd want it any other way!"

"Than to be seduced by beauty you perceive as existing outside yourself?" He smiled a little sadly, and this sudden incomprehensible *tristesse* was as compelling as his confidence. He took my wayward hand with his other one, turned it palm-side-up, and raised it gently to his lips. His mouth on my palm made me shiver. This was the secret erotic place for me. Warm them and sweet fire burns through my limbs and into my belly. How did this man know that?

"We all want to be seduced," I said. I felt reckless and took a sip of bourbon to bolster the feeling. I cleared my throat. Was I going to say something invitational? Not after the disaster of my last relationship. Yes. No. My mouth, like my hand, had a mind of its own. "Want to come back to my place and discuss seduction?" I murmured.

He gave me a frank, searching look, the kind that sears you all the way into the lonely messed-up sanctum of your soul, the place where you almost never let anyone peek, because you're so afraid they'll see how tainted you are in there. The place where you think you deserve to have a boyfriend who treats you badly, because of all the flaws you can't hide from yourself. He was looking deeply into my core, and with such a lack of judgment that I shivered again. This time the tremor came with some feeling I couldn't identify, though it had something to do with self-acceptance. I hadn't had much of that lately. He said, "I must decline your kind offer. I wouldn't add you to my list of regrets."

"I regret your saying no," I said, wishing I could think of something lighter, more flirtatious. But part of me was relieved, too. Silence spread out between us, thick and viscous and crimson.

An older man in a trench coat passed behind us. I didn't see his face, only his form, tall and stocky as my dad had been. Or maybe still was. My father, who was my best friend for most of my life, had been missing for five years, since I was twenty-four. It was one more miserable thing to avoid thinking about, along with the recently dumped boyfriend, the stalled dissertation, and being just about flat broke. But this was the worst, the one I tried to prevent from entering my consciousness at all costs. I turned around on my stool, holding the bourbon and watching the old guy. He wasn't my dad, of course, though I would never have been able to control the impulse to check.

"Sandro Filipepi," the Italian said, in a musing tone. I turned back to him. He smiled. "Who took his brother's nickname, Botticelli."

"You know about him." I smiled back. "Yes, that was the nickname given to his brother Antonio, who was a goldsmith."

"No, he took it from Giovanni. He had that kind of relationship with Giovanni. Competitive, complicated. Antonio he protected."

"I never heard that about those relationships, and I've studied him for years! What's your source?"

"I must have read it somewhere." The Italian shrugged.

"Really? And what else have you read?" I leaned toward him again, intrigued, and not because he was the hottest man I'd ever met in person. Okay, not only because of that. My thigh rubbed up against his, which was as hard-muscled as his arm.

"He had a rich sense of humor that he used to hide his melancholy. When he told the most jokes, he was the most depressed."

"Go on."

"He was, oh, I don't know. Who knows what I read, it could have been something from a bumper sticker, or a bathroom wall." He fixed his gaze on me. He was quiet for a few beats during which I swam in those exotic eyes. I felt myself dissolving like sugar in hot water. I couldn't make out his motives; was he hitting on me, or not? Why was he so connected one moment, but refusing me the next? Quietly, he asked, "What are you looking for?"

"What am I looking for? Redemption, love, adventure, money to pay the rent, my father—"

"In Botticelli." He waved to Tomar the Israeli bartender and indicated a refill for his mug. Tomar bustled over and swept up the mug, shooting me a glance that seemed a bit alarmed. He'd never seen me get friendly with another customer.

"Right. My thesis." I pushed my glass away, a spastic gesture. "I'm blocked. Looking for a breakthrough insight. Some way to make Sandro Filipepi, a.k.a. Botticelli, meaningful to modern life." I smiled. "I'm Don Quixote, taking on an impossible quest."

"Better than being Dulcinea," he teased. I grinned back. "Botticelli is special to you," he said. His fingertips grazed gently over my cheekbone. "Look within yourself. The divine feminine resides within you. It will break the impasse."

"I don't think of myself that way," I said. There was little that was divine in my musty nooks and crannies. Dust balls and mouse droppings, sure. At best, moments of kindness and generosity. Lots of love, well-intentioned but too often errant, for my family, my roommate Fern, a few cousins, and old friends. Although lately, since my father's disappearance, I'd had a hard time connecting with my mother and brother. Yet another impasse in my life.

His hand remained on my face. "Mythology, then. Stories and legends. Especially the old ones. There are truths in them. Literal truths, figurative truths. Those can spark your inspiration so you can write." His fingers fluttering over my skin laid down a delicious filigree of molten lava.

"You could help me access my divine feminine." I couldn't help making another offer! Might as well go with it, I decided. I smiled and leaned close, nuzzled his cheek with my nose and lips. I breathed him in: amber and oak, pepper and leather, and something else, something sensual and indefinable. I could taste it, him, on my tongue, the rich maleness of him, and I quivered all over. His body twanged like a guitar string. I had a moment of triumph: he wasn't immune to me after all. He ran his palm along the side of my neck. He took a deep breath and I could feel his chest rise and fall next to mine. "Let yourself...."

"No!" he said forcefully, his voice hoarse. "I'm leaving, before I do something that I'll regret." He pushed back from me, jarring me so that I almost fell off my stool. I steadied myself with a hand on the scarred wooden bar. He said, "You don't know what you're offering. You, of all people...."

"Me of all people, what?"

He shook his head. "Don't drink so much. Keep your eyes open, see what's around you. You have more than just a thesis to write. You have a destiny." His smoky green-gray eyes were obdurate, and there was high color in his cheeks. Curiously, I wasn't offended, despite the rejection. I sensed that something was going on that I wasn't privy to, and that the Italian wanted me despite himself.

I reached into my purse for my wallet. He put his hand on mine. "I've got it. Least I can do for a fellow art lover."

"My name is Laila Cambridge." I smiled at him. "Look me up." He nodded and slapped two twenties onto the bar. With a spring in his stride and perfect posture, he left the bar.

That's when it hit me: why the Italian's face was so familiar. The *Primavera*. One of Botticelli's ravishing masterpieces. The yummy Italian looked just like Mercury, the dark-haired youth standing at the far right edge of the painting, scattering fog. I riffled through pages, found the image, and gasped. Botticelli's Mercury looked uncannily, photographically, like the Italian. The Italian's hair was shorter, but it was the same color. The features were exactly the same.

I leapt off the barstool and bolted outside, hoping to catch him.

It was a beautiful, crisp spring night in Manhattan, full of sparkling street lights, fresh air breezing in off the Hudson, pedestrians stepping quickly, and laughter swirling up like white blossoms as shoppers walked past windows. He was nowhere to be seen, though he couldn't have gotten far. Standing on the street, I started to laugh, too. I'd never, ever been turned down before. This was a completely novel experience. Intriguing, as the man was. And I'd never had a response like that to anyone, ever. I took a shuddering breath, remembering his touch. Then I laughed some more. I felt lighter and more hopeful than I had in months. I had no reason to feel this way; I simply sensed that things in my life were changing and I was ready.

Chapter 2

I WAS STILL HAPPY THE NEXT MORNING. There must be a few motes of truth buried in those Pollyanna theories about people creating their own reality, because right off the bat I got an unexpected call from Tour Time Manhattan, my part-time employer. A group wanted to be guided around the Metropolitan Museum of Art. They would pay well for the privilege, and Tour Time would pay me well, too. Cash. Sorely needed cash. Not enough cash to keep away the landlord, but it would buy some groceries.

At noon I took the subway uptown, enjoying another warm spring day. I thought about the sexy Italian, his ironic smile, his fingertips on my cheek.

Things got lively right away. As I always do, I first took the group to the bathroom, so we could spend the next two hours focusing on the art in the museum. You know, paintings and sculptures, the reason people actually come to the Met. We were down on the ground floor by the wheelchair-accessible entrance. I stood out by the elevator, chatting with one of the security guards, and when the elevator doors opened, someone brushed against me on the way into the elevator. I was almost knocked over. I shouted, "Hey!" But the elevator doors closed before I could see anyone.

When I'd gotten my bearings again, I realized that I was holding a small piece of paper. It said, "Laila, meet me in the bookstore. Urgent." The handwriting was small and fine, with a perfection of form that had once been called copperplate. Curious.

I called to one of the tour members that I'd be right back, and when the elevator doors re-opened, I rode up to the main floor. I trotted into the bookstore, swept around, and, with my usual klutziness, knocked off a badly-stacked pile of books about de Kooning. I knelt to gather them together, smiling and flushing as I remembered last night and the gorgeous Italian's fervor for de Kooning. A man knelt beside me, to help.

"Ironic that art books should be so gracelessly placed," he said. "But then you don't really consider this art, do you, Laila?"

"You!" I cried. I found myself looking into cat-like hazel eyes, and I do mean feline: his pupils were elliptical black slits. The next moment his eyes were normal, and I shook my head to clear the illusion. "I wondered if I'd ever see you again."

"You got my note." His eyes were hot and smoky on my face. "Thank you for coming."

"I left my tour group alone, which isn't a good idea. The question is, did you know I'd be here today?" I asked. We both stood up slowly, keeping the distance between us narrow. I was breathing faster, my heart racing. I said, "You did, didn't you? You sure seem to know a lot about me."

"Nothing you wouldn't want me to know." The resonance in his deep voice suggested a smile.

"I don't know what I want you to know about me. If anything. Particularly since you rejected me last night."

"I didn't reject you. Far from it. I simply declined to add to my bad karma." He walked around the table to the other side, looked down at the books as he straightened them. I was tempted to tell him that bad karma was more fun than good karma, but his shuttered face discouraged such levity. His mood shifts were mercurial, disturbing. Who was this man?

"What do you need to talk to me about so urgently?" I asked.

"I need to speak to you privately. About an urgent matter."

"Let's have a drink this afternoon. I'll be out of here by four."

"I think you're drinking too much."

"What do you suggest?"

"The park, when you're done here. By the Balto sculpture."

"I don't know," I demurred. "Why should I meet you? I think you're playing me, teasing me for fun. What kind of game is this?"

"I'm not teasing you!" he exploded. "It's no game. It's urgent. It concerns your father."

I stiffened. "What do you know about my father?"

"I've known him for years. He's alive and well."

"That's not funny."

"I'm not joking," he said sharply. "Your father's alive, but he's in danger. He needs your help. Meet me by the statue when you get out and I'll explain."

My mind was dizzy with possibility: my father was alive? Robert Cambridge, my best friend, my sweet, funny, smart daddy, who hadn't said a word to me, or to my mom or my brother Brad, in years? It had been five years, three weeks, and two days, since the last time I spoke to him, over lattes at a coffee shop in Midtown. Even for me, obsessed as I was with art, it was hard to focus on the Rodins in the sculpture garden and deliver the expected interesting patter to the tour group. It was hard to think about anything else at all. But, as luck or karma would have it, my old nemesis and obsession came back around to bite me in the tushie. Some punk kid in the tour group sniggered. "I can photoshop a smile onto the Mona Lisa. Or put this golden angel beside Johnny Depp next to the Eiffel Tower. Now that would be great art!"

It was like a bullet cracking over my shoulder. Thoughts of my father receded, at least a bit. Hadn't I shucked off questions for the day? And shouldn't great art be obvious? To all but teeny boppers whose brains have been fried by iPod exposure, that is. Art was redemption and salvation, isn't that what Botticelli believed? Did I? If an expert forger could replicate Botticelli perfectly, what did it all matter?

The teenager stared at me expectantly. When his beady dark eyes dropped away from my face to wander all over my anatomy, I recognized him as Sam, an undergraduate in an art history class in which I was a teaching assistant. He wasn't a teenager at all, just a youthful smartass. I wondered if I could smack him and still keep my job. Probably not.

"Great art, like—" I looked around, wondering where we were in the tour. Good Lord, was I actually standing in the early Italian Renaissance room? What was wrong with me, that I hadn't noticed before? Hello, autopilot! "Great art like Giotto's *Epiphany* here does more than entertain for a few seconds." I pointed to the exquisite panel, one from a series about Christ's life painted around 1320. "It enhances life, expresses emotion, exalts the spirit, and communicates something poignant and universal about the human experience." I smiled sweetly at the wastrel. "Look at the tenderness in the Magi's gaze toward the infant Christ. The Madonna's concern. So much is said, and it crosses time and cultures—"

"I get it, she's worried about what's going to happen to him," Sam said. "But how does that relate?

"We can all relate to it. I'm sure your mother worries about what will happen to you," I replied, with a lilt.

A plump woman at the back of the tour group giggled. "I don't worry, I always know he's in trouble!" she called out.

"The Met has a fine collection of paintings from this era," I went on, "though it was Giotto who, according to the early art historian Vasari, made the art of painting dynamic again, with his naturalism and ability to express kindness in his figures." I waved the group forward. "Moving on to the next room," I chirped, "and taking a right and another right into the Northern Renaissance." They were forty-five people, a family reunion. The group flowed onward, and I caught demon spawn Sam by the scruff of his scrawny neck.

"Listen, you freckled undergraduate twerp," I hissed, prepared to lecture him on art and redemption.

"Hey, do you have a boyfriend?" Sam interrupted. "We could meet later to discuss this over drinks."

"You're not old enough to drink," I said. I gave him a little shake, listened for the sound of rocks rattling around his cranium, then released him.

"Did you hear about Angela Carlone?" Sam asked.

The post-doc visiting from Italy. "What about her?"

"They found her dead. Here. Yesterday."

"Here? At the museum?" I was shocked.

"Yeah, it was weird. They're really being hush-hush about it, but it's some sort of sick murder. She didn't have any blood in her body at all."

"Murder's always sick," I said. Poor Angela. I had met her only a few times, but she was well-regarded. She wrote on seventeenth century French painters, and she had a nice way with it. Lots of art historians couldn't write to save their lives. Not that it had saved Angela's, apparently. Until today, when the Italian had told me my father was alive—assuming there was any truth to it—I had always wondered if something like this had happened to him, if that was why he'd vanished one day: he'd been murdered, had bled out somewhere without anyone to find him and call 911, and so he'd simply been erased from the planet like a chalk line smudged out on a cosmic blackboard. It was the thing I, my brother, and my mother all avoided saying out loud; it was the reason why we could barely speak to each other now. But today it had all changed. The Italian had said my father was alive.

"...So they'll announce it in a whitewashed way at school and then hold a memorial service," Sam was saying. He certainly had the goods. Impressive, for a scrawny twerp.

"How'd you find out all this?"

"I saw some art history professors in here, Professor Hetson and Professor Diamond. They didn't see me but I overheard them talking about it. Big scandal—they don't want everyone at Columbia hearing about it."

"Pay as close attention in class as you do to eavesdropping, and you might learn something. Otherwise, don't think I won't get Professor Hetson to fail you. Now, out!" I snapped my fingers and pointed. He winked obnoxiously and trotted off after his group.

Right, *my* tour group. I glanced around guiltily. I wanted to be sure that no one from Tour Time had witnessed me manhandling a customer.

Chapter 3

AFTER THE TOUR FINISHED, I FIELDED THE usual questions about other bathroom locations, how to score cheap Broadway tix, and where to eat cheap. Then I escaped and made my way outside.

The day was corkscrewing into weirdness. A visiting post-doc was dead, and the Italian claimed to have information about my father. I was deep in these thoughts when a low chuckle sounded. From behind the sculpture of Balto, the brave Alaskan dog, emerged the Italian. He was smiling, and he was looking fine. Something about his long, muscular limbs, balletic carriage, and effervescent eyes made me want to ravish him on the spot. I didn't think he'd go for it, though; he'd already turned me down once. He said, "You put the pup on your tour in his place."

"My tour?" I said, startled. Had he been watching? I hadn't noticed him at all. Was I that out to lunch, or was he just invisible?

"Your comments about the paintings were perceptive. I followed for a while."

"I shouldn't have been so harsh with Sam."

"Nonsense. He deserved every word."

"I don't want to talk about some skeevy undergrad," I said. "I want to hear about my father."

"Walk with me," he said. He looked around while gesturing us forward.

"Tell me your name," I said, not moving yet. "You know mine."

"John Bolingbroke."

"Doesn't sound very Italian," I muttered. I stayed planted in the spot where I stood.

"I told you, I've wandered the world. Now, do you want to hear about your father?" He placed his hand on my lower back and ushered me along the path through Central Park, which was green, sunlit, and whispery with a soft breeze. My whole back palpitated from his touch. He pulled his hand away.

"How do you know my father?" I managed.

"Several years ago, he helped me acquire a painting. A Pollack."

"A Pollack?" Uh-oh. This could be bad. I thought my dad knew all the forgeries? "Which one?"

Bolingbroke grinned. "Not one of yours, sweetheart. Though I'd feel privileged to own one."

I winced. "Just tell me about my dad."

"I'm a collector and amateur historian, specializing in the post-modernists," he began. I couldn't help putting a finger to my mouth and miming a gag. He shrugged. "They appeal to me, as we discussed last night."

"There's no accounting for taste."

He raised one dark eyebrow and gave me his ironic half-smile. The way he tilted his head, I was struck again by his resemblance to Botticelli's Mercury. He saw my double-take. "What?" he asked.

"You look exactly like the Mercury in Botticelli's *Primavera*. You don't just resemble him. You look photographically identical to him."

Bolingbroke looked straight ahead, focusing his gaze on a tree. "I've an ongoing acquaintance with your father. I saw him again two weeks ago."

"Two weeks ago?" My mind reeled again. "Where?"

"At the Avery Fine Arts Library. He was looking for a painting."

"The—the Columbia library?" I sputtered. "I'm there all the time! I didn't see him. He didn't try to see me? How could he not let me know he was alive? He just vanished and left us all to worry about him! For five years!"

"Some questions only your father can answer, Laila," Bolingbroke said. His voice was somber. "Though it's safe to say that he vanished to protect you."

"How could it protect me not to know whether he's dead or alive?"

"Focus, Laila," Bolingbroke commanded. "After I saw your father, I overheard some, ah, people talking. Very bad people. They plan to follow your father, take the painting from him, and kill him. The problem is, I can't reach your father now. He's out of communication. His cell phone is disconnected and his last e-mail account is bouncing my e-mails back. It's not in service."

"Slow down," I said. I seated myself on a nearby bench and put my head in my hands. Some nannies pushing squalling kids in carriages went past. Bolingbroke sat beside me, stretched out his long legs. I closed my eyes. "What painting? And why?"

"He was looking for a Botticelli. *Coming Forth by Day.*"

"That painting's been lost forever. Hell, it may even be apocryphal! I mean, come on, a painting about a secret pagan rite, on which supposedly Leonardo da Vinci himself collaborated? The only known collaboration between Botticelli and da Vinci? It's every art historian's, museum's, collector's, and treasure hunter's wet dream! After the Ark of the Covenant and the Amber Room, that's the single most sought-after historical treasure!"

"Your father said it was real. He's looking for it."

Too much, too strange, this information. Moving too fast, spinning away from me. Let me start at the beginning, I thought. Which was: Dad was alive. Bolingbroke saw him two weeks ago. Or so Bolingbroke claimed. "Proof of life," I snapped. "How do I know you're telling the truth? That you've actually seen my dad?"

Bolingbroke nodded. His striking, roughly-hewn face wore a hooded expression. "He mentioned your birthday passing two months ago. That you were now twenty-nine."

"My date of birth is a matter of public record."

"He said your mother is painting again."

I jerked upright. "He contacted her?"

Bolingbroke shook his head. "No. She doesn't know he's alive. But he showed me a small panel. Very fine. A still life with fruits. Reminded me of—"

"Gotcha! My mother is famous for her landscapes. You've made your first mistake, John Bolingbroke. Or whoever you are. What do you want from me, anyway? Money? I have none. Restitution? Is this about that Pollack? One of your relatives met me in Berlin, when I was posing as a dealer? Crap, are you related to Vivian Goran? Is this about her? I was cleared of involvement in that."

Bolingbroke didn't move a muscle, but I could sense his energy coiled within him like a panther or a cobra about to strike. I got very still. Was he going to hurt me, now that I'd found him out? Bolingbroke's voice was soft. "Laila, your mother is now painting still lifes. I own two of her landscapes, *Yellow Midnight Stockholm* and *Jardin de Tuileries*. Superb pieces. The still life was very much in her hand, which, as you know, is distinctive. Her fame is justly earned."

"I know my mother's talent," I said, and tried to keep the bitterness from my voice. I'd never had what she did. I couldn't create, I could only copy. And even though I could copy anyone, literally, any painter in history, that wasn't real art. It was forgery. And it was loathsome. And someone had died because of it.

"I know of Vivian Goran, everyone connected to the art world heard about that ugly matter. It's a gossipy community. But I'm no relation and don't particularly care. She should have had a better alarm system," Bolingbroke continued. "This isn't about restitution. My Pollack is authentic. Nor do I want your money. I have more than enough for any ten humans."

"Then what do you want?" I whispered.

Bolingbroke leaned toward me. His eyes were close to mine and I noticed how long and thick and minky his lashes were, without being the least bit feminine. "I want you to help me find Robert Cambridge and the painting. And we don't have long. The group I overheard is powerful and dangerous. They have unlimited resources. They're closing in on him. We have a week at most before they get him."

I got up and ran. I admit, just took to my heels and fled. I'm not usually chicken-shit; I'm a six-foot-tall red-headed babe who can conquer anything with her ten languages! I have a tattoo on the small of my back that says "Rock You"! But all of this, about my dad being alive and in danger, was too much, too shocking, too uncertain. It tore too deeply into my heart where I didn't have defenses, where hair color and height and ink and linguistic flair don't mean anything, because love is all that matters, anyway. So I ran. Bolingbroke did not follow.

I didn't go home. I found myself on the subway to Columbia. A notion roiled around my cranium that I was going to argue again with the rare books librarian about a missing art history folio. Then I realized that I was going there to see if my dad had been there. Or if—a billion-to-one shot—he was there still.

But the folio was actually a good place to start. I needed it for my thesis. And if my dad was looking for the legendary lost Botticelli, he would want to see the folio, too. It contained some fascinating and unusual essays about Botticelli and beauty and salvation. It touched on my area of interest, the redemption the artist sought in Savonarola, that fiery monk who had imposed the fury of his asceticism upon Renaissance Florence. The painting was rumored to have been done right at that pivotal time at which something inside Sandro Filipepi had shifted. Further, the author of the essays had some strange musings on Botticelli's private life, musings that sounded oddly as if he'd personally met the artist. It would be a crucial resource for someone tracking a lost Botticelli.

The lost Botticelli.

Yes, the folio was a good starting point. For my dad, and for me. It had been published privately in England a hundred seventy years ago in limited numbers. Only five copies still existed. One was in the Hermitage—I saw it there as a little girl—and one was in Paris, one in Vienna, and one in England. Somehow, the fifth copy had landed here in New York, at the Columbia library. I had examined it a year ago, but it had been missing ever since. I suspected that the evening librarian knew who had it and was shielding the person.

A few hours later, I was in luck: the librarian came in for her shift. I decided to confront her about her knowledge. There was something sneaky and knowing about the way she smiled. She was a petite woman in the Snow White mold, with veinless white skin and black hair. She wore a heavy set of dark glasses that I suspected she wore for the same reason I did my horn-rims: to ward off unwanted attention. She was curvy enough that plenty of men would find her attractive, even though she swathed herself in scarves, turtlenecks, and long black skirts. Before I allowed myself to lose my temper, I insisted that she check the reserves for the folio.

She came back eight minutes later shaking her head. "Still not here. Sorry." But a coy little grin played on her face. She wasn't sorry at all. That's when I started yelling.

"Look, it's not right to shelter a book thief. That's a rare, precious folio that was set aside for serious researchers. If you know who has it, you have a moral obligation to tell me!"

"It's not your place to tell me my moral obligations," she said, in a voice that was too silky to be honest.

"This is an institution of higher learning, and book theft——"

"Happens. Can't be prevented. It's not my responsibility to hunt down book borrowers so you can finish your paper."

"It's my doctoral dissertation!" More importantly, although I didn't say it aloud, I thought that I'd be able to tell if my dad had been handling it. Somehow I'd know, maybe just through some vaporous psychic sense of daughter-father-connection.

The librarian shrugged. Then she moved to help another student without another glance at me.

"Excuse me, miss." I barged up and shouldered the student out of the way. "Can you tell me if anyone else has recently been asking about the folio?"

"Now you want my help?" she asked scornfully. She laid her glasses down on the counter and glared. "How would I know who's been looking for a particular book? Are you aware that there are more than eight million volumes in our collection, and more than twenty-seven thousand students, more than four thousand full-time faculty members, and countless others who use these facilities?" Vitriol came from her eyes, but I wasn't deterred by her statistics. I didn't like math. Or people who recited it.

"He would be memorable," I said. "Tall man, red hair like mine, there's some gray in it." And suddenly silence blanketed the library the way it's always supposed to but seldom does. I couldn't figure out why, and then I realized that the librarian was staring at me in a way that sucked all the noise out of the room. Along with all the air, energy, motion, and life.

"You have reason to believe that a man like that has been here?" she asked.

I felt wary. Scared, truth be told. I shrugged. "Not really. I just wondered."

"If he shows up, whom shall I say is looking for him? Where shall I direct him?"

"Forget it," I said. What had straightened out her panties? Why was she suddenly so interested? I backed away as she stared at me. Then the other student coughed and rustled some papers, so she slowly turned back to him.

As I'd done several times, already, I meandered through the aisles of books, scanning every man as though he might be my dad. Of course, none of them was. Nor did I pick up any mystical residue of him. So much for the psychic friends network. But maybe it was just that I was obtuse. Finally, I sat down at a desk with the big Zollner book on Botticelli, pulled out my notebook, and pretended to jot down notes. I sent a snake-eyed look over towards the librarian, and found her staring at me with a cocked head and an equally jaundiced expression. Her lips were drawn back in a sneer that exposed the points of her teeth, like fangs. Weird. I bent over my notebook and tried to collect my thoughts.

How was I going to check out Bolingbroke's story? I wanted to know that the Italian (if he really was an Italian) was telling the truth before I leapt into anything. Although I was worried that if Bolingbroke's story was real, I was wasting precious time that was better spent looking for my father.

Absently, I started a list of my favorite bars for martinis, arranged by neighborhood. My roommate Fern had taken me to a place in SoHo that served the best in the city, in my humble opinion. Fern. Maybe she could help. She would certainly have a thoughtful perspective on all this.

Chapter 4

WITH EVENING PURPLING THE SKY, I TOOK the subway from Columbia to the West Village, where Fern and I shared an outrageously over-priced fourth-floor walkup in a brown-stone which we would never, ever leave. We had sworn that to each other so many times, over various bever-ages, that it was almost a blood oath. An oath we were in danger of violat-ing through eviction, if we didn't come up with several thousand dollars real quick. But I brushed those thoughts aside, because I could worry about only one thing at a time. And right now my attention was on my father, and on Bolingbroke's story.

It was seven o'clock when I got off at Christopher street. I walked slowly to Barrow, enjoying the windy spring evening and the bustling streets, the human-scale buildings and the riot of shops and restaurants. The Village is the best part of Manhattan. Those of us who love Manhattan think that anyone who lives anywhere else has got to be kidding. Manhattan is the pumping, pressurized heart of the universe. In August, it's more like the armpit, but for most of the year, this city is simply more alive than anyplace else. And I've lived in enough places to know.

Before my father disappeared, he was in the foreign service. When I was a kid, we lived all over, most places for nine months to a year. We weren't rich, we just got to travel, and I loved it. The adventure of going from place to place, of learning a new language and a new way to be in the world, the delight of creating a new self in a new setting. My dad loved it, too. I remem-bered talking about it with him. We were sitting outside, in one of the green glacier-carved pastures near Lake Lucerne. I was weaving a chain of bluebells and primroses, daisies and harebells, all the fragrant flowers that grow close to the sky on the Alps.

"Next week we go to London," he told me.

"I like London but I won't get to learn a language," I said. I finished the wreath and laid it on Daddy's red head as a crown. That was Daddy, the king of my heart.

He grinned at me, squeezed my hand in his. "That's my favorite part, too, Little Goofy Bird. Hearing the languages. Seeing people talk and live differently."

"Not in London, Big Goofy Bird," I teased him. "The only way they live differently is that they carry umbrellas everywhere!"

He laughed and put a daisy behind my ear.

So we had this bond between us, of enjoying the freshness and the exploration. But my little brother, Brad, had hated it. Where I had seen limitless opportunity and expansion, he had seen chaos and insecurity. Which perhaps explained why he was already a banker, married and settled comfortably in Greenwich, Connecticut at the age of twenty-seven. Or was he twenty eight now? We were only fourteen months apart, and, as Bolingbroke reminded me, my birthday was two months ago.

"Hey, pussycat, why the big frown?" Fern asked as I came through the door. She spoke in a fake Asian accent, as she did whenever she wanted to make me smile. Fern's half Chinese, a quarter Japanese, and a quarter German, and she speaks English perfectly. She should; she's getting a doctorate in English Lit. Her parents were government foreign service wonks too, and we'd been sent to the same boarding school in Switzerland for a few years. When we found ourselves together at Middlebury as undergraduates, we'd decided it was kismet for us to be friends. We'd lived together ever since, except for those lost years between college and grad school when I let myself be taken over by the dark side of the force.

Fern sat on our dilapidated settee in the front room, which was our living and dining room. Our apartment consisted of three rooms in a line, railroad style, with a tiny kitchen and an even tinier bathroom off to one side. The middle room was my bedroom while the back room was hers.

"Brad," I said. "Isn't it his birthday this week?"

"Last week," she said. "You sent him a card."

"I did? Fern, you're the best," I said gratefully. What was left of my family was in disarray since my father's inexplicable disappearance. I had always told myself that someday I would rectify that, and until then I had alcohol and denial to help me cope, and Fern to do the dirty work of making contact with my mother and brother when it was necessary.

But now the game had changed: Bolingbroke had claimed that my father was alive. I threw myself on the settee beside her. "I had a weird day. Upsetting. You won't believe what I heard! I'm not sure I do. And I don't know what to do about it."

Fern blinked. Her face registered concern for me, but not worry. She was unflappable even in the midst of my worst dramas. Like some months ago when I realized that my stage-actor boyfriend was cheating on me with not one but *three* women, and I had thrown a huge hissy fit, complete with flying vases. Fern plugged her iPod into the speakers, blasted the Dixie Chicks, and gave me a broom and dustpan to sweep up the shards, without one word. Then she made margharitas, and I substituted heartache for blistering headache: the perfect consolation. Fern always looks perfect, too, with her toenails pristinely pedicured, her dresses neatly pressed, and her hair and makeup immaculate. She's flawlessly beautiful in an exotic Eurasian way; she'd be easy to hate, but she's so kind and thoughtful that you can't. When I grow up, I want to be Fern.

She asked, "Is this one of those occasions where I'm making margharitas? And you ask for an IV to deliver them?"

"I wish." I paused. "I ran into this unbelievably hot guy last night. Bought me a drink but turned me down when I offered to throw my naked self at him."

"Buying a drink, that's classy. Very polite," Fern said, in a musing tone. "I always like that in a man. 'For courtesy wins woman all as well as valor may.'"

"Milton? And I don't think rejecting me was so polite."

"Tennyson, girlfriend. And maybe he's just trying to get to know you before he surrenders to your womanly wiles. It's gallant, you know. When you do more than hook up and move on. Didn't you tell me you wanted more out of a guy?"

"I don't know how gallant this one is. Today he found me at the Met and told me he'd seen *my dad* two weeks ago."

"Whoa!" Fern held up one hand.

So, in a low voice, I told Fern about the bar, the tour, Bolingbroke talking to me by Balto, the snarky librarian, and the dead end at the Columbia library.

"So you don't know if Bolingbroke's telling the truth," Fern said. Thoughtfully, she wove a slip of tissue paper between her slim fingers.

"No, and I don't know what to do."

"If he's telling the truth and you delay, you endanger your father. If he's lying, he leads you into some kind of wild goose chase, for no good reason," she said, sympathetically. "Plus you get your hopes up. Hard to know what to do."

"My instincts scream, 'Trust him!' But you know how my instincts have been."

"Held hostage by your lust," Fern said. She shrugged. "Don't sweat it, Gonzo. Happens to the best of us."

Fern was also between boyfriends. For two years she had dated the lead guitarist of her rock band, but he'd taken up recreational drugs in a way that wasn't recreational at all, and she'd dumped him, out of her life and out of the band. It hadn't been pretty, though she would never show how hurt she was. Where I practiced denial and drama, Fern chose the high road of stoicism. I was probably the only person who knew how sad she really felt.

"There's got to be a way to find out, quick," I said. "This is my dad we're talking about. If there's even a one percent chance, a one-tenth of a percent chance...."

"There's a way," Fern said quietly. She gave me a steady look, then rose and went to gaze out the window. "I'll call my drummer Dex and we can borrow his car."

"No," I said. "No, please."

"I'll be with you," Fern said, in a cajoling voice. "It won't be bad. We'll keep it short. Just long enough for you to see for yourself. That part of his story will be easy to check out."

"I don't want to." I cradled my head in my lap. "It will bring everything back up. Everything. Everything I want to forget. Everything I don't want to think about. My past. Everything!" I would have kept ranting but there was suddenly a loud staccato thumping. Fern and I jumped.

A huge black bird beat its wings against the front windows. I ran to look closer, and gasped. Three big windows ran along our front wall, and the bird was throwing its body against the middle one while its wings stretched from outside window to outside window: more than five feet in span. It looked into my eyes. I was aware of intense, predatory intelligence. It and I both shrieked. It sort of floated backward into the purple twilight like a hummingbird or a balloon caught in a backdraft. Then it was gone, scattering dark scrims of light in its wake.

"That was some bad-ass mutant raven," I muttered.

"Not a raven," said Fern, who had considered biology as a major in college because she liked the taxonomy of things. I think it soothed her. But *Paradise Lost* and Nirvana had won her heart, so English Lit and rock singing it was.

"Whatever it is, it can't be a good omen," I said. A shiver of dread crawled up my spine. "You don't want to see a giant mutant raven before you go to an ashram. It's bad juju."

"Coincidence," Fern declared. "Now put on a dress your mum will be happy to see you in. We're leaving in ten minutes."

Soon enough, we were sitting in Dex's Mini Cooper, crossing the George Washington Bridge and then heading up the Palisades Parkway, up to the ashram where my mother had taken refuge when it became clear that we weren't going to hear from my father. Fern was driving. I stared out the window and hoped my mother wouldn't notice the dark circles under my eyes. My mother didn't need anything to worry about. She was, well, fragile.

"How do you contact the hot guy if you verify his story?" Fern asked.

"He'll find me, I guess. He's done a good job of that."

"Or you google him and find his address online," Fern said. She tossed a glance across her shoulder at me before concentrating on the road. "I don't think you should mention your father to her."

"You think? But wouldn't it be fun to get her hopes up, get her all riled up and agitated? Make her blood pressure skyrocket?" Now I was being snotty.

"We got another phone call from our landlord about the past-due rent," Fern said, as though I were being as sweet and reasonable as she was. "I've got a gig next month that will bring in something, but we're still short."

"I'll sell the Diebenkorn."

"No, no, Laila, don't go there. You'll never forgive yourself." Fern pursed her lips together for a moment. "We could go to the park and set out a hat. I'll play the guitar and sing, and you dance."

"The last time we did that, a social worker asked if I was off my meds. How about, I'll play the guitar and you dance?"

"One, you don't play the guitar, and two, something about those long red-headed legs of yours drives men wild. You don't even have to dance. Just smile and flitter your skirt around and they'll drop dollars into our hat."

"I'm too old for that now," I said. "Besides, my long red-headed legs didn't drive Bolingbroke wild."

Fern snuck a look at me. "We need a cover story, why we're driving up at night, unannounced, to see her." Fern always had my back. Did I mention that I love her?

"I don't deserve you."

"Sure you do. You're always there for me." Fern smiled. "Remember junior year, the rugby party, beer pong with vodka?"

"That was ten years ago. That doesn't count."

"Oh, it counts. That will always count!" She giggled and I had a flash of that party, the drunken gang of rugby players circling her, and the way I'd heaved her over my shoulder and brought her back to our dorm room. "For a cover story, something about her two paintings that hang at the MOMA?"

I considered but then shook my head. "They'd contact her, not me. And I don't want our topic of conversation to be her paintings. I don't want her to know we're snooping to see if she's painting again."

"She's an expert on da Vinci. And crazy passionate about him."

"Attribution of a possible da Vinci? I could make up a rumor from the art history department," I said. "That would intrigue her."

"That's my girl," Fern approved.

"I'll try to make it believable." I always could lie to my mom. Never to my dad. Dad, who was maybe in lethal danger. Had he really disappeared to protect us? I sank down into my seat, which, considering how tall I am, is a feat in itself. It means I fold up my legs and collapse my shoulders down and stare at the crescent moon scar on my left knee, from when I was eight years old and tripped on a Stockholm street. I slipped free of my dad's hand and ran laughing past a yellow building, never dreaming that one day he'd slip free of me, and all the pretty yellow buildings in the world couldn't tell me where he was.

Chapter 5

AN HOUR LATER, WITH THE CATSKILLS ROLLING green and lustrous even in the night, we got off the interstate and followed a winding road. After about six miles, we came to a wooden clapboard gatehouse by a pebbled drive. Fern pulled up under a brilliant halogen floodlight and waved to the guard, who smiled and let us pass. Fern has that effect on people. It's not just that she's gorgeous, but also that she emanates a kind of sweetness that functions as a free pass in life. People expand when she smiles at them. Next lifetime, I'm going to do that, too. I mean, I get attention and lots of ogling, but my natural feistiness radiates out. After the look-see, I get a squinty glance and set jaw. It's all in the aura. Mine waves a red flag at people.

Fern parked and we got out. We left the parking lot and followed a lamp-lit dirt path cut through a manicured emerald lawn toward a large, brightly-lit chapel-like structure which I knew to be the central meeting hall. There was a flow of people, most dressed in white salwar kameez, the long tunic over loose trousers that southern Indian women favor. I checked the time: 9:30 p.m. We'd arrived after a meditation.

"This way." I led Fern around the meeting hall, past a barn-like dormitory structure and a large dining hall, toward a grouping of bungalows in a grove of oaks, poplars, and elms on the outskirts of the campus. Big white globes on posts shed soft spherical radiances, and the moon was near full, its platinum light almost as bright as day. Tall leafy trees threw oblong shadows which were thinned by shifting opalescent spots of moonlight. Lilac scent floated out on the damp night breeze, an owl hooted, and a distant melodic chanting rose and fell softly, like the sea.

"'Nothing is so beautiful as Spring—When weeds, in wheels, shoot long and lovely and lush; Thrush's eggs look little low heavens, and thrush Through the echoing timber does so rinse and wring the ear....'" Fern quoted softly.

"Tennyson?" I ventured, spying the bungalow which my mother occupied. I hoped her roommate wasn't around so we could speak in privacy.

"Hopkins," Fern answered.

Then someone was calling my name, and my mom, in a long white tunic, was standing in the door of her bungalow with a big smile on her face. The next thing I knew, I was in her arms. My eyes were a little wet. Probably from the drive.

"Laila, what a wonderful surprise," she laughed, hugging me hard. I squeezed her fiercely, then stepped back to look her over. She was just as always: small but stately, with flittery bird-like bones that always felt like my arms would crush, if I squeezed as hard as I really wanted. Her blond hair was streaked with gray and her oval face sagged a little, more from loss than from time. She'd always been so pretty and youthful, until my father's disappearance had desiccated her. They were divorced when he vanished, but it struck her hard anyway. She was eying me just as closely, and she frowned, seeing something that worried her. "You're too thin," she said, pinching my arm. I grinned at her. I'm not too fat, but then again, with the sturdy Scandinavian farmer's bones I inherited from my dad, I'm not too thin, either.

"I wish," I said. "Then I could eat more of Fern's baked goods!" My mother smiled, a brightening that didn't alleviate the underlying shadow, and looked past me to Fern. "Fern, how lovely!"

"Eleanor," Fern said, and they embraced cheek to cheek, cooing at each other. That quirky smile of my mom's, from when she was pleased—like when I got a rare A in math or Brad got an even rarer one in French, or Dad got posted to a favorite city—struggled at the corners of her mouth. She motioned us to come in. We stepped inside the bungalow, which was one room with two beds and two bureaus, a tiny kitchen alcove off to one side, and a bathroom off to the other side. A threadbare braided rug in brown and red circled around the floor. On top of one bureau were stacked some blank, primed canvases, and beside them lay a pile of paint tubes.

"You're painting?" I asked, breathless and struck to the core. Bolingbroke was telling the truth. About my mother, at least. I walked over and touched one of the canvases. They were ready for her extraordinary gift, and there was a palette splotched with pigment lying nearby. There were no brushes in sight, which meant they'd been used and cleaned and put somewhere to dry. I could smell turpentine, that old familiar sharp scent that had followed my mother around when I was a child. Somewhere there were painted canvases, and I would give a lot to know what they looked like. Still lifes? Had my mother truly given up the landscapes that had made her famous?

"Brad sent supplies a while ago, so I've been dabbling." My mother sort of shrugged, too studied in her offhandedness. "You know it was his birthday last week."

"Laila sent him a card," Fern said.

"Uh-huh," my mother said, tilting her head to one side like a curious sparrow.

"Fern signed my name," I said brightly, eliciting a wry smile from my mom. She knew I couldn't remember Brad's birthday. I only remembered my own because of the prospect of presents and champagne.

"There must be some reason you've come to see me," my mother said. She sat down on a small wooden stool, folding her hands in her lap. "Not that you need one." She turned her face away and I knew she wished I came more often.

But I didn't go down that pot-holed road of guilt and regret. Instead I pasted my biggest, brightest, falsest smile on my face. "Ah, mother dearest, a delicious rumor, and I had to bring it to you," I said. "A painting, a possible attribution. Professore Pedretti has a secret. It's all hush-hush and under wraps. I found out by accident at the Met."

"This can only be a possible Leonardo!" My mother raised an eyebrow and brightened some more, for real this time. "Tell me everything!"

"I don't know too much, and I don't want to get you too excited," I cautioned. "Just some whispers I caught earlier today when I was leading a tour. I saw Professor Hetson and Professor Diamond in the Met bookstore. They didn't see me so I went behind a stack of books and overheard them discussing it." My, what a cool liar I was. Might as well get a really good whopper going. "They mentioned Pedretti. Pedretti had been in touch with Mario Bigetti—"

"Bigetti, that sly Roman dealer of arts and antiquities and all things that want to be!" Mother clapped her hands like a little girl. She was leaning forward on the stool. Her eyes were wide and luminous, her face smoothed out with pleasure. I had not seen it thus for many years, maybe over a decade. She laughed. "He'll be in court forever about the possible Caravaggio. He's up to his old tricks?"

"Bigetti found a panel in an attic in Lazio. Legs had been nailed into it, turning it into a little makeshift stool," I fabricated. "It impressed him enough to call in Pedretti. Pedretti was impressed, too. That's what I heard." It was an appealing story. We all long to find hidden treasure. I myself had once nurtured the usual pedestrian fantasies of finding a priceless antiquity in someone's old barn. Which I would donate to a museum, and so receive a substantial financial gratuity in thanks. This was a fantasy that my demons had corrupted long ago, by showing me another way to replace lost works of art.

"Who knows what's in all those old countryside villas!" My mother looked thrilled. I closed my eyes because it hurt to lead her on. Only for my dad, I told myself, fiercely. "I'll make a few calls," my mother enthused. "An examination will be set in motion. Infrared, x-rays. Surface-texture topographical imaging. Pigment analysis."

"Well, there you have it," I chirped.

Her face puckered in on itself, all seams and ridges like a drying apple. "Laila, you didn't... it's not...."

"No! Never again, you know that!" About this, at least, I was not lying. My mother may have started painting again, but I would never again forge a masterpiece. No matter what the temptation. I walked back to the bureau and fingered the tubes: cobalt blue, ultramarine, cadmium gold extra, alizarene red, titanium white, raw sienna and burnt umber dark. I wondered where the greens were. I thought of old lead tin yellow, and how hard it was to get a decent quantity of that stuff. Or the right kind of cadmium yellow, almost impossible to lay hands on a tube of it. Verona green. What wouldn't I have given to have a supply of it? One thing that forgers have to worry about that real painters don't: authentic materials. My fingers trembled a little, thinking about it. But I was out of the life. I shouldn't be thinking this way.

"There will be underpainting." My mother smiled and flushed. "Wooden panels themselves were precious and Leonardo was ever mindful of the cost.

He was such a slow painter, with new ideas all the time, that he would just paint over and re-do something he'd already started. It's his signature, the underpainting, what makes it truly his. You will never find a Leonardo panel without some fascinating underpainting." She spoke with intimate certainty, as if he were her friend. I felt that way about Botticelli. After researching him intensively for the last few years, I even dreamt about him. Wasn't that just what Bolingbroke had advised me to do? Bolingbroke.

"Mama," I said. She gazed up, barely seeing me through the haze of con-templating a newly discovered painting by her great hero, Leonardo da Vinci. She had once told me that he had inspired her landscapes, the ravishing land-scapes that had brought her worldwide acclaim. Seeing the *Virgin of the Rocks* as a girl had given her a thirst to paint like him. Now her idol was going out on tour with a new hit. She looked like she'd seen a rock star and he'd kissed her. I cleared my throat. "Did you ever meet an acquaintance of Daddy's named John Bolingbroke?"

"Bolingbroke?" Her veiled-over eyes snapped back into focus. "Sure, I met him once. Tall and attractive. Quite. He and your dad were in some sort of club together, some men's thing. Your dad didn't talk about it much."

"A club? Dad belonged to a club?"

"Not a club, per se. Like a group or an organization of some sort. He mentioned something and I had the idea that he was smoking cigars and drink-ing brandy with other men. I didn't pay much attention. He was very secretive about it." My mom knelt beside her bed and pulled a box from underneath it.

"And that's where he met Bolingbroke," I murmured.

"Um. Then your dad introduced him to a collector who was selling something." She opened the box, which was full of books. With a flourish, she pulled out an old leather-bound volume, a da Vinci catalogue. "One of the post-modernists, I think."

"Pollack," I said, before thinking. Fern made a tiny sound. I'd forgotten she was here. I turned toward her. She made her face really, really blank, which meant, "You've fucked up, Laila."

"You met him? Did he know about your father's disappearance?" The pearlescent pleasure drained away from my mother's face, leaving it as gray as when we'd first arrived. "I don't suppose he saw him after we did? No one did." And there was no avoiding it: the very subject we wanted to avoid discussing, Bolingbroke and my father's disappearance, stood before us, as broken and ugly as a charred corpse.

We left an hour later, having narrowly avoided analyzing Bolingbroke and his connection to my father. Fern, ever resourceful, had managed to bring the conversation back to da Vinci. My mother walked us out, holding my arm loosely. I could feel her fingers, small and fine as a child's, on the inside of my elbow. It made me want to protect her, which also made me angry, because wasn't she supposed to protect me? That old conundrum that had haunted me since childhood twisted up my gut and kept me silent. She was silent, too. Then, as the ashram fell away behind us and the parking lot approached in all its packed-earth glory, she said, "Did you ask Mr. Bolingbroke if he'd seen or heard from your father?"

"I didn't talk to him for long," I answered tightly. "Chance meeting. Over quick."

"I never thought to ask Robert's club if they knew anything about his disappearance," she said, her gaze troubled. "I wouldn't know how to contact them. As I said, your father was exceptionally private about them."

"I'll see what I can find out. But let's not get our hopes up."

"I don't want you to get your hopes up and get hurt," she said gently.

I felt that prickle of irritation I always felt when my mother got too maternal toward me. Immediately I felt guilty, as well; she'd suffered when my father disappeared. And wasn't I just wishing she would protect me? "I'm a big girl, mother. I can take care of myself."

"I still love him, you know," she said softly. "I always will."

"You were divorced when it happened," I said, before I could stop myself. My mother looked glum. I stopped in front of Dex's car. I was relieved to be leaving, but also troubled by my mother's feelings. I still had to ask: what was she painting now? I looked into her drawn, lined face and knew she didn't want to tell me. All these blank spots in our dialogue now. It's what no one tells you, what you can't be prepared for, when you're confronted with an inexplicable loss: that collateral emptinesses open up like holes in the ozone, letting in cancerous radiation. But, because, potentially, Dad was at stake, I couldn't baby my mother. "Mama, what are you painting? Landscapes?"

Fern heard the tension and slipped her arm around my mother. "This ashram must be such a lovely subject, Eleanor. 'The evening beam that smiles the clouds away, and tints tomorrow with prophetic ray.'"

"Byron, how appropriate," my mother said. She laid her head on Fern's shoulder for a moment and I didn't know who to be jealous of: Fern, that my mother was so easy in her affection toward her, or my mother, for nailing Fern's quote. My mother lifted her head and smiled at Fern. "I'm painting still lifes. It's new for me, intriguing."

"They must be so beautiful!" Fern gushed.

"Everything you paint is superb," I said. "And your hand would be distinctive, no matter what the subject. You are a master."

"I think people at the ashram are enjoying them, because some have disappeared." My mother made an open-palmed gesture: what can you do?

"I am sure they are magnificent, and so very tempting to people who love beauty." Fern smiled. She leaned forward and kissed my mother. "Don't be anxious, Eleanor. Laila's not alone in this." My mother nodded and watched us get in and buckle up. Then she turned away very quickly, her white tunic fluttering around her, her head drooping forward.

Chapter 6

He sat in his library in front of a lit candle. Bolingbroke didn't need its illumination, but the flickering yellow flame helped him focus, brought him quickly into the internal alignment he needed for astral projection. He wanted to find Laila, see what she was doing. She didn't realize the danger that stalked her and her father—how close it was, how coiled and ready to kill. Bolingbroke had twice promised Robert that he'd protect the girl: the first time five years ago, when Robert Cambridge took on the highest mantle of his secret society, and disappeared in order to protect his family. And then again a few weeks ago, when Bolingbroke saw Robert at the library. Bolingbroke had promised, and he kept his promises. It was a matter of honor, of *soul*, that thing that vampires lacked and that Bolingbroke prized above all else. That nearly indefinable thing of which he had a precious half.

Shadows like gray strips of gauze hung down from the intricate wood paneling, heightening the brightness of the bobbing flame. Outside his brownstone, a woman walked by, laughing. For a moment, Bolingbroke's hunger surged. All of his unquenchable desire for blood erupted, and Bolingbroke could taste it in his mouth: sweet, coppery, the essence of life seeping into every starving fiber of his being. And wouldn't Laila be delicious, in his arms, skin against skin, her vanilla and violets and daisies and bergamot scent on his tongue? Her sugary blood draining into his throat while pleasure tore through her soft flesh....

He hadn't expected her to be so luscious, so intelligent and humorous, so complex and yet simple in her appetites. He had known she was beautiful, had enjoyed the pictures of her as a tall skinny girl that Robert had shown him when they first met. He'd admired her from afar when she was forging. Bolingbroke cherished mastery, and Laila Cambridge was a master forger. But meeting her, now that she was a grown woman, that changed everything. It was no longer about impersonal appreciation. He wanted her like no woman he'd met before. He was honor-bound to protect her. But who would protect Laila from him?

Bolingbroke repeated his mantra within his head, concentrating on it syllable by syllable, disciplining himself into the inner stillness he demanded of himself. The effort was tremendous. It left him dripping with sweat. The rewards were equally vast. Peace spread through his being, followed by an intense, upwelling lightness. A moment later, his consciousness disentangled from his body. He was floating, floating, flying.

He landed beside her. It was so palpable that he could smell the perspiration of nervousness and emotional overwhelm on Laila's tall, finely-knit body. Humans did not know that there were a thousand scents of sweat, each one specific and delicious, just as there were a thousand flavors of tears. Blood chemistry changed with each emotional nuance of the human in whose veins it ran, which made humans a feast for connoisseurs. Vampires never tired of their sole food source because each meal was a symphony of flavors, fresh and unpredictable, evolving during the course of the feeding. Bolingbroke no longer needed to feed on living people, but he could still smell them in ways they couldn't begin to understand. He could sense them better, in fact, since he'd received his half-soul. Because now he could see the luminous aura in which they lived. Traveling like this, in what the ancient Egyptians would have called his ka, and what Asians would refer to as his chi or ki, and what modern Westerners would call his astral body or spirit form, he could see Laila's aura with clarity and pleasure: beautiful, bright, complex colors, swirling in a symphony of light and feeling. God, she was beautiful. He wanted her. He started his mantra again.

Fern and I drove back in silence, the kind of comfortable quiet that only best friends can share. The kind of quiet that is without masks because we've already seen each other at our worst, as well as at our best, and at every point in between, so there are no excuses and no conceits. Besides, I knew what she was thinking, and it was what I was thinking: that Bolingbroke's story had borne out. I had to contact him and tell him that I wanted to find and protect my dad. That I was desperate to do so. That I'd do anything to save my father, anything. Even though it still hurt that he'd vanished without a word or a trace, and left me and my mom and my brother in the cruelest kind of pain.

We returned the car to Dex, who wanted to bullshit about the band's upcoming gig. Fern fended him off and we walked slowly back toward our apartment.

"Buy you a drink?" she offered.

"Mmm," I said. I was thinking of Bolingbroke. I couldn't get him out of my mind, in fact. He filled up my thoughts as if he were standing beside me. I could almost smell him. If I closed my eyes, I could: amber and the woods and some indefinable rapture. It weakened my knees.

"Hey, Laila, alcohol?" Fern poked my ribs.

"I'm drinking too much." Like an automaton, I repeated Bolingbroke's words.

"Has that ever stopped you before?" She linked her arm through mine. "Chop chop, round eyes, we go bar and drink whiskey."

No, I had to find Bolingbroke. "I want to get started. Right now."

"I thought you'd want to get a good night's sleep," Fern said. "Start in the morning."

"It's my dad, Fern," I said, but she already had out her smartphone and was typing into its Web browser.

"I know, you don't want to waste a minute, he could be in danger," she murmured. "There's a J. Bolingbroke on the Upper West Side."

"He said he had enough money for any ten people."

"Nice address. North of the Museum of Natural History." She nodded and showed me the Google entry. I kissed her cheek and held out my arm for a taxi. Then I ran out into the avenue in front of one, because in Manhattan, the best way to hail a taxi is to stop one with your body.

"Need cash?" she called.

"I've got the laundry quarters," I hollered back.

"You think your dad's life is worth me wearing stinky clothes?" she teased. She shook her head with fake regret. My dad's life. Adrenalin burned through my body. It was after midnight. Sleep could wait, though, if I had only a week to save my dad, as Bolingbroke had said.

The taxi stopped outside a brownstone on West 89th off Columbus. I paid the driver—I hated to relinquish those precious laundry quarters, but there were only just enough for the fare plus tip—then ran up the steps. I was trembling as I rang the buzzer.

A moment later, the door opened. It was Bolingbroke. He wore a loose white shirt and jeans. Our eyes met, his transmogrified into cat eyes, and he lifted me up into his arms and kissed me. I wrapped my arms and legs around him and gave myself entirely to the moment, to his mouth.

Then we were inside the parlor floor apartment, cozy with mahogany paneling and shelves and shelves of books. An antique English desk with gargoyle faces carved into the drawers stood near the window. We sat in a leather club chair, me in his lap.

"I shouldn't do this." He groaned and rubbed his lips gently over my neck.

"I want you!" I said. I was shivering as if with cold, but I was bursting with juicy warmth. All of my bones were liquefying with desire.

"We have work to do." He lifted his head. Whimsy and desire and regret chased each other over his face. I laid my hands on his cool cheeks, felt his strong bones under my palms, and kissed him. He groaned again and it became a kind of growl as we kept kissing. "Stop!" he cried. He pushed me away as far as he could, which wasn't too far, given the dimensions of the chair.

"Don't you want me?"

"More than anything." With that, he slid himself out from under me and sprang up. He paced around the room. He reminded me of a panther, feral and pulsing.

"So keep kissing me!"

"It's complicated," he said. He ran his hand up through his hair and I noticed again that he looked exactly like Mercury in Botticelli's *Primavera*. I smiled. "What?" he demanded.

"Mercury," I said softly. "Come back and kiss me more, sweet Mercury."

"You're in danger, Laila."

"My father is in danger." I sighed and leaned back in the chair.

"He is. But that group I told you about, they're interested in you as well."

"Group... I saw my mother today and she mentioned that my father used to belong to some sort of club or group. Is that the same group who's after him now?"

"Oh, no. Different groups." Bolingbroke laughed shortly. "Opposing groups, actually. Your father's group, his society, is leading a fight against the, ah, evil group."

"Evil group, like terrorists?" I puzzled.

"Not exactly, more like, ah, La Cosa Nostra. Or the yakuza, the Japanese mafia. They're vicious and bloodthirsty. They don't want anyone to stop them, and your father's group has pledged to do that, so your father's become a target. Right now it has more to do with the painting he's looking for. They want it."

"The legendary lost Botticelli!" I jumped up and wandered to the corner of the room, where a white marble bust sat on a sleek black granite column. I ran my hands over the bust's eyes and curly hair. "I know what he was doing at the Columbia library. Looking for clues in a rare folio about Botticelli."

"Folio," he repeated, and his face took on that strange shuttered expression I'd seen a few times before.

"I've been looking for that folio for my dissertation," I said. "It's over a century old and has some unusual comments about Botticelli. If my father is searching for a lost Botticelli painting, he'll start there. He was the first one to show me the folio, years ago. In the Hermitage." Into my mind's eye flashed a quick image of my father and me walking along the River Neva in St. Petersburg, talking intensely about the Botticelli folio, da Vinci's *Madonna Litta*, Giorgione's *Judith*. I was bursting with impressions, my words a kaleidoscope of excitement and awe. My dad listened carefully, as if I were the most fascinating girl in the world. He had a way of doing that, not just with me but with everyone: focusing with total acceptance and absorption.

"What do you know of the painting?" Bolingbroke asked, interrupting my reverie. He sat on the window alcove and crossed his arms over his chest. His back was very straight, his head poised elegantly and with authority on his strong neck.

"I know the legends. Not sure I believe them. Sandro Filipepi went through some sort of troubled passage in his life. Had to do with the monk Savonarola and his fire and brimstone sermons. There was a clash between Savonarola's ferocious calls for reform, which correctly pointed out the corruption in the Church, and the liberal humanism that the educated class had developed. They were all in a fervor of translating ancient texts, you know, and had adopted the pagan gods and goddesses as philosophical ideals. Savonarola despised that. He was a purist."

"I have found, over the course of my life, that the necessary end of a purist agenda is terrorism," Bolingbroke said. His lids drooped and for a moment he looked timeless and ancient, inscrutable as a force of nature, a carved god. I wondered what he had witnessed in his life to bring him to such a painful conclusion. Had he himself suffered as a result of someone's purist agenda? But then he was half-smiling at me, and jerking his chin as a gesture for me to continue.

"During this time Botticelli painted a masterpiece, of a pagan rite," I burbled brightly. "It was said to be his last mythological painting, and was painted after *The Allegory of Spring* and *The Birth of Venus.*

"It's said that Leonardo da Vinci contributed to the painting. Lots of different stories about how that came to be. Leonardo got drunk one night and painted in a god on a dare. Botticelli asked Leonardo to collaborate. Another rumor claims that Leonardo, who had a particular passion for faces, was so entranced by the beauty of the female faces that he begged to be allowed to paint one of the gods in the painting. Supposedly this comes from Vasari himself, though I've never found the reference. And I've read the complete *Lives of the Artists*, in the original Italian. Every friggin' page, and Vasari isn't fun when he starts pontificating. He is one long-winded PR guy."

"He's a useful reference for an expert forger recreating lost masterpieces."

I didn't take the bait. I had been stroking the bust, which was certainly Baroque and struck me as both masterful and familiar. "Is this a copy of a Bernini?"

"No," Bolingbroke said. He smiled.

I shrugged. "Reminds me of the Bernini bust of Costanza Bonarelli, his mistress."

"It's not a copy," Bolingbroke said. "What else do you know about the lost Botticelli? What are your thoughts on it?"

"It's all legend, rumor, and hearsay. One rumor says it was the first painting Botticelli threw in Savonarola's bonfire of the vanities. It just kills me to think of Sandro Filipepi throwing in his own work to be burnt! What a tragedy for humanity!"

"I understand," Bolingbroke murmured. "But you must consider the time. There was widespread disgust with the Church, and unease about the Medici, who ruled with complete disregard for anyone's welfare other than their own. People were electrified by Savonarola. His words were persuasive." Bolingbroke stopped and the corner of his mouth lifted in that ironic half-smile that caused my heart to stutter. "Savonarola was ushered into power on a platform of change. His followers were the first crowds to scream, 'Yes, we can!'"

"Modern day liberals would not appreciate the analogy," I said, dryly. "Anyway, I never believed that the painting still exists. I guess Dad does. Otherwise he wouldn't look for it."

"It exists," Bolingbroke said. His strange hessonite eyes speared me with their passion. I was transfixed, immobilized. He said, "*Coming Forth by Day* is real, and it's one of his greatest works. It was carried out of Savonarola's abortion of a bonfire by one of Sandro's intimates. It was given to a Roman nobleman and Medici supporter, and then it vanished."

I couldn't speak at first. Finally I managed, "You're sure?" Bolingbroke nodded. I asked, "What's your source?"

Bolingbroke looked away, freeing me from the spell of his eyes. "It's unimpeachable. And that's what I told your father when he contacted me. That's why I went to the library to meet him."

"Why is he looking for that painting?" I wondered. "Why do the bad guys want it?"

"It's valuable."

"Valuable enough to kill for?" I mused. "I guess it's worth untold millions of dollars. A hundred million, perhaps. But there are other paintings that would fetch as much or more on the market. Why this painting?"

"Someone else knows for sure that it exists," Bolingbroke said. He stalked around the room again.

"I suppose it could have surfaced recently, gotten everyone in a tizzy of coveting it," I said. "Maybe my father is looking for it to fund his group. And if my father is looking for the painting, tracking the painting is the best way to get to him."

"Before the other group does," Bolingbroke added.

"Dad and I don't have the same resources, though," I muttered. I was thinking now, calculating, plotting my course. "We know the same books and paper trails. But we'll have different trajectories. This is actually a bet that my path will cross his."

"You have contacts your father doesn't. In the art world. Its underbelly, I should say. Those contacts will serve us."

I looked up sharply and found him grinning. It wasn't funny. I raised my chin and spoke primly. "I don't appreciate your insinuations."

"I'm not insinuating. I'm stating a fact. You were part of a network; you studied with the best forgers in the world; you know the best who are currently operational."

"I was the best," I said, wearily but truthfully.

Bolingbroke dipped his head, affirming what I'd said. "You even had a run at selling your forgeries yourself."

"Big mistake." But fun, too, the peculiar kind of intimacy that comes from looking a mark in the eyes and putting a grift over on him. Or her. I shivered with revulsion at myself. *Never again*, I swore.

Bolingbroke was relentless. "Given the stakes, why would you indulge yourself in qualms about your old contacts? Crooked dealers, crooked distributors, crooked provenance manufacturers, crooked collectors. They have a wealth of information. Especially about rumor and legend, which is what we've got to go on."

"Crooked, is that your word for it? Qualms, ha—you don't know the half of it," I muttered. I collapsed on the leather chair. "They'll try to drag me back in. They'll remind me of the old life. There's a thrill. The temptation.... You don't understand."

"I understand too well about temptation," he said. He turned his back on me so I couldn't see his face. "You're the one with the contacts. What's our first step?"

I thought for a few minutes. Where to start.... Did I jump right in, call my old fence? No, she didn't necessarily know about Botticelli, or about this painting. She just knew people willing to pay top dollar for paintings from the hand of a master. Not that it was hard to find them. Even I had managed to collect a clientele during the year I'd sold my own stuff. There's a thriving market for stolen or dubious art; a surprising number of collectors don't give a damn about the provenance of a great work, if they desire it. Something about a masterpiece makes normally honest people salivate like starving apes and abandon all pretence of integrity.

But a lost masterpiece. That was a differently striped, and far more intriguing, beast. A fabulous beast, like a griffon or a unicorn. Where to start? As I mused, a strategy took shape in my mind. I knew who had a wealth of information about art, especially about lost art. Misappropriated art. He lived nearby. He had issued a standing invitation to me to call him. I had something he wanted.

"You have a car?" I asked. He nodded. I said, "Good. We're driving to the Hudson Valley. We'll stop by my apartment first." I sprang up and went to Bolingbroke's door, let myself out into the cool night air.

"Now, the middle of the night, there's someone we're going to see?" Bolingbroke followed me out and locked the door behind us.

"It'll be fine, he's kind of a vampire—"

"Vampire!" Bolingbroke tensed.

"Dude, chill, it's an analogy." I touched his arm gently. I was standing close to him and moved my hand to his broad muscular chest. Bolingbroke grunted and pushed me away. Wise, since otherwise I might have slowed things down. *Focus, Laila,* I told myself. *You have a job to do.* "He's an eccentric collector, keeps late hours. Told me to call him at night, the later the better."

"A collector," Bolingbroke repeated. He took my elbow and led me down the stairs toward Columbus Avenue.

"More than a collector. And more than eccentric. Reclusive, a genius of sorts. A billionaire." I had always wanted to introduce my father to this man. My father had enjoyed unusual people. He told me once that he collected misfits rather than paintings, because as much as he loved art, he loved curious people more. Also, for all our travels, we were not rich, except in experiences. My dad. "Bolingbroke," I asked, "what did my father say to you, when you saw him at the library?"

Bolingbroke was quiet as we went down Columbus toward a parking garage on one of the cross streets. A group of drunken kids passed us, and various lawyer and banker types, coming home late, clutching Blackberries and briefcases. Lots of Manhattan professionals work a hundred hours a week. It's kind of nuts. Finally, he said, "He made me promise to take care of you." It was so exactly like what my father would do that it silenced me. My eyes got a little damp again, and I thought it must be from the chill in the night air. We approached the garage and a sleepy Hispanic man sitting on a folding chair recognized Bolingbroke and bolted inside.

"You must tip well," I commented. He shrugged. We stood in the pale pointillist oval of a light by the garage front. And then the garage door clanked and scrolled open, and a Bentley rolled out toward us. I whistled. "Sweet!" I said softly. My dad, who adored cars and motorcycles and anything with wheels, would have loved this automobile. I probably had that kind of thought twenty times a day, every day, and had since the last time I'd seen him.

Chapter 7

FERN WAS STILL AWAKE WHEN I USHERED Bolingbroke into our apartment. She sat on the couch with her Riverside Shakespeare in her lap. Her straight black hair fell down loose around her shoulders and she wore a close-fitting tank that said "OM" and drawstring trousers, as if she'd just come from yoga class. Did she ever not look perfect?

"Hey, Gonzo, you're back," she called, before laying eyes on my guest. She leapt to her feet, smiling.

"'Gonzo'?" Bolingbroke asked, *sotto voce*. I slapped his shoulder. His luscious, hard, rolling shoulder.

"Fern, John Bolingbroke; Bolingbroke, my roommate Fern Takahasi." I waved my index finger around, pointing to the appropriate individual, even though my mom had always yelled at me for pointing at people. She wouldn't have loved the etiquette of this introduction at all. But Fern did. She leapt up with a huge smile on her face.

"Nice to meet you," Fern said, extending her hand.

"The pleasure is mine, Miss Takahasi." Bolingbroke took her hand in both of his and bowed over it. His lips grazed her palm. Fern quivered. Maybe I'd have to remind her about the strict terms of our dibs policy.

"Fern, we're going to see Kristofer Hahnemann," I chirped. "I'm going to call him. Be good while I'm gone, you two."

"Did you say Kristofer Hahnemann?" Bolingbroke asked. He dropped Fern's hand and twisted his face into an expression I couldn't read.

"You know him?" I asked.

"Know of him," Bolingbroke said.

"I always wanted to meet him," Fern said. "Laila says such interesting things about him. Though she claims he's obsessed with old conspiracies that are better left shrouded in time. 'Oh leave the past to bury its own dead. The past is naught to us, the present all.'"

"'What need of last year's leaves to strew Love's bed? What need of ghosts to grace a festival?'" Bolingbroke recited the next lines of the poem. He smiled and clasped Fern's hand again.

"'Then let us love and leave the rest unsaid,'" Fern murmured.

"How delightful to hear Wilfrid Scawen Blunt quoted. One doesn't often encounter him these days."

Fern beamed at him, and her cheeks turned pink. "He's only a minor poet....."

"Play nice, you two, but not too nice," I said. Really I growled. I marched to my bedroom. I slammed the door good and loud, so they'd remember me while I was out of the room. I went to my closet, pulled out shoes and a suitcase to clear a path, and brought out the boot box. In this box I store a pair of tall white patent-leather boots that have pinched my feet from the moment I bought them. I wear them anyway; they're the perfect accoutrement to a black-and-white kilt miniskirt that I wear to Fern's gigs. I stroked their shiny white surface, thought about how racy these boots always make me feel. I stand over six feet tall when I put them on, but I decided long ago that if my karma made me tower, I wasn't going to hide it. Anyway, Bolingbroke was at least four inches taller than me. I wondered if he'd like the boots.

I smiled and replaced the boots, set aside the box. What I was looking for was stored in the way back, behind the box. A flat package, wrapped in cellophane. I pulled out the package and tore off the wrapping. Rich, dappled colors. A masterful manipulation of color and light, a luminous palette of saturated color. I had used layers of paint to achieve a rich, complex impasto. Purples, lavenders. A lively line. One of my best. And only two people in the world, maybe three if that French critic's eye had improved, could tell that it wasn't a genuine Diebenkorn.

I sat down on my bed and picked up my landline. The phone company was going to shut it down soon, had sent us threatening letters for weeks.

Hahnemann answered on the second ring. "Laila Cambridge, are you ready to sell me the Diebenkorn?"

I had to smile even while I grimaced. I'd known Hahnemann for ten years. What could I say? We ran in similar seedy, nefarious circles—me to create and sell great works of art, him to acquire great works by any means possible. He had even acquired mine, knowing full well what they were, praising me for their authenticity and execution. He's always the same, always rockets in for the bottom line like a wasp going in for a sting. Kinda have to admire his focus. "Hello, Kristofer. How are you?"

"I've been waiting for this call for two and a half years."

"I've got it right in front of me."

"Finally." He took in a gulp of air. Acquisitive, that one. Relentless. "What was my last offer?"

"As if you didn't know, and the price is double that," I snapped.

"Agreed," he said, too swiftly, and I knew I should have said triple. Damn. But at least Fern and I wouldn't have to worry about scrounging for laundry quarters for a long, long time. What was it my dad used to say? That's right: "Bears make money, bulls make money, pigs get slaughtered." So at least I hadn't been a pig.

Hahnemann said, "Send a car?"

"Huh? No, I've got a ride. I'm bringing a friend."

"Your lovely Eurasian friend?" Hahnemann sounded perky, and I made a mental note to warn Fern. I wouldn't put it past Hahnemann to collect people as well as paintings.

"No. But you'll like him."

"Him? I already don't. The bum. Why are you bringing him? You know how I feel about strangers." He was disturbed, and a German inflection dipped in over his speech like a shadow. I thought about answering him in German so I could hear his accent. The German language is a multifarious business, and the split between High and Low German gives way to regional dialects and accents that yield a wealth of information about family and status to an attuned ear. For whatever reason, without deserving it at all, one of those flukes of the genetic lotto, I had such an ear. Given Hahnemann's proclivities, I could use this ear to get the goods on him, in case I ever needed an ace up my sleeve.

I said, merely, "He's an art lover and a collector. He's one of us."

"Bah. When will you arrive?"

"We're leaving in a few minutes."

"You have the address." Hahnemann hung up. I cradled the Diebenkorn in my arms and carried it out to the living room, where Fern and Bolingbroke were in the midst of a heated discussion about obscure Victorian poets.

Bolingbroke looked up and whistled.

"I'm getting the rent money," I told Fern. "Beats dancing in the park for money thrown into a hat. Don't want that social worker calling me again. I narrowly avoided Bellevue last time."

"She had no sense of humor," said Fern.

"You, dance in the park?" A wide grin broke over Bolingbroke's face.

"Laila's a great dancer," Fern said, arms akimbo.

"I don't doubt," Bolingbroke agreed, in the kind of voice that speaks of doubt and nothing but doubt. He took the painting from me, hoisted it up into the light, and perused it carefully.

"Laila, you want to do this?" Fern laid her hand on my shoulder. "You'll feel bad tomorrow. Soiled."

"No, I won't. It's for dad. I need information and Hahnemann probably has it. Besides, he's not a victim. He knows exactly what it is."

"A breathtakingly beautiful work of the highest caliber," Bolingbroke said, in a reverent tone. "Absolutely indistinguishable from the artist's own hand. Magnificent. You have some talent, Laila."

"Talent is what my mother has, the ability to produce an original in her own unique voice. I'm, like, a scanner with red hair. A copier. A wax model maker from Madame Tussaud's."

"You underestimate yourself," Bolingbroke said, with his customary authority. "I hope you haven't undervalued the painting. On the open market, it would fetch a tidy sum."

"Yeah, I can price a painting. A lot better than I can dance."

"Of that, I am sure."

"That's the address," Bolingbroke said, just after his GPS announced it. He pointed to a vast, purple silhouette against the indigo night. I'd heard about Hahnemann's place but never visited before, and I couldn't believe how big the house was. "House": the thing was a megalithic castle, sprawling all over a set of hills overlooking the Hudson River in Tarrytown, New York. I've seen European villages that were smaller. I've seen European countries that were smaller!

"Damn, that's some spread!" I said, gawking.

"Vulgar display of wealth." Bolingbroke sniffed. Was he the tiniest bit jealous?

We drove through a vast iron gate, along a winding road to a circular drive, and stopped in front of a set of looming wooden doors that must have been brought over from a medieval palace. Floodlights came on as Bolingbroke parked. He came around to open the car door for me but I had already sprung out. He rolled his eyes.

"Welcome, welcome, Laila and guest," said Hahnemann, as we approached. He stood in the threshold in a tube of yellow light, a lean, blond gentleman with fine, erect posture and a sophisticated mien. As always, Hahnemann was dressed in a well-cut Italian suit—this one was fine navy wool with a thin purple stripe—and custom shoes. My father would have approved; he always said that clothes made the man. This man reeked of money and status and fairly buzzed with culture and taste. But I knew that he was stone cold acquisitive, and not afraid to get his hands dirty to get what he wanted. He kissed both of my cheeks in greeting.

"Kristofer, may I present my boyfriend, John Bolingbroke," I said. "Bolingbroke, this is Kristofer Hahnemann." The two men shook hands, and Hahnemann looked slightly less peeved because I had introduced him so formally. He gestured us up the steps. I paused to admire the heavy oaken doors with their ornate carving.

Bolingbroke leaned close and whispered, "Boyfriend?"

I shrugged. "This reminds me of the Zwinger palace," I murmured, running my hand along the door.

"You have a keen eye," Kristofer said. "Of course, we always knew that about you."

"I thought the Zwinger doors were destroyed by fire some time ago," Bolingbroke commented.

"The doors were quietly saved and reproductions were installed. Then there was a flood in 2002." Hahnemann motioned for us to step inside.

"A flood in Dresden, yes, I remember," I said.

"You should. You were there, restoring a very nice but damp Rembrandt that would otherwise have rotted." He smiled and waved for me to precede him into the foyer. "You worked feverishly, without stopping to eat or even to use the facilities."

I stepped into the cavernous hall and wanted to exclaim at the beauty
of the antique crystal chandelier that hung overhead, big as a Volkswagen,
shedding millions of rainbow slicks of light. But I was too absorbed in what
Kristofer was saying. "You saw me in Dresden? What the hell were you doing
there?"

"Money was required for the rescue and restoration efforts." He waved
his hands again and the doors closed. "Grateful Dresden officials gifted me
with these doors."

"Convenient," Bolingbroke said. Hahnemann gave him a sharp look.
Bolingbroke lifted one corner of his mouth in a lop-sided something that
resembled a sneer.

"Golly gee whillikers, I left the painting in the car!" I said, trying not to
sound as brittle as I felt.

"Allow me," Bolingbroke said. He stalked back toward the door. I followed, and pulled him aside when we were far enough away from Hahnemann
to avoid being overheard.

"Behave yourself," I whispered, grabbing his sleeve.

"He's carrying a pistol in his right jacket pocket," Bolingbroke breathed
into my ear.

"Hahnemann? No way," I scoffed. But then a Raphael painting, an actual
Raphael, caught my eye. It hung in the place of honor on the wall at the end
of the foyer.

I raced past the profusion of priceless paintings, sculptures, tapestries,
and Ming vases to the Raphael. It was a portrait of a young man with a fur
mantello over his shoulder—not a work I recognized instantly, but I knew the
hand. Raphael's sweet sensibility and eye for composition, his use of color and
geometry, were as unique as a thumbprint. Some disowned part of me began,
automatically, to analyze the technique for what I myself could use. *No, Laila.*
I shook my head to clear out those sleazy, tantalizing thoughts. Then I recognized the painting. And Hahnemann was standing right beside me.

"This was stolen by the Nazis! Hans Frank, Hitler's lawyer, was supposed
to have it, but when they arrested him, it wasn't among his possessions."

"Hans Frank was a bloodthirsty bum and I sang at his execution,"
Hahnemann said. I turned to face him, not realizing how close he was. His
body, so near mine, gave off a faint warm crackle, like electricity. His cool

blue eyes were only a few inches from mine and he gently smoothed a lock of hair away from my nose.

"But you got the painting from him first?" I asked, barely able to breathe. Hahnemann nodded.

"You remind me of the German lasses of my youth," he whispered. "But that red hair...it's exceptional." There was warmth in his gaze. I found myself blushing. He smiled, even white teeth in a symmetrical face. A mysteriously youthful face. Was he thirty-five, or seventy-five? If he had met Hans Frank, he had to be getting on in years.

"How old are you, Kristofer?"

"How old do you want me to be?" His face softened, so that he looked twenty.

"Where shall I put this?" called Bolingbroke. Kristofer and I turned toward him. Bolingbroke held the painting.

"Oh, yes, *mein Gott*—the painting, at long last!" Kristofer clasped his hands together and sped toward Bolingbroke. Beaming, he took the painting from Bolingbroke and practically skipped down the hall. "Follow me!"

We marched through a maze of ornate rooms, passing masterpiece after masterpiece. Off one gallery, a door hung open. A delicate floral fragrance wafted out. I couldn't resist the urge to peek in. Sculpted amber panels, inlaid with jewels, covered the walls. I stepped in and golden light, heady and rich, enveloped me.

"Holy *shit*!" I exclaimed. "Oh my *god*!"

"We'll discuss this another time," Hahnemann said.

"That's the Amber Room! The whole world is looking for it!" I was stunned. The Amber Room: a complete chamber decoration made in 1701 of amber panels backed with gold leaf. So astonishingly beautiful that it was called the eighth wonder of the world. Seized by the Germans during World War II, and lost in 1945.

"Let the world look," he said. He set his jaw. "While they look, I will preserve it for future generations."

"Preserve it or hoard it for yourself, like the Raphael?" Bolingbroke asked.

"This is none of your concern," Hahnemann said. He sounded irritated. "I went to a lot of trouble during the war to protect this, this irreplaceable part of humanity's cultural heritage."

"I'd say you went to a lot of trouble to profit from the war," Bolingbroke said.

Hahnemann blanched. "I hid Jews and gypsies. I created a scheme whereby homosexual men married made-over gypsy women and both were saved. I was part of an underground German resistance movement that tried to prevent the worst excesses of the Nazi party. I did this at risk of my own life. I sent thousands of people to safety. I am not a criminal!"

"You ended up with a palace full of stolen art that you haven't given back to the rightful owners," Bolingbroke said softly.

This was getting ugly. I was as appalled as Bolingbroke was, but I wasn't here to judge Hahnemann. How could I judge, with my past? I was here to get information so that I could find my father before he was killed. Had Bolingbroke forgotten about that? "Gentlemen, let us agree to disagree, for the moment," I snapped. "We have business to conduct."

We ended up in a spacious alcove, in which hung six paintings that I knew all too well: a Lorenzo Lotto Madonna, a Hans Memling portrait, an El Greco landscape of Toledo, an Ingres portrait of a young woman, a Corot seascape, and a wildly energized Pollack. A pristine empty space in the center of the six attested to Hahnemann's determination to obtain this one, one of my finest ever, the Diebenkorn. Bolingbroke looked intrigued and went to study the Pollack close up.

Hahnemann had a complicated hanging system with which he was fiddling, trying to get the painting up on the wall, as he talked. "The trick, of course, is not to let the collector know that they own a genuine Laila Cambridge, rather than a genuine, well, whomever you were forging. What a fascinating diversity of hands you possess!"

"Not proud of it."

"But you should be: you're a master in your own right," he said. "To convey another artist with such utter believability, as if you inhabit them, or they you, for the duration of the painting. Breathtaking."

"It is, was, a kind of possession," I murmured. And I flashed to it: the profound absorption of painting, as if I myself were Lorenzo Lotto or Jackson Pollack. With the paintbrush in my hand and every painting of the artist burning in my mind, all of my senses were heightened. Time stopped. The single moment NOW was preternaturally vivid. Everything fell away, all the extraneous detritus that we carry around with us and don't need. What was left was naked, real, and the essence of who I was. I was most alive then. What did that say about me? Nothing good. And Vivian Goran had died rather than surrender a Masaccio she was convinced was authentic. I closed my eyes. "I don't do it anymore. It's wrong."

"I'm close to acquiring another Corot you did. The deal is taking some time. As I said, I don't want to disillusion the owner."

"Lazy bastard," I muttered.

Hahnemann started. "Oh, I've—"

"Not you. Corot. Made him easy to, you know...."

"Forge?" he supplied. I nodded.

"Which Corot?"

"There's more than one more out there? Interesting." He looked intrigued. I opened my mouth but he held up his hand. "Don't tell me. Part of the fun is finding them. It's like a treasure hunt."

"As you wish," I said. Hahnemann had finagled the painting onto the wall and he stepped back to view it, sighing with pleasure.

"Payment?" Bolingbroke said, over his shoulder.

"Is your old account active?" Hahnemann asked me, ignoring Bolingbroke. "I'll have the money wired in."

"I'm out of the life. I closed the offshore account. I have a regular bank account," I said. "I'm legit now. I pay taxes."

"What a waste," Kristofer sighed. He wasn't referring to the taxes.

"One more thing, Kristofer. To close the deal."

"Don't you dare try to extort more money out of me!" he roared. "We agreed on a price!"

"Easy, Herr Kommandant, stand down," I barked back. "I want information. If you don't tell me what I need to know, then we don't have a deal! Screw the money. I'll take the painting with me and burn it in the street."

"She'll take the money," Bolingbroke said. "With the information." He placed his large, warm hand on the small of my back, exerting control, warning me to silence.

"What kind of information?" Hahnemann said. His eyes had gone silvery blue, cold and frigid like an ice floe in the arctic moonlight. The rest of his handsome ageless face set itself into still lines. I wondered if there was any limit to this man's anger, when he was crossed.

I took a deep breath. "What do you know about Botticelli's *Coming Forth by Day*?"

Hahnemann's face relaxed. "Ah, the holy grail of lovers of the Early Renaissance. The legendary lost Botticelli, which bears a god painted by da Vinci. The only known collaboration of the two masters. Botticelli's most ravishing masterpiece, depicting an ancient, magical, and potent pagan rite. As well as the secret signs of the most secret and ancient of societies, the Illuminati."

"The Illuminati? What?" I asked.

Hahnemann laughed. "I thought you would ask me something important that I don't want to reveal, like who shot Jack Kennedy or whether there were alien ships at the Apollo moon landing. The location of Camelot. The resting place of the scrolls from the Library of Alexandria. *Mein Gott, Zaubermaus*, you can't imagine the secrets I hold. And you're inquiring after a lost painting?"

"It's important," I said. "We can discuss Camelot another time. Please, Kristofer. Do you know where it is?"

He smirked. "That information is lost in the sewerage of time."

"Do you know where it is?" I repeated.

Hahnemann shook his head. "Why the sudden interest in this painting? This painting, of all others? I can tell you the locations of two lost Giorgiones."

"I don't want to know about two lost Giorgiones." Not this time, anyway. Maybe in the future? When my dad was safe.... I swallowed. "I need to find this painting. Must."

"The trail has been cold for so long," Hahnemann murmured.

"You must know something," I pressed. "Anything."

Hahnemann shrugged. "Don't tell me what I must know."

"You're lying," Bolingbroke said, in a neutral tone of voice.

"What? I don't care what *you* think!" Hahnemann cried.

"Not think. Know. Your heartbeat has increased in tempo, as has your breath. Your vocal pitch has inflected. You are sweating, and your face and hands have paled. You are lying," Bolingbroke said calmly. His face turned hard, and his look at Hahnemann reminded me of the librarian's scowl at me—it drained the room of life and energy.

"I don't know where the painting is," Hahnemann insisted. He reached his hands toward his jacket pockets.

"If you attempt to pull out that pearl-handled pistol, I will rip out your throat," Bolingbroke said softly. Hahnemann's hand kept moving. The next thing I knew, faster than I could even blink, Bolingbroke stood beside Hahnemann. It was as if Bolingbroke had dematerialized and then, in the same instant, rematerialized across the room. Bolingbroke's hand encircled and crushed Hahnemann's. In Hahnemann's crumpled fist was a small pearl-handled handgun. It looked too pretty to be lethal, but that was probably deceptive. Bolingbroke took the gun from Hahnemann, put it in his own pocket.

Hahnemann gaped. He looked as if he was about to say something, but then walked to the Lotto Madonna and stroked the antique gilt frame. I remembered acquiring the frame from a dealer in Milan. I paid good money for it, because an authentic frame went towards authenticating the painting. I had sold the Lotto to a pharmaceutical heir in Lausanne. How had Hahnemann obtained it?

"I had no intention of aiming the weapon at you," Hahnemann said, tightly.

"You looked for the Botticelli," Bolingbroke suggested.

"At one time, yes," Hahnemann agreed. Lightly, trembling, his fingers traced the curving cheek of the Madonna. "I have my own reasons for wanting to find that painting...." He seemed vacant, unsettled, angry, regretful, and achingly sad. Why such complicated feelings?

"What did you discover?" Bolingbroke asked.

"Not much, and I am an expert at discovering things," Hahnemann said. He took a few fast, shallow breaths, then turned toward us. "But I know who has a strong connection to it. Giovanni Belzoni."

I groaned. Not Belzoni!

Hahnemann's smirk returned. "You know him, of course."

"I heard he was dead."

"Nonsense! He's very much alive, in Paris. I spoke to him a few weeks ago. He asked me to send him Mallomar cookies. Says he can't get them in Paris."

"That sweet tooth of his," I murmured, glumly.

"He's got a place in the twelfth, Rue Guillaumot, says twenty years ago junkies hung out on the stoop but now it's clean and upscale."

"He preferred the junkies," I muttered. "They helped him find whores."

"This Belzoni knows about the Botticelli?" asked Bolingbroke. Hahnemann nodded but didn't look at Bolingbroke. Bolingbroke raised an eyebrow at me. I nodded. Made sense; Belzoni knew everything about the art world, especially about what was hidden in it. And Belzoni, like me, revered Botticelli. If anyone knew about the painting, it would be him. "We'll be on our way, then," Bolingbroke said. "Laila, give him your account information."

"I wrote a check. In case Laila was so foolish as to capitulate to bourgeois notions of financial rectitude," Hahnemann said. He withdrew a folded piece of paper from his breast pocket. I took it—okay, snatched it—out of his hand. A check made out to me. In the right amount, with the right number of zeros. Yeah, baby. My knees weakened with joy. I couldn't help it—the straight life wasn't a lucrative life, at least not right now, for me. Fern and I were tired of eating discount peanut butter.

Bolingbroke turned on his heel and strode back the way we'd come. I trotted after him. Hahnemann came after me. We passed by an alcove filled with Meso-American *objets* and Hahnemann grabbed my arm, drew me in behind a giant grinning Olmec head.

"Laila, I must make a request," he whispered. His blue eyes pleaded with mine with such intensity that I was taken aback.

"What?"

"If you find the painting, please, turn it over to me. I beg of you."

"You? Why?"

"It's important to me. Vitally important. I will pay you. Ten times the amount of that check. Twenty times. One hundred times! You know I am good for my word!"

"I don't know," I said slowly. That was a vast sum indeed. Fern and I wouldn't have to worry about meals and rent until we were little old spinsters with an apartment full of kitties who would eat our rotting corpses when we died over our knitting. Hell, we could buy the whole townhouse and still live comfortably till we were a hundred and two.

"I'm desperate. I will pay, and I'll tell you anything. Anything!" He kneaded my hand close to his chest. His fingers were bruised where Bolingbroke had smashed them together. "Please, Laila, I beg of you," he whispered again. Kristofer Hahnemann, making a heartfelt plea? This was the first I knew that he had a heart.

"The painting's not the end-game for me, but I can't make any promises," I temporized. I tried to wriggle from his grasp, but Hahnemann gripped me and pulled me closer.

"Beware of that fellow, there's something about him that isn't right," Hahnemann whispered. He let me go so abruptly that I sprawled out backward, arms and legs flailing in four different directions. Bolingbroke was coming back to see what had kept us. "You'll be wanting this," he said to Hahnemann, and tossed him the little gun, which was now crumpled like a coke can. Then he reached an arm down to help me up.

"You, dancing in the park?" He seemed to struggle to keep a straight face.

"I'm very graceful when I dance!" I hissed.

"If you say so," Bolingbroke returned.

"Belzoni will be glad to see me," I said, as Bolingbroke opened the Bentley's door for me. I smiled softly and cast my lashes down, as if with dewy amorous nostalgia. Bolingbroke didn't say anything, but his face got taut. I could swear fangs protruded from his upper lip; he immediately slammed the door behind me. He walked around the front of the car to the driver's side, slid in next to me. The light inside the car illuminated his face. No fangs, but yep, an unmistakable snarl tightened his face.

"That thing you did with Kristofer's gun," I started.

"It was old," he said. He didn't look at me. "How well do you know Belzoni?"

"Extremely well," I said. His face puckered in on itself, which spread glee through my being, from my shiny red hair all the way to my Shanghai Red pedicure. I didn't mind one bit if Bolingbroke was jealous. He didn't know that Belzoni and I were anything but lovers. I mean, I'd loved Belzoni, after a fashion. I'd hated him more. He was my teacher, I was his apprentice. We were never friends, never confidants. He had taught me to forge, developed my craft, incited my passion for it. I would never forgive him.

I always figured I'd kill Belzoni some day, as payback.

Chapter 8

IT WAS DIFFICULT FOR BOLINGBROKE TO CONQUER himself
when Laila sat so close. As he guided the purring Bentley through the night,
he struggled to make up his mind. "Call my travel agent," he said abruptly to
Laila. "In my phone, under Sheila." He passed his cell phone to her with one
hand.

"At four in the morning?" she asked.

"When the machine answers, say my name. She'll take a call from me."

"I just bet she will," Laila said. Her voice spun with implication but she
didn't look at him. He listened to her make the call on his cell phone, her
untuned alto voice full of whimsy and exhaustion and impatience. She was
blissfully unaware of how luscious she was. She'd offered herself to him. He'd
declined. It was one of the hardest things he'd ever done, turning down her
innocent and wicked proposition. Her soft throat had pulsed just inches from
his mouth, and her lovely skin had beckoned his fingertips, his lips, his teeth.
He'd been wildly aroused. But he couldn't risk it. He no longer needed to feed
on humans, but he still could. Human blood still nourished him in ways he
craved. That hunger swept over him during love-making, hot and uncontrollable. The last time he'd taken a woman to bed, the results had been disas-
trous. He could not repeat that mistake. It was a matter of honor.

Who would have thought that receiving back half the soul he'd prayed
for so passionately would have brought with it full celibacy? Celibacy that
he, once upon a time the lover of thousands of women, imposed on himself.
Because he would not endanger a human woman, and vampires disgusted

him. And he had no intention of revealing himself, his differentness, to them. What would they do? If they saw him as a threat, they'd try to eliminate him. That's what they did. Assure their own survival, at all costs.

"I don't know how she did it, but we're on a ten a.m. flight to Paris," Laila said.

"Doesn't leave much time to pack," he observed.

"Pack? Who needs to pack?" Laila unzipped her purse and held up a zip-loc baggie with a pair of underwear and a passport in it. "I'm ready to go at a moment's notice!" She pulled out the panties, which looked more like a strand of black lace than like an undergarment. "Check out my thong!" Playfully, she flicked it at his cheek.

"Not while I'm driving," he said.

She leaned close, wafting her scent all over him in a way that shook him. "Can I do it when you're not driving?" She giggled, a ripple like a lyre calling to a courtesan on a Venetian bridge. He had to steady his hands on the wheel to keep from crashing the car.

"Laila," he growled. They both fell silent.

He drove the Bentley to the curb and got out to open the door for her. He smelled something faint, something on the air that he didn't like, and he walked her up the stairs of the brownstone. "I'll pick you up at seven. See that you're ready."

"I'm ready now," she said, leaning close again.

"Laila, restrain yourself!"

"If you say so." She smiled, still leaning close to him. He held up a hand and kept her far enough away that he wouldn't be tempted to sink his teeth into her delicious curving neck. Did she not realize that she was tempting him into a madness from which there was no return? Of course she didn't.

He descended the stairs, watched the door close behind her. He drove the car another block, parked, and walked back. The dark was full, plummy, and moist, as vampires loved night to be. They were out now, and nearby. Bolingbroke meant to make sure that they weren't waiting for Laila.

The wind shifted and flicked that particular acidic strand of scents to him: vampires. A moment later, Bolingbroke saw them, turning onto the same street where he stood. He melted deeper into the night, leaning against a building. He reached into his pocket and pulled out a small silk pouch. Out of it he took his mala, his strand of one hundred eight sandalwood beads, which he slipped around his neck. The mala had been given to him by a Shaivite pundit in the Himalayas over two centuries ago, and it was Bolingbroke's most treasured possession.

For some reason Bolingbroke did not fully understand, the mala rendered him invisible to other vampires. He thought it was because he had chanted mantras on it for so long that it had become imbued with its own— what should he call it, a living resonance, a palpable vibration, an aura? It brought up the whole unsolved, unsolvable question of what, exactly, a soul was. Whatever the definition, this mala had acquired its own presence, which was one of silence. When he wore it under his dark cloak, it invested him with itself. It shielded him from the acute senses of nearby vampires. Humans picked up on the silence itself, as an entity in its own right, and turned toward him with curiosity. But vampires glided past him as if he weren't there. Since that night at the Metropolitan Museum, Bolingbroke carried the mala with him at all times.

No sooner was the mala draped over his neck than Intihuaca and the young black-haired female, Kadja, flitted past him. And why were they here, when Intihuaca had said to wait on taking Robert and Laila? They were using vampire wind speed, and Bolingbroke caught just a few words of their conversation:

"... find the painting," Intihuaca said.

"... will take her before she...." responded Kadja. Then they were too far past for him to make out their words, even with his fantastically acute hearing. Vampires traveling at wind speed appeared to shapeshift into large black birds, and they moved too fast to be easily overheard.

But Bolingbroke could move at superhuman speeds, too. Faster even than vampires. He had an ability that they lacked. An ability they could not even imagine. He had gained undreamt-of abilities when he had gained back half his soul. He could transform himself into an energy column that struck down like lightning wherever he wished. It was nearly instantaneous. He did that now, willing himself onto Laila's stoop. Almost faster than he could think, he hovered there.

A few seconds later, Kadja and Intihuaca stood on the street in front of the stairs. Bolingbroke willed his energy column into stillness.

"Did you hear that?" Kadja asked. She seemed to look directly into the whirling column of electrons into which Bolingbroke had dissociated himself.

"Some human on the next block breathing," Intihuaca said. "I smell the girl. She passed through recently. Probably out drinking."

"There's another smell, one I know too well. Very faint, as if it were on her. As if she were with him. Him!"

Intihuaca tilted his head, sniffing. His eyes streamed amber light. Bolingbroke felt a flicker of fear. If they were going to perceive him, it would be now.

"I smell the girl and her roommate. Why did you insist I come, Kadja? I told you, it's not time now to take her," Intihuaca said. He looked through Bolingbroke, then looked around, shifted from foot to foot as if nervous. But Intihuaca was sixteen hundred years old and never got nervous.

"She said her father was at the library!"

"So? It's not time yet. They're not close to the painting."

"What about the roommate? Maybe we should take her as motivation," Kadja said.

"Kadja, you must be patient. There is no reason to do that yet, and we do not wish to tip our hand too early." Intihuaca looked annoyed. "You wish to feed and spread fear. Fine. Go find a kindergarten class and drain a few children." He spread his arms and entered wind speed from a standstill, a testament to his great age and power. Kadja had to take a running start. She was about to launch herself into the air when she paused and glanced around. She seemed to look again at Bolingbroke. She shivered. Her beautiful, feral face twisted with something like fear. Then she was gone, a dark, moving shape in the darker, honeyed night.

Bolingbroke dropped out of the energy column. He landed on his knees on the stoop, exhausted. He was covered with sweat; vampires did not perspire. But he always did, the half-souled former vampire, after shape-shifting into the energy column. Shape-shifting drained him, left him weak and unfocused. He would need sustenance. Blood was the best, but he abstained from it. What he ate now was the prasadam, the sweets, left on altars in Hindu temples at the completion of rituals. Holy foods of all kinds nourished him: the wine and bread of Christian communion, meals offered to ancestors in Buddhist worship, maize used in native American rites, and Sabbath challah blessed by Jews. Prasadam re-invigorated him the quickest. There was a temple in Brooklyn. Bolingbroke stumbled back toward the car. After the temple and the prasadam, he would accompany Laila to Paris, protect her by any means necessary. He would not allow Kadja or the other vampires to take her. No matter what.

"Oh, first class. Sweet!" I sang. "Remind me to send your travel agent flowers. Though she probably wants them from you."

"Probably," Bolingbroke said, in a neutral voice. "Take your seat, Laila. You're holding up the line."

"They can wait. I'm in first class!" I couldn't help but giggle. The stewardess scurried over, unctuous and eager to please. With my best affect of noblesse oblige, I handed her my backpack and the bag of Krispy Kremes I'd bought en route to the airport. I watched her fret with the donut bag, taking care to place it in the bin so it wouldn't get smooshed. Then I slid into the roomy seat. I hadn't slept at all, too fired up to even pretend to doze. I was getting on a plane! Flying to Paris! If my father's life weren't at stake, I would be writhing with ecstasy: nothing was better than traveling, not food, not even sex.

I stole a look at Bolingbroke, who looked cool and relaxed in a tailored white button-down shirt and black pants. OK, maybe traveling wasn't better than sex. He caught me staring at him and raised an eyebrow. I grinned. The stewardess had scurried back with a little tray bearing glasses of champagne.

"A little early for me." Bolingbroke waved her away. I leaned over him and grabbed a flute.

"It's never too early for champagne!" I said. "That's my motto in life." I lifted the glass. "To Paris!" I took a deep sip. I finished the glass while the plebians in economy filed past enviously. Next time I flew, I'd be one of them again, but for now, I was enjoying the privilege!

I was still in a good mood when we reached cruising altitude and the stewardess came to take our lunch orders. I had her tell me about both the lamb ribs and the linguini con funghi, because half the pleasure of ordering was listening to her describe the entrees. That's when another stewardess came over and popped my happy bubble.

She was a frowsy blonde serving economy class, and she looked frazzled. "Are you Laila Cambridge?" she asked. She didn't wait for me to nod but thrust an envelope at me. It bore my name on the outside. It took me a second to place the writing. Then I yelped.

"Where did you get this?" I cried. She was already trotting back to economy. I scrambled over Bolingbroke, practically sat in his lap as I tried to get to her. "Did someone on this plane give it to you? A tall red-haired man, graying? Is he on board?"

"A little boy at the airport gave it to me," she called back over her shoulder. "I have work to do!"

Bolingbroke's arms tightened around me. "Are you all right?"

"This is, this is my dad's writing," I said. I took a deep, shuddering breath. Bolingbroke nodded slowly, his gaze on the envelope. Right, I should open it. I tumbled back into my own seat. My fingers shook as I peeled back the flap.

Laila, you must have a million questions. I cannot answer them now except to say, I love you, Little Goofy Bird. I would not have left you except for your own safety. The stakes are greater than you know; the world is involved. Find out what your mother knows. All my love, Big Goofy Bird. I blinked to keep from weeping. Big Goofy Bird, Little Goofy Bird—he remembered our nicknames for each other. I passed the note to Bolingbroke.

"Your mother? Didn't you speak to her?" Bolingbroke's voice was thoughtful. "What did she tell you?"

"Nothing. She didn't know anything about Dad or his disappearance. Except she said something about some private men's club he was in, and that she should have asked them about him."

"Private men's club...."

"She didn't know how to contact them." I dashed the tears away with the back of my hand. "All these years, not knowing if he was dead or alive. Every day, wondering." I leaned back in my seat and closed my eyes, champagne and butterflied lamb chops forgotten. How could my dad have left me in anguish this way? Luckily, before I could struggle much more with this unbearable question, sleep came down over me like a soft black bag, tucking me inside a velvety vacuum.

"You're what?" I asked, in disbelief, as we stood in de Gaulle airport.

"I'm going out. I have personal business to attend to," Bolingbroke said.

His eyes, fast and level and shimmering with lightning, swept the terminal. He made me think of a tiger scanning the jungle for prey. I was suddenly uneasy, and for no reason I could pinpoint right away. What had Hahnemann, that rich old Nazi crook, said to me? *"Beware of that fellow, there's something about him that isn't right."* What did I really know about Bolingbroke? Besides what my hormones told me, which was that he was unbelievably sexy? That he smelled like every good thing I'd ever wanted to hold?

"You're going out now?" I snapped. "It's almost midnight!"

"You can find your way to a taxi and thence to the hotel, can't you, Laila? The Hotel Raspail Montparnasse in the Sixth, the Montparnasse district. We have two rooms."

"The travel agent didn't tell me that," I said.

"She tells you everything?" Bolingbroke handed me his leather shoulder bag. Like me, he traveled light, carry-on only. He gave me his ultra-sexy one-corner-lifted half-smile, half-sneer. "Please leave this in my room. Unmolested. I'll know if you rummage through it."

"I certainly wouldn't——" I spluttered.

"You certainly would. But I'll ask you not to. I'll see you in a few hours." He turned and left so quickly that it was as if he blinked out, like a candle flame breathed into nothingness. I was left aghast, dizzied, unsure of what my eyes had actually seen. He was gone, though, of that much I was sure. I immediately unbuckled his leather satchel and lifted the flap to peer in. A pair of pants and two more immaculate white shirts, all folded flawlessly, as if by a professional launderer who'd ironed them first. Gingerly I moved them out of the way, careful not to disturb the creases. A toothbrush, Crest, and a hairbrush. A pair of Dolce & Gabbana sunglasses. A candle. Nothing else. Nothing strange. What didn't he want me to see? I closed the flap and rebuckled it.

Passengers, arriving and departing, eddied around me. They wore the blank, unscathed faces of people who weren't heartsick over a threat to a missing loved one's life, who weren't traveling with a mysterious, possibly dangerous man. But I didn't envy them. I was finally doing something productive, something concrete, about some of the misery I'd been wrestling with over the last few years.

Chapter 9

I DIDN'T GO TO THE HOTEL. INSTEAD, I told the taxi driver to take me to Rue Guillaumot in the twelfth arrondissement. Of course he overcharged me. I retaliated with a gentle tongue lashing in my best French, which is pretty damn good, if I say so myself—and I always do. He looked cowed and offered me a two euro piece back. I waved it off. It felt good to be arguing in another language besides English. That's part of the fun of speaking lots of languages. Each language has its own rich resources for scolding, cursing, and quarreling. I know enough expletives in the romance tongues to fill a large dictionary. Okay, a medium-sized thesaurus. But still, it's impressive.

We stopped at a tiny street, only four apartment buildings long. I stood in the middle of the block, waiting for people to come home. When they got to one of the doors and started punching in an entry code, I courteously described the man I was looking for. A lady coming into the second building on the right knew exactly who I meant. She looked me over and rolled her eyes. I knew what she was thinking. That I was one of his whores.

"Belzoni, you sick bastard," I called, by way of greeting. I came in the apartment and closed the door behind me. Belzoni still kept a key behind the fire extinguisher down the hall, as he did in all his flats. He ought to change his habits. Someone who wasn't as nice as me could get in and hurt him. On second thought, he could keep on as he was.

"Laila Cambridge, my prize pupil," he said. He took a drag on his cigarette and blew gray-green smoke all over his salt-and-pepper beard and hollow chest. "Laila Cambridge, the Michael Jordan of forgers. The Tiger Woods, the Lance Armstrong, the William Shakespeare of the faux arte demi-monde. Rain Man with a paintbrush. Laila Cambridge, with hair red like cherries and sin, *comme il faut*. I knew, *certo*, you'd show up at my door one day." He was speaking the bastardized Italian-English-French patois of his illustrious forbear, the great archeologist and artifact-looter Giovanni Belzoni.

"Fuck you." I threw the bag of Krispy Kremes at him. He beetled his black eyebrows at me.

"Reminds me of when you showed up at my studio in Berlin, a skinny kid with red pigtails, twelve years old, and a mouth like a Parisian sewer."

"I was fifteen!" I roared.

He laughed uproariously, leaning his back over his wheelchair. "Thirteen. Braces, knock knees, acne, and all. You used to get *molto grande* zits on the tip of your nose!"

"Almost fifteen!"

"You came early to your gifts!" He laughed again and blew more of that nasty Gauloise smoke at me. Everything in the apartment smelled like cigarettes: the dozens of canvases, the palettes, tubes of paints, easels, the few chairs, the table with no chairs, the bed, even the two fluffy gray cats. They'd have to tear down the walls to get the stink out. This being France, they'd probably market the flat with a premium attached for the tobacco fumes. He flicked his cigarette, spewing ashes. "You're here bearing gifts, like the Achaeans at Troy, eh? What the hell do you want?"

"I would have been fifteen in a year, give or take." I took a hard look at my old teacher. He looked almost the same: gaunt, seamed face with a wild black and white beard, buzz-cut white hair, long lean frame with big shoulders and arms and withered legs, fingers stained amber with nicotine. Except he looked a million years older than the last time I'd seen him, only seven years ago. "You look like shit."

"Wish I could say the same about you." He took the deepest kind of drag on his cigarette, the kind that leaves a ten centimeter stack of ashes after one puff, and I imagined the alveoli of his lungs singed beyond recognition. He held the smoke in, the way dopers do weed. Letting it out in slow sooty rings, he said, "You grow more beautiful every year. Bellissima. Too bad you're not my type. You still don't charge for pussy, right?"

"I thought Gauloise were banned."

"That's ever stopped me?" He opened the bag and lifted out a powdered donut, sniffed, and flicked his tongue through the hole suggestively. Nothing from his waist down worked, he'd once told me, when I queried him about the unending queue of cheap hookers. "But everything from the neck up works, and that's all that matters in sex." I never figured out if he was right or not. I had a momentary, dizzying flash to Bolingbroke, wondered about his opinions on the topic. Bolingbroke, who'd gone off on his own on some unnamed errand. I threw down the two bags, mine and Bolingbroke's.

"I need information," I said.

"Of all the gin joints in all the towns in all the world, she walks into mine," Belzoni said.

"Shove it," I said, but in Italian, where I could cast all sorts of aspersions about his ancestors' purity. Not that he minded. Belzoni bragged about being the bastard son of a bastard son, and so on, all the way back to the six-foot-six-inch muscleman who dug up Karnak and carted away Egypt's precious heritage in 1817. "Do you have anything decent to drink?"

I didn't wait for him to answer but marched into his kitchen, opened the freezer door, found the Belvedere, and swigged directly from the bottle. I closed my eyes as the vodka burned up my gizzards. Even the bottle stank of Gauloises. That nasty smell. I never thought of Belzoni without seeing him surrounded by a burnt-tar cloud of poison, and myself as a tall ungainly kid with a paintbrush in her hand and a song in her heart. The happiest days of my life were spent in Belzoni's studio. It made me hate myself all over again. And hate him more.

"You can drink my hootch, but you can't avoid me," Belzoni called, taunting me. I took another swig and carried the bottle out with me. Then I sauntered over to look at what Belzoni was working on. As always, he had one of his custom easels set on a low table and two halogen lights goosenecking at the canvas.

"Vermeer? How trite."

"When in doubt, *magari*, go back to basics!" He shrugged. "*Ce n'est pas mal*, really. My old teacher Hans van Meegeren would have approved."

"The impasto is for shit, and the face is too modern."

"It's really *in de trant van*," he said, defensively.

"It's not at all in the style of the Old Masters," I snapped. "The light in the interior is all wrong. When is the last time you actually looked at a Vermeer?

And look at this brush you're using. Please. What are you, a second year art student in some pleasant little atelier?"

Belzoni didn't answer. His eyes were closed as he chewed, reverently, a glazed raspberry-filled. "Jesus and Mary in heaven, this is good." He moaned a little. "I used to think the Germans made the best sweet cakes, but you Americans, you really understand decadence. How it has to be cheap and trashy to be fulfilling."

"What are you doing snacking now? It's the wrong time of day."

"I'm much less rigid in my dotage," he said. He finished the donut in a spray of yeasty crumbs. "I've abandoned my old routines. I snack whenever it pleases me and drink wine all the time."

"Go back to your old routines so you can paint again." I pointed at the half-finished Vermeer and then pinched off my nose to indicate that it stank. "Isn't there anyone to critique you? Who's running you these days?"

"A Spanish woman, went to Oxford, speaks six languages, very classy. Started out at Sotheby's and had one of those fancy careers before she went out on her own. You'd like her; she doesn't sell her pussy, either."

"Yes, that's what makes me like people: they're not prostitutes," I said brightly. "Put your thinking cap on, Belzoni. I have some questions."

He grinned and tore into a cinnamon twist as if it were his last meal. "Oh, *porcinella mia*, do you think you're going to show up here with a bag of sweets and I like a cheap *figa* will spread my asshole for you? Not hardly."

"It's important. Life or death."

"Bullshit."

"I don't lie to you, Belzoni!"

He roared with laughter so intense that it shook his long frame in his wheelchair. Even shrinking with age, Belzoni still stretched out to six feet four inches. "What a load of *merda*! You're a born liar. You'd rather climb a tree and tell a lie than stand on the ground and tell the truth."

"Tell me about Botticelli's *Coming Forth by Day*," I said. I closed my eyes and took a few deep breaths to calm my rattled nerves. In, count to four, hold, count to four, exhale, count to four. Old yoga trick, works every time. Except this time. My eyes popped open. Belzoni was staring at me with a rapt, starry look that I'd seen on his face only once before: when I finished my first copy, of a Rubens, when I was fourteen. When he knew he could sell it as something Rubens himself had produced. I cleared my throat. "You don't know the painting?"

"Of course I know the painting. I know all about the painting. I know about all paintings. I am Belzoni." He smiled and reached into the bag, took out a chocolate-iced custard-filled. He grinned as he masticated.

"How much do you want? I don't have a lot on me."

"Not money." His eyes flicked to the Vermeer. The unfinished Vermeer.

"No."

"A few more hits of the Belvedere, you'll want to, you know you will," he said. He grinned widely, carving a yellow-stained bone crescent in the thicket of his beard.

"I don't do that anymore."

"You know you want to. You look at my inferior work and see everything that you can fix and make beautiful, make perfect and right and worthy of Vermeer himself."

"No, Belzoni."

"You said it was life or death. This is the price."

"I'll give you money."

"I don't want money."

I backed up, found myself collapsed in a heap on a rug soiled by dirty cat hair and slicks of oil paint. "I do not do it anymore. NO!"

"A talent like yours, one in a billion painters can do what you can do, you really think you're going to give it up? You think you can? You're deluded." Belzoni laughed and wheeled himself over to me. He plucked the vodka bottle from my hand and took a long swig. "Come on. You'll enjoy yourself. It's not like I'm asking for a good blow job with *ingolo*."

I retched. "Vivian Goran."

"Vivian Goran was a stupid hag who deserved what she got." Belzoni swigged again from the Belevedere bottle and then slapped it into my hand. I took a long, long, long draught.

"Vivian Goran was a kindly old lady whom I swindled."

"She could have kept her front door locked."

"She has two daughters, a son, and seven grandchildren, who miss her every day."

"She chose to fight. She could have handed it over to the burglars. They'd have let her live. There's no sport in killing a little old lady. It's even more tedious than fucking them."

"She fought because she thought it was a real Masaccio, worth millions of dollars. A masterpiece, a priceless treasure created hundreds of years ago."

"Joke's on her," Belzoni shrugged the way only an Italian can, with complete insouciance. "Finish the Vermeer. Then I'll tell you everything. And trust me, *bomboletta mia*, what I know is worth it."

"Fuck you," I yelled. I called him 'bastard' in every language I knew, and some I didn't. He smiled.

"The painting is real. It is ravishing. Isis and Osiris."

"What? No," I said. "That can't be right. Botticelli's pagan imagery was Greco-Roman. And, of course, Roman Catholic."

"Not in this case," Belzoni wore a smug expression. "*Cara mia*, Egyptian mythology is at the center of our very world. It's of fundamental importance."

I rolled my eyes. "You only say that because your ancestor dug up Egypt and gave its treasures to the Brits."

"Isis and Osiris are the foundation of everything," Belzoni insisted. His hand shook a little as he lifted his Gauloise to his mouth. "The Freemasons have kept the ancient rituals alive. Ancient, mysterious secrets, *magari*, things we can barely believe today. Magic that is real. *C'est vrai*."

"Secrets, Freemasons, magic, baloney!" I scoffed. "Tell me about the painting."

Belzoni stared hard at his fake Vermeer. "I would be happy to. When you finish my painting. There's so little left. You'll be done by tomorrow morning," he pressed me. "I've seen you do it. You go into a fugue state and your eyes are empty and your hand moves with the speed of a hurricane. How I envy you. You are Mozart, I Salieri. I would give my testicles to have your gift. I've already sacrificed my legs."

"But I promised myself: never again!"

"Bah, silly girl, promises are made to be broken. Especially promises to yourself."

"Stop it, Belzoni."

"I still have a stock of the good pigments my papa took from a coffin. You remember the story, *Lailetta mia*? Minor painter, buried in a crypt in Umbria. Papa found a reference in an old will in a private library, the painter asked to be buried with the tools of his craft. One moonless night, my heroic papa honored our lineage, and broke the silence of that crypt. Found the pigments. I will fetch them for you. Only for you."

The right pigments, I could practically smell them, earthy and dusty at first, and then, when the oils were added... Sweat trickled down between my shoulder blades. I couldn't talk, and just stared at Belzoni.

He smiled, a mocking crescent in his tangled beard. "Don't look at my ugly face. Look at the painting. It needs you, Laila. It needs your hand. It's calling to you."

I took another swig of vodka. It would be for Daddy, I could easily justify it, easily forgive myself.... My eyes turned to the painting. The interior light, I could fix that first. It wasn't so bad, it wasn't as if I were starting a forgery from scratch. I was just participating on one someone else had made. It was a lesser sin. It wasn't even a sin, because it was for my dad.

"You say it's life or death," Belzoni mocked me. I was almost persuaded.

But Vivian Goran's kindly, seamed face rose in my mind. I could not forgive myself for her death. I could not forgive myself for the lust to forge that set my hands trembling. Who knew what misery this forged Vermeer would bring upon the world? Would Belzoni know enough to make it worthwhile? No. If he knew where the Botticelli was, he'd have it. He'd have sold it and I'd have heard about it. No. He knew a piece of the puzzle, but not a big enough piece. I took a deep breath. "I'm too good to forge."

Belzoni laughed. "Capomaestro Michelangelo himself engaged in the gentle art of forgery. You think you're better than the greatest artist who ever lived?"

I upended the vodka, poured it over Belzoni's head. He sputtered, laughed, and cursed at the same time. I grabbed up the bags, walked out, and closed the door firmly behind me. I stood in the hall, breathing air free of the stench of Gauloise and wrong living. Two girls came toward me. They wore pleather miniskirts and torn hose and mascara that ringed their faces with raccoon masks. They looked at my hair and boobs and their eyes did mercenary calculations. I posed suggestively, as if I plied their trade.

"Ladies," I said brightly. "He's ready for you. Let me save you some time and tell you what he likes."

Chapter 10

BOLINGBROKE STOOD ON RUE GUILLAUMOT. HE COULD smell Laila, and he was annoyed. Hadn't he told her to go to the hotel? But of course she had come directly here, when he couldn't accompany her. He'd had to feed, had gotten off the plane weak, famished, his flesh crawling, he was so debilitated by hunger. He'd almost succumbed to the temptation to feed on a human. He'd gone to one of the seediest suburbs, where burnt-out shells of cars lined the streets and the disenfranchised and unwanted slept on sidewalks. He'd stood over an old homeless man and almost....almost.... almost gorged, almost thrown away the ideals he clung to despite his some-times outrageous desire. Then he'd noticed a church at the end of the block. He sneaked in and stole some communion wafers. They strengthened him enough to find other nourishment.

Laila was here. He followed the scent to the door of one of the buildings. He paused, breathing in her scent, wanting her. He refused to give in to it. Last time he'd taken a human to his bed, she ended up near dead, bleeding from puncture wounds all over her body. Bolingbroke had abstained from human blood for so long that he had lost his mind, gone wild with thirst, when he ran his tongue over a paper cut on her index finger. He gorged on her like he was an animal. He saved her by changing her into a vampire. It was the only way to ensure that she continued, and it was criminal. He'd dishonored himself. He would not do it again.

As for the long-ago woman, what of her? She was no longer alive, she was undead. She still continued. Or was that a good thing? To exist from blood feast to blood feast until fire, the sun, or a wooden stake through the heart ended it all. To live from the coppery scent of one pulsing jugular vein to the next pulsing jugular. He had taken from the human her hopes and dreams, her aspirations and longings, her internal environment full of love and joy and anguish. He had destroyed her creativity, because vampires did not create art. They did not write sonnets or symphonies, even the ones who had been masters in their human lives. He had taken from her the blessing of a heart connection with another living being. All for a few hours of physical bliss. It still saddened him. He would not do that to Laila. She was all heart and humor, that one. It made him smile.

Bolingbroke laid his hand on the locked apartment door, willed it to unlock. Metal was so cooperative. *Click.* He opened the door and went inside. He could hear Laila upstairs, talking.

I found Bolingbroke on the landing downstairs. I smiled at him, relieved to be away from Belzoni. I felt as if I'd dodged a bullet. The bullet of temptation. Then I wondered how Bolingbroke had tracked me here. Hahnemann had mentioned Rue Guillaumot in the twelfth arrondissement, but not the building number, and Bolingbroke didn't know what Belzoni looked like. Bolingbroke couldn't do as I had done, query people until he located the right building. He kept doing this, showing up when I least expected, after disappearing when I least expected. What was he, part bloodhound, part commitment-phobe? "Hey, how'd you find me?"

Bolingbroke frowned. "Laila, that was not kind of you," he remonstrated. "What you told those girls to do."

"You could not possibly have heard what I said."

"Acoustic thing. Voices carry down stairs." He shook his head.

"He can't even feel his bottom," I said brightly. "He's in a wheelchair."

"That makes it worse. Have you no pity?"

"Not for him," I said, more viciously than I meant to. "He doesn't deserve pity!"

Bolingbroke wasn't fazed; he just arched an eyebrow at me. "You were far more generous toward that old Nazi in Tarrytown."

"Hahnemann has some redeeming qualities," I said.

"If you say so. I see you've been into my bag."

But I was already moving down the tiny street to look for a taxi stand. "Not at all. What makes you think that?"

Bolingbroke let Laila kiss him in the taxi. Not just let her: he craved her, and when she put her arms around him, he succumbed to his craving and crushed her into his chest. What an armful she was! How long would it be before he couldn't resist her tantalizing flesh? He knew he was endangering her, but he couldn't summon the will to push her away. He of the iron discipline, he who lived by the unbending rule of personal honor, could not summon his own self-restraint. She was so soft and vital....

It was almost more passion than he could stand, and he nuzzled her neck with his lips, wanting desperately to sink his fangs into her. Everything in his being thrummed to taste her. But Laila's luxuriant red hair smelled of cigarettes, and when he lifted his head to tease her about it, he noticed the taxi driver watching them in the mirror. He gave the driver a cool glare, its meaning clear in any language. The driver shivered, afraid for his life.

"Let's go back to the hotel," Laila said, in a husky voice.

Bolingbroke pushed her away. The effort was enormous and made him sweat, but he pulled her off him. He gently scooted her onto her side of the seat. It would not do for him to lose control and feed on her here in this taxi. He'd have to explain to Laila what he was. She wasn't ready to hear it. Then he'd be forced to kill the taxi driver to keep him quiet. A messy and inefficient scenario. Bolingbroke hated inefficiency. "We don't have a lead. We need to plan. We have a mission, we have work to do. We're not on a honeymoon."

"I wish we were," she whispered. She sat back in her seat and closed her eyes. Bolingbroke wondered what she was thinking. He didn't ask.

We were back at the hotel, where I was feeling woebegone. I kept striking out with Bolingbroke, but the rejection I was getting used to. What was worse was that I had almost given in to my abandoned former self, the evil twin who owned a bigger piece of the real estate of my soul than did my current righteous self. I had almost picked up a paintbrush to finish Belzoni's forgery. To improve it, so it would be indistinguishable from the hand of Vermeer. When I thought about Belzoni's second-rate efforts, my hands tingled as if with a thousand pins and needles—I wanted to hold a brush and fix the painting that badly. Would it have been so bad? I'd be one step closer to finding Daddy.

"Perhaps we don't need him," Bolingbroke said, as if he'd been reading my mind. I started. He smiled a little. "You must have other contacts."

"I don't know who. I've been racking my mind, trying to think of someone."

"We're in Europe. Who among your old contacts is still around?" Bolingbroke persisted. I shrugged. He stroked his chin. "I'll take you to a late dinner. That might jog your memory."

We sat by a window at a charming restaurant called L'Avant Goût in the thirteenth arrondissement, on Rue Bobillot. It was one o'clock in the morning, but somehow Bolingbroke had charmed the owner-chef into staying open and serving us food. Charmed and bribed, I suspected, in rapid, old-fashioned French spoken directly into the owner's ear at a volume just below what I could hear. The shop front was modest, but the food was divine. I sipped a parsley soup with a single creamy oyster in the bottom—it was inventive, creative, astonishing on my palate, salty and sweet and piquant with parsley. I moaned with pleasure. Bolingbroke was playing with a steak tartare appetizer, and he lifted his head and smiled.

"I wager you sound that way in bed," he said, grudgingly, as if the words escaped him despite himself.

"Try me and find out." I sipped and moaned a little more lasciviously. He rolled his eyes. So it was a bit overdone this time, what with my heaving bosoms and all. The parsley soup wasn't that good. Almost. Not quite. Bolingbroke would be, though. I gave him a big smile. The excellent food was a tonic to my spirits. I was in Paris, after all.

He shook his head. "Do you have any notions about who among your old chums might know something about the painting?"

"I can't think of anyone right now. Maybe it's the jet lag." But I never suffered from jet lag. Traveling made me too blasted happy.

"You and your family lived and traveled extensively throughout Europe. You were here when you were forging. Surely there's someone among your contacts...."

"My studio was outside the walls of Lucca," I murmured.

"Yes, in a picturesque but ramshackle farm house, complete with rats and bats. Rather a dump. How did you find it?"

"It wasn't a dump!" I said. Then I shrugged. "Maybe a little bit of a dump. But I didn't need much back then. It served my needs.... A friend of Mama's rented it to me. Mama, she might know someone, she's a painter and art historian...." I drained the shot glass with the parsley soup and then went outside with my cell phone. Not to call my mother. To phone Fern. With the cell phone that still worked worldwide, because when I was forging paintings, I had needed such a thing. I had clung to the expensive cell phone despite my vows to never forge again. What did that say about me? Nothing good. *Laila, you bad girl!*

But now was not the time to castigate myself. Now was the time for action, for progress. Mama might know someone who held another piece of the puzzle. Fern would have to try to contact my mother at the ashram and take the calls when my mother deigned to call back. But for Fern, my mother might respond quickly.

"How's it going, doll face?" Fern asked sweetly, and my heart brightened.

"Better, hearing your voice." I smiled into the phone.

"Seduce Mr. Gorgeous yet?"

"No, and what's worse, Belzoni was a bust."

"*And*?" Fern stretched out the word to several syllables. She heard what I wasn't saying, what I hadn't told Bolingbroke, what I could barely admit to myself.

"He would only tell me what he knew if I finished a Vermeer for him." I sighed.

"I'm proud of you, Laila."

"Fern, I really wanted to. I wanted to so badly, I was sweating." It felt good to confess that. Liberating.

"You did good, Gonzo. I'll buy you a drink when you get back. Several drinks. So, what do you need from me?" she asked briskly. Fern was so smart and practical. How would I ever live without her? If I ever got married, my future husband—and I felt sorry for the poor sucker already—was going to have to realize that I was a package deal. Fern came with. I asked her to contact Mama and delicately inquire as to who might know about *Coming Forth by Day*, without letting on to what was happening.

"Don't mention the painting by name. Tell her I'm snooping for the Leonardo." That was a lie grounded in truth, sort of. Anyone who knew Botticelli would know Leonardo. And Leonardo was said to have worked on the painting with Botticelli.

"I'll get back to you. You keep trying to lure Mr. Gorgeous into bed. I expect to hear good news on the slut front. And I want details!"

"Doing my best, but he's not succumbing."

"Not like you to give up, Gonzo!" Fern was laughing as she hung up. I went back in, smiling, and sat down to a second course of lamb paté with white bean salad. The paté was as good as the soup. Had I died and gone to heaven?

"Why does Miss Takahasi call you 'Gonzo'?" asked Bolingbroke.

I gave him a sharp look. "How do you know she did?"

"The way you smiled, along with the faint blush along your clavicles. It has some privileged meaning between the two of you." He looked at me expectantly.

"You'll have to sleep with me to find out." I gave him a crooked smile. He looked away. I sighed. "What about you, John Bolingbroke? What's your story?" He gave me a blank look. I sighed again. "You're not making this easy for me. Tell me about yourself, okay, mystery man?"

"I love art and I want to help humanity," he said softly. He pushed his tartare away. For a moment I had that blurry vision, where I thought I saw him with fangs and cat eyes. I blinked and it was gone. He was himself, the handsome, dark-haired man whose strong bones looked aristocratic from certain angles and rough from others.

"That's so boring! Not at all what I meant. Take the stick out of that fine, tight tushie of yours and tell me a story."

"There's no stick in my bottom," Bolingbroke growled. "Unlike your besieged friend Belzoni."

"He deserves what he gets, trust me," I muttered. "Come on, give it up. An anecdote. From your life. Your favorite story from when you were a kid."

He raised both eyebrows, then leaned back in his seat, crossing his arms over his middle. I dug into the paté and waited. Several minutes elapsed.

I finished my dish and Bolingbroke's butternut and ham salad with shaved parmesan. Delicious! Finally, he said, "When I was a boy, I, one day, ah, my father was hosting a dinner, several important men from the town. My mother and her servants had prepared a lavish feast."

"What town?" I interjected.

"Do you want to hear the story or not?" he asked, dryly. I nodded and the chef's wife brought us another appetizer, marinated sea trout with rutabaga and cumin, so I filled my mouth with food to keep myself from interrupting. He continued, "My father put out his best wine. In Venetian carafes. On a dare from my little brother, I stole in and drank an entire carafe. It made me very ill, dizzy, and I dropped the expensive carafe, which shattered...."

"My father called us all in so he could interview us and discover the culprit. I could barely stand upright. I'd be demolished if he smelled my breath. He belonged to, ah, to that generation of men who believed, 'Spare the rod and spoil the child.'" Bolingbroke smiled grimly and his agate eyes dissolved into some far, far away place. I waited.

"I stood in a line with my two brothers and sister, and just as Father was about to step forward and sniff each of our breaths in turn, one of his guests, a painter, claimed that he had drunk the wine. He was quite well-regarded, and offered my father a small but rather nice devotional piece to recompense him for the wine and the carafe. My father believed him because, well, the painter was who he was, a person of prominence. Also the painter had been drinking prior to his arrival at our home. He had quite the stench about him." Bolingbroke smiled. He stared off again, as if he were finished.

"Then what happened? Did you thank the painter?" I asked.

"Oh, yes. I took myself to the painter's workshop the next day to thank him, and was promptly pressed into service. I spent the next two years running his errands. The unsavory ones." He shook his head with a wry and regretful expression.

"Two years for some wine and a glass decanter? Not a good deal for you."

"Quite a bargain, actually. My father's wrath would have known no bounds. I got to be around the workshop, and the painter tried to teach me his craft. Unfortunately, I am all, how do you say, left thumbs." His lips quirked in a sardonic, self-deprecating grin, something I'd never seen before on his face.

"It's a genetic thing, those kinds of small motor skills. Don't fault yourself. And it's not just in the hands, it's in the eyes. The perceptual senses must be developed in order to see correctly to guide the hands," I told him. Then my phone buzzed. A text message. Two words: "Cromer Amsterdam."

"Of course," I said, slapping my forehead. "Obviously. I should have known! Lord William Cromer."

"That was fast work on Fern's part," Bolingbroke murmured. "I know the gentleman in question. He's both distinguished and respected."

"He's no gentleman, he's a rat bastard of the slimiest kind," I said. I picked up my wine glass and drained it. "Cromer is the best faker of provenance documents in the world," I said. That was why I hadn't thought of him: I hadn't wanted to. I still had a hard time facing my past. Cromer was a big part of that past.

"Lord Cromer? Are you sure?"

"He's almost as good in his way as I am in mine. As I *was*." I ran my hands over my face. "I'm exhausted."

"Lord Cromer is usually in London; I've dined with him there. I wonder what he's doing in Amsterdam," Bolingbroke mused.

"Faking papers for a Frans Hals," I replied, with an edge to my voice. "Perhaps a Holbein." I made a rude noise with my lips. "If *Coming Forth by Day* is in play, he'll have heard about it. Can your travel agent get us to Amsterdam?"

"I'll make a call," he said. He stepped away from the table. I sighed.

Belzoni, Cromer. The sins of my past had come home to roost.

Chapter 11

FERN CALLED ON MY CELL PHONE AS we disembarked the next day from the high speed Thalys train at the crowded Amsterdam Centraal train station.

"You got my text?"

"You work fast!" I said. "Thank you."

"Are you okay?" she asked.

"So-so," I answered.

"Hm, I don't like the sound of that."

"I'll get over it. How are you? Anything up?"

"Hmm," she repeated. "Tall Hot'n'Hunky ought to take better care of you. I don't hear my Laila's usual sparkly spunk."

"Yeah, well," I said, as the hot man in question touched my elbow to guide me through the station. It was true, I didn't feel so sparkly, after my close brush with my darkest sin: forging an Old Master. I still thought about the life every day. But if I picked up a paintbrush at Belzoni's behest, I would hate myself for it. Even if I did it to get closer to my father. And then there was the rejection, which had lost its novelty and was starting to wear thin. Bolingbroke pulled me to him and then pushed me away. He let me kiss him until we were both in a lather, and then he shut me down. I felt like a yo-yo. I didn't understand. Now I was going to see Cromer. My old partner in crime.

Walking through the train station was not the place and time to try to resolve anything. Amsterdam Centraal was more than just a hectic hub of transportation, it was a majestic neo-Renaissance building and tourist attraction in its own right. Of course it was eternally under construction, and had been since it was first erected in the 1880s. Bolingbroke paced ahead of me to part the throngs. Languages swirled around us: French and German, English and Dutch, Danish, and even two different dialects of Frisian, that standoffish Teutonic tongue spoken by natives in Holland who stoutly defend their non-Dutchness. My ears pricked up at the tapestry of foreign words. Languages were the juice of life for me. A little of my sparkly spunk ebbed back in. "I'll be fine! Cromer was a good call. I can't believe my mom got back to you so fast."

"She did because she loves you," Fern said.

"Loves *you*," I corrected.

"Laila, sweetie. I won't keep you. I just wanted to tell you that Kristofer Hahnemann called four times. I finally gave him your cell number. Don't know what he wants, but he sounds desperate. I thought you said he was richer than God?"

"Richer than God's banker," I said. "Thanks for letting me know. Love you."

"Love you, too," she said, and clicked off.

"Miss Takahasi?" Bolingbroke asked. I nodded. He steered me out of the building. Amsterdam Centraal was in the bustling heart of Amsterdam. The sun was high overhead. The bustle of pedestrians, bicyclists, trams, and signs sent a wave of exhausted dizziness through me. I swayed on my feet.

"You need to rest," Bolingbroke said. "Let's get you to the hotel." I didn't argue. I'd barely slept last night, and my days and nights were getting upended like the bottle of vodka I'd dumped on Belzoni. We made our way along the Leidseplein as rapidly as I could walk through the haze of my fatigue. We stopped at a coffee shop for a coffee and pastry. Some foam from his latte brimmed Bolingbroke's lip, and I found myself wanting to lick it off. The sting of his dismissals couldn't shut down my desire for him. He noticed my gaze fixed on his mouth and wiped brusquely. We moved on toward the Rijksmuseum, and to a clean but unassuming hotel near the museum. Poster reprints of Amsterdam Impressionist paintings lined the walls, but I didn't take in the details. I couldn't even lift my head as we climbed to our rooms. I was asleep in mid-air, flopping onto the narrow four-poster bed.

It was dark when I woke. I sat up, groggy, still tired, wondering what had woken me. My cell phone tinkled and I picked it up, saw a message. Rubbing my face with one hand, I used my other hand to play the message, which originated from a blocked number. It was an extended period of silence. Complete stillness, but with a sense of presence. Someone was there. I strained to hear breathing. Was it a man? A woman? Usually an in-drawn breath gives a clue, some subliminal sense of maleness or femaleness, but there wasn't any sound at all in the voicemail. Just silent purposefulness. Creepy. Made the peaks of my spine tingle with foreboding. Was it Hahnemann? Fern said he'd been trying to reach me. But it wasn't his style to remain silent. He'd leave a pithy few sentences with no preamble, telling me exactly what he wanted and what I should do for him, immediately if not yesterday. Not Hahnemann, then.

Could it be my father? My heart lifted as I wondered, but on the heels of that question came another. What if it was one of the people out to hurt him? If my father could get a note to me, he knew I was tracking the painting and therefore him. Who else knew I was on the trail? It occurred to me that there were details missing from the story I had, and Bolingbroke could fill them in. Maddening, elusive Bolingbroke. I brushed my teeth and then went in search of him.

Bolingbroke was not in his room. The blonde desk clerk could offer only that he'd departed from the hotel with alarming speed a half hour ago. "Practically at a run," the woman whispered, in Dutch. It was such a pleasure to practice my Dutch that I felt cheerful and almost forgave Bolingbroke for running out on me again in the middle of our quest for the lost Botticelli painting and, more importantly, for my father. I inquired about internet service and a computer. I was courteously shown to the business center. One great thing about the Dutch, they work hard and expect that everyone else wants to, also.

Twenty minutes of googling around the internet and I found Cromer. He'd left his phone number and address in a post on an art bulletin board. The woman who'd initiated the thread had a pix next to her handle, and wow, she was a brunette cha-cha-cha. How'd she get her cleavage up so high, so close to her face? Neat trick.

I used my cell phone to place the call. I'd have a huge bill, but what the hell, I was flush right now. I had Hahnemann's money. The line rang. "Cromer," a voice answered.

"Bill, I need to see you," I said. My voice was a little breathless because I didn't know how Cromer would respond. Our last meeting had not gone well.

"Laila Cambridge, I never expected to hear from you again!" He was smiling. "At least, not until God herself sent a pillar of light to guide you to a perfectly preserved seventeenth century canvas and corresponding blocks of pigment and then placed a brush in your hand. Wasn't that what you told me, last time we spoke?"

It was gallant of him to leave out the invectives I'd hurled along with my vows to never again forge a painting. When I'd heard about Vivian Goran, I'd been shattered. How could someone have died because of my painting? Her death was like a razor slicing clean and hot through the layers of my denial and self-delusion. I'd been working out a provenance with Cromer at the time and, since he was standing there beside me, he bore the brunt of my eruption. "Try to forget the last time we saw each other. Please."

"For you, anything, Laila. How are you, duckie? I don't suppose you're traveling with a lovely piece of art requiring papers and a home?"

I closed my eyes. Just as I'd expected, I was going to keep being reminded of my sordid past. And just as I'd feared, I kept feeling a flicker of interest. The flicker was stronger now, since Belzoni's request. The inner wall was showing holes; the promise that I'd never again forge, the vow that was my bulwark against my worse self, was wearing thin. And didn't I just wish I was toting some gem of a masterpiece for Cromer to authenticate? Wouldn't it be fun to have something juicy to show him, a nice little lost Rembrandt, maybe a hush-hush Giorgione? Hahnemann knew of two; maybe I could lay eyes on them, get some ideas.... I almost salivated at the prospect. I was going to need serious psychopharmaceuticals when this was all over, to put the genie back in the bottle. Alcohol would do. I swallowed. "I need information."

"Anything for you, of course, darling. Why don't you come round to my flat tomorrow morning?"

"Uh-huh, and where would that be?"

Cromer snickered. "Duckie, if you've found my mobile, you've surely discovered my whereabouts. You're just that clever. Around ten, shall we say?"

"Brilliant," I snapped, mimicking his upper-crust accent. He hung up and so did I. Then I went upstairs and showered, let the water wash away the slime of my temptation. It was a warmish trickle, the way showers in Europe always were, but it helped. I emerged with a firmer grasp on my virtue, such as it was. I changed panties and shirt, slapped on a coat of paint to hide the dark crescents under my eyes, slicked on some lipstick, and toddled back down to ask about Bolingbroke. Still absent. I clarified the address with Astrid, the nice Dutch lady, and set off.

The building was in the nicest part of the Jordaan, with a view of the Westerkerk church tower. Even with the indigo of night smoothing down over everything, the charm of the area was obvious, with its lit-up labyrinth of narrow streets and little canals, windows with lace curtains and well-kept flowerboxes, and courtyards with lovingly tended gardens. Not long ago, the Jordaan had been in disrepair. Almost overnight it had been gentrified, though a good number of artists still lived here. The exact address led me not to one of the cheap artist's residences, but to a renovated house. *Très* picturesque, *très* expensive.

Light spilled out from a front window. I peered in, but couldn't see anyone. I went to the door, but it was locked. Was I going to let that stop me? Oh no. Certainly not. In my naughtier days I had picked up a few sly skills, because the life was inherently dangerous and because, well, Cromer wasn't wrong. I was that clever. This was such a small sin, too. No one could get hurt from it. There was an old tool set wrapped in cloth in the bottom of my purse. I dug out the little bundle and pulled out two tools.

My fingers have a precise, fine coordination. They have a delicacy of touch that pianists would kill for. It was just one of those freak gifts, like my red hair. But then, I'm never going to win the Fields Medal for Mathematics. In fact, if my high school teacher hadn't pitied me, I'd have failed math, and I'd still be trying to graduate. I'm not getting any prizes for scholarship at all, and I'll be lucky if I scrape by my dissertation defense. Nor will I ever win a foot race, dance in a way that doesn't remind everyone of the Funky Chicken, or sing so that dogs and children don't howl in agony. But I can paint. And I can pick.

Two minutes later, the door swung open. Two minutes? Slow for me. I was rusty.

The front parlor was empty, but muffled sounds wafted forth from the back of the house. I tiptoed down the hallway and then threw open a door.

There was Cromer. In bed, naked. On the bottom. Straddling him was a magnificent white-skinned, black-haired woman who was just as naked as Cromer. Her body was pale as alabaster and curvy as a sculpted marble figure-eight. Her nipples were black as polished ebony—body paint, I thought—and the contrast with her white, white skin was breathtaking. Black hair streaming around her shoulders, she lifted her head and laughed. She had fangs.

Now I was hallucinating. I slammed the door and sprinted back to the living room. My heart was pounding and my brain was telling me that I hadn't seen what I thought I'd seen. I was willing to believe that.

I waited, but no one chased me. After a few more minutes, it became clear that Cromer and his lady friend were not going to come after me any time soon. I sat down on a small, elegant couch to wait. The sounds from the bedroom got louder. Cromer started screaming. Hey, who am I to judge? I'd probably be screaming if Bolingbroke was on top of me. An old copy of Dutch *Avant Garde* magazine lay on an end table, so I thumbed through it. I ignored the screams, moans, and laughter bubbling out of the bedroom.

Maybe an hour later, Cromer came out wearing a man's silk houserobe. He was pale, and his hands shook as he tied his belt. Otherwise, he looked the same as always: medium height, slim, with the typical oval face and substantial nose of inbred British aristocracy. He was fortyish, but the mercurial play of intelligence made him look thirtyish, or even younger. Even postcoital, he wore an air of erudition and refinement. He looked like he quoted Shakespeare even while doin' it doggy style. But he really was much paler than usual.

"Bill, are you okay?" I asked. I cleared my throat, wished I wasn't so damn happy to see him and to be reminded of our adventures together. I couldn't help beaming at him. The scene from the other room faded.

"Bollocks, Laila, you were supposed to wait until tomorrow!" he muttered. He ceased fidgeting with his belt and threw himself down on a chair across from me.

"It's urgent."

The black-haired woman sauntered out. She wore a gossamer dress in iridescent silk, with her black hair tumbling all over her back and shoulders. She was tiny, but gave an impression of being statuesque. I felt sort of dwarfed, although I had at least eight inches on her. Something about her was ferocious, menacing. I shrank down in my seat.

She leaned over Bill and tongue-kissed him, running her hand inside his robe. She pulled her hand out and licked her fingers. Then she threw a disdainful look over her shoulder, and my breath caught in my throat. I knew that face. How was this possible? What was *she* doing here? Shock and disbelief paralyzed me. She kissed Bill again, and then moved with lissome grace toward the door.

"You!" I cried, leaping to my feet. "The librarian! What are you doing here? Did you follow me from New York? What's going on?"

"You must have me confused with someone else," she said, with a smile and a sneer. Definitely the skanky librarian from Columbia.

"I'm not one bit confused. I know exactly who you are!" I shrieked. "But why are you here?" She erupted into silky laughter. The next moment, faster than I could blink, she stood in front of me, gripping my wrist. Gone were the layers of swathing and the heavy glasses. Gone also was the mask of civility. In its place was a beautiful, feral woman who grinned and clamped my wrist with unexpected strength. I couldn't shake her off. I cried out in pain. Her eyes widened, her pupils dilated hugely, and the room swam around me. My brain imploded in a perfect round middle-C note, and all my senses collapsed into a single naked singularity.

A voice spiraled toward me, breaking the spell. "My travels are my business. You want to make something of it?" It was her, purring. I might stand eight inches taller than her, but she was pulverizing my wrist in her hand. Terror gagged me.

"Kadja, please," Cromer begged. "Please, enough." She looked at him. She threw my hand backward. I staggered. Her eyes did that catlike thing I'd seen Bolingbroke's do, but it appeared and disappeared so quickly that I couldn't be sure of what I'd seen. Was I so tired and out of it that I was hallucinating?

"It's not time yet," she said. I caught myself and rubbed where she'd squeezed. Sure enough, an ugly red and black bruise circled my wrist. And then she was gone, simply vanished from the house, as if she'd never been there. Cromer and I were silent in shock. Neither of us knew how to verbalize the strangeness of her behavior, and of her seeming disappearance before our eyes. I hoped I wasn't losing my mind. The last person I wanted to distrust was myself.

"That was dodgy," Cromer said finally. He let out a stuttering exhale as he raked his hands through his sandy hair.

I recovered my voice. "That woman is a psycho freak! Why is she in Amsterdam?"

"You weren't supposed to meet her, you know," he said, shrugging. "I invited you for tomorrow. Morning."

"I couldn't wait."

"Patience is one of the virtues. You are going in for those these days, aren't you?" He gave me a crooked grin and I noticed again how pale he was, even for him. "You look lovely as always."

"You don't look so hot. Are you okay?" I was worried he'd pass out in front of me.

"May I offer you a drink? You aren't abstaining from spirits as well as the bringing forth of beauty, are you?" He rose unsteadily and went to a bar by the window.

"I'm abstaining from criminal activity, that's all."

"Is that the rhetoric? How charming."

"Bill, you're wobbling on your feet." I didn't want to have to give him mouth-to-mouth resuscitation, not after he'd been playing tonsil hockey with that vile woman.

"What would one expect after shagging such a creature? Leads one to believe in demons and succubi and all sorts of fairy tale characters that should not populate our realms." He poured himself a brandy. He gulped it, refilled, and then remembered me. He raised one sandy brown eyebrow and the crystal decanter at the same time. I nodded, and he poured a glass for me. Then he downed his second glass, refilled it, and brought over my drink. He seated himself again. The brandy did not restore his color.

"So what do you want to know? Not that it's less than wonderful to see you. Even when you catch me in flagrante delicto." There was an edge of sarcasm in his voice.

"I need information. What's it going to cost me?" I asked. "You don't do anything without your percentage." The scent of oak permeated my sinus cavities before I tasted the liquid. I sipped, subtle amber magic on my tongue, burning me from the inside out. "This is an armagnac, and XO." My father had a bottle of it. Dad. My heart wrung itself inside my chest. Was I any closer to finding him? Was using my old skills all for nothing? Breaking and entering didn't matter, if it led me to him. But what if it didn't, and nothing I did led me to him?

"Your discernment, as always, is exquisite, Laila," Cromer said. "As far as price, that depends on what you're seeking. Information about what?"

"*Coming Forth by Day*," I said.

Cromer whistled. "What is it about that painting?"

"As if you didn't know."

He smiled again, bitterly. "You know what it depicts?"

"Belzoni says a pagan ritual, with Isis and Osiris."

"But of course you've been to see Belzoni!" Cromer straightened and brightened. His gaze bored into mine and I could see dollar signs flashing, ka-chink, ka-chink, in his eyes. "Belzoni, that old scoundrel is a mercenary of the highest order...."

I knew what he was thinking: that if I'd gotten information out of my old teacher, I'd have had to pay for it. And there was only one form of remuneration Belzoni wanted from me: paintings. Old Master paintings. That meant there was one in his possession, needing authentication, needing a buyer. Cromer wanted in on the action.

"He asked, I refused," I said quietly.

"Couldn't tempt you back, eh?" Cromer said, regretful. I looked away, to stifle the intrigue that rose in me, as fresh as if I'd never walked away from it. I stared around, then down at the floor. That's when I noticed a trail of scarlet drops spattering along the floor where Cromer had walked to the bar and back. Was this the source of his pallor? What had she done to him?

I asked, "Are you bleeding?"

Cromer pulled his houserobe tighter across his chest. Was that a dark stain spreading across his front? Hard to tell because the robe was a plush, inky-red paisley. He coughed. "It's nothing. Who's running Belzoni these days?"

"Some Spanish woman from Oxford who speaks a lot of languages, and who, I quote, 'doesn't sell her pussy.'" I paused and Cromer snickered on cue. "He seems happy. She keeps him in wine and hookers."

"That's why he hasn't been calling me with business lately." He scowled.

"What do you know about the painting, Bill?"

Cromer rose and tried to walk around, but he only managed a few steps before he wobbled and had to return to the chair. "I want an introduction."

Uh-oh. Who was he planning to screw? Who would he sucker in with his British poise and polished accent and prestigious title? Was I about to take on the guilt of setting up an old mark for more abuse? Someone I'd already ripped off, who didn't deserve that, and who certainly didn't deserve to be scammed again? Brows knit, Cromer watched me, looking pastier by the minute. But I wasn't thinking about his white face, I was contemplating myself with horror: *some part of me wanted in on it with Cromer.* I played with my hair, which I only do when I'm really, really upset. Were my ends split? Was I actually just a bad person, because of my past, because I'd enjoyed my past? Would I never be redeemed? Cromer cleared his throat. I noticed that the sclera of his eyes was tinted over with red. I said, "You don't look well. We should find a doctor for you."

"When you were in business for yourself, there was a wealthy Japanese collector. Mr. Yamamoto. He got one of your best, very happy with it. The van Gogh."

"I hated that painting."

"A stunning piece. I'd buy it, if I could afford it. Vincent himself would have thought he'd painted it and forgotten during a mad spell. I often think that's how you do it, you actually let them inhabit your body while you paint. It's the only explanation. Possession by an outside force." He paused and shivered a little, as if chilled. I didn't respond. Visibly he took hold of himself. "I want to meet Mr. Yamamoto. There's a sweet Gauguin floating around that he would like. That's his period, isn't it?"

"And I am sure its provenance is spiffy."

"Pristine." He smirked. "You have the greater talent, my dear Laila, and my own poor gifts pale in comparison. But what I do, I do very well."

"You are a virtuoso with the paper trail, Lord Cromer." I rose and walked along the trail of blood drops. I concentrated on them instead of paper trails and cons. The drops were sparser where he'd walked over to the bar. The pattern was thicker where he'd walked back. "Bill, seriously, you're bleeding, and it's getting worse."

"I can take care of myself," he said brusquely. "Now, Laila, you want something I have, and I want something you have. Let's do this and move on."

I couldn't face another dead end. The clock was ticking. I had to pay Cromer's price. There was no avoiding it. *For Daddy.* I snapped open my cell phone. I winced, remembering how polite Mr. Yamamoto always was. So sweet and generous. I was scum for scamming him before, back then. Here I was again, teeing him up for another player to take a swing. But maybe Mr. Yamamoto had better art counsel this time. Maybe he wasn't still collecting. And maybe potatoes would sprout wings and fly over the Louvre dropping *frites* like snowflakes. I still had Mr. Yamamoto's cell number programmed into my cell. Why? Why hadn't I thrown away his contact information? Had I always subconsciously known that somehow, some way, I would be back in the thick of things?

After the initial ceremonies, the conversation went quickly. I told Mr. Yamamoto that my colleague would be calling him and hung up before he could offer to fly me to Tokyo on his Lear so I could eat dinner at the most expensive sushi place in the world, his treat, of course. And would I need a new outfit for the occasion, because he had accounts at all the best clothiers? I clenched my hand around my cell so tightly that it would have groaned, if it had had intestines.

Cromer was listing to one side in his chair but he was also smirking. "Yes, the Botticelli painting is real. It originated in Florence."

"Wasn't it burned in Savonarola's bonfire of the vanities?" That was the legend.

"It was saved from the bonfire by a supporter of Botticelli, a model who worked for both da Vinci and Botticelli, I have seen his diary," Cromer said. "He writes of singeing his knuckles as he snatched it out of the fire. A group tried to stop him as he carried it away...." I had a flash of the scene. Maybe it was the exhaustion and strangeness of this quest. Maybe it was the stress of looking for Daddy and of resisting extreme temptation. Maybe it was a hallucinogenic oyster in the parsley soup. Maybe it was Kadja's strange glance that had thrown my brain into disarray. But I had a flash of that night in Florence, so palpable to touch and sight and sound that it was as if I were there experiencing it....

February 1497. The streets of Florence are filled with people. Thousands of people in the somber dress that Savonarola, that fiery reformist Dominican, made mandatory. Groups of children called 'weepers,' like bands of thugs, wander through the throngs, demanding that people give up their vanities, tearing clothes and striking people when they demur. In the Piazza della Signoria, a pile of discarded items grows: mirrors, cosmetics, books and sculptures and paintings considered immoral or lewd, lutes and lyres and game pieces, fine dresses and women's fur-lined cloaks and hats made of sumptuous fabrics, ornaments, jewelry except for rosaries, playing cards, books by pagan writers—anything with which Savonarola's hatred could find fault. Botticelli himself stands at the edge, hunched over, his hands covering his face. He's thrown in several paintings. How will he even support himself, with his paintings destroyed? But he will eschew anything that leads him away from Savonarola's harsh God, even his own vision, even his own work....

So Sandro Filipepi had doubted himself and agonized over his actions. I could relate. I inhaled woozily and tried to focus on Cromer. All I saw was the gray stone square in front of the Palazzo Vecchio. I heard the roar of the throngs and smelled the smoke rising from the precious objects consigned to the bonfire. I didn't understand the hallucination: it was three-dimensional and intense, and I was fascinated by it....

The pile of vanities rises a dozen stories high. A tidal wave of hoarse sounds shakes the piazza, the throaty cries of bloodthirsty mobs. A young man wrapped in a black mantello, horror in his eyes, snatches a painting from the flames. He hurries to conceal it in his cloak, is set on by a gang of Savonarola's furious disciples. But this young model is brave. He stands and fights. Two of the disciples are knocked down, then trampled to death as Savonarola's sermon grows in fervor. The model uses the pandemonium to escape....

"Belzoni said the painting showed Isis and Osiris," I said, struggling to ground myself in present-day sanity. "Couldn't be, though, could it? No one read Egyptian then. The Rosetta Stone wasn't translated until...."

"1822, and that is Belzoni's purview," Cromer said. "But Greek was widely known. The great philosopher and linguist Marsilio Ficino, founder of the Platonic Academy, came by a Greek scroll that he translated and shared only with Leonardo, who was a great favorite of his. A scroll about rites of king-making and resurrection—"

"Speculation!" I interrupted. "No one has proved a relationship between Leonardo and Ficino. Even Vasari—"

"All history is bunk," Cromer said. "No one knows that better than me. I've manufactured quite a lot of history. It leads one to wonder... how much of what we accept as truth in the timeline is actual fact? How much was engineered for purposes of power? Burning books and paintings isn't the only way to control the minds of the masses. The better way is to write and promote books containing the desired history."

His words could not hook me in because I was flashing back to Florence, the smoke, the model's horror. Cromer resumed his story. "The model took the painting to Rome. He held it until his death, bequeathed it to his best friend: an Orsini, who, in turn, left it to his eldest son. It was written about in the secret diary of an Orsini cardinal, where he also made note of his two mistresses, seven children, and youthful boyfriend, and his provisions for all of them."

I felt a little queasy and shook my head, trying to clear myself of the hallucination. "Really, Bill? Or am I being treated to some of your creative talent?"

"The archive wouldn't let me borrow the diary, but I did manage to sneak some photos of it on my mobile. It's rather extraordinary. Even I'm not that good. Do you know, the lusty Cardinal bought a palazzo in Civitavecchio and installed his entire bloody brood there, with both women and the boy?"

"More efficient that way," I mumbled. It felt humorous to me, despite the vertigo of temporal dislocation. The haze of the past rolled back in like a fog, veiling my sight. I could barely see the outline of Cromer's head.

"Indeed. This painting seems to have been bathed in blood. It was taken out of Rome on May 5, 1527, when Charles V's troops sacked the city.... Cromer was talking, but I couldn't hear him. The vision had consumed me again.

May 1527. Harquebus fire and screaming. Germans and Spaniards climbing scaling-ladders, clambering over and through the breached walls of Rome. A thick mist rising out of the Tiber. Homes and shops burning. The Spanish Infantry rampages through the Hospital of San Spirito, slaughtering patients with pikes and swords, or else throwing them into the river. The children of the Pietà orphanage are massacred, most chopped into bits, piles of small bloody limbs and torsos. Church doors are smashed open, tombs and convents and palaces broken into and looted, nuns are raped and strangled, priests and nobleman maimed and mutilated and tortured to death. Nothing, no one, is sacred. Amid the screams, one woman dresses herself as a beggar boy, takes with her two paintings bundled to her back, and runs through the streets. She is allowed to climb out the walls of Rome after hollering Spanish endearments she'd learned from her first lover....

"It was a woman who saved the painting when Rome was sacked," I murmured.

"Yes, I said that. An Orsini mistress. Made her way to Paris. She was beautiful and found powerful protectors. She left the painting to her daughter. I've seen that will. The daughter also had political savvy and stayed on the correct sides of the religious wars. She married well, a minor nobleman with land holdings, and kept the painting in the family. It hung in a private place of honor in a Parisian palace for two centuries."

But the strange vision of the painting had spun forward in time, and I saw another time of horror and death and bloodshed. "The reign of terror, the storming of the Bastille," I said numbly.

July 1789. Riots, chaos, looting. Oppressive heat. Unruly mobs, hungry and angry, scouring Paris for weapons and ammunition. The Bastille, a medieval fortress and prison with eight towers on the Seine, a long-time symbol of tyranny, is rumored to have 250 barrels of gunpowder. The drawbridge ropes are cut, not one guard is spared a quick and horrible death, and within a few hours the commander, the Marquis de Launay, is beaten, stabbed, and decapitated. His head is paraded about on a pike.

On the outskirts of Paris, a young nobleman gathers his family, his wife and two small children. He collects just a few prized possessions: some jewelry, the painting that his forbear brought to Paris. He flees the city within hours of the Storming of the Bastille.

"...Ghent for more than a century, then ended up in Amsterdam," Cromer was saying. "On the very eve of the Nazis marching in."

I jumped up and raced to the bar, literally sprinted those few yards, to shake off the incoming vision. Inhabiting the past so viscerally fascinated me, but I would not, could not, experience the Nazis marching into Amsterdam. My hand shook as I poured a large glass of cognac and drained it. The liquor burned and re-attached my feet to my legs and my legs to my trunk. The haze scrolled back from my eyes. Once again, I could see the room. I was scared and curious at the same time. What was happening to me? Trembling, I went back toward the couch.

Cromer kept talking, as if nothing I'd done was unusual. "This is where the trail cools. A Polish priest seems to have come into possession of it. He was a marked man, wanted by the Gestapo. Not just for being Polish. He had destroyed records about Jews and created false identification papers for them so they could escape. He fled Amsterdam. Took the painting to Rome."

"Rome?" I was pinching the inside of my arm, the soft spot that really hurts, to make sure that I was awake. And that I didn't lose myself again in a dream of the past.

Cromer nodded, but feebly, and his pale lids wavered. "I saw something when I was working on export bills out of Rome...."

"Faking them," I corrected. And the devil on my shoulder wondered what he had been running, and if it was successful.

"They have to come from somewhere," he returned blithely. "How else is an old family, fallen upon hard times financially, reluctantly parting with a prized Caravaggio that's been in the family for centuries, going to prove that their clever forebears acquired the painting legitimately?"

A Caravaggio—how delicious. Aloud, I said, "Cromer, for shame. Such fictions you create. To think the rest of the world believes that you're an honest art historian and researcher."

"Why shouldn't they, I've written three highly-regarded scholarly books that prove I am!" He smiled.

"Just for shits and giggles, who did the Caravaggio?"

Cromer gave me a sly look. "Goldberg."

"Alain?! That Israeli commando has the sensitivity of tree bark! He's got hands like a lumberjack. I bet it looked like something painted by Grandma Moses after she went blind!" The quick crest of amusement helped me feel more like myself again. The hallucinations dimmed like a light bulb shorting.

Cromer was laughing from his belly. "He did a nice job of it. He's improved. Duckie, you've no business criticizing when you've decided you're too good for the rest of us and have retired from our specialized line of work. Unless you're coming out of retirement, in which case, let me be the first to welcome you back...." He gave me a hopeful, avaricious look. I looked away.

"We had a grand run, though, didn't we, Laila? Remember the Corot, the seascape, the Swiss couple, and the randy professor? I still think of you fondly whenever I see a pair of lederhosen."

"I try to forget that." But I couldn't smother the grin that spread all over my face. I've never minded making a fool of myself. Okay, I do mind, but if I can't laugh at myself, I'm in big trouble. I figured that out a long time ago.

"Oh, come on, you really don't miss it, the risk and the thrill of the life?"

"No." But it was a lie, and we both knew it.

He grinned. "Examining the old ledgers, that's when I first saw a tax bill for an unknown Botticelli painting entering Rome. Mussolini didn't put a stop to taxing art imports." He went on, as if the conversation had never taken a detour into the no-man's-land of my deepest desires.

"I recognized the name," Cromer was saying. "I'd heard it before. It was the alias used by the traveling priest. Moreover, he noted that he was returning from Amsterdam. The painting was described as "in the hand of Botticelli," an implication that it was a copy, so the tax would be less. But it was the narrative attached to the painting that caught my eye. A god and goddess in strange costume, enacting a pagan rite."

"As Belzoni said," I murmured.

"Indeed. It was to Belzoni I turned then for information, just as you did."

"That sick bastard wouldn't tell me anything unless I fixed a stupid Vermeer for him! And the interior light was all wrong!"

"There you have it, the interior light is everything," Cromer said softly. "You cross his threshold, what do you expect him to do, Persephone? Not offer the pomegranate?"

"I hope he rots in hell forever," I muttered. I chewed my lip. "So it probably returned to Rome around May, 1940. What then?"

"I've tried to discover that." He shifted around in his seat and I noticed the sludgy scarlet line of blood dripping over his knee, streaking along his calf to the floor.

"Bill, your bleeding is getting worse. We've got to do something."

"I'll take care of myself momentarily, when you leave. The last piece of information I uncovered was from a nun who knew the priest. If you ask me, he'd been in her knickers, and vow of celibacy be damned. She had a gleam about her when she spoke of him. An intimate, womanly gleam. History changes, people don't, that's a fact."

"Um, you're losing quite a lot of blood there, Billy boy."

"Do you want to hear this, or not?" He was losing patience along with his sanguine life force, but then patience had never been his most salient quality. Urbane brilliance, classy charm—those attributes sprang to mind when he was mentioned. Because I knew his hidden side as only a handful of other people did, I also thought of cunning, conniving, lying, and cheating. But patience, never.

"Try not to bleed to death until you've finished the story. This is urgent."

"I asked Sister Marina what he did when he returned from Amsterdam. Of course, I had to listen to her reminisce about his selfless courage and all that codswallop. All in keeping with my cover as a pious art historian. She says he left soon after for America. He took several paintings with him for safekeeping in a parish house in New York."

"The painting's in the U.S.?" I froze in place. "No way!"

"Think of the times. Germany invaded Poland in the fall of 1939. Mussolini was afraid the Italian army wasn't up to fighting, but he joined the war anyway, in June, 1940, only a few days before France surrendered. The times were uncertain, the Gestapo was everywhere—it even had a special division for looting art. Europe was in chaos, works of art were vanishing. Many people knew that relations between *il Duce* and *der Fuhrer* were strained. And our priest was a wanted man, hated by the Gestapo, in possession of several works of art. He set out on a steamer under his alias."

"How do you know he brought *Coming Forth by Day* with him?"

"I found the evidence!" He brightened. "In the parish house registry, there was a list of what he stored there when he arrived. The description was almost exactly the same in English as in the Italian tax bill: 'after Botticelli, a god and goddess performing a ritual.' It can only be the lost Botticelli."

I returned to the couch and perched on the edge. "Okay, then what?"

"There the trail grows cool. The parish house was under renovation when I visited, and they'd moved everything they kept in storage to a warehouse in New Jersey. Of course, they were snidely secretive about it, and refused to let me explore the warehouse." Cromer made a small moue of discontent.

"That stopped you?"

"I managed to find out which warehouse facility." He shrugged. "It wasn't the only possibility. In the 1990s, one of their naughty priests finally had to pay for buggering a couple of altar boys, so the parish house quietly sold some paintings to finance it. It was all done on the sly, very hush-hush. Four major collectors were contacted, offered a chance to purchase in exchange for extreme discretion. I've made a list." He pointed to the bar. "That folder by the Armagnac. That's for you. It contains copies of my research. The whole trail, as I've pieced it together."

I rose and went to the bar. How did he know to put together a folder of documentation for me? Of course—"Belzoni told you I was coming!" I was aghast, disgruntled, angered, but not surprised. Belzoni wouldn't tell me what he knew about the painting, but he would tell Cromer I was looking for it. This was the downside of the life: not being able to trust a colleague. Because we were each in it for ourselves, and don't you ever forget it. I didn't miss that part of it. I felt relieved that there was something unappetizing for me to cling to, even as the old allure seeped back into my bones. I thought of Fern and how she'd do anything for me, any time, and always tell me the truth. She was my true North.

"He called and said you'd dropped in on him with questions and might come to see me. Giovanni owes me a favor," Cromer smiled, a hollow, knowing thing that sent chills down the sensitive peaks of my cervical spine. There was a reason we couldn't trust each other, in this life: we each drew the line at a different level of moral apathy. I didn't believe that people should be hurt. Giovanni didn't believe people should be hurt. But Cromer believed people's pain was their own business. He didn't draw any lines.

I knew exactly what Belzoni would and could do. I hated him and I loved him, and I knew he'd do nothing more and nothing less than forge and sell paintings. He was a child, not a criminal. Some people might take exception to my lax definition of the word "criminal,"—you know, uninformed folks who don't get what a service forgers are doing in providing classic beauty to a grateful humanity.... What was I saying? Forgery is wrong, a form of lying, a terrible sin. But still: Belzoni wouldn't hurt a tiny creeping insect. I wasn't sure he didn't just regale all those trashy hookers with stories, and really, anyone forced to listen to Belzoni's stories deserved to be paid. The girls would probably prefer to perform a deviant act than listen to him. I know I would.

But Cromer, he was a different bird altogether. He was conscienceless. For all his urbane air and aristocratic mien, he had never exhibited a single qualm about anything. Not about the cons he perpetrated, not about the means he used for his ends. Not about any suffering that resulted from his choices. I'd watched him in action, and it wasn't pretty. He didn't reflect on the consequences. I wondered what kind of favor Cromer had done for Belzoni. I probably didn't want to know.

I picked up the file and leafed through it. Photocopies and pictures, lists and notations, wills and bills and inventories. "Impressive. How much of it is real?"

"Laila, I'm wounded!" He pouted. "There is honor among us. That folder represents the absolute best that I'm capable of. I put it together for you. Only you. There are others looking for the painting, you know." He blinked and straightened suddenly in his chair, as if he'd revealed too much.

I ran to him and gripped his robe by its lapels. "Who else is looking for it? Who has contacted you?" I would have shaken him, but he put one enervated hand on my wrist. Even his fingernails looked wan and bloodless. "Bill, goddamn it, you're going to keel over and die from blood loss!"

"Laila, you Amazon, remove yourself from my garb," he snapped. But I didn't. I scrunched up the robe more tightly in my hands. The robe gaped open and showed bloody puncture marks on his chest, under his clavicles. He cried out and shrugged the robe closed, despite my grip.

"Tell me, Cromer, right now, or I'll let some key people know what it is you actually do. Who else is after *Coming Forth by Day*?"

"Back off," he snarled. It was an acquiescence. I released him but did not step back. He ground his teeth. Probably needed a retainer to prevent that, should call his dentist. Or I could just knock his teeth out for him, to thank him for manipulating me into setting up Mr. Yamamoto. I wanted to punch him, longed to do it, yearned, but never would. And that's what separated me from him. That's what kept me out of the game.

"Spill it."

Cromer said, "There's a consortium. They contacted me three years ago, asked me to find the painting for them. They send money, finance my research. She's one of them." By "she" he meant Kadja the librarian. So that was why she was in Amsterdam. That was why she was so hostile to me at the library. Of course, I was right all along; she did know about the missing Botticelli folio. She'd probably taken it herself, hoping to find clues to the painting's location at the time the folio was written, a marker in its travels through space and time. I wondered if Bolingbroke knew she belonged to the "evil" group. Cromer moaned and sank down in his chair.

"You're working for them. But you gave information to me?"

"I know you," he muttered. "You gave me an introduction that only you could, a fair trade. I've tried to get to Yamamoto many times. He's not accessible." Cromer shifted uneasily in his seat, rewrapped his houserobe. "They're not nice people, Laila. They're dangerous. I'm not sure they'll let me live if I find the painting for them. I'm sure they won't if I don't. If I turn up dead," he said, indicating the blood draining down his thigh and calf, "at least you'll carry on, and probably find the painting. Using my research. Part of me will live on in that way. I don't have children, you know. Never wanted the shackles of marriage and children. My work is my progeny."

"Great sob story, Bill. I almost believe it." I strode back to the bar and took the folder. I was angry. Angry that he'd work for a deadly group that was tracking my father, angry that he appealed to my sympathies, angry that he hadn't told me up front that Belzoni had told him I might come by to see him. I hated to feel sorry for him.

"You'd better believe that they're dangerous, Laila. Because they know you're looking for the painting. And they're watching you." He said it with more vigor than he'd managed all evening.

"Call a doctor, Cromer. You don't want to die tonight," I said. I walked out, clutching the folder. I suppose I thought I'd see him again, some day. Without defining it to myself, I vaguely figured I'd encounter him again and we'd share a few laughs over a cognac. Don't you hate being that wrong?

Chapter 12

BOLINGBROKE HEARD THE CALL AS SOON AS evening fell. It was the lavender dusk hour when vampires roused from their deathsleep and stalked human prey. They chose individuals, sometimes children, sometimes the homeless, who wandered off on their own, like straggling gazelles that attract the attention of lions, and were cut down just as remorselessly. The early hour indicated that a group of vampires had fed promptly and coordinated immediately. A human life had been snuffed out, because the group needed every precious drop of life from its victim in order to send the call.

He's in place, stay with him!

Bolingbroke heard it without being able to localize it. The call originated in Europe, yes. Holland, certainly; Amsterdam, maybe. To his telepathic senses, it was received like a chorus of voices, and he had the distinct impression that one of the voices was familiar to him. It made him uneasy. Who had followed them from New York? Bolingbroke took up his leather bag and opened the lining. Inside was a sharpened wooden stick, fourteen inches long. It was made of cedar wood, which he'd discovered was the surest, swiftest killer. He shrugged on his jacket and placed the stick in a specially designed interior pocket. Inside the pocket there were other sharpened sticks: hawthorn, birch, dogwood. They had different uses, and Bolingbroke believed in being prepared against all eventualities.

The infamous red-light district was the obvious place to look for vampires. As an old and tolerant city, Amsterdam hosted a dozen covens, had for centuries. They were naturally drawn to the Rossebuurt, with its brothels and erotic toy shops and the live sex show venues that lined its cobbled streets, with its gabled, Gothic buildings leaning at odd angles, and with its tree-shaded canals. The Rossebuurt was the glittering center of Amsterdam's night life, and food would be readily available.

The area was already raucous and bathed in garish fluorescent red light. Hookers in bikinis and spiky high heels stood in windows on the ground floor or leaned out from windows on upper floors. A woman asked for directions and as he answered, a pedestrian bumped into Bolingbroke, melted away fast. It was a burly young man, blond and acne-stubbled, and he'd have gotten away seamlessly except for Bolingbroke's superhuman speed and coordination. The woman, an accomplice, sprinted off.

"You will return my wallet to me," Bolingbroke growled. He clamped one hand around the youth's neck and lifted him until his feet dangled off the sidewalk. The man squeaked and nodded, the whites of his eyes gleaming with fear. He handed Bolingbroke his wallet. Bolingbroke shook him. "The others, also." Three more wallets were forthcoming. Bolingbroke squeezed the neck harder, and two more wallets were handed over, hastily. Bolingbroke set the young man on his feet.

"Be gone, and trouble me no more!" he commanded. The young man left at a dead run. Bolingbroke passed the wallets to the next pair of stunned-looking married tourists who walked by, innocents out for an adventure they could not possibly compass. He could see from the husband's white socks and black shoes beneath his khaki shorts, and the wife's shiny white teeth when she smiled nervously, that they were Americans, probably Midwesterners, those nearly universally honest creatures.

"These were retrieved from a thief," Bolingbroke said. "Give them to the police!" He used the Voice, the spell-binding voice of command that vampires used to enslave humans, when vampire charisma alone wasn't enough to bend the fragile creatures to their dark will. The couple nodded and bolted from the Rossebuurt, holding hands. Bolingbroke returned to his search.

Dealers walked by muttering, "Coca, coca," but Bolingbroke ignored them. He was looking in windows, glancing around at the tourists. Mostly, he was smelling. Sooner or later he'd catch the unique and subtly vitriolic scent of a vampire. He passed by the Sexyland Erotic Supermarket, where a group of young women laughed at a giant dildo that one of them was waving around with gusto. Then, there it was—a whiff of vampire. Bolingbroke looked around until he spied a young blonde woman in a second-story window. Her face was plump and innocent, and the smile on her lips was absolutely guileless. But Bolingbroke knew at a glance what she was.

He went to the doorway of the building, where a large man with a shaved head stood smoking. He wore an ill-fitting suit and shifted his weight from foot to foot. When Bolingbroke stepped onto the stoop, the man held out his hand and asked for seventy-five euros, in Dutch with a Russian accent. Bolingbroke paid without negotiating. The man stood aside and jerked his chin at the door. Bolingbroke went through.

As he climbed the stairs, he slipped the mala over his head. Stealth was necessary. There was no telling how old she was, how much power she had accumulated over the length of her unholy years. Bolingbroke was tall and had immeasurable strength, but an older vampire, whether male or female, would be stronger. A fight could get ugly. Bolingbroke had no intention of letting that happen.

When he got to the second floor, he opened the door soundlessly. The vampire's keen hearing caught something, but she couldn't see him, so she flicked an incurious glance over her shoulder. Bolingbroke glided up behind her. She had a curvy back and ample buttocks, slightly plump by this age's standards, the pinnacle of female perfection in an earlier era, and luscious at any point in history. Her yellow hair hung down to her waist in a clean, silky sheet. She glanced back again when Bolingbroke stood only a few inches behind her. Her blue eyes were wide with puzzlement. But the mala cozened her evil senses and she couldn't see him, so she turned back to her window.

That was her fatal mistake. Bolingbroke retrieved the wooden stick from his pocket. His hand moved as a fast as a hummingbird's wing, and the stake went through her left breast: just above the heart, but close enough to kill her.

She groaned and staggered. Bolingbroke caught her as she fell.

"Who's there? I can't see you!" she cried. Her limbs trembled. Bolingbroke placed her on the ground. He slipped off his mala beads. Her face changed. "What, what are you?"

"The stake will kill you, but not for three minutes," Bolingbroke said. "I placed it so you'd have some time to talk."

"You smell like a vampire, but also you smell unlike one. You're not human, you're some kind of forbidden mix, and now you've done this to me! Why?"

"Two minutes, fifty seconds. Were you part of the call this evening?"

But she was babbling, clutching her breast. "This cannot happen to me; I am too old! I was turned by Flavius Constantinus' vampire, after his mother convinced him to disown the vampire and profess her Christianity." Emperor Constantine: he ruled in the fourth century after Christ. This was an ancient vampire. "Had I seen you, I would have killed you with one blow," she grated. She gripped the stake and wrenched, but, of course, the stake would not be moved. Bolingbroke had placed it with exactitude. "What are you, foul thing? What have you done to me? To me, who has killed tens of thousands, hundreds of thousands, of human cows. Now you have killed me!" She moaned. Her body jerked. Her undead flesh had turned black and purple around the protruding hilt of the stake. Coppery dark lines fanned out from the wound, staining her white skin. Her left arm swelled and mottled over with purple and brown striae. True death was coming fast. She howled, "Noooooo...."

Bolingbroke looked at his watch. "Two minutes. Who was involved in the call?"

Her face puckered, and uncontrollable writhing took over her limbs. Bolingbroke stepped back to avoid being hit. She gasped, "Why should I tell you anything?"

"If you answer my questions, I will have mass said for you," he told her. It was a powerful inducement for a vampire, who knew that hell awaited, and that her only hope was the prayers of true believers. She looked at him with contempt. Then a violent seizure spun her body on the floor like a top, set her left arm to drumming like a jackhammer. The seizure passed and her contempt changed to anguish.

"I was part of the call. There were three covens. We took down two children, twins, Spanish tourists. Delicious, so young and fresh. Unspoiled, sweet blood. After the feast, I joined my mind to the covens'."

"The call was about Robert Cambridge?"

"He cannot be allowed to give that painting to his death squad!" She lurched over onto her side, like a fish flopping on a dock, and vomited black blood. "We have feared them for too long. When he finds the painting, we will take it from him. Then we will launch an all-out attack on their society that will make *Kristallnacht* and the mass arrest of the Knights Templar look like child's play! We will not be stopped!" But her right arm and both legs were bloated and blackened, and her spasms were growing slower. She was stopping.

"Were there any outsiders at the feast?"

She nodded. Her voice came in a hoarse bark. "Two. My name is Geertje, daughter of Adelbert, when mass is said...."

"Who were the outsiders?" Bolingbroke asked. Her lips moved with almost no sound. He leaned over to catch her words. Then her skull imploded, followed by her torso, and her four limbs rolled out on the floor and then imploded, as well. All that was left were slicks of black and scarlet blood on the floor, and the spatter on his shirt.

Bolingbroke thought he'd caught one name.

I found Bolingbroke waiting for me, pacing around the lobby of our hotel. He had a strangely hyper affect. It made me nervous. He tilted his head as I came in the front entrance. He lifted his face as if scenting something. Was I sweating that badly? He said, "You've seen Cromer."

"Uh-huh. Do we talk here or elsewhere?"

He bit his lip as if the question were of the utmost importance. "My room," he said. "I'll have food brought." He spoke in rapid, old-fashioned Dutch to Astrid, who looked at him with the moon-faced adulation that gorgeous Bolingbroke always inspired in women. When he was done, he focused himself on her by way of a smile and flowery expression of gratitude for her immeasurable abilities. Poor Astrid. She practically dissolved into a puddle of goo. I rolled my eyes as he took my arm and ushered me up the narrow staircase ahead of him.

"Oh, please," I said in a low voice, looking back at him over my shoulder.

"What?" He feigned innocence but there was a kind of gleam in his eyes that reminded me of Cromer's words about a woman gleaming over a man she'd slept with. That led my mind to that incredible moment when I'd burst through the door and seen Cromer in the middle of coitus with Kadja. Kadja, who belonged to the group looking for the Botticelli painting at any cost. Something about her face, that moment when she'd looked up and laughed, was tickling my brain. I'd seen her wearing a similar expression recently. But where? Not at the library. Somewhere else. A painting?

"A portrait of Kadja...." I murmured.

Bolingbroke stiffened. He grabbed my arm. "What do you know about Kadja?"

"She's the librarian at Columbia, and she's here in Amsterdam." I shook him off. "The question is, what do *you* know about Kadja?"

Bolingbroke said nothing. Then we were in his room. I went immediately to his bed and flopped down. "These have been the strangest few days of my life. Nights have become my days, so I don't even know what day it is anymore. I barely know what's going on. I've discovered that a fabled lost Botticelli painting on which Leonardo collaborated is real, and is probably in New York. My dad has been looking for it, and there's a violent group looking for him because of that. He's alive but in danger. I feel terrified and exhausted and frustrated. I never know what's coming next."

"Anxiety is held in check by strategy," Bolingbroke said.

"Strategy?" I laughed. "All I can plan is to go the next step, then the next, along the path to finding him before they do."

"That's a workable strategy," Bolingbroke assented. "Find him and find the painting, protect them both. Efficient. What's this about New York?"

"Why is this painting so important to that group?" I wondered, with some frustration. "To both groups, my dad's and the dangerous one?" Bolingbroke gave me a sideways glance but didn't say anything. I gargled with frustration. "Did you know, Bolingbroke, that it has a strange and bloody history? And that I'm having hallucinations? I don't even know if I can trust myself anymore. I've made contact with my old partners! Now I'm at the mercy of these hallucinations that feel so real...."

"What kind of hallucinations?" He seated himself on the edge of the bed, turning to face me so he could stroke the hair off my face. His funny, ironic half-smile lifted one side of his mouth. Something softened in his hawk-like eyes.

"When Cromer was telling me about the painting, I, well, I went to the places and times he talked about. I experienced them. It was so real, all the sights and sounds and smells!" I held my breath a little, wondering what he would think. Maybe it would give me a clue about what I thought.

But Bolingbroke only nodded. Somberly, he said, "I have heard it said that the painting possesses mystical powers. Perhaps you're attuned to it, Laila, and so it communicated its history directly into your consciousness. You are an artist."

I laughed, a little shakily. "I don't know about mystical powers. I know all about paintings, since I've made one or two myself. Their power is in their beauty and truth and inspiration. About the way they kick us out of the coma of our everyday lives and lift us up and transform us into our better selves." I turned my cheek to nuzzle his hand. He smiled. I said, "That's what the modernists don't get, that art isn't a solipsistic pursuit in the mind of the artist, and beauty isn't irrelevant. Beauty's the whole damn point."

He drew the tip of his index finger down my nose. "I'll debate the point with you another day, when we're back in New York. Tell me about Kadja."

"She was at Cromer's place."

"Start at the beginning. You know Kadja from the Columbia library?"

"She takes the late shift a couple of nights a week. How do you know her?"

"Has she ever threatened you?" Would he ever give me a straight answer?

"She never threatened me before tonight. At the library, she just beamed radioactive waves at me. Tonight she did this." I stretched out my arm so Bolingbroke could see the bruise I wore as a bracelet. He took my wrist between his hands and stroked my hand, arm, and wrist. His long fingers moved gently, rhythmically, along the delicate bones and veins. Soft, sweet warmth grew wherever his fingertips touched. At first, my wrist throbbed harder. Then the throbbing eased, and my wrist relaxed. The relaxation spread from my wrist through my whole body. The anxiety began to seep away.

"And she was with Lord Cromer this evening?" Bolingbroke repeated. I was so lost in the delicious heat in my battered wrist that I hadn't answered him the first time.

"With him? Oh boy, was she with him! I didn't recognize her at first, without all her clothes on." I groaned a little. "That feels amazing! How do you do that?"

"They were in bed." He looked absorbed in his own thoughts. But his fingers continued their swirling motion.

"She was on top," I drawled, suggestively. He cut his eyes at me to acknowledge the suggestion. Then I glanced at where the purple bruise had been. It was nearly gone! I gasped and sat upright. "How did you do that? I figured that would take weeks to go away! Are you some kind of healer?"

"A skill I picked up in my travels," he said. "Lie back and let me finish."

I closed my eyes, overcome with worry about my dad, who was looking for a painting with a history fraught with Nazis, wars, and blood, a painting coveted by the rapacious Kadja and her cohorts. If they were anything like her, they were bloodthirsty bastards; that was clear. How would I protect my dad from them, once I found him? I opened my eyes to ask that question, found Bolingbroke gazing at me intensely. His eyes did that quick transformation from predatory cat's eyes to regular eyes; well, not that regular, because they were so absolutely gorgeous and penetrating. He released my hand gently. The bruise was entirely gone. I smiled with thanks, and he ran those warm, warm fingers over my lips. I caught his hand and kissed those magical fingertips gently. His breath caught, and he shuddered. He rose from the bed as if tearing himself away.

He leaned against the wall, his long legs stretching out before him. His eyes bored into the floor like laser beams that would start fires in the knotty wood. He looked at the wall and the furniture, anywhere but at me. I felt a thrill: he wanted me! He was fighting himself! He asked, hoarsely, "The painting is in New York?"

"That's what Cromer said. That's where the paper trail leads. The story makes sense," I said. I summarized it for him: from Botticelli's model to the libidinous Orsini to the resourceful mistress and her quick-witted descendent who fled Paris. Then to the priest who took the painting first to Rome and then to the parish house in New York.

"Plausible, but unlikely. None of the gossip has ever placed the painting in the States. Your father is probably in Europe." He drummed his fingers against the wall.

"Cromer gave me copies of his research notes. They lead back to New York. If Dad discovered the same information, he'll be back in New York. Maybe that's why he was in the city when you met him at the Columbia library. And the next clue is there."

"I must talk to Cromer," Bolingbroke said. He pushed off the wall and began to pace.

"He might be in the hospital by now," I said.

Bolingbroke swung toward me on his heel so fast and so furiously that I was taken aback. He did have mercurial mood shifts, didn't he? Who was this curious man, and why was he helping me find my father? What was Bolingbroke's interest in the painting, after all? Clearly he knew more than he was telling me, and why wouldn't he come clean? He looked so ferocious, waiting for me to explain, that I swallowed. "Cromer was bleeding. Kadja had bit him or cut him or something. Weird, huh?"

"I know you're tired, Laila, but we have to go *right now* to see Cromer. Can you do it?" He was already at the door, holding it open for me. I jumped up. The room spun around me. I had to lean into the wall to steady myself. Did I have a choice? Not the way things had been going lately, when so many of my choices seemed to be foregone conclusions, planned in some chess game to whose players' thoughts I was not privy.

Chapter 13

"THROUGH ALL OF THIS, I GET THE feeling that you know a lot more than you're letting on, Bolingbroke," I said. We were hurrying along the Leidseplein. In fact, his long strides were eating up big stretches of street while I trotted beside him. I panted, "Time to give it up!"

"The time for that will come," he temporized, without slowing the pace. He refused to speak again, just increased his speed so that I was now galloping. And remained just as frustrated and stymied as I always was with him.

He didn't pause until we stood in the Jordaan, in front of Cromer's house, which was strobed by the rotating lights of three police cars and two police motorcycles parked next door. Bolingbroke swore softly. There was a scurry of official activity in the yard between Cromer's house and the building next door, and other pedestrians had paused to gawk. I marched up to a young police officer and stuck out my boobs, which was the universal request for a little consideration, please. It was understood and honored in all languages. He was a barrel-chested blond buck, and he smiled back in friendly fashion. Then he remembered his position and scowled with importance.

"So what happened?" I asked, in my sweetest Dutch.

"Don't know." He shrugged. I stepped closer and shook my boobs a little in his face. His eyes widened in appreciation.

"You're so smart, I'm sure you've got some idea," I cooed.

He pushed his blue cap back on his head and scratched his ear. "Well, miss." He inched toward me. "A killer went through here. At least three people dead in this building, and the English fellow leasing the house next door is missing. The house is bathed in blood, and our first thought is that he was taken from the premises and killed. We might still find him over here. Expect to, actually. His bloody clothes are in the other building, and the bodies are all torn up into pieces!"

"Terrible!" I gagged a little. "What are you going to do?" I backed away.

"Don't worry, we're the finest police force in the world," he boasted. "Look how quickly we shut down the bums who were dumping Smart Cars into the canals. And we have excellent crime scene scientists. We'll find this murderer and put him in jail!"

I made all the expected sounds of admiration and then raced back to Bolingbroke. "The cop says there's a killer—"

"I heard," Bolingbroke said, somewhat crisply.

"What is it with you and your hearing? You're like a dog. You could at least let me have the satisfaction of telling a really grisly story," I complained. Then it hit me. "Cromer's missing. They think he's dead. Torn up into pieces!" I felt stricken; I didn't expect to care so much. I didn't trust Bill, after all. I knew him too well for that. But we had spent time together, cooperated to pull off a few sweet cons, and respected each other's skills. Hell, I'd enjoyed his skills! I'd enjoyed him. Why hadn't he gone to the doctor when I'd asked him to? He wouldn't have been caught unawares, and killed. I felt a riff of sadness. Cromer wasn't a virtuous man, but he didn't deserve a horrible death.

"He's not dead," Bolingbroke said. He didn't elaborate, but pulled my arm to swing me around and direct me back whence we'd come. "But your DNA is all over his flat, so let's get you out of here." He set forth with that race-walking stride of his, clutching my arm so that I had to lope to keep up.

"How do you know he's not dead?" I panted, wishing I had some running shoes.

"I know," he said.

"If you say so," I said, as dryly as I could.

He didn't speak again until we were safely away from the Jordaan. Then he was curt. "I have a friend with a plane. I'll call to ask for a ride back to New York. Pack your things and be ready to go soon. I know you're tired—"

"I'm not so tired. My second wind blew in. I've gotten used to being up at night and sleeping during the day. Cromer talked about demons and succubi; maybe I'm turning into a vampire," I quipped.

Bolingbroke halted abruptly and raked me with a glare so frigid that I actually stepped back from him. What was this guy's deal? One minute he healed me with the warmest, most honeyed touch ever, and the next I was terrified that he was about to harm me. He stepped several paces away and took out his cell phone. Bolingbroke spoke in a murmur too low for me to make out his words. But then, I didn't have the canine super-hearing that he did.

He snapped the phone shut. "Two hours," he said.

"Sure, and do you think I might get your cell number? In case I need you."

"Of course." He opened his phone.

"My number is...."

"I know your number," he cut me off, pressing buttons. My phone rang. PRIVATE, the screen said. Big surprise there! I opened my mouth to tell him the number was blocked, but a second later, the number came through. I saved it under his name.

"You know, I received a strange call from an unknown caller earlier," I said. "Just silence. Not even breathing. Couldn't figure out who it was."

"It was them. Probably Kadja," he growled. He grabbed my arm again and hurried me back along the Leidseplein toward our hotel.

"'Them.' Who exactly are 'them'? You explained that they were an evil group, like the Japanese Mafia, and my father's society was pledged to stop them. But what is their name? What's the name of my father's society?"

"There'll be more explanations in the fullness of time, I promise, Laila. But right now I want to get you safely away from Amsterdam, and back in the States, where you can resume your search for the painting."

"It's not the painting that matters, it's my father," I reminded him. We had nearly reached our hotel, and he was practically shoving me in the door. Then he paused.

"I simply don't feel that the painting would have left Rome for New York."

"Why not?"

He shook his head and hustled me into the lobby. "It's the first I've heard of it leaving the continent. If it were in New York, wouldn't they have found it before now? Or your father? If it really were so close at hand."

"Not if they didn't know where to look. Hey, why are you so frantic to get me out of Amsterdam?"

"Frantic?" He snorted, the first ungraceful thing ever to have come from him. "That is one word that does not describe me. I move always with deliberation."

"You're sliding me up the stairs like I'm a mannequin on a tray, and I'm six feet tall," I said. It really was undignified. I tried to push him off so I could climb the last few steps to my room in peace.

"Cromer's dangerous. He's been, ah, co-opted by the evil group, and you were the last person to talk to him before the, ah, co-opting. You're imprinted on him. He'll be looking for you."

"Cromer would never hurt me! He'd use me, lie to me, sure, scam me out of money if he could, but hurt me physically? Never!"

"You'd be surprised what those people can make one do," Bolingbroke said. His eyes blazed. We stood at the door to my room, and I had the key out. He took it from my hand. I couldn't help it—he stood so close, and smelled so good, like vanilla and leather and lush bergamot and male musk—even with my fear about my father being in danger, and my dislocation over the events of the last few days, and the anxiety and frustration, I was still human. I slipped my arms around him and kissed his lips, softly, quickly. Then I stepped back. His agate eyes half closed and he shivered, the most sensuous movement I've ever seen a man make. Then he smiled, that sardonic half-grin that spoke of knowing and mastery and exquisite pleasure. He opened my door and thrust me inside.

How was it that a search for my missing father, and the painting he was looking for, had allied me with this potent man? My father. Then something occurred to me. Someone. Of course. "Hey, I know who we could talk to about Rome," I said. He raised an eyebrow. "My mom," I said. "She lived in Rome several times, studied painting there. We were posted there with my dad when I was a kid. And her best friend lives in Rome. Aunt Emilie, though she's ill now."

"Good idea. You have that note from your father," Bolingbroke reminded me. "She'll want to see it. Let's get you back home, and we'll see your mother. You have twenty minutes to pack, then we're going to the airport."

Chapter 14

FERN AND I WERE BACK IN DEX'S Mini Cooper. It was the next day. At least I think it was. The sun was high in the sky, but I'd given up on the compartmentalization of "day" and "night," and their arbitrary division from other days and nights. I surrendered calendar distinctions, did what I could to get closer to my dad and the lost Botticelli that so many people wanted, and tried to grab a few hours of sleep whenever possible. Time sort of flowed around me, shrinking every second.

I kept thinking about the hallucinations that had dragged me into the lost Botticelli's past, how real they'd felt, down to the shrieks of dying people in my ears, Savonarola's thundering voice, the battered bodiless head of the Marquis de Launay, and the smell of burning buildings in my nostrils. I was convinced that somehow, in some magical way, I had actually been present at those scenes. What was time, anyway, that I should be mindful of it? It was all so bizarre. I was happy to be back with Fern, in a tiny car that forced me to collapse my knees against my chest, driving up the Palisades to visit my mother. This, at least, felt familiar.

"Tell me again what Cromer said about the painting being taken to the parish house," Fern said. I'd been replaying Cromer's story for her, letting her beautifully analytical intelligence crunch through his tale, searching for flaws and inconsistencies and similarities. My beloved roommate's mind was a wonderful thing. She could find patterns that no one else could. She could also spot a lie from a hundred yards, with her eyes closed and a beribboned poodle playing a violin to distract her. I patted her shoulder to let her know that I was grateful she was my buddy.

Fern tossed me a quick smile so I'd know she read my mind. Then she focused on the road. I said, "The priest, the one who helped all the Jews, was wanted by the Gestapo, so he escaped on a ship under an alias and brought some art with him. He stored it here at the parish house."

"And why doesn't Bolingbroke believe that?"

"Says the painting would have been found by now if it were there. Says he thinks my dad's in Europe. I think it's really just a gut thing."

"He has nice guts," Fern reflected. "You haven't managed to get in his pants?"

"No, and not for lack of trying," I said, glad to be discussing this topic, too. If anyone could figure out Bolingbroke's recalcitrance, it was Fern. I rubbed my wrist, which was whole and flesh-colored, with no trace of the ocher and black bruise that Kadja had left. "He's interested. He's holding back."

"Maybe he's afraid he'll hurt you," Fern suggested. "I see the way he looks at you when you're not aware. He's ravenous for you, but there's more to it. He's protective."

"Really? Then why does he disappear every time I have to see someone and find out about the painting? If he's protective, he'd want to tag along and make sure I'm okay!" I was frustrated. As soon as his friend's jet had landed out in Islip, Bolingbroke had bundled me into an airport limo and told me to hie myself home. He had an errand.

"You always run out on me when I have to take the next step!" I'd accused him before we'd reached the car. "It's hard for me to keep thinking of you as the great love of my life when you do that!"

Something whimsical and even vulnerable then impressed itself onto his beautifully boned face, like the mold of an archangel's face impressed onto soft wax. In that moment, didn't he again look exactly like Mercury in Botticelli's *Primavera*? If I were Botticelli, I'd have wanted to paint him! Hell, maybe I would, when all this was done. I'd paint him in the manner of Botticelli, a nice big canvas with an outdoor scene of nymphs dancing, a faun in the background. My fingers twitched, hungry for the brush. Then my hand balled up into a fist, rigid with chagrin. *Laila! Down girl! Stop it!*

At the airport, Bolingbroke had repeated in a bemused voice, with less than his usual supreme self-confidence, "The great love of your life?"

"You know what I mean!" I'd stood with my arms akimbo, tapping my foot. I had been acting nonchalant, and I deserved an academy award for it. Really, though, I felt incredibly vulnerable. And I wanted Bolingbroke to know that I had feelings for him. It wasn't just lust, although yes, lust was present. I sighed in agony like Meryl Streep. "I had to find Belzoni myself, I had to find Cromer myself, now I have to break into the warehouse in Jersey myself! What kind of great love allows that?"

"I'll accompany you to the warehouse," he said. "Too much illicit fun to miss. But you can visit your mother with Miss Takahasi. You don't need me for that." He kissed me swiftly, fiercely. Then he took a strand of wooden beads out of his pocket and slipped them over my head. "Since I'm the great love of your life and all, you'd better wear this." He took my chin between his thumb and forefinger and gave me a scorching look that I'd not soon forget. "Don't take it off!"

"Earth to Gonzo," Fern was saying. "Gonzo, you're being paged by your best friend, who has memorized the entire first act of *The Tempest* by now, and who still wants to know when you're breaking into the warehouse!"

"They say memorization is a lost art." I giggled.

"They never met me," Fern said, coolly.

"They would like to." I played with the wooden beads around my neck. They had a soft, comforting feeling to them, and felt imbued with Bolingbroke. Did they mean we were going steady?

"Breaking and entering, Laila?" Fern prodded me with her elbow.

"Soon. Tonight. I have a feeling that the time to find my dad is growing short. I'm a step behind him, and they know where he is."

"They, the evil group," Fern clarified.

"Uh-huh."

"And why doesn't Bolingbroke tell you explicitly about this group?"

"That's the question, isn't it?" I mumbled. I slapped my head for being an idiot, because how could I fall for a guy who was obviously keeping things from me, crucial things I needed to know as I raced to save my father?

"You're not an idiot," Fern mused, gazing at the road. "When he's sitting on information, it's hard to trust him completely. Even though we want to. I mean, what's his agenda? Why is he after the painting, and what's his interest in your dad? What secrets is he keeping, hot'n'sexy as he is? But still, there's something about him; he's trustworthy."

I couldn't answer, and fell into a reverie about secrets and hidden agendas. My father had joined a group, a secret society, and I'd never known. He'd been missing for years, and suddenly he was alive and searching for a lost Renaissance masterpiece that I'd always believed was apocryphal, not real. He had kept a lot from me, even when it hurt me. Now I was going to visit my mother to show her the note he'd sent, and to find out what she knew about *Coming Forth by Day*, and what she thought of it being transported from Rome to New York. Now I had to wonder, though it saddened and mortified me to do so: what was my mother keeping from me? Was there no one in my life who was what they seemed?

My mother was cleaning brushes in her cottage. I saw her a few seconds before she saw us. She wore a threadbare green smock and her pretty oval face was furrowed in concentration as she cleaned a brush. A hog-hair flat, size 4. She was squeezing the bristles from the ferrule edge outwards with her fingers. I'd performed the same action a million times, but never with the same certitude, the same faith, as hers. She was a real artist, who conveyed her personal vision onto canvas with sublime skill. People who got to see her work were transported. It was a genuine experience of revelation.

I felt again, sharply, the inadequacy of my own abilities in comparison to hers. I was a master forger, yes, but a forger only. No matter how I tried, when a blank, primed canvas stood on the easel in front of me, what flowed forth was someone else's hand. Sure, Belzoni and Cromer praised me, but they were scoundrels. The whole world had adored my mother for her landscapes. In comparison, I had accomplished nothing. I couldn't even get a handle on my dissertation, which was supposed to redeem me from my squandered life of cheating others. All my bad feelings about myself swarmed in like a cloud of locusts eating up whatever new green shoots of self-worth had dared to grow.

"Laila!" My mother's face lit up. She laid her brush on a rag and rushed over to hug me. She wrapped her arms around me but kept her hands lifted, careful not to stain my shirt. "Fern, too! What an unexpected pleasure! I haven't seen you girls in months, and now twice in one week."

So, a side of guilt to go with my entrée of self-loathing. But now was not the time to let her serve that to me. "Sit down, Mama. I have something to show you," I said. She scanned my face and hers fell into grim lines. She went back to her bureau with her head hanging, used a clean rag to wipe her hands.

Still holding the rag, she seated herself on her bed. She looked fragile and tiny, with her pretty creased face and puckered mouth. In the roomy sleeves of her smock, her arms were very thin; she was up to her old tricks, not eating. It made me mad to see it, and anger fortified my resolve. Mama wound the rag between jittery, paint-stained fingers. I produced Daddy's note from my purse. "After we talked, I took a trip to Paris and Amsterdam," I began.

My mother looked startled. "That was fast! Oh. Was it, are you...you made a painting?" Her voice held that delicate note of reproach that had made me wince all through my childhood. It still made me wince. Other kids had moms who yelled, and I would have preferred that to the reproof that was too meek to fight. I felt myself sinking into the constant feeling of unworthiness I'd had as a girl and then as a teenager at my mother's side, when she was so petite and talented and acclaimed, and I was a large ungainly person and a fraudulent artist. But I could not afford—no, Daddy could not afford for me—to indulge the feeling. *Tomorrow I'll beat up on myself.* Lately I hadn't been so good at keeping my promises to myself, but the thought still bolstered me.

"No, Mama, it wasn't about a forgery, though I was tempted."

"Laila, after all the times—"

"Let me finish," I snapped. She collapsed a little, and I wanted to smack her. I couldn't help it. I shuddered, hating myself for the feeling. No one could make me hate myself like my mother could. I took a deep breath. "Mama, I went in search of a painting. One that Daddy's looking for. *Coming Forth by Day.*"

"What?" she cried. "That painting? Your dad's looking for it, you're sure?" I passed her the note from the airplane. "Robert," she whispered. Tears welled up in her big blue eyes, and now I wanted to pet her and comfort her and stop her from feeling sad. Was there ever a moment when I wasn't regressing, when I had to deal with my mother?

"Mama, what's going on? Because John Bolingbroke says that Daddy's looking for that painting, which I never even believed was real, and there's an evil group pursuing him because they're looking for it, too. What do you know about this?"

She shook her head, hunching her shoulders and curling the hand holding the note into her chest. High-pitched keening shrilled out from her.

"Mama, focus! Daddy's in danger. Come clean. Right now!"

"Robert's alive," she whispered. She huddled up inside herself like a distraught child and rocked back and forth on the bed. "Robert, thank God, you're alive." She lifted her tear-stained face. "I thought he'd been murdered. I didn't know. I didn't know what happened. I didn't know he was looking for that painting!"

I forced myself to count to ten. Then, in as calm a voice as I could manage, I asked, "What do you know?"

Fern brought Mama a cup of water. I don't know how Fern found it, I hadn't heard her moving about, but I was grateful. Mama gulped the water. It calmed her sobs. Fern to the rescue, as always! Fern stroked Mama's gray-streaked blonde hair. Mama smiled at her and gave her back the cup.

"I don't know where to start." She knit her forehead into deep lines. "The group your father was drafted into...."

"I thought he joined on his own," I interjected. "That's what you implied last time." I had been standing, but I sat down on my mother's roommate's bed, opposite her. Fern sat next to me. I flashed her a thankful glance.

"They invited him. Pressed him, really, because they needed his unique set of skills. Have you ever heard of the Illuminati?"

"The Illuminati?" I repeated stupidly. "Oh, someone else mentioned them to me recently. Who are they?"

"A Bavarian secret society founded in the late eighteenth century," Fern supplied. "A group of freethinkers, an offshoot of the Enlightenment. They called themselves the 'perfectibilists.' Goethe was a member." She smiled. Fern loved Goethe. She loved that era of literature, too. I loved it about Fern that she loved Goethe, though I privately wondered why anyone would bother with poetry when there were paintings?

"That's one of their incarnations," Mama murmured. "Actually, they are an ancient secret society, and it survives to this day."

"Fascinating," Fern said, leaning forward. "What are your sources?"

Mama smiled. So did I. Fern was using her most professional grad-student-about-to-get-her-Ph.D-voice. I could practically see the antennae standing up on her head. She was really intrigued. Mama said, "I'll get to that. The Illuminati were founded by the ancient Egyptians for two purposes: to carry on the secret knowledge of the mysteries, and to combat vampires."

"Vampires?" I burst out laughing. Mama stared at me.

"I'm not joking, Laila," she said softly. "Vampires are real. I don't know the whole story, but there is coded reference to vampires in the Egyptian *Book of the Dead*, and to how they came to be. In the earliest times, a high priest of Osiris was angry over the loss of his great love, a priestess who died during a rite of passage in the mystery school. He blamed the gods for her death. He cursed Osiris during a ritual, and Osiris, angered at the betrayal, struck back. The priest's *ka* and *ba*, elements of his soul, were separated from his *khat*, his body. The goddess Sekhmet gave his *ka* strength, and it fought free of the tomb. It was hungry. She told it to drink blood, and it went in search of both blood and psychic energy to drink."

"Vampires? Mother, really."

"Laila, do not doubt my word," Mama replied, her voice suddenly steely, surprising me. "Vampires are real," she snapped. "The Illuminati were created to fight them, to keep them from overrunning the earth. Vampires see humans as their prey, and they kill people indiscriminately."

"People consider the Illuminati a shadow government that controls and manipulates world events," Fern mused.

Mama nodded. "In every era, there are world leaders who are members of the society. It's been that way all the way back, through the Knights Templar, back through the Greek and Gnostic initiatory cults, all the way back to the Illuminati's origins in Egypt, in the temple of Osiris. Sometimes the leaders are inducted into the Illuminati after they've risen to leadership positions. But often people rise through society because they've been taught esoteric skills of mastery by the Illuminati."

"Was Winston Churchill among the Illuminati?" asked Fern. She raised a slim eyebrow at my mother.

"Fern, you aren't taking this seriously!" I said, incredulous. "You were almost a scientist! Come on, secret mystical societies? Vampires?"

"Literature is full of references to powerful creatures who drink human blood," Fern said. "William of Newburgh, who wrote the *History of English Affairs* in the twelfth century, told of corpses sallying forth from their graves. In the Middle Ages, they were called 'revenants.' The English philosopher-poet Henry More wrote about vampires in *An Antidote to Atheism* in 1652. There is continuous reference to them through centuries of English literature."

"Not just English literature," Mama said. "The stories of supernatural entities who feed on the blood of the living are found on Babylonian tablets, in Indian tales of the vetalas, in Persian poetry drawn on pottery shards, in Jewish folklore about the demon Lilith. Greek minstrels sang of the goddess

Empusa who seduced young men and drank their blood. And, of course, vampires appear in the Egyptian *Book of the Dead*."

"You're awfully well informed about these legends, Mother," I noted, and I couldn't keep a dry note of disbelief out of my voice. But an intolerable thought nagged at me: was she losing her grounding in reality?

"After your father vanished, I found a notebook. Just one page in the middle of the book had writing on it. Your father had written a couple of sentences about vampires. He must have left it for me to find, so I'd have an idea about what he was up to. He had told me a little bit about the Illuminati, and the notebook said that they were at war with vampires. So I did some research," she said swiftly. Her chin rose a little with pride. "Do you know the real title of the Egyptian *Book of the Dead*? It's the *Pert em Hru*."

"Impressive," I said, with undisguised sarcasm. I got up and wandered over to the brushes on her bureau. Flats and filberts, even a few pencil-thin riggers, which was a new thing for her. Most were meticulously clean. I held up one that bore flecks of Egyptian blue, a blue copper silicate, on the wooden handle. The number 4 flat she'd been cleaning.

"I'm not done. The title translates to 'Coming Forth by Day,'" she finished, in a smug tone. The brush dropped from my nerveless fingers.

"What do you know about that painting, Mama?" I asked, as I bent over to retrieve the brush from the floor. My heart palpitated in my chest. I should have thought to ask Mama about the painting before now. She knew everything about da Vinci. Everything. Not just what was authenticated, but every rumor, every scrap of hearsay, every anecdote muttered through the centuries. Why hadn't I thought to ask her about it? Because I was protecting her? But what about protecting myself? Maybe she could have spared me the trip to Europe, the meetings with my old cronies Belzoni and Cromer. Maybe I wouldn't have had to be tempted to forge again. Maybe I wouldn't have had to set up Mr. Yamamoto for a con. Maybe I wouldn't have had to stray back into a world that I craved but rejected. My heart hung heavily in my rib cage.

"I know how it came to be."

"Botticelli painted Isis and Osiris," I said, baiting her. I paced around the room, feeling wild and restless. Under her bed, on the side opposite where she sat, I spied the corner of a canvas poking out. Her back was to me, so I used my toe to prod the canvas out a smidgen. Handwriting? Mama turned around, and I nudged the canvas back.

"Sandro painted the Isis. She was ravishingly, astonishingly beautiful. Leonardo painted Osiris. Leonardo loved handsome youths, you know. He used to dress them up as women——"

"And parade around with them in public, I know, mother," I said impatiently. Hadn't I grown up with endless stories about Leonardo, as if he were a close personal family friend?

"But he also loved beauty wherever he found it," Mama continued, primly, as if I hadn't interrupted. "Sandro was suffering from melancholia and painted Isis. Leonardo was so struck by her beauty that he begged to paint the Osiris. Sandro let him."

"What are they doing in the painting?" Fern asked.

"They're standing over a boy who is bleeding, Osiris at his feet, Isis at his head. The staff and key of Isis are in her hand. Lots of green leaves." Mama swiveled back around to look at Fern. I used the moment to nudge the canvas out again. Definitely handwriting, and a tree? Wasn't she doing still lifes? This glimpse didn't even look like a real painting, but like a preparatory study for some other work. What was she up to? Intense curiosity flooded me. My mother was keeping secrets.

"This story is in none of the histories, diaries, or memoirs I've ever read," I stated, in a skeptical voice. "I've read them all."

"The Illuminati have an archive of histories, diaries, and memoirs that have never been revealed to the public," Mama said. She pulled up her legs and swung around on the bed to face me. "Their library is more secret than the Vatican's. There's some overlap, I understand. And a few powerful cardinals have been members of the society, so certain materials have made their way from the Vatican to the Illuminati archive. I was allowed to look at some things after your father disappeared."

"I thought you didn't ask them what happened to Daddy."

"I didn't ask them what happened to him," she explained. "I was afraid to. Afraid they'd tell me he was dead. I asked to look at their references on da Vinci and Botticelli. I pieced things together from the source material. So I could keep my hope alive."

"Go on with your story, Mama. I still don't believe that Leonardo and Botticelli painted Egyptian mythology."

"Leonardo discussed the myth of Isis and Osiris with Sandro, and Sandro loved female goddesses. It captured his imagination."

"How did Leonardo know the myth?" I pressed.

Mama smiled. "Leonardo had Marsilio Ficino's translation of the *Pert em Hru*."

"Never seen concrete proof that they knew each other."

"Of course they did! Both were intimates of Lorenzo de Medici. Ficino was one of Leonardo's teachers."

"The *Book of the Dead* isn't even a book, it's a loose collection of hymns and spells," I objected. "It wasn't codified like the Bible. And the first versions of the *Book of the Dead* weren't published until the 1840s, centuries after Leonardo and Ficino. I heard all about this from Belzoni, because his illustrious ancestor Giovanni Belzoni, the circus strong man and thief of cultural heritage objects, discovered the tomb of Seti I. That tomb has one of the most complete records of the *Book of the Dead*, so Belzoni felt genetically obliged to read and reread it, and to pound it into my uncaring head. I've never heard of a Greek version!"

"Your not having heard of it doesn't mean that it doesn't exist," Mama replied. Her voice was fierce. "The Papyrus of Ani was translated into Greek; Ficino had that scroll."

I shook my head. "If what you're saying is true, that the painting is named after the *Book of the Dead*—"

"And the origins of vampirism are contained within the scroll, then what's the relationship of the painting to vampirism? Is the dead youth the priest who was the first vampire?" Fern finished, following my train of thought exactly.

Mama shrugged. "I thought your father had been killed by vampires. I didn't know about them until after he, you know...."

"After he disappeared."

"From what I can tell, the Illuminati have a sweeping plan for decimating vampires. Robert was part of it, though he never told me about vampires or his role in the war against them. But the Illuminati must have wanted him to find the painting; he was an art expert and spoke twenty languages, knew collectors and important people all over the world." Mama huddled into herself again. "He must have disappeared to protect us. He was afraid of putting us in jeopardy." She sniffled. "I know Robert. He's noble like that." Her face and voice grew soft with longing.

"You were divorced!" I snapped, before I could restrain myself. Mama's head sagged down onto her chest. I didn't know who I felt more frustrated with, her or me. She should be able to hold it together. I should be able to talk to her without being mean to her. I knocked my head backwards against the wall a few times. The pain on the back of my head cleared it. My fingers found their way to Bolingbroke's beads, and I rubbed one between my thumb and forefinger. The motion was oddly soothing. The bead had a sweetness that seeped into my hands and calmed me. Peace had been scarce lately and I appreciated the feeling. I'd have to remember to thank Bolingbroke.

"Lord Cromer told Laila that the painting is in New York, in a parish house," Fern said.

"How is William?" Mama asked. "I haven't seen him in ages. Loved his last book."

I thought for a moment. How much of the truth should I tell Mama? "He was, um, suffering from some health problems."

"I hope he sees a good doctor," Mama said, biting her lips. "Once you reach a certain age, you know, it's not easy. The body is frail."

Fern went over to sit next to her, picked up my mother's hand and squeezed it, working her irresistible Fern magic on Mama. Fern said, in a coaxing tone, "The painting went from Florence to Rome, then to Paris, then Amsterdam. It was in Amsterdam until World War II, and then it was likely taken to Rome. Then it was brought to New York, along with some other paintings, to keep them safe from the Nazis."

"Of course, the Nazis knew about *Coming Forth by Day* and wanted it desperately," Mama said. "Adolf Hitler had had an experience with a vampire. It was the source of his obsession with esoteric mysticism. He wanted to create an army of vampires, the vampire *Reich*, who would fight and kill at his behest."

"Vampires, bah," I muttered.

Mama rose and went to her bureau. She picked up her rag and went back to cleaning her brush, the number 4 flat with Egyptian blue spattered on the handle. Her back was to us. "When I first heard the rumors about a lost Botticelli on which Leonardo had collaborated, I wondered if it was real. Then I came across a passage in an Orsini diary that described the painting."

Cromer had mentioned that diary. "Where was the diary, Mama?"

"One of the private archives, I don't remember." She tossed me a smile over her shoulder. "You know how it is. There are so many of those private family archives in Italy, also in Spain, and old families are protective of their privacy. Maybe it was one of the ones on the Adriatic Coast. Maybe it was in Civitavecchia. Hard to remember. At that time of my life, I was taking master painting classes in Italy and researching Leonardo for my dissertation. I was all over the country in old libraries and archives, working and writing day and night, when I wasn't painting. It's all kind of a blur now."

"You're sure it describes *Coming Forth by Day*?" Fern asked, with that soft smile of hers that elicits total trust.

"Oh, yes, Fern. Osiris, with pale green skin stood at the feet of a wounded youth whose chest flowed with blood. Isis stood at the head. She was ravishingly lovely, as only Botticelli could paint a woman, with long flowing black hair. Such sweetness of feature and expression, as she stared yearningly at her husband. In his outstretched hand, Osiris held a seed sprouting into wheat. Gorgeous. A life-changing painting."

"That's some diary description," I murmured.

"Indeed." Mama finished with her brush and laid it down, plucked up another one. I slid the canvas out from under the bed a little more and stared hard at it.

"What are you painting, Mama?" I interjected.

"Still lifes. I told you last time. Have you seen John Morra's work? It inspires me. I like what he does with light."

"Anything else?"

She selected another brush to clean, though it looked pristine to me. Had it even been used? Was she nervous? Was that why she was cleaning brushes that had never been used? "Still lifes. Bottles, fruits, eggs, tea kettles, glassware. Things from the community kitchen. That's where my easel is set up. I clean and prime here, but I work there."

Lies and secrets. Who can someone really know, anyway? A door inside me slammed shut. "We've got to get back to the city," I said brightly. I pushed the canvas back under mother's bed surreptitiously. "I'm looking for Daddy, which is why I'm on the trail of the painting. I want to check out the New York lead."

"Laila feels there's some urgency about it," Fern said softly. Mama nodded. She seemed as done with the interview as I was.

"Okay, then," I said, with more false cheer. I hugged Mama, Fern hugged her, and we went out and walked along the path to the parking lot.

Just as we were getting in Dex's Mini Cooper, Mama raced up to us.

"Laila, you'll let me know, please? When you find your dad? And tell him I think about him every day?" she begged. Her face was woebegone. "I must know that Robert is safe. He's the love of my life!"

"I'll ask him to call you. You can tell him," I said. The words were stiff, but my voice wasn't, and I let her hug and kiss me one more time. Then she fled back toward her cottage and her mysterious painting.

"That was sudden," Fern said, as she turned the key in the ignition. "Did the door hit us on our way out?"

"I couldn't stick around, knowing that my mother was lying to me."

Chapter 15

F ERN ERUPTED WITH QUESTIONS, BUT MY CELL phone rang, pre-empting the answers. "Hello," I said. And if I sounded grumpy, I think I had a right to.

"Laila, have you found the painting? Can I have it?" Hahnemann asked. "Where are you? What did Belzoni say? Tell me now, damn it!"

"Kristofer, what is so blooming urgent?"

"Are you with that man?"

"Bolingbroke? No. He's not with me. Why?"

"He's not what he seems to be. I don't know what he is. Maybe he's a, he's a..." Hahnemann paused. "It's hard to explain. He's a, ah—"

"Vampire?" I supplied, with a sigh.

"So you know about them? Yes! I think he might be one. I thought I remembered his face, and I searched my library until I found him in an old photograph. He's standing beside Crown Prince Rudolf in Vienna, one day before the supposed suicide of the crown prince and the murder of his mistress Marie. That friend of yours is holding a gun, the same kind of gun implicated in the incident. It's him, I tell you! The bum was involved in Rudolf's death! Rudolf's hands and body showed signs of a terrible struggle. Bolingbroke killed him!"

"Kristofer, this is crazy talk! He's not a vampire. He's not a killer. He didn't do anything to Rudolf. That happened decades before he was born. A half century."

"You can't tell when a vampire was born! They don't age, the soulless demons."

"I don't believe vampires are real. If they were real, they'd, I don't know, drink Rudolf's blood, not stage a suicide."

"It's him. The face is the same," Hahnemann insisted. "You're in terrible danger!"

"He's not the guy in your photo. He has that kind of face, the way it's boned. He looks like someone. I've thought that, too."

"You must protect yourself, Laila! The world will be deprived of an awesome talent if that monster hurts you. You may have stopped forging now, but you'll be back at it. You're too good at it—it's your destiny. You must be spared!"

"I don't have talent, Kristofer. If I had talent, I wouldn't be forging. I'd be creating in my own individual voice. Now, was there anything else?"

"I am warning you. If you don't listen, *Zaubermaus*, it's on you. Now—tell me about the painting."

"It's real. I'm tracking it."

Hahnemann waited, hoping I'd say more. I didn't. He didn't need to know about Cromer. Hahnemann made a rude noise. "Bah, you're keeping secrets."

"Aren't we all?"

"Remember my offer." He hung up before I could answer.

Fern snuck a sideways look at me. "Hahnemann?"

"Crazy bastard. Wants me to know that Bolingbroke killed Crown Prince Rudolf."

"Really? Hmm." Fern looked thoughtful.

"No, not really! Bolingbroke wasn't even a twinkle in his grandfather's eye when that happened. Come on, Fern. You can't believe that business about vampires."

"But Laila, your mother told us...."

"My mother is lying to us."

"You don't know that!" Fern was indignant. "You have issues with your mother, Laila. She's got the whole fragiler-than-thou thing going on, and it bugs the crap out of you. It's excessive, I agree. 'Everything in excess is opposed to nature,' yes—"

"Proverbs?" I asked, to identify the quote.

"Hippocrates. Your mother is an artist, and artists often have extreme edges to their personality. They express themselves differently and must be given latitude."

"Latitude, I'll say—Mama does need that!" I snickered.

Fern tightened her hands on the steering wheel. "You resent your mom's fame and accomplishment, and you're pissed that she divorced your dad. Maybe she has her failings as a human being, but, you know, we who live in glass houses.... Eleanor is a lot of things, but never a liar!"

"She lied to us, all right," I said grimly. "Lied to our faces."

"About what?" Fern demanded.

"What she's painting. She said all she's doing is still lifes. But I saw a painting under her bed that was definitely something else." I ruminated on what I'd seen without describing it aloud. *Indecipherable handwriting, a cypress tree, an angel wing: a Leonardo study! But why?*

"So? Your mom's doing other stuff, too. So what? Maybe she's branching out and she's protective of it. She doesn't want anyone to know what she's doing. That she's doing something new. Maybe she's playing and amusing herself with her skill, and she doesn't think it's anyone's business."

I shook my head. "Fern, my mother always loved to show people her process. She was a real exhibitionist. She liked to gloat—"

"It's not gloating, Laila. She's justly proud of her work," Fern said. Her usual placid patience had returned to her voice. She wasn't going to let me needle her.

But I wasn't thinking about Mother and her secret study anymore. I was watching hilly green pastures roll past us. And I was thinking about Hahnemann. "I just realized something. It was Hahnemann who mentioned the Illuminati to me. You know, that superstitious group that my dad joined."

"Superstitious!" Fern giggled. "That's some spin!"

Let her laugh. I wasn't convinced about the whole of my mother's story, not when I knew she was lying to me and hiding something. "Hahnemann told me and Bolingbroke that the secret symbols of the Illuminati are painted in *Coming Forth by Day*. Maybe Dad really was, or is, in this mystical group, and there's a group that opposes them. Not vampires, per se, like in the movies—maybe that's just a metaphorical description of them. Maybe they're a blood cult of killers or something. Like the Mafia or the yakuza or something.

But they want the painting so they'll know all the secret signs and symbols of the Illuminati. So they can identify anyone belonging to the Illuminati. That's their interest in the painting."

Fern sighed. She put the blinker on and changed lanes. "Okay, I get it, that would be a good reason for them to hunt for the painting. But, Laila, a blood cult of killers? Wouldn't it just be easier to go with the vampire theory?"

"No," I said. With that, we rode in silence.

Bolingbroke showed up at our apartment at dusk, wearing black trousers and a long-sleeved black turtleneck that stretched tight over his ripped pectorals and hugged in at his surprisingly narrow waist. It made me want to tear off the shirt and lick his navel until one or both of us was moaning. Fern and I were dressed in dark clothes, the kind that fade into the night and obscure the wearer. I tucked up my bright red hair in a stocking cap so the sheen didn't give us away. The thing about breaking and entering is, and yes, I have some experience in the matter—is that you've got to stay hidden. But that was beside the immediate point, which was how scrumptious Bolingbroke looked, all lean and dangerous in black. He made me forget the danger and terror of looking for my dad, and the disillusionment of knowing that my mother was lying to me.

"You look good enough to eat," I said enthusiastically. I threw my arms around him and kissed him. Just for a moment, he responded. His passion was intoxicating. It was worth forgetting everything for! Then he peeled me off, holding me by my shoulders, and gave me a wry look.

"Are you wearing the mala?" he asked. He ran his hand along my neck. I shivered. He pulled up a bead between his index finger and thumb and smiled. The sweetness of the bead bound us together, almost as intimately as an embrace. He leaned in toward me.

"It's a mala?" I repeated. I was about to ask what a mala was, but he released me abruptly, disconnecting utterly.

"Miss Takahasi," he said, inclining his head toward her.

"Please, call me Fern!" she cooed. She couldn't help it. Bolingbroke had that effect on women. I elbowed her anyway. "Oof!" she said.

"The car is at the curb," he said. He cocked his head toward the door. I settled my strappy canvas bag of goodies on my shoulder. Fern locked the door behind us.

Bolingbroke opened the car door and ushered us in. Fern took the back seat out of deference to my long legs, which, even in Bolingbroke's fancy Bentley, would prefer to stretch out in the front.

"Nice car," Fern told him when he got in.

"How'd it go with Mrs. Cambridge?" he asked, in response.

"They're divorced, have been for years," I said, exasperated.

"Eleanor says the painting is about vampirism," Fern said.

"Interesting," Bolingbroke said. He gunned the car through a red light and onto the West Side Highway.

"My mother is lying," I said. "Kristofer Hahnemann thinks you killed Crown Prince Rudolf of Austria."

Bolingbroke flicked a glance at me. "What's your mother lying about?"

"Nothing important," Fern said. "Laila's overreacting." Her voice implied that overreacting was typical for me. Bolingbroke nodded a little, as if agreeing. I wanted to slap them both.

"A lie is like a cockroach: if you see one, there a thousand more hidden in the cracks that you can't see," I said, defending myself. "It *is* important."

"So?" Bolingbroke prodded.

"I asked what she was painting, and she said still lifes. But I saw something tucked under her bed, and it wasn't a still life."

"Artists." Bolingbroke shrugged. "They're odd about their work."

Not my mother, I thought, but I decided not to argue the point. Whatever my mother's game, I'd have to figure it out for myself. I asked, archly, "So, did you kill the crown prince?"

"That happened in 1889," Bolingbroke said. "How old do I look? How old do you want me to look?" The corner of his mouth lifted. It wasn't a denial. It hovered on my tongue to discuss the vampire theory with him.

"Are you a member of the Illuminati?" I asked instead.

"No."

"Daddy was. Is."

"I'm not."

"How do you know if someone's a member?" Fern piped up, from the back seat.

"There are signs and symbols, very secret. Like the Freemasons have," Bolingbroke said. He scowled into the rear-view mirror at her. "Jewelry, handshakes, code phrases. Car medallions. Flags. A pattern woven into a tie."

Fern, with her laser-precise mind, was focused on something. "So the painting, if it shows those symbols, would be important to a group which is opposed to the Illuminati."

"The painting could help that group ferret out secret members of the Illuminati," Bolingbroke agreed. "If those signs and symbols are represented on the painting. Buildings, institutions, private dwellings could be identified as Illuminati strongholds. Individuals with the symbols on their person would be at risk. It would be very dangerous for that painting to fall into the wrong hands."

"Plus there's the vampire element," Fern said. "What's your take on vampires?"

His eyes took on a flinty gleam in the rearview mirror. "We're going to Hoboken, isn't that right?"

"I don't believe in vampires, either," I offered. "Yes, Hoboken. I gave you the address." He grunted and lapsed into silence. The kind of loud, deafening silence that clobbers you over the head and shrieks, "Don't talk to me!" I turned around and gave Fern a palms-up gesture. She waved with one hand, perfectly painted nails gleaming like pearls in the rich, dark car interior. That was a whole dialogue for us, me saying, "Go figure, the hottie thinks vampires are silly," and her replying, "Doesn't matter, we've got a handle on things; we'll find the painting and your dad, and it will all turn out just fine." Turns out we were both wrong.

The storage facility was on River Road, not far from the Hudson, in a run-down neighborhood where a row of dilapidated warehouses rose up out of an asphalt road littered with broken glass and crumpled Dunkin' Donuts cups. Spotlights and street lamps cast dull white ovals on the ground, showing where weeds grew up out of cracks in the cement. Overhead, black cables were strung as thickly as a rainforest canopy of leafy branches. We drove through the area and past it, along the road by the river, until the buildings grew spiffy again. In New Jersey, a block or two could make all the difference.

"Security cameras, several of them," I said.

"A guard in a booth," Fern observed.

"There'll be alarms, too," I said. "That's a cheap facility, but they're trying to be secure."

"Uh-huh," Bolingbroke said. He continued on and turned a few times, took us two miles away to a suburban hospital. He parked in the outpatient parking lot, between a Mercedes and a beat-up Volvo, the square station wagon type from the '70's that will probably still be running after the four horseman of the Apocalypse eradicate civilization and leave us back in the Stone Age. He said, "I'll run ahead and take care of the surveillance. Meet you two there." We got out of the car and he clicked his key to lock the doors. Night had set in, but the omnivorous light pollution of Manhattan and environs showed the wry expression on his face clearly when he tilted his head and grinned. Then he was gone.

"Hey!" Fern cried. "Where'd he go?"

"Beats the hell out of me." I was, somehow, not surprised. Something about his ironic smile had tipped me off: he was going to surprise me. Maybe I was getting used to seeing what I couldn't believe was real, because of the hallucinations and all.

"How'd he do that?" Fern asked. I shrugged. Her eyes widened. "You think he's a...vampire?" She whispered the last word.

"No!" I spluttered with laughter. "No way. He's as warm to the touch as he is hot to look at. I've seen him drinking beer. And coffee. And eating Dutch cookies. I don't know anything about vampires, but surely they don't eat cookies. They drink blood, right? And aren't they, like, dead? Cold?"

"Undead. You have to admit, that was beyond weird, the way he disappeared," Fern said. She shivered a little and buttoned her black sweater, which neatly matched her black turtleneck. They were a twin set. Someday I would be chic enough to go breaking and entering in a matching cashmere twin set.

I shrugged. "Maybe he was a soldier and he's trained in that. Maybe he's a magician. I don't know. Don't know anything about him." Was I ever going to know? Or was vagueness and frustration a new way of life? I settled my bag on my shoulder, held it tight against my ribs with my elbow. Its solidity was comforting. "You're the one with the sense of direction. Where are we going?"

"This way," Fern said, pointing.

We hoofed it fast, and it still took twenty-five minutes. When we arrived at the warehouse, the whole area was cast in shadow. The street lamps and spotlights had gone dark. The security cameras were still and limp. There was no sign of the guard in the booth. There was no sound except for the wind rustling scraps of paper on the ground.

"Hope he's not dead," I muttered, referring to the guard.

"I'm officially scared of him," Fern said, referring to Bolingbroke.

"Don't be," Bolingbroke answered. He was walking alongside us as if he'd been with us the whole way. He brushed up against me. "I don't have the immeasurable talents of our Laila, but I do possess a few skills of my own."

"I'll bet you do," I said tartly, unable to restrain myself. Bolingbroke's long fingers slid across the back of my hand. I felt myself blush, as if he'd left a hickey on my neck.

"The guard...?" asked Fern.

"He'll wake up in a few hours with a headache." Bolingbroke ushered us toward the far side of the building. "I'm more concerned about the cameras. The company will notice they're not functioning and come to investigate."

"So what do we have, a few minutes?" I asked.

"Maybe twenty," Bolingbroke said.

"This doesn't really look like storage units," Fern said. "It looks like an empty industrial building. Maybe the parish house is on a budget?"

"Maybe the art isn't stored here," Bolingbroke said.

"It wouldn't surprise me if everyone was lying to me, not just my mother—Cromer too," I said. "The painting's not here. It's in a grass hut in the Australian outback." I couldn't keep the bitterness from my voice. Fern gave me an especially eloquent specimen of her patented reproachful looks. She'd be more sympathetic if the people she loved most were deceiving her!

"I know why you suspect your mother, but why Cromer?" Fern asked.

"Cromer admitted that he's working for the group that's after my father. I found him in bed with Kadja. There's no telling what he's up to or where his allegiance lies."

We arrived at the back door of the rusty, crenellated warehouse. I slipped on thin gloves and fingered the lock, planning with half my brain how to pick it. That was when the memory shook loose from my unconscious and catapulted itself into the forefront of my mind. Kadja: where I had seen her smiling portrait. It had bothered me since the night she was with Cromer, a constant low-level irritation like an itchy bug bite. Now I remembered. That beautiful uplifted face, so haunting when I saw it, because it was open and innocent and young, not sinister and knowing. In a painting that I'd been led past at a trot, so that I glimpsed it out of my peripheral vision. *At Hahnemann's mansion.*

I stiffened.

"What?" Fern grabbed my arm. "You okay?"

"I just realized. There's a portrait of Kadja at Hahnemann's house," I said. I shook my head. "What's her involvement with him?"

"Kadja, the librarian who was in Amsterdam when you were there?" Fern puzzled. "Why would there be a painting of her in Hahnemann's house?"

"She's his daughter," Bolingbroke said. "If we're going to do this, we should do it now. We can discuss Kadja later."

I was so stunned by this unexpected revelation that all I could do was stare at him. Was there no end to the strange twists of this quest to find my father and the painting for which he was searching? Finally, remembering that I had a task, I pulled myself together. Out from the bottom of my goody bag came my little wrapped set of tools. It seemed easier to get on with breaking and entering than to ponder the meaning of Kadja being Hahnemann's daughter. These days, I wasn't sure what the meaning of anything was. Bolingbroke was right: better just to follow the strategy we'd set for finding my father than to try to parse the depths.

Two minutes later, the lock groaned and sprang open. I was still rusty.

"Hahnemann's not one of the bad guys, is he?" I asked Bolingbroke.

"Depends how you define 'bad guys.' He's not one of the group that's out to get the painting from your dad and kill him." Bolingbroke thrust me out of the way and entered the warehouse first. I followed him in. Fern trailed in after me.

I pulled out two flashlights and gave one to Fern, and we flicked them on at the same time. The beams of light showed a vast and cavernous space, partly empty and partly filled with disorganized piles of wooden and cardboard boxes, furniture, old kitchen appliances like refrigerators and dishwashers, storage chests, lockers, and junk of every stripe. The air was cool, musty, and inky. A thick inch of dust sueded every surface, from floor to ceiling. It smelled, too, of something that had rotted, something that had once been warm-blooded and sizable, like a dog or a family of squirrels. Now it was fetid hamburger with cheap perfume sprinkled over it.

"Ew," Fern said, pinching off her nose. "What's that smell?"

"Something dead," Bolingbroke said. He glided away into the shadows.

"The painting's not here," I said, my shoulders slumping. I just knew it—I don't know how, but I was sure. I felt disappointed. I shouldn't have.

I should have heard the legato of subterfuge in Cromer's story. He who lies for you will lie to you. Not one of Fern's classy quotes, but it summed up the situation.

"Cromer's paper trail...." Fern said, stepping around a wooden pallet covered with old magazines. Our flashlight beams intersected on the cover of *Cosmopolitan* from October, 1996. Cindy Crawford and her famous mole. What was it about beauty needing contrast to be appreciated? Maybe truth needed lies in the same way.

"A pleasant fiction. At least part of it. Hard to tell when it veered away from reality." I stepped around a washing machine with its tub sitting atop its lid. "I'm beginning to think that this painting makes everyone a liar or a crook. It warps everyone who sees it, and brings out their worst impulses." I was following my nose to the source of that icky smell, which grew more putrid as I got closer. I stepped behind a high wall of open shelving holding stacks of dishes, the sturdy earthenware kind used in diners, and found both Bolingbroke and the source of the smell.

A body lay curled up on the ground.

"Damn," I said. My stomach rolled over inside my abdomen.

"Shit!" Fern was coming up behind me, and she jumped. "A body? Is it a man or a woman? How old? How long has it been dead?"

"About a week," Bolingbroke said, in a neutral voice. "Notice the maggots?"

I swore. I hate maggots. "Looks like a woman, from the bracelet on the wrist."

"Yes, female, mid-twenties, mixed race," Bolingbroke paused. "Exsanguinated."

"You got all that from the smell?" I demanded.

"Exsanguinated, like bled to death, as if a vampire had fed on her?" Fern whispered. The beam from her flashlight trembled on the body.

"Vampires, plural," Bolingbroke said. I waved a dismissive hand and meandered off to explore further. The smell of putrefaction diffused, but it didn't disappear. I passed a box labeled "SPARE PARTS." Was there anything here from the parish house, or had Cromer just plucked a storage facility off the internet, sight unseen, to fool me? Was this place important in and of itself, and if so, why? Was it a message to me? Some part of me didn't believe that Cromer wanted to hurt me. Yes, he'd scam me, and yes, he'd strong-arm me into forging pieces that he could authenticate and sell, if he found the right leverage. But hurt me? After all we'd been through together as conspirators in various cons, lederhosen and all? Hard to accept. I didn't want to accept it.

In fact, I didn't want to accept any of this: the dead body in the warehouse, Kadja and her vicious friends, my mother's lies, Cromer's misdirection, Belzoni asking me to finish his forgery. I didn't want my old self. I wanted it all to be like it had been a few weeks ago, before I'd met a hot Italian in a bar. But even if time could magically loop backwards and splice into the past to produce a different present, wouldn't my father still be missing, presumed dead? Wouldn't he still be an absence that hung on my heart like an anvil? Wasn't it better to be here now, in a warehouse with a dead girl, carrying my mother's lies, and to know that my father still lived, and that, perhaps, I could save him?

As I struggled with my ambivalence, I picked my way through an aisle of mannequins, old-fashioned wooden ones like dressmakers used to use. I went around an old woodworking table with clamps and a lathe. I almost bumped into a man who stood there, still and unbreathing as a sculpture.

He looked to be about thirty and of native South American heritage. He had very black hair and eyes, a big nose, and a sloping forehead. He peered at the beam of my light with a quizzical expression, then looked around as if puzzled. His eyes never landed on me. I held my breath. He put out his hand to touch the flashlight, as if it were floating in the air, as if he couldn't see me. His fingers patted the rim of the flashlight. They were very white, with scarlet-black cuticles.

Then Fern screamed, and the man was startled. He leapt up off the floor. The next instant, he twisted himself into a giant black bird that hovered up near the rafters.

Its wingspan, from feather tip to feather tip, was tremendous, maybe eight feet.

Then it was gone.

My limbs shook, and my teeth chattered as if I'd spent an hour in a meat locker wearing only a bikini. If there was somewhere to run to, I would have run. There was nowhere, though, so I retraced my steps. I had never felt such terror, and I couldn't believe I was walking slowly, quietly. Being in my own body was a surreal experience. I ended up next to Fern, who had found another body a few yards from the first one, under a pile of ragged blankets.

She shined her flashlight onto it, and I saw an octopus tangle of arms: not a single additional body, but many more. And those weren't blankets; they were clothes, some still on the bodies, some stripped off. She swept the beam of her light to another heap of cushions or pillows nearby. Again, I saw first a lifeless hand lolling out, followed by a spray of arms and legs. Then I saw that those weren't cushions, either; they were heaps of bodies.

Dozens of bodies.

"This is a killing ground!" Fern cried. She grabbed my arm. Tears streamed out of her eyes. I felt the terror of the proximity of murder, and I felt her fear, and I wanted to protect her. *Fern must be saved!* Then I remembered that I had to protect myself, too. I had to find my father.

"Let's leave. Painting's not here. Cromer lied." I was panting and gagging.

"We're lucky there's no one here to kill us!" Fern said. Her flashlight swept to a scaffolding on which I thought lay odds and ends, flotsam and jetsam. But the detritus resolved into bodies—hundreds of them—desiccated into blackened logs, stacked up on the shelves. I leaned over and retched. Fern was vomiting beside me. Reminded me of college, minus the booze, with corpses added.

There was someone here to kill us. I remembered the hungry, curious look on the Indian's face. Had Cromer known the Indian would be here? Had Cromer sent me here to become another body in this macabre place? Was Cromer that far gone, in his work with the people who wanted to hurt my father? My head snapped up, and I met Bolingbroke's eyes. He saw something in my expression and lifted an eyebrow. I looked at Fern and shook my head, pointedly.

"Let's go," Bolingbroke said tightly. We left far faster than we'd entered, and I kept looking around for the Indian. He was gone, but his handiwork remained.

And perhaps his friends were nearby.

Chapter 16

"LAILA, COME BACK TO MY PLACE. I need to speak with you,"
Bolingbroke said, as he pulled up to our curb.

"Am I safe?" Fern asked plaintively, when Bolingbroke opened her door
to let her out. She stood huddled on the sidewalk, her arms tucked into her
black twin-set sweater. A crescent of stomach grunge stained one sleeve,
where she'd wiped her mouth. She smelled like vomit. I did, too. We'd both
had another round of it in the car, on the way home. The beige glove-leather
interior of Bolingbroke's car wasn't so pretty anymore.

"Yes, I think so," Bolingbroke said softly. He squeezed her shoulder.
"Courage, Miss Takahasi. You aren't one of the players in these machinations.
You're a bystander."

"Were all those corpses players, or bystanders?" she asked. Her voice was
so earnest and full of fear that it wrung my heart. Whatever I was involved in,
I should not drag Fern into it! From now on, I would pursue the painting and
my father without her. I would not endanger my dearest friend. She put her
hand through my window and touched my cheek as if she'd read my thoughts.
Bolingbroke squeezed her shoulder again. She ran up the stoop and unlocked
our front door. Once she was inside and the door had closed behind her, he
got back in the car.

"I'm a player," I said.

"You're not safe," he stated, matter-of-factly. "What happened in the
warehouse?"

"There was a man, watching. I came right up to him before I saw him. But he didn't see me. And I was right on top of him because I hadn't seen him standing in the shadows. It was weird. He touched the flashlight, but he acted as if I weren't there."

"Describe the man."

I did. "Bolingbroke, he transformed himself into a giant black bird before my eyes."

"That's what they do."

"But I don't believe in vampires. I've been having hallucinations lately. I had them about the painting, while Cromer was describing its history, and I used to go into that weird possessed state when I was forging. I'm seeing things, that's all!" I insisted. I gripped the dashboard as if his car were flying up the avenue at a hundred and fifty miles per hour.

"Is that the first time you've seen a vampire in raptor form?" he asked.

"One was at our window, early on," I said quietly. "Right after I met you." Admitting this dampened my denial. That was way before I'd had a hallucination about *Coming Forth by Day*. Bolingbroke was smart enough to keep quiet.

At the parking garage, he tossed his keys to the attendant. "It needs detailing," he told the man. "There's a substantial tip in it for you, in addition to your fee, if it's clean."

The man's face was wreathed in smiles. "Yes, sir, I make your car beautiful and perfect!" He opened the door. The sour smell wafted out. He grimaced but squared his shoulders.

"Sorry about your car," I said. "I've never seen anything like that. So many bodies in one place. All those people." A wave of sadness gusted through me, an ache and a tear through my heart. All those lives, ended too soon. Would my father be one of them? Would I? Fern?

"That's why they must be stopped," Bolingbroke said, somberly. He took my hand in his, and we walked to his townhouse. What was it, two in the morning? This hour had become mine, like an old friend with whom I played cards and drank mint juleps, after the last several days of being awake for it.

I fingered the bust that looked like a Bernini reproduction. The woman's face was slightly turned, her features beautiful and dynamic, as if caught in a fleeting instant of time. Her neck was long and her hair was curly and wild with life. Her expression was immediate and full of the drama of her sweetness and vitality, her imperiousness and her humor. Like the bust of Costanza Bonarelli, this one was incredibly lifelike, with all the theatricality of the Baroque in general and Bernini in particular. I didn't recognize the model, which was odd, because I knew Bernini's work intimately. Maybe the woman who'd posed as Daphne in his breathtaking *Apollo and Daphne*? She was beautiful enough to captivate a god! That piece was now on display at the Villa Borghese in Rome, so perhaps I could check it out next time I was there.

"We're at a dead end again." Bolingbroke came up behind me and laid his hands over mine on the marble bust. I could feel the heat of his body radiating into my back. His breath fanned my hair.

"This isn't a Bernini copy," I said, in a low voice. My eyes closed, and I trembled to feel him so deliciously close to me. The fear and worry and horror melted out of me. I leaned back into him, wanting him.

"No."

"It's a real Bernini."

"Yes." He matched each of his fingers to mine so my hands were cradled in his. His fingertips stroked upward along the backs of my hands and circled my wrists. All my nerves sang with pleasure and longing. This man's touch was magical!

"Kadja is Hahnemann's daughter. That's why he wants the painting," I whispered. "She's a vampire. The painting concerns vampires."

"Has he asked for the painting?" Bolingbroke was now caressing my wrists and the soft fleshy insides of my arms. It got harder for me to think. Why did I want to think, anyway, when all that came to mind were unanswerable questions, impossible scenarios, and overwhelming odds? Thinking was over-rated. Feeling was the thing!

"He begged me to give it to him when I found it. Offered me millions of dollars."

"He has it to offer, rich bastard."

"Is he a member of the Illuminati?"

"No." Bolingbroke stepped closer and nuzzled my neck, puffling my hair. I turned and he caught me in his arms, pulled me close. He groaned and then kissed me, and my knees turned into pudding. His mouth was hard and demanding, and then soft and inquisitive, his chest pulsed against mine, and every part of me that could soften and open, did.

He carried me up a set of stairs with a mahogany banister. He laid me on his bed, a carved wooden four-poster affair with a lacy white canopy arching overhead. He lay atop me, kissing me. His weight on me was full and lush, like the most satisfying dessert. We took turns pulling off each other's shirts. I pulled off the mala and tossed it on the floor after my shirt, then reached for him. My palms passed over his rolling chest and hard belly. His mouth was all over my breasts. I had never been so aroused and was writhing a little, about to explode. He put his lips on my neck and rubbed his mouth back and forth across the hollow of my throat. I rocked my pelvis up against his and fumbled with the zipper of his pants.

That's when he rolled off me.

"Hey, come back here!" I gasped. "Don't stop!"

"I have to," he said, raggedly. His eyes were closed and his body was rigid. The vein on the sides of his neck stood out, as did the ones at his temple.

"No, no, no!" I said. I squirmed around and straddled him. Frustration tore through me. "Look at me, Bolingbroke! You're not leaving me hanging now!"

"Laila, please, you don't understand!" He moved his hips so that he rotated us, and I was flipped underneath him again.

"I like this position!"

"No, no!" He groaned. Then he kissed me, a deep, searing tongue kiss that I felt in the deepest reaches of my being, physical and emotional. He came up for air. "If we go down this path, I may hurt you. Probably will."

"I'll take that risk," I panted. "Please, take off your pants!" I reached for his zipper again. He caught my hands and held them down on the bed, over my head. His pupils were widely dilated and glowing in the dim light of the crystal lamp on his nightstand. I was rendered thoroughly enrapt by his eyes.

"Laila, I want you, but I will not risk hurting you."

"I'm a big girl. I can take care of myself," I said. "Come on, you got me ready! Don't leave me like this. It's not fair!"

"Believe me, Laila love, this is far worse for me than it is for you." He leaned down and looked piercingly into my eyes. His eyes burned like hessonite on fire and transformed into ellipses. Just as I swam out of consciousness, I thought I saw fangs through his parted lips.

Bolingbroke was seized by tremors, like an addict's shakes, as he covered the girl with blankets. He should not have kissed her, should not have given in to his desire for her. So close he'd come to hurting her beyond repair! He sat on the side of the bed and buried his face in his hands. In this moment, he would have given up the half a soul he cherished, for which he'd practiced austerities and worked so hard and so long, to have held her naked and screaming in his arms, to have given himself fully to her and taken her fully in return. It was ironic. He couldn't help but smile. Because if he hadn't possessed that precious, indefinable half of a soul, he would not have restrained himself. He would have ravished her as thoroughly as every thread of his being lusted to do, and then he'd have drained her sugary bubbling blood, sucking her into his body so that she was, forever, a part of him. Even if she no longer lived.

But Laila must live. Bolingbroke lifted his head and stared at her sleeping face. So lovely, so innocent, although she'd argue with that term. This naïve, sweet woman thought that forging paintings made her wicked! She had little understanding of true evil, even after what she'd seen today in the warehouse. She did not want to take in what was actually going on, that she'd been swept up in a merciless battle between the forces of good and the forces of evil. She did not want to understand what she could lose if Bolingbroke lost control. More than just her life; the irreplaceable immortal spark that made her Laila. So he'd used his vampire hypnosis to put her to sleep.

He seldom used the old vampire ability to command a human's consciousness, didn't enjoy the feeling of having a living person at a disadvantage. Bolingbroke, since Bernini's *St. Teresa* had awakened him, didn't want power over others. He wanted power over himself. He wanted to control himself utterly until that moment when fate or a capricious god gave him back the other half of his soul, and he was human again. Or until he was no more. He would never give up.

He rose and paced around the room. He found his shirt on the floor and pulled it back on, though it was so imbued with Laila's scent that it drove him to the frayed edge of madness to wear it. When was the last time he'd controlled a human being with his mind? Decades ago, before he'd sworn fealty to the Illuminati. He could never join them fully, because they knew what he was: half-human, half-vampire, a taboo creature, as the vampire Geertje in Amsterdam had said. But he'd offered to help them, and they'd accepted him on those terms. Not as one of them; Bolingbroke could never be one of them until he was human again, if that ever came to pass. But as a fellow soldier in the war against the undead who killed and consumed humans with impunity. Who were even now pursuing an unholy scheme to kill Illuminati members and to have free run of the earth.

What had Geertje said, that vampires were planning a mass attack on the Illuminati? Robert Cambridge had told him as much a few weeks ago, when they'd met at the Columbia library. Bolingbroke had passed on the information to his contacts. It was time for him to see them once again, to let them know that the attack was imminent. The vampires were waiting only for the painting. They knew where Robert Cambridge was, and they were closing on him as he got closer to the painting. Bolingbroke wasn't sure he and Laila would get to Robert before the vampires did.

I woke, and it was still dark. I was confused and disoriented. Then I remembered Bolingbroke. His hands, his mouth, his eyes—and then unconsciousness. I swung my legs over the side of the bed and let myself sit and breathe. He was not anywhere nearby, and his absence pealed through the space like a bell. I ached with the emptiness of it. The room was dark, but I remembered a lamp on a nightstand, and I felt around with my hands until I found the switch and turned it on. The light roused me and settled me at the same time. I got up and retrieved my bra and shirt.

I found a light switch near the door and flipped it on. An overhead brass fixture shed soft luminescence on the voluptuous, finely-crafted furniture. These were the objects of Bolingbroke's intimate life, which gave me a voyeuristic thrill. Every day, he pulled open the drawers of this Chippendale kneehole bureau with undulating carved shells. It was made of densely grained mahogany and retained its original brass hardware. It was a work of art in itself, sumptuous in design and flawless in execution. Antiques were not my specialty, but I recognized a good one, probably from all the time I'd spent perusing Sotheby's catalogues. They'd have been proud to represent this bureau.

On the other side of the room was a late Victorian desk, kidney-shaped and polished to a high blond sheen. As I got close, I could make out the inlaid

satinwood and tulipwood marquetry. It had a number of small drawers at each
end. I couldn't restrain the impulse to open a drawer on the right. Then the
one below it.

What I saw in the fourth drawer stunned me: a Botticelli folio. I pulled
it out. It was the missing folio from the Columbia library! I sat down on
Bolingbroke's bed and leafed through it. It wasn't Columbia's copy of the folio,
though; it was some sort of proof, and retained the author's marks and comments. I had heard that only five copies still existed; but clearly, here was a
sixth, which pre-dated the others! Why hadn't Bolingbroke mentioned it to
me when he knew I was researching Botticelli? I scanned one of the notes:
"Sandro's wit," it began. That sentence wasn't in the proof, but it had been in
the final version; I remembered reading it.

Then I knew where I had seen that distinctive copperplate handwriting.
It was in the note that John Bolingbroke had given me, when he met me at the
Met, on my tour.

Bolingbroke had written the folio.

The folio fell, pages fluttering. How was this possible? Was I going crazy?
What *was* Bolingbroke? How old was he? What did I know about him, or
about anyone? I had my cell phone out and was dialing Fern's number. Her
soft, sleepy voice answered, and I shrieked. "I don't know what to think! It's
all so strange! He wrote the folio!"

"Laila, calm down! Where are you?"

"I'm at his place. The Upper West. I don't know what to think! Fern, we
almost, almost, and I wanted him so badly, and then he stopped, but somehow
I fell asleep, and now I don't know what to think!" I was exhilarated with the
strangeness of it, and bereft, too. I was terrified, as I had been so frequently
lately. What was Bolingbroke? I wanted him, but I didn't even know what he
was!

"You're not making sense, Laila. Slow down. Breathe." I could hear Fern
take a deep inhalation, demonstrating.

But I couldn't force open my lungs to take a breath. I kept shrieking, my
voice rising in pitch with every sentence. "I found the missing Botticelli folio,
and it's all marked up with the author's comments. But the author's writing is
his!" I wailed. The folio was at my feet, and I kicked it across the plush antique
bedroom. A loose page skittered out onto the silk Persian carpet. The carpet
was also an antique. What had he said—"I have more than enough money

for any ten humans"? He wasn't human! He'd admitted that to me. He was hundreds of years old!

"Laila!" Fern was shouting into my earpiece. "Pay attention! I'll meet you halfway. We'll go get a drink. Tomar will open the bar for us!"

"Okay, okay, right. Yes. Um, Twenty-third and Seventh?"

"I'll meet you there in fifteen!" Fern hung up. I had a flash, one of those dislocated hallucinations that had dogged me since Cromer's, of her tearing off her pink Hello Kitty pajama set that I gave her for Christmas last year. Then she was slipping on a pair of jeans, the ones with the butterfly patch, and her black trench coat.

Right. I had to get myself downstairs and out the door and into a cab so I could meet Fern.

That sounds like a simple task, but I was so unraveled and wild that it was like moving in a field of molasses, in a dream. One of those sweaty, heart-thumping dreams where fiends are chasing you and you can't get away from them because you can't move at more than half a mile per hour. How could I want Bolingbroke so badly, when he wasn't human? How could I ever trust myself again? Eventually, eventually, I found myself at the bottom of the stairs. Bolingbroke's door was dead-bolted—*how the hell did he let himself out and leave the door dead-bolted?*—and it was a tremendous effort of brainpower to slide the bolt. But I got out onto the street. Still captive to slow motion, I made my way to Columbus Avenue and flagged a cab. The guy was reassuringly Hindi and human. He gunned the cab south on Columbus. He turned up his radio and complained about the MTA, and it was all so pedestrian that I could have kissed him.

I got out on the corner where Fern was already waiting. I sort of tumbled incoherently into her arms. I was crying, so she led me down the street aimlessly for a few blocks, murmuring soothing words like "You'll get over him" and "There are other fish in the sea." Then she pulled me under the eaves of a shabby building on Twentieth Street, underneath an anemic street lamp. She hugged me until my hiccups stopped. "So, what's going on?" she asked, when I could finally speak.

"Yes, what *is* going on?" purred a soft voice. "Laila Cambridge, are you weeping for your father?"

Fern and I jumped. Kadja stood five feet away, by a garage door in a run-down structure sandwiched between townhouses.

"Aren't you supposed to be in Amsterdam?" I said, numbly.

"I finished my business there," she said. She grinned and undulated like a cat that had finished the cream.

Cromer had been horribly hurt by her, and now he was missing. I didn't know anymore whether I could believe Bolingbroke's assurances that Cromer wasn't dead. I was jarred back into the present. "You finished off Cromer, you mean!"

"He's still around." She waved a hand dismissively and stepped closer. "Not a very imaginative lover, though, would you say? Or did you have him in bed? Too tame for you, I imagine."

That's when I saw that she was dragging someone behind her. One hand gripped the back collar of his navy blue blazer, so that the man faced down. Fern spied him at the same time and she leapt backward with an exclamation.

"Oh, him," Kadja said. She curled her arm as if lifting a dumbbell, and his body flopped up into the air like a rag doll, though he was a grown man and not a small one. He moaned. His hands scrabbled and his feet kicked in protest, but weakly. Both his legs were broken, which, even in the pale streetlight, was clearly revealed by the jagged femur bones sticking out through the meat of both thighs. Kadja hissed and long fangs shot down in her mouth. Her other hand swiped faster than my eye could follow, and his shirt front and tie were in tatters. She sank her fangs into him, sucking noisily. Blood spattered out onto the street, onto us. It drew crimson lines down her chin. Then she raised her smeared face. I thought of the contrast with the portrait in Hahnemann's house—how young and lovely she'd been, how fiendishly lethal now. I had never been so terrified.

"I'm done with him." She hurled him down the street nearly twenty yards. He never made a sound. Probably dead, and a good thing. It would have hurt to be flung across a parked car with that kind of force.

"What do you want?" Fern asked, keeping her voice steady.

"What all vampires want." Kadja giggled, an oddly girlish tinkling. "I want blood. Blood and the power to get it whenever I choose, from whomever I choose. Unconditional access to my sustenance." She circled around us, licking her lips like a tiger about to strike. Fern and I spun around on our heels to keep her in sight. "Blood, the juice of life, the elixir of heartbeats. The warm and fragrant nectar of circulation, which grants its drinkers immortality. The only food worth eating."

"I prefer chocolate myself; you don't have to deal with veins and bones," I said nervously. I bit my tongue to keep from babbling, which I tend to do under pressure.

Kadja's gaze fixed on me. The sclera of her eyes glowed ruby red. "I tracked you here tonight because I want to know: what were you doing with my father?"

Her father? Right: Hahnemann. "He wanted a painting I had, so I sold it to him," I said. It was an effort to keep my voice neutral. Terror was spiking through me, hammering my heart, which felt like a glass thing about to shatter. Was Kadja going to do to me what she'd done to that poor man?

"Yes, Daddy dearest has an obsession with art. Like your father—isn't that so, Laila?" Kadja wound around us again, making her circle smaller and tighter.

"Lots of people like art," I said huskily. I looked around for an escape.

"You leave Laila's dad alone," Fern said, in soft, firm tone of command. Kadja laughed derisively. With deliberate insult, her gaze scrolled slowly down and then back up every inch of Fern's slim form.

"You're a luscious piece of Asian meat," Kadja said, with a sneer.

That was when clarity clicked in, and everything else vanished. I had to save Fern. Nothing else mattered. If something happened to me, well, I'd been warned. Bolingbroke had told me up front that I was messing with vicious and amoral people, back when he enlisted my aid in finding my father. My father, not Fern's. It was not her battle. She had no business being caught up in this danger. She was an innocent bystander. I had to make sure she got out alive.

I decided to draw Kadja's focus, give Fern a chance to run.

"How'd a bitch like you get made into a vampire?" I asked. I inched away from Fern. "I mean, you're a lousy librarian, got the personality of a moray eel on steroids. What idiot vampire would be stupid enough to turn you and keep you around?"

Kadja hissed and glared. "Be careful, human. You're no match for me!"

"I get it, you're strong. Big deal. You're still a heinous bitch." I stuck out my tongue at her and made a raspberry noise. My knees were shaking, but only my bravado showed. I took a step to the side, away from Fern.

Kadja was standing directly in front of me, nose to nose, though I'd never seen her approach me. One moment she was a few yards away, the next she

was in my face, reeking of blood and something faintly corrosive. Her hair
crawled around her head like snakes rearing up. She growled. My hand was
down by my hip, and I pointed with my index finger so that Fern would get
the hint and get away. Kadja howled. "I will drain you, forger, after ripping
your legs and arms off your body. I will suck every last drop of your blood and
scatter pieces of your body so that even dogs can't find them all!"

"Like you did to those people in Amsterdam?" I said. My voice shook; I
couldn't help it. Fern took a step toward me. I gestured with my hand: *Back!
Go!* We'd been friends long enough for her to interpret the motions. Why
wasn't she getting away? *Come on, Fern, I'm doing this for you!*

Kadja's hand reached up, landed softly on my cheek. She caressed my
cheek and throat and neck. I swallowed tremulously as revulsion coursed
through my entire body. She said, "That wasn't me in the Jordaan. But I think
you'd be a fine meal, big as you are. I'm hungry now; that silly man only whet-
ted my appetite."

"Leave her alone!" Fern barked. Kadja threw her head back and laughed.
The next split-second, faster than lightning could sizzle the air, she had
thrown Fern over her shoulder and was running down the street. Fern was
shrieking, and though they were a blur of movement I could see Fern pounding on Kadja's head.

"No!" I screamed. "No!" I bolted after them. "Put her down! Take me!"
I chased them as fast as I could, faster than I'd ever run in my life. I sprinted
down street after street, following a receding blur. They disappeared into
Union Square Park. It was now about four in the morning and there were few
people even in that clotted part of the city. I hunched over, panting painfully.
What could I do? How could I save Fern? What resources did I have?

Bolingbroke. I straightened slowly. I didn't know what he was, or how
old he was, or what that meant for us. I didn't think he was a vampire. He was
warm and humorous and drank coffee. He was something, well, supernatural, with his centuries of life. But he wasn't the only one with an inexplicable
gift. I, too, had a special talent: I could channel dead painters and paint as
them, and my work was indistinguishable from theirs, because…it was theirs.
I had never admitted it to myself this way, but that's exactly what it was:
channeling. As Cromer had said. Desperation drove me to admit it. I, Laila
Cambridge, could step aside and let another consciousness inhabit my body

and mind. That was how I was able to forge so truthfully that it shocked and delighted the cognoscenti.

If I could do that inherently paranormal thing, let myself be possessed by Vermeer or Corot so that I could make a bundle of money, then surely I could do something extraordinary to rescue my dearest friend. I could send Bolingbroke a mental plea for help. It was my only hope. It was her only hope. I couldn't close on Kadja fast enough to save Fern, though I'd give my life for hers if I could. There just wasn't enough time for that. I closed my eyes and focused. But I felt too scared to concentrate.

Then I remembered his mala, which I had stuck in my pants pocket. I pulled it out and clutched it. Its sweetness radiated through me, intensified and narrowed the play of my mind. I had to reach him; nothing else mattered. Fern's life was at stake. *Bolingbroke.* I thought of him as fully as I could. Every line, every pore of his face, every hair, the ironic half-smile which always seemed like such a tease, the luxurious taste of his tongue on mine. *Bolingbroke.*

Chapter 17

BOLINGBROKE STOOD BESIDE ME. HIS ARMS ENCIRCLED my waist. "How'd you do that?"

"She's got Fern! Kadja! She took Fern into the park!" I grabbed his sleeve and pointed. "There! Please, don't let her kill Fern!" Bolingbroke broke into a run, the same kind of high-speed blur that Kadja had used so effectively. I galloped after him. Terror palpitated through me: would he be too late? Had Kadja drained and disposed of Fern like an empty wrapper? What would I find when I arrived? How could I go on if my best friend had been killed because of me? I raced toward the park.

I found them by some trees on the grassy pavilion. The murk of night was punctured by clusters of shining yellow globes on lamp posts, by humming white street lights, and by after-hours spotlights on shuttered storefronts around the three-acre park. Tomorrow a greenmarket would set up here. Now Fern lay on the ground, unmoving. Kadja stood over her. Bolingbroke was not there. However, a whirling column of brilliant white, red, and green light spun around Kadja like a top, and she was clearly frightened of it. She kept batting at it, and once, when her hand touched it, she howled with pain. Thick muddy blood spewed from her ripped-off fingertips.

The column shepherded her away from Fern. I ran to my roommate, knelt next to her, checked for blood and bite marks. There were none. I clasped her wrist and found a pulse. "Yes!" I cried. I felt her arms and collarbones; they didn't seem broken. I ran my hands over her ribs; they seemed whole. Her femur bones didn't protrude from her flesh. She was breathing lightly, as if asleep. I said her name, but she didn't wake. I cradled her head in my arms and stared at Kadja, whose skin was burned and split on her face, arms, and thighs. Sludgy black blood had beaded up on the long gashes.

"Show yourself! What are you?" Kadja howled. She dropped to her knees and quivered. A bolt of lightning hit the ground, and Bolingbroke appeared on the spot of scorched earth between her and us. "You! You were one of us. But now you're not...."

"I've been changed," Bolingbroke said. He yawned and there were fangs in his mouth. *So I wasn't hallucinating that*, I though dully. It was a small measure of comfort to know that my mind wasn't playing tricks on me. He said, "I have all the old vampire powers, and new ones as well. You will leave these women, or I will kill you!"

"What will Lilith think of you, when I tell her?" Kadja sneered.

"I no longer answer to her," Bolingbroke said. "These humans are under my protection. Go now, or die!"

Kadja laughed. "You may have them for now, taboo creature. It doesn't matter. In a few days, we will strike and recreate the world in our own image." She struggled to rise, but couldn't. Bolingbroke stepped toward her. She threw her head back so that her black hair swirled around her shoulders, smearing her black blood. Her mocking laugh rang out again. "Soon we will possess the painting, and we will know all the secret signs of the Illuminati. We will identify the hidden members and those who live more openly. We will attack the Illuminati en masse, in their homes and at their work, in their places of worship and the schools of their children. We will torture them and kill them and drink the blood of their families. We will eradicate them. Never again will we fear their death squads!"

"Your plan will fail," Bolingbroke said. "The Illuminati have secret resources they have stewarded in case of such an attack."

"Their puny extrasensory abilities are no match for what we vampires can do," Kadja said, scornfully. "What is prescience and alchemy against our strength and might? We will take the painting and torture the Illuminati for their secrets, possess them as our own. Then the world will be ours!" She held her arms out and gazed at them. The long cuts slicing down her arms glowed vermilion red. They began to mend, splicing together like fabric weaving itself whole. I was beyond being shocked at such magic. I was just happy to hold Fern, who was still breathing. I was also pleased that we had a few more days, that Kadja and her unholy crew hadn't yet found the painting. That meant my dad was still alive!

"We will get the painting first," Bolingbroke said. "We will show it to your father."

"I curse my father!" Kadja shrieked. Her red eyes bulged. I thought her head might explode, so great was her fury. "He tries to capture me and turn me back, but I will never let him! I'll kill him first! I'll break his neck and drink his old blood and leave him in a sewer for the rats to chew!" She burst upright in molten rage like a volcano spewing lava. She glared ferociously at Bolingbroke, and then she ran. After a few feet, she morphed into one of those huge black birds and flew away, fast.

Bolingbroke stumbled backwards. First he sat, and then he flopped onto the ground. He stretched out completely. I laid Fern's head down gently and ran to him.

"Are you all right?" I asked. I cupped his face with my palms. There wasn't an ounce of tension in his body; he was limp and lolling, completely enervated. He'd given everything he had to save Fern. I loved him in that moment as I'd never loved a man before. After all the teasing, this was the real moment, knowing that he wasn't human like me, and not caring because he'd been willing to sacrifice himself to save my best friend. "Bolingbroke, what's the matter?"

"I held it together until she left, that's all that matters," he said. He gave me a crooked smile. "If you really want to ravish me, now would be the time."

"How can I help you?"

"I need food, special food. Holding the form of an energy column debilitates me. I can do it, but it leaves me completely exhausted for hours. Unless I get special food."

I swallowed. "Blood? You don't drink that, do you? I mean, you're not still a vampire, isn't that what you told her?.... "Look, you saved Fern. I owe you. If you need my blood, you can have it." I pushed up my sleeve and held my wrist to his mouth. He could drink all of my blood, after what he'd done for Fern. I owed him. His lips grazed my skin.

"Laila...." He hesitated. His eyes looked bloodshot and weary, and purple half-moons sagged under them. His strongly-boned face was gaunt and anemic-looking, as if he'd run a marathon, and then another one immediately afterwards. His gaze blazed up just for a moment, then dulled. "Remove your flesh, woman. Do not tempt me. I'm a half-vampire. I can drink blood. But right now, I need something else. A communion wafer. Baptismal water. A sacramental offering."

I didn't bother to question it, because what was the point? I didn't understand any of it anyway. Vampires and energy columns: they were a whole new world for me! Everything was strange and different. I was just lucky to survive from one moment to the next. If Bolingbroke needed wafers, I'd find them.

I looked around. It was 4:30 in the morning; people were beginning to walk through the plaza, shoulders hunched, cups of coffee held out in advance of their bodies. The guy in the newspaper kiosk on the south side of the park was taking a few bundles of newspapers from a guy in a delivery truck. It wouldn't be long before someone spied Fern and Bolingbroke and got inquisitive. I asked, "Is there a church near here?"

"Broadway at Tenth Street. Go to the hall, not the main church. There's a maintenance man who has an arrangement with me. I pay him well. Tell him it's for me, and he'll give you what I need." Bolingbroke's lids flickered. His eyes rolled up into the back of his head, and he was unconscious.

I dragged Fern and then Bolingbroke to a tree and propped them up. For good measure, I pulled his arm around her shoulders and leaned her head against his chest. They looked like a couple taking a rest, perhaps after a night of carousing. It was the best I could do for them at the moment.

Desperate, I sprinted down Broadway to the church. It was a Gothic Revival masterpiece, taking up a huge chunk of prime Manhattan real estate. A light shone in the door to the adjacent hall. I rapped on the window, and an elderly African-American man in a gray Fair Isle cardigan opened the door for me.

"May I help you, Miss?" he asked.

"I'm here for John Bolingbroke," I said breathlessly. He nodded and held up one finger, signaling that I should wait. He closed the door and departed back down the hall he'd come from. I waited, heart throbbing from running, and from post-adrenaline let-down, and from fear that I'd return to Union Square and find Fern and Bolingbroke gone. Or dead.

The man in the cardigan reappeared at the door. He held out a small plastic container, the kind moo shu chicken gets delivered in. I took it and he retreated, closing the door firmly. I raced back up Broadway.

They were exactly where I'd left them, which was a tribute to the New York policy of non-interference. Some people read it as rudeness or coldness; New Yorkers know it to be no-bullshit courtesy. Fern and Bolingbroke were both still unconscious. I knelt beside Bolingbroke, opened the plastic container. Inside were some wafers and a vial containing a few tablespoons of water. I pulled the stopper out of the vial and poured the water down his throat. The effects were immediate: he opened his eyes and sat straight, unfurling like a flag in the wind. He took the container and devoured the wafers. Color washed across his high cheekbones and strong nose. He was rejuvenated! He smiled at me, set aside the empty container, and turned to Fern.

"She's been put to sleep through hypnosis," he said, as he lifted her eyelids.

"Why would Kadja do that?" I asked. I shivered and wrapped my arms around myself. "She could have just, well, you know."

"Good question. I don't know why, unless it was to use her to get information from you." He pulled Fern into his arms and stood, lifting her as gently as if she were a sleeping baby.

"Before she grabbed Fern, Kadja asked why I met with her father. I told her he wanted to buy a painting from me. Then she mentioned my father. Do they know where he is?" I stood up beside him.

"We'll find him."

"We're out of leads," I said dully.

"We'll find new ones," he said.

I took a deep, deep shuddering breath as all the dams inside me burst at once. I knew what I had to do. It was a small thing, compared to what I had just witnessed. It would be worth it to protect Daddy from what Kadja and her kind could do. To protect us all. "We have to go back to Paris."

Bolingbroke cradled Fern in his arms. "Why?"

"Cromer misdirected us to New York to give the vampires the lead. They're paying him, after all. But I know who will know where the painting really is."

"Belzoni?" he asked. "But he knew nothing."

"He knows." I smiled sadly. "He just demanded a high price for the information. It's time for me to pay it."

Bolingbroke settled Fern against his chest. "Laila, I'll fly her back to your apartment. I know how inquisitive you are; you must have questions. We'll discuss them on the plane when we have more time, yes?"

"Yes," I said. He nodded and then was suddenly gone. There was no transition, just absence. I heard something like the soft whir of windmill blades and looked up into a sky that was brightening with pink and yellow tendrils of dawn. Above me hovered a giant black bird. Fern drooped from its talons. Then it was gone.

So Bolingbroke could fly. I was a mere mortal: I had to flag a cab.

Chapter 18

MY APARTMENT DOOR WAS STILL LOCKED, BUT Bolingbroke was already inside. Arms folded across his chest, face tight, he watched Fern from the foot of her bed. "We have an early flight. Pack," he said.

"Aye, aye, sir!" I snapped a salute. But I went to Fern first and checked. Her delicate features were soft and relaxed, her mouth open as she breathed. She appeared to be sleeping deeply. She was snoring, which she seldom did, and which she found humiliating when I teased her about it. It didn't bother me; I snored like a sailor in a seedy port town after a rotgut binge. "Is she okay? Will she wake up? Do I need to do anything for her?"

"She'll sleep for a while and wake feeling refreshed. There's nothing to do. A vampire put her under. She has to wake up from it. Fortunately, she will wake. She wasn't drained and killed." His head was cocked, and he was looking at me, not at her.

"Is that what you did to me in your bed?"

"Yes."

"Condescending form of coitus interruptus. But not lethal." I rubbed my face and trudged back to my bedroom. When was the last time I'd slept for eight hours, through the whole night? I couldn't remember. I threw my breaking-and-entering goody bag on the bed, got my ballistic nylon travel bag from where I'd parked it a few days ago by my bureau, and went to the bathroom to retrieve my toothbrush. Better brush my teeth first, to get the taste of death and near-death out of my mouth. A dollop of Colgate and some elbow grease.

I leaned over the sink and spat, stood up, found Bolingbroke staring bleakly at me in the mirror. His face was drawn and taut, his mouth pursed.

"Don't ever do that again," he said.

I turned around slowly. "Do what? Take a cab, fight a vampire bitch, call you mentally, kiss you in your bed? Because I rather liked that last one. And I am really, really glad I found a way to reach you, because Fern would have died if I hadn't."

His jaw was set and his eyes gleamed. "Offer me your blood. Don't do it." He stomped out into my bedroom.

"You don't want my blood?" I asked sweetly, following him. I gave him an angelic smile as I pulled the collar of my shirt down and ran my fingers over my exposed neck. I flared my fingers over my jugular invitingly, like a game show girl exhibiting the merchandise. He snarled, the tips of his fangs peeking out. In my most saccharine voice, I cooed, "I have other bodily juices…."

"It's not funny."

"I'm not laughing. I'm trying to tempt you. I want you!"

"I want you, too." He went to my window and looked out, his spine and neck rigid. "But I care about you. So don't tempt me. I could hurt you. Would."

"Because you're a half-vampire?" I went up behind him and wrapped my arms around his muscled chest, rested my head against his broad back. His large hand caressed mine, where they clasped together at his heart. I felt a resounding sweetness that began in his hand and palpitated through me. I didn't care if Bolingbroke was a half-vampire. I wouldn't have cared if he was a whole vampire. I just cared about him. I murmured, "How is that possible?"

"Long story, and there's no sex or forgery involved, so I won't bore you. Half my soul was returned to me. It came with additional abilities."

"What's between us is not just about sex," I murmured. "I reached out to you with my mind and you felt me. You heard me. You came!"

"Shocked the hell out of me," Bolingbroke said, with a short laugh. "You amaze me, Laila. I've never met anyone who surprises me the way you do."

"You saved Fern." I would never forget that!

"I'll protect you, too, with everything in my being. Until I'm finally, truly dead."

"So hold me!" I cuddled closer into his back. He felt so good in my arms. He smelled good, too, and after all the horrors of the night, that lush male leather and bergamot scent reassured and comforted me. I felt safe holding him. I'd forgotten what safety felt like, over the last few weeks, with my world turned upside down anew with every fresh hour. And for the years leading up to now, with my father's painful and perplexing absence, I'd never felt whole. This peacefulness and spaciousness I felt close to Bolingbroke, this was the first time I'd truly let down and relaxed in years.

"In the act of lovemaking, the vampire part takes over. It's savage. Relentless. Uncontrollable. The last woman I took to bed, she was dying. I had to turn her. It's an unforgivable crime to do that to a human being, to take away their soul and turn them into a blood-lusting, undead creature." He pulled one of my hands to his mouth, kissed my palm. "I will never do it to you. Never." His warm lips started a fire in my hand that burned up my arm and blazed through my whole body, all the way down to my toenails.

I inhaled deeply. "When you do that...."

"I know. I'm sorry. It's wrong of me." He let go of my hand and disengaged me. "It's all I can think about, holding you, kissing you. Your scent, your laughter. It started out as a promise to your father to watch you. Then I was intrigued by your astounding skill as an artist. Then I met you...."

"Not an artist. A forger. A cheat." I laughed, feeling wistful and self-effacing and admired and cared for, all at once. I felt hope, hope that I'd finally get the closeness I had been craving, without even knowing that I missed it. Here was a man who could stand with me without judging me. A man who was honorable and trustworthy. When was the last time I'd felt this way? It was like waking up after a long cold sleep.

"You're too hard on yourself." He kissed my forehead. "I won't take the risk of killing you in the throes of passion. You matter too much to me." He paced restlessly around my room, touching my things: my big Zollner Michelangelo book, the stack of reference materials about Botticelli, the scissors and notebook on my desk, a bottle of l'Occitane hand lotion. He smiled. "It's arousing to me, handling your intimate belongings, knowing you touch them every day."

I felt the same way in his bedroom. "I'll take the risk," I whispered. "I trust your self-control. I trust you!"

He was fingering a purple scarf I'd left draped over my chair. "What if a sweet, elderly woman was interested in purchasing a Corot, a stunning piece of art, and she thought it was a real Corot, so she would be willing to risk her life to defend it from thieves who'd broken into her flat? Would you sell her the painting, knowing she'd risk everything? Would you sell it for a million dollars? For ten million?"

Vivian Goran. I felt sick. I was directly responsible for the death of an old lady whose only sin was loving beautiful art. A grandmother with a brood of loving children and young grandchildren who would grow up without her presence in their lives. My shame rose up in such brilliant living Technicolor and TXH surround-sound that it blotted out the room in front of me. I saw Vivian Goran as she was the last time I'd seen her alive: a dignified, vibrant white-haired woman, the kind of dame who'd gone to an all-girls' school back in the day when women were first encouraged to be assertive people. She'd have burnt her bra and looked elegant doing it. She was formidable but possessed of such graciousness that no one was intimidated. I swallowed. I'd promised myself that I'd never again let one of my paintings be sold, to anyone. I'd promised myself that I'd never again set up anyone for a con. I'd promised myself that I'd never again forge. I'd broken all of my promises but one. And now I was headed to Paris to break the last one, the one that really mattered. Bolingbroke's strong arms couldn't save me from myself. My throat was scratchy as I said, "I sold a painting a few days ago."

"To Kristofer Hahnemann, who knew exactly what it was, and who's guarded better than Fort Knox. He'd vaporize thieves before they got close to him."

"It's the promise that matters," I rebutted. "The promise to myself."

He smiled bitterly, his eyes kindling on my mouth. "That's what I think, too."

"You win," I murmured, feeling nauseous, and not from the bodies in the warehouse or Fern's brush with death. I took a deep breath and let go of Vivian Goran. There would be plenty of time later for me to flagellate myself about her. After I found Daddy.

"Hollow victory," he snapped.

"Does this mean we'll never get to be together?" I asked, plaintively.

"Not as long as you want to live."

I couldn't answer that. I wanted Bolingbroke. More than I'd ever wanted any other man. But I also wanted to live. I stared at my toothbrush hard, as if it held the answer. Just bristles, no solutions. But Bolingbroke and I weren't finished—I knew that. Vampire or half-vampire though he be, this thing between us would eventually demand consummation. Waiting wasn't my strong point, but I could do it. I smiled at the toothbrush, even if it insisted on remaining silent.

I tossed my inscrutable toothbrush into my travel bag and opened my top drawer. Three pair of panties. Two mercerized cotton shirts, one black, one navy, because they shake out wrinkle-free. My slinky black skirt which goes with both tops and looks good no matter how squashed it gets. A pair of socks. I'd travel in jeans. My Curious George shirt to sleep in. I threw everything into the bag, returned to the bathroom for toiletries. I zipped them into a small clear cosmetic case and brought them back out to the bag. My usual spunk was eking back in, and I gave Bolingbroke a cheeky smile. "Ready to go! Do we need to stop by your place for a black cape?"

Bolingbroke lifted one corner of his mouth in his trademark half-grin. "Vampires can grow them at will. The better to suck your blood with." He affected a Transylvanian accent and we exchanged a real smile, a sad smile. It made me want to kiss him. His face changed, one of those mercurial twists of expression, and for just a second, vulnerability erased his irony. During that defenseless space, I pulled the mala from my pants pocket and slipped it over my head. His expression gentled. I stepped toward him, and he toward me. We were leaning in toward each other to kiss, but a clear bright voice stopped us.

"Where are you going?" Fern asked. Blinking and stretching, she stood in the doorway to my room.

"Fern!" I shrieked. I ran to her, had to squeal on my brakes before I bowled her over. I hugged her and squeezed her, stood back to feel her forehead and check her color, hugged her some more. "You're okay! Are you?"

"I'm wonderful! I feel like I slept for a week!" She hugged me and laughed. "Why are you packing?"

"Going back to Paris," I said brightly. I went to get a scarf out of my drawer.

Fern narrowed her eyes at me. "Back to Belzoni?"

"We're at a standstill here. Gotta shake loose some new leads."

"You know what it will cost," Fern said. She grabbed my elbow. "Are you sure about this?"

"It's a one-time deal. I'll be fine. It's necessary."

"Hmm," she said, slitting her dark eyes at me. Her scowl was saying, "Don't do it, Laila!"

I clasped her shoulders with both hands. "We've seen what they can do. We know what the stakes are. After what happened to you, it's not theoretical anymore. I don't want my dad to be hurt, like that man was. Like you almost were! I don't want him to end up like those bodies in the warehouse."

Fern nodded slowly, then slipped inside my grasp and hugged me fiercely. Into my ear, she whispered, "Does Bolingbroke understand what this will do to you?"

There was no answer to that. I stepped back. "Meantime, you should carry protection, Fern. I'm not talking about Trojan magnums. Bolingbroke, how do we arm her, in case Kadja returns? Are the old stories correct? You kill vampires with wooden stakes?"

"Stakes, yes. Burning and beheading," Bolingbroke said. "Silver stops them. So does sprinkling germinated seeds around them. They're paralyzed, and can be staked or beheaded. It's not always easy to find germinated seeds, of course. Better to have sharpened stakes of cedar or hawthorn."

"Germinated seeds?" I looked at him quizzically. "My mother said something about Osiris holding sprouted wheat grains in his hand, in the painting."

"Fascinating. I wonder…." Bolingbroke's voice trailed off. Then he snapped back into himself. "I carry sharpened stakes. They're small but efficient. I'll give you a few, so you can see how to make some for yourself. Carry them always on your person." He opened his jacket and displayed a pocket with several thick pencils. He removed two and handed them to Fern, and they weren't pencils at all. They were nine-inch-long sticks, whittled at both ends to pin-prick sharpness. "I have larger ones, too, but these will work."

"Aren't you the prepared one," I commented, wryly.

"Yes," he stated.

"These will kill someone like Kadja?" Fern asked, doubtful.

Bolingbroke smiled, the coldest, most humorless expression I'd ever seen on anyone's face. "Kill within five minutes, if thrust anywhere into the torso or belly. Disable for long enough for you to escape or strike again, if jabbed into the leg or arm. Kill instantly if lodged into an eye socket, the hollow of the throat, or the heart."

"This little stick?" Fern asked.

"Lethal to a vampire," he said. "You have my word on it."

Chapter 19

I STOOD ON RUE GUILLAUMOT, IN FRONT of Belzoni's apartment building. It was the evening of the next day. At least I think it was. The sky was a honeyed violet color. I had slept on the plane, curled up against Bolingbroke's strong shoulder, and these days, I slept during the day. That meant it was now night, ipso ducks-in-a-row. It was the night when I stopped pretending to be better than I really was. The night I owned up to the truth of the worst that I feared about myself.

The anticipation was killing me.

Bolingbroke laid his hand on the heavy glass-and-steel door; magically, it clicked and swung open. "Sweet," I commented. "You can do that, and you've been letting me pick locks?"

"You enjoy picking the locks so much." He smiled and gestured for me to precede him. I put my hand on his arm. "I have to do this by myself. Don't come." My shame and my glory were one single, indivisible, inescapable thing, and I wanted to be alone with it.

"Laila." He touched my mouth gently, my lower lip. He didn't tell me I didn't have to do this. He didn't ask if I was going to be okay. He kissed my forehead and stood back, watched as I went to the stairs. For the first time, I noticed the wheelchair lift that was attached to the banister. The small cage sat on the landing, by Bolingbroke.

The key was in its usual place, and the opened door let out a wave of pungent fumes that made me choke and cough. I went in wordlessly, didn't see Belzoni. The Vermeer was still on the custom easel on the low table.

The gooseneck lamp was turned off. The apartment seemed quiet, hazy with stale gray particulates, the kind you hack out of your lungs in bloody clots when you're dying. Belzoni must have gone out to buy cigarettes and booze and sugar cookies, maybe to pay some cheap hooker to sit on his face. Took me back to when I was a teenager. Good times. I wanted to cry and, on cue, chartreuse snot leaked out of my nose. I wiped it with the back of my hand.

Brushes and tubes of paints were scattered about the table haphazardly, along with glass jars filled with crumbly pigment. Natural ultramarine blue made of costly lapis lazuli: Vermeer's favorite. White lead, grainy and coarse. Lead tin yellow, lemony and poisonous. My pores opened hungrily to take it in. Yellow ocher—I unscrewed the jar and smelled it: from France. Walnut oil. Linseed oil. Mortar and pestle and a wooden palette. I turned on the gooseneck lamp and looked at the painting. Belzoni had been trying to fix the interior lighting in the days since I saw him. Trying, and failing. Poor Belzoni. It seemed his hands now worked only as well as his manly parts. Which was to say, not at all.

But my hands knew what to do, and could do it perfectly. They throbbed with glee.

There's that first segment of time, the preparation, about an hour. How do I describe it? The peculiar fascination, the chill and thirst of excitement. Every nerve, every axon, every synapse vibrating with thought, life, joy. Even though I wasn't painting a whole masterpiece, just finishing one, I was completely, exuberantly alive. I ground some pigments by hand and then threw detritus off the table until I found Belzoni's last hand-made squirrel-hair brush, the kind used by geniuses for centuries. There's no cutting corners when you're producing a seventeenth-century masterpiece. I examined the canvas. It was suitably old, had boasted a cartoonish Madonna which Belzoni had sanded off. The framing was fair, but I bent a few old nails to better direction, so the canvas wouldn't pull improperly. Then I set to work.

Vermeer gusted in like a fog, and inhabited my body and mind. Johannes Vermeer, the Dutch baroque painter who specialized in domestic interior scenes during the mid seventeenth century, possessed me. It started with flashes of color: cornflower blue and yellow. Then his personality seeped in and filled me.

Joannis was his baptismal name. He was slow, patient. He was curious about everything. He didn't rush, but there was always the bright crackle of thought and a steady thrum of sexual awareness. Extraordinary sensitivity to light. This was the characteristic I've always noticed when an artist possesses me: they actually see the world in the same way they paint. For which reason I only once forged a Van Gogh. Poor suffering slob actually saw light and color bulging everywhere, an anguished and haunted universe in which I had no desire to exist. I vomited after the Van Gogh, which was now ensconced in Mr. Yamamoto's collection. Not one but two world-renowned experts had authenticated it.

But Vermeer was sane, stable. A pleasure to host. He slipped his hand into mine with the ease of putting on a fine glove, we both sighed with pleasure, and we were off.

The last grace note on the girl's hand where she held the book: and I was done. It always happened with a thud, an audible, palpable thump. The artist left my body. I stepped back, shaking with a post-adrenaline high.

"*Che bello*," Belzoni breathed. He wheeled himself next to me, held a smoldering Gauloise next to his face. When had he come in?

"Amazing—a masterpiece," Bolingbroke said, from behind us. *Bolingbroke?* I turned around. He was standing there staring at the painting, without a glance at me. He looked awe-struck, bedazzled. I wondered how long the two of them had been watching. Bolingbroke stepped around me to examine the canvas.

"Beautiful," Bolingbroke murmured. "Sublime."

"No," I said. I threw myself on one of the few chairs, an old wooden bench carved with cherubs. "It's not beautiful. It's a scam. A lie. And I'm a piece of shit for making it." I was only too aware that some part of me adored myself as a piece of shit. I covered my face with my hands.

Bolingbroke examined the Vermeer. "It's perfection. What do you do about the oils drying? They'll be dissolved easily by alcohol if anyone tests that way."

"There's a laser that dries them as if they've been drying for hundreds of years," I said. I rubbed my hands over my eyes. Pale beams of light streamed in through Belzoni's tobacco-fume-glazed windows. "If Belzoni doesn't own the laser, his handler will."

"A laser—fascinating," Bolingbroke said.

"They use lasers to discredit us, the poor hard-working artists who contribute to the beauty of the world by the sweat of *la testa, magari*, why shouldn't we use lasers to help ourselves?" Belzoni lit another cigarette with the butt of the one he held.

"Even the smell is right, the smell of the oils," Bolingbroke marveled.

"Belzoni has a stock of pigments that his father got out of a coffin." I noticed an open bottle of Bordeaux on the table. I picked it up to drink from it, but Bolingbroke grabbed it from my hand. He set it back on the table.

"Can you do this?" Bolingbroke asked Belzoni, gesturing at the Vermeer.

"*Signore*, please. No, *certo*. I can not do this. Vraiment, a million million artists cannot paint this way. Only Laila. Beautiful Laila. Laila who does not sell her pussy." He threw a wink over his shoulder at me. "She does not have to. She can sell paintings."

"You disgust me, Belzoni," I said. "I hate you. Someday your blackened guts will explode and you'll die in agony. I'll dance on your grave."

"*Perché?* Did I not give you the keys to your own talent? Did I not teach you everything, only so you could surpass me in every way? You are my finest creation, Laila. I could not love you more if you were my own bastard child."

"I am your bastard child, dirtbag. Spiritually speaking." I went to his kitchen, splashed water on my face. I cleaned a wine glass and gulped down a lot of water. In the cupboard behind his pills, I found aspirin. They were expired but I took two anyway, on the theory that expiration dates were marketing ploys. I peeked in on the men and they were still staring at the monster I'd created, gushing solemnly.

I could only hope no one died because of it. *Only for Daddy*, I told myself. I felt queasy and violated. And happy. And full of self-loathing. And fulfilled. I opened the freezer door, found a bottle of vodka, and swigged. A long, long, long swig. Then I swigged some more.

"Tell me about the Botticelli," I said, when I came back out.

"*Oui*, a bargain is a bargain," Belzoni said, nodding. He spun one of his wheels, fast, so he whipped around to face me. "Cromer told you it was in Amsterdam for many years."

"Thanks for warning him, by the way. Gave him time to put together a nifty little paper trail and send me on a wild goose chase," I said sourly.

"Those are the best kind, *Lailetta mia*." Belzoni stroked his beard. "A priest discovered the painting there. He was having an affair with a young woman in a noble family. *Magari*, I go back to the beginning. Do you know what the painting shows?"

"Isis and Osiris in a pagan ritual," I said. I went to the window and tried to open it. It wouldn't budge. Belzoni hated fresh air. He had nailed it shut. I picked up a ratty chenille blanket hanging off the back of a chair, wrapped my hand, and punched through the window, making a big hole, splattering shards of glass—like my integrity—everywhere.

"Laila," Bolingbroke reproved. I smiled brightly and hugely, exposing all my teeth. Belzoni shrugged. He knew the look on my face too well to challenge me. He flipped me off, and then resumed his story.

"Isis and Osiris stand guard over a bleeding youth, Isis with her staff and key in hand," Belzoni said. "Osiris holding a sprouted grain."

"Mama told me that," I said, impatiently.

"How much vodka did you drink, Laila?" Bolingbroke asked. He stood beside me, his nostrils flaring slightly, as if he were sniffing my breath from above my head.

"Lovely Eleanor," Belzoni sighed. "So talented. Almost as talented as you."

"Not enough vodka," I muttered. "Belzoni, cut to the chase."

"Patience, *porcinella mia*. The youth was—"

"The first vampire?" I guessed.

"A newly-turned vampire. Isis and Osiris were healing him."

"Returning him to human?" Bolingbroke exclaimed, leaping, exploding, toward Belzoni. Startled, Belzoni jerked backward in his wheelchair. Bolingbroke visibly leashed himself. His cheeks were flushed and his face was rapt, but he said softly, "The painting shows the cure for vampirism?"

Belzoni nodded, eying Bolingbroke warily. "Botticelli's brother Antonio was turned. Botticelli went wild with grief and fear. He appealed to Leonardo for help."

"Never heard or read a whisper of such a story," I growled. "Wouldn't there have been one tiny shred of gossip about it in the historical record?"

"All history is bunk," Belzoni said.

"Public history is bunk," Bolingbroke muttered. "Sanitized for the masses. Spun for PR purposes." Belzoni gave him a sideways glance, then grinned.

"*Si*, there is a private history, more accurate, kept in secret by the secret societies," Belzoni said. "We cannot have the unwashed masses who must be controlled knowing the true chronology of mankind."

"That would be, let me guess." I tapped my lip, then waved my index finger victoriously. "Aliens from the Pleiades genetically engineered human beings out of Cro-Magnon man and their own DNA...."

"Laila, let him finish!" Bolingbroke commanded.

"You do know everything, Bellissima," Belzoni said, sarcastically. He puckered his face at me. "*Mille grazie* for whispering to my whores the other day. I couldn't sit for two days."

"You're welcome," I chirped. I didn't bother to state the obvious—that all Belzoni did was sit. When he wasn't letting hookers sit on him.

Belzoni rolled his eyes. "Leonardo was moved by poor Sandro's plight. He went to his dear friend, the great philosopher and linguist Marsilio Ficino, founder of the Platonic Academy. Ficino had come by a Greek scroll that he translated and shared only with Leonardo, who was a great favorite of his. A scroll about rites of king-making and resurrection: the Greek translation of the Papyrus of Ani. Leonardo took Ficino's translation and decoded the cure for vampirism."

"My mother went on and on about the Papyrus," I said.

"Eleanor, she does know everything about Leonardo," Belzoni said.

"Leonardo cured Botticelli's brother?" Bolingbroke asked. "And Antonio survived the cure?"

"*Oui! In fatto*, Leonardo, with Ficino's translation and Botticelli's aid, did cure the boy. It is the only known cure of vampirism. Botticelli painted *Coming Forth by Day* to memorialize it. Leonardo fell in love with the face of Isis, her glorious beauty, and contributed to the painting. The painting shows how Leonardo cured Sandro's brother."

"Why didn't Leonardo just tell the Illuminati how he did it, or write it down so the cure was available for anyone who needed it?" I asked.

"Good question," Belzoni admitted. "No one knows. *Peut-être* he was threatened. *Peut-être* the vampires of that time, when they saw *bello* Antonio was human again, threatened to turn someone Leonardo loved, if he revealed the cure. Perhaps the cure was extreme, and Leonardo couldn't tolerate it. All we know is that *il Maestro* Leonardo figured it out and rescued Antonio, but he never again spoke of it. Ficino's scroll, and the translation, both disappeared. Botticelli painted *Coming Forth by Day* to preserve the cure, but it is disguised in the painting, at Leonardo's direction. *Il Maestro* had a subtle and complex mind, and one would have to know how to read the painting."

"So the lost Botticelli shows the cure for vampirism, and that's why Daddy's after it. And why the vampires are after him." I perched myself on the edge of the wooden chair.

"Vampires want to suppress the information, the Illuminati want to use it. They are at war with each other," Bolingbroke said. He moved to the window and looked out.

"That is a war I wish to avoid," Belzoni said, shuddering.

"Where is the painting now?" I asked.

"Imagine. May, 1940. The Nazis march into Holland." Belzoni's grizzled head sank down onto his chest. "My mother, she was half-Jewish. Her mother was Jewish."

"Your mother was a Lithuanian whore, you brag about it all the time," I said.

"It's a happier story, no?" Belzoni spun his wheel and rolled over to look out his broken window. "She was sent to Kamp Vught. She was one of a group of women who tried to save another woman, so the Nazis pushed seventy-four of them into a cell nine square meters big. She died in there."

The room fell quiet except for the sounds of Paris waking, sirens in the distance and the laughter of children as they entered the school across the street, the hum of cars and trains.

"I didn't know," I said, still skeptical. "I'm sorry."

"No, Laila, better that she died," Belzoni spun around and gave me his old mocking grin. "The ones who lived were *pazzo* ever after. Crazy."

As *pazzo* as Belzoni? But I couldn't mock him, even if I believed him to be lying. I shook my head. "Is the painting still in Amsterdam?"

"*Non.* It is in Rome. A Polish priest who was bent on saving Jews and paintings fled to Rome with it. It was given for safekeeping to a prestigious Roman family. French-Roman, actually. A family who knew how to keep secrets."

"Cromer's fake provenance said it left Rome in the forties," I said.

"No, Bellissima. It was in Rome in 1965. I was staying with the family." Belzoni paused. "I saw it there."

Bolingbroke and I both jumped. "You saw it?" we chorused.

"Me and two friends who were a little younger than me," Belzoni said softly. He gazed out the window resolutely, as if avoiding us. "They were twelve. I was seventeen. Emilie Bouchard and Eleanor Sidwell."

The room whirled around me. I couldn't breathe. Emilie Bouchard was my godmother, my mother's closest friend, and had been since my mother stayed with her for a year as a girl. Eleanor Sidwell was—of course, of course, of course—my mother. My deceitful, manipulative mother. I sat down, heavily, onto the slatted wooden chair.

"Just briefly, in the dark, I saw the painting," Belzoni said. "By flashlight."

"What were you doing in Rome with my mother and Aunt Emilie, Belzoni?" I asked, my voice hoarse. I bent over and laid my head in my lap.

"Eleanor Sidwell is your mother?" Bolingbroke clarified. "Fascinating."

"We were all three taking painting lessons," Belzoni said. "From Gino Severini, Umberto Boccioni—"

"My mother was learning from Futurists?" I asked, still folded up onto my lap.

"Not just from Futurists," Belzoni said. "From any great artist who would give us lessons. Emilie's parents were richer than Croesus. They wished her to have every opportunity to develop her talent. They happily paid whatever outrageous sum an artist asked, so that Emilie could be exposed to the best. Even Bob Thompson, dying of his heroin, gave us a few lessons. It was the best of times, with the best of friends!"

"I should have asked long ago how you knew my mother." I felt sick.

"I went on from that summer to Hans van Meegeren. I was ready for him then," Belzoni reminisced.

"Hans van Meegeren died in 1947, just before he was to serve a prison term," Bolingbroke said. His voice sounded strained. Had he purchased one of the forgeries?

Belzoni tsk'ed his tongue mockingly. "*Signore*, public and private histories, *oui?* In 1947, things looked bad for Nazi collaborators. Jews everywhere wanted vengeance, rightfully so, and not everyone believed my wily teacher's story that he was conning the Nazis. He was sentenced to one year in prison. He determined to avoid that."

"Hans van Meegeren was always a trickster and a cheat," Bolingbroke said, dryly.

"*Magari*, my wily teacher decided that the wisest course of action was to stage a plausible death. He was reincarnated as a kindly art professor in Venezuela." Belzoni smirked. "He lived to be almost one hundred years old."

"So. You and my mom and Aunt Emilie painted and played together," I said. It made me gag a little.

Belzoni nodded. "Emilie discovered a secret passage in her villa. Antiquated palazzo, decrepit where it wasn't renovated. Plaster behind some wallpaper had crumbled, the wallpaper got wet and tore. *Ecco*, a hidden opening! The tunnel was dark. Emilie had been afraid to enter. With us to accompany her, she had her opportunity. We crawled through to a room. There was the painting. I still remember shining my flashlight on it. *Dio mio.* Breathtaking. More beautiful than anything I had ever seen. Like a bolt of lightning in *il cuore*."

"You saw the cure," Bolingbroke said, in a dazed, almost inaudible voice.

"I saw Botticelli's Isis. The most beautiful woman I have ever seen. Even now I think of her every day. I will die with her face before me. Ravishing. *Bellissima.* Leonardo painted Osiris. A handsome youth, breathtaking. That painting changed my life. The power of its beauty was so great that I knew I wanted to do that, I wanted to make masterpieces. I became what I am—"

"Why didn't my mother tell me she saw the painting?" I asked, plaintively.

Belzoni laughed. "Your mother tells you everything? You think *bella* Eleanor has no secrets of her own?" He laughed some more. I thought about hitting him over the head with something, cracking his skull and watching the gray matter slosh out.

"What were the gods doing in the painting?" Bolingbroke asked, his deep voice hoarse. "What were they holding?"

Belzoni shook his head. "I remember little, *signore. Mi scusi.* It was so long ago, and I was blinded by the face of Isis."

"Mama described it. 'Osiris with pale green skin stood at the feet of a wounded youth, whose chest flowed with blood. Isis stood at the head. She was ravishingly lovely, as only Botticelli could paint a woman, with long flowing black hair. Such sweetness of feature and expression, as she stared yearningly at her husband. In his outstretched hand, Osiris held a seed sprouting into wheat. Gorgeous. A life-changing painting.'" When it came to spoken or written descriptions of paintings, I had perfect recall. For good reason.

Recreating paintings is my life. Was my life. I gulped. "I should have heard it. I should have known. Her words were too... alive."

"*Sì*, that painting made us all who we are," Belzoni mused. "Your pretty mama had not yet committed to her painting. She dabbled until that moment. When we left the room, she turned to me and said, 'Giovanni, I will be a great painter.' And did she not live up to her vow?"

"She did," I snapped.

"Emilie, *che vergogna*, she knew she was no painter. She never painted again. But she cherished art ever after, even now." Belzoni exchanged a mournful look with me.

"What happened to the room?" Bolingbroke asked.

"We heard something, a haunted sound, chains dragging, or like a fire.... The *ragazze* screamed and ran. I followed. The next day, we went back. I had a kitchen knife." Belzoni laughed. "Someone had bricked up the opening."

The cold, unrelenting hallucinatory state of a few days ago washed over me. A clear image rose, filling my vision, blotting out the apartment and Belzoni and Bolingbroke in front of me. Instead, I was present with two girls and a lanky, black-haired youth gripping a butcher knife. They were whispering, filled with self-importance, eager to explore a secret passage. My mother Eleanor in a blue dress that matched her eyes, long blonde braids, and patent-leather shoes. Aunt Emilie with a chic bob and white dress with smocked bodice, cigarettes and a pack of matches hidden in her pocket. Belzoni standing tall: walking. Still whole. It was hot in Rome and the smell of car exhaust, thyme and basil baking in the sun, and artichokes cooking in olive oil floated through the air.... I shook my head and blundered, unseeing, to Belzoni's bathroom. The vision faded as I drank water from the sink's spigot.

"So, the Bouchard villa," I said, when I returned. "If what you say is true, Belzoni."

"Everything I say is true, except what isn't. But there is good news," Belzoni said. "The painting is still in Rome, still in the villa. You will find it there."

"Bolingbroke, how soon can your magical travel agent get us to Rome?" I asked.

"I'll make a call," he said. He gave Belzoni a funny salute as he left.

"Good-bye, Belzoni. I hope I never see you again." I looked at my old

teacher and shook my head. I felt weary, soiled, and exhilarated all at once. It
had been years since I had forged. I hated the part of me that felt good doing
it again, that felt whole. I hated him for returning me to the woman I used to
be, the woman I had vowed to leave behind. I hoped it would all be worth it
when we got to Rome.

"Don't go." Belzoni wheeled himself next to me and grabbed my hand.
His fingers were dry and cool and stained with paint and nicotine, his skin
papery thin and flaky. "Stay and talk. I'll make *caffe* for us. I've missed you so.
You're so lively and funny. *Per favore*. Humor an old man who cares for you."

"I told you, what I'm doing is a matter of life and death. It won't wait." I
shook his hand loose.

"*Lailetta mia*, don't hate me so. You're only hating yourself." Belzoni
wheeled back to his table and spun around to face the canvas. "She's got the
laser. She'll bring it. She'll be so pleased."

"I hope you get a lot of money for it. It's really good now."

"I'll get enough to keep me in pussy and wine!"

I went to the door, cursing under my breath. "You're killing yourself
with all those cigarettes."

"Have to die of something," he called back. "*Cara mia*, wait." His voice
was suddenly so thready and indistinct that I stopped and looked back over
my shoulder at him. He frowned. "That man, I don't like him. He's not what
he seems."

"None of us is, Belzoni."

His mouth twisted into a complex and sardonic shape. "Out of the
mouths of *bambini*."

Outside, in the taxi, Bolingbroke felt dazzled, restless, unsettled. He could
barely rein himself in. After all this time, a cure! Centuries of longing, about
to ripen into fulfillment! It was shocking, wondrous, tantalizing. He had to
steel himself to the work that lay ahead of him, before the cure could be
attempted. He and Laila still had to find the painting, hide it from the vampires, and escape with their lives. Laila was saying something, but he had
missed it. He said, "You'll take a shower, change, and eat breakfast before we
board the plane to Rome."

"You're not going to make me shower alone, are you?" Laila whispered. "After that, that—what I had to do to get the information?" Her voice held a mournful note. It had cost her to finish the Vermeer. He knew that she'd worked ferociously to leave her past behind her. It was part of what he admired about her. With her rare talent, it must torture her not to exercise that gift every day. But this was not the time. Not now, when he was so close to being able to have her without hurting her, when he was so close to having a life with her.... He looked away, into the milky Parisian morning, at the *bouquiniste* stalls along the Seine where tourists rummaged through old books and yellowed postcards.

"You're strong," he said. It was a dismissal, and she flinched away from him. He grabbed her arm.

"What?" she snapped.

"Your mother's friend, the Bouchard woman. You know the location of her villa?"

"Emilie Bouchard. I don't remember where her villa is exactly, just that it's near the Vatican. I'll figure it out when we get to Rome." She paused, suddenly smiled. "You're not present. It's the first time I've ever seen you so distracted."

"The painting is on my mind."

"The painting?" I asked Bolingbroke.

"It shows the cure," he said. Hope and longing burst over his face like the sun after a storm, and he gazed at me as if with sudden possibility. What could light him up like that? Then I understood!

"The painting shows the cure! When we find it, you can take the cure. You can be cured!" I cried. Cured: and then he would be human again, and wouldn't endanger me. We could be together! All the promise of love and intimacy that I felt in his arms would be a real possibility for us! I wouldn't have to worry about being killed, and he wouldn't have to fear killing me. I leaned toward him with gladness and song in my heart.

But Bolingbroke had already retreated back into his shell of invulnerability. "There are many reasons to find the painting. We must protect the

Illuminati, too." His tone was brusque. Then my cell phone rang. I answered it, giving him a frosty glare. "Yes?"

It was Fern, and her voice was funny. She said, "Laila, there's someone here in our apartment who wants to know where you are. Exactly where, right now."

My breath froze. "A vampire?"

"No," Fern replied, swallowing. "Hahnemann. He has a gun in his hand, and he's aiming it at me."

In the background, the old German shouted, "Tell me where you are, Laila Cambridge, or you'll never see her again! I *will* be with you when you find the painting! I demand it! If you want this girl to live, tell me where you are. I will bring her to you."

I held the phone to my chest and stared at Bolingbroke. "Hahnemann has taken Fern hostage."

"I heard," Bolingbroke said, shrugging. He looked unconcerned. "Tell them to meet us in Rome."

Bolingbroke mused to himself that he would take care of Hahnemann later. While he was still a halfling, before he was human again. Bolingbroke would enjoy one last good kill.

Chapter 20

FIUMICINO AIRPORT AT DUSK. GETTING OFF THE plane in Rome, I'm always surprised by the human warmth of the café workers and taxi drivers. Yes, big-armed men carrying machine guns sweep through the terminals, and everyone smokes as if they believed in a cigarette fairy godmother who magically prevents lung cancer. Still, there's a kind of affable openness that's alien to New York. The coffee at the bars is delicious, too. Can't help but wonder why we Americans put up with so much bad food in our public venues.

Bolingbroke and I had carry-ons, so we didn't have to wait for baggage. Passengers never know when their luggage will deplane at Fiumicino. Italy time is different from time in, say, Holland or Germany, where if they say the bags will be out in six minutes, then the bags will be out in six minutes and zero seconds. That kind of timekeeping is unheard of in Rome and the southern part of the Italian peninsula. After all, the espresso is so good that everyone has to stop working and grab a demitasse every half hour.

I was finishing a latte macchiato that Bolingbroke insisted we drink when a familiar voice sounded behind me.

"You'll thank me later; you need me." The faint German accent and lack of preamble: Hahnemann. He bustled up toward us, carrying a large Gucci valise. Fern trailed him. I ran to hug her. "Are you okay?" I asked. She nodded, looking chastened—and angry.

"Miss Takahasi, you haven't been harmed?" Bolingbroke asked.

"Just my dignity," Fern said dryly.

Bolingbroke stiffened, and looked as if he would hit the man. Hahnemann held up a hand. "I came to help."

"We don't need your help," Bolingbroke said, in a forbidding tone. "Just the girl."

Hahnemann's brilliant blue eyes focused on Bolingbroke. "Please. I am as invested in this painting and the cure for vampirism as you are."

"Because Kadja is your daughter?" I asked. I slipped my arm around Fern. "She tried to kill Fern! And you threatened Fern!" It infuriated me. And it scared me, how close I'd come to losing Fern.

Hahnemann's unlined symmetrical features melted in on themselves. He suddenly looked decades older. "I know, she's become a terrible creature. You can't believe the things she's done. Killing and eating children, women, innocent men…. It breaks my heart. I must save her! I would not have hurt Fern. She's far too beautiful. You know how I feel about beautiful objects, they are to be treasured."

"I am not an object! I'm a person, and pointing a gun at a person is a threat to kill them—which you also verbalized," Fern said, furiously. Her dark eyes simmered. I'd only ever seen her so angry twice, and both times ended badly for the folks involved. She said, "Having armed bodyguards carry a bound and gagged person onto your private plane and travel to Rome without a moment's notice is way beyond rude. You are a *very* bad man. You're a nasty old Nazi!" She was fuming. She was too angry even to quote poetry.

"Would you like me to kill him right now?" Bolingbroke asked her. "There's a janitor's closet behind the duty-free store. It will only take a few minutes. I can be very efficient about it." His hand moved so fast that we never saw it grab Hahnemann. We just saw Hahnemann dangling a foot above the floor. Bolingbroke was gripping Hahnemann by the collar of his jacket and smiling with pure enjoyment. His lengthening fangs made soft bulges in his grinning upper lip. Bolingbroke shook Hahnemann, who squeaked.

"Please, please, calm yourselves. Fern, I will recompense you well for your time. Very well. Laila, Mr. Bolingbroke, you will need me. Put me down. I have some items that will greatly aid you if you encounter vampires. Please, you must hear me out."

"I hate Nazis." Bolingbroke hoisted Hahnemann higher. "Hated them from the first moment the German Workers' Party hung posters and barked about the treaty of Versailles." His grip on the back of Hahnemann's neck tightened. Hahnemann writhed, the soles of his handmade buttery leather Italian loafers knocking together.

"I hated the Nazis more than anyone, I worked from inside them to help people! Please. You must give me an opportunity to save my daughter! I love Kadja—she's everything to me. All of what I have done, bringing Fern to Rome, it is for Kadja, to save my beloved child. It is what a father must do. I can be useful to you."

"There's no saving her; she won't allow it," Bolingbroke said. "What we do is our task, not yours. You are useless. Your life has continued long enough." He smiled, and his eyes traveled past the duty-free store to a little side door. His chrysoberyl eyes sparkled. It was a side of Bolingbroke I'd never seen before: his ruthless joy in killing. I shivered.

"Uh, Bolingbroke," Fern said.

"Please, she's my daughter," Hahnemann begged. Sweat beaded up on his forehead. "I can help you. I know all about those creatures. I've brought weapons."

"Maybe he can be useful. Anyone would want to rescue their child," I said. Bolingbroke gave Fern and then me a sour look. He dropped Hahnemann. Hahnemann flashed us a look of gratitude as he righted himself and straightened his jacket.

"How about you just hurt him a little bit?" asked Fern. "Maybe break his kneecaps later? He is trying to help his child, after all." She wore a crisp white cotton shirt with a Peter Pan collar that wasn't at all crinkled from the journey. I hugged her.

Bolingbroke's lip lifted in a sardonic sneer. "It's not just that she's his child. He's the reason she was turned."

"What do you mean?" Fern demanded. She gave Hahnemann a scathing look of contempt and disbelief.

Bolingbroke shrugged. "He found out about vampires and wanted to study them. He tried to catch one. He used her as bait."

"You used your own daughter as vampire bait?" I asked in disgust, as Fern physically turned her back to Hahnemann. Revulsion plunged my stomach to my knees, making me feel seasick. So that was the real tragedy in the portrait on Hahnemann's wall: Kadja would never again be that laughing, innocent young woman, so full of beauty and hope—and her own father was the reason why. I gagged. "Jesus, Kristofer. Even for you, that's cold. I mean, you're slimy about art; I've gone there myself. You feel entitled to sequester the world's treasures in your palace. But to use your own daughter that way?"

"I never dreamt...." Hahnemann quailed. His head drooped and his shoulders quaked. He opened his suit jacket, which was, as always, an immaculately hand-tailored affair made of the finest fabric. "I brought these. Please. Let me come with you. There'll be a battle, you know it. You can't rely only on these two women and the sharpened sticks Fern was carrying." He took a vial out of an inner pocket, reached out with it toward Bolingbroke. There was a long minute as Bolingbroke stared at the vial in open contempt. Then he took it and studied it. Hahnemann said, softly, "Silver nanoparticle spray. Hard to make in the right concentration to be effective. Very costly. I have a few dozen, the fruit of decades of experimentation. I brought all that I have."

"The Illuminati will want this technology," Bolingbroke said stiffly. He passed the vial back to Hahnemann. Bolingbroke's face was impassive but we all knew that Hahnemann was now part of the team. Fern gave me a look that told me how angry and disgusted she was with Hahnemann. I wished with all my heart that Hahnemann hadn't brought her here.

"I brought six dozen sharpened hawthorn stakes and two guns that fire them," Hahnemann said. He was babbling with relief. "I'll give all the technology I've developed to the Illuminati. Please, just don't kill my daughter. We'll have the painting; we can use the cure to turn her back."

"You know what the painting shows, and you didn't tell me when I sold you the Diebenkorn?" I asked, softly. Hahnemann's eyes dropped away.

"I can't promise she won't be killed," Bolingbroke said. "Still, your technology is the price of admittance to this search. You will surrender it. And your research."

"Gladly, gladly. I'll hand everything over," Hahnemann said. "I want the chance to save her. Please—she's everything to me. She's all I have."

"Maybe you shouldn't have used her as bait, then," Fern said.

The four of us got into a taxi. I scooted into the back seat between Bolingbroke and Hahnemann, who sat with his head in his hands. His eyes were closed. The driver wanted to talk about American music. This topic was owned by Fern, the rock musician, but she stared out the front window with fierce concentration. Bolingbroke, whom I wouldn't have expected to care, took the gambit. His Italian was rapid and flawless, and he lapsed into North Tuscan dialect with its soft g's and c's and funny shortening of the verb *fare*, to do or make. Fascinating: Bolingbroke was Florentine. Originally.

I wondered how many centuries ago he'd been born there. I gave Bolingbroke a sideways glance as he argued with the driver about Lenny Kravitz. I caught him in a reflective pause, and he tilted his head and smiled.

Then we were driving down the Via Tiburtina, and even in the twilight, the palm trees struck me as exotic. And ancient. This road was built by Marcus Valerius Maximus more than two millennia ago. I glanced westward from the palm trees, to the purple outlines of cedar trees on the distant hill of the Vatican, and I knew that the painting was here in Rome. I could feel it. It was speaking to me again. Maybe Bolingbroke was right, the painting possessed mystical powers. Or maybe something in me had awakened. Because I also knew that my dad was here. Knew it in my red-headed bones.

After all the years of his absence, I could feel his dear, familiar presence in this eternal city. Perhaps it was the way my mind had been stretched lately, by forging and hallucinating; some long-closed gate in my consciousness had banged open. I sensed things in ways I never had before. I believed things that, a few weeks ago, I would have scorned.

"We're not going to a hotel," I said, in Italian. I leaned forward and spoke directly to the driver, who draped an arm around Fern to help himself turn in the seat and listen to me. "Unhand my friend and mind the road. But take us toward the Vatican."

"You remember the location of the villa?" Bolingbroke asked.

"I will when we get there," I said. I felt my heart beat faster. *Daddy.* I would see him again. After all these years! I had so much to say to him, most of which boiled down to "I love you," and "How could you do this to me?" I imagined hugging him and slapping him. Then I remembered the painting, and the others who were also looking for it, and for my father. I didn't want to find him and then lose him right away! I leaned into Bolingbroke. I whispered, "Are they here?"

His face shuttered. "Yes."

"How long do we have?"

"A few days, perhaps. Or a matter of hours."

"So Hahnemann's right: there'll be a fight," I said. It wasn't a question. Bolingbroke nodded. "Did you bring weapons?"

He tipped his head at me and his eyes like chrysoberyl changed to green with silky red-orange trillings. "I am a weapon," he said. But I wasn't, and as I leaned back in my seat, I realized that I should have done what Hahnemann had, and thought ahead. In typical Laila fashion, I'd leapt at the chance to find my father and lay hands on a ravishing lost Botticelli painting, without considering the whole situation and the consequences. Now I was rushing toward my father with an unwinnable battle hard on my heels.

I instructed the driver to turn down various Roman streets. Fern seemed frozen inside herself. Hahnemann and I used our phones to try to find the Bouchard villa. No luck. It was now quite dark, and the driver was getting frustrated, both with our uncertainty and with Fern's imperviousness to his unsubtle blandishments. He finally offered to call his uncle, who had been a taxi driver in Rome for thirty years and who was now enjoying life on Elba. He used Hahnemann's phone and naturally sped up to enjoy the conversation with his Zio, because all Roman men know that driving one hundred sixty kilometers an hour while not looking at the road is a sign of extreme virility. We careened aimlessly around the *vicino Vaticano,* with the driver laughing into a cell phone and ignoring traffic and pedestrians.

After we narrowly missed running over an old lady in a black dress and matching lace shawl, I thunked the driver on his shoulder and demanded to speak to Zio. Our intrepid chauffeur described for Zio my cherry-red hair and lavish endowments, which earned him a flick in the ear from Bolingbroke. Then I got on the phone.

"It's an old villa, sprawling, near the Vatican. The family was originally French, settled in Rome around the year 1800. They intermarried with Romans but kept the name intact," I started. I kept describing. Zio hadn't a clue. Finally, desperate, I said, "The signora, she's pazzo now…."

"Oh, *si!* I know exactly!" Zio laughed. "Give me my nephew." And five minutes later we turned down a dark cul-de-sac, one of those surprisingly antique streets you stumble upon when you explore the modern city of Rome. Bolingbroke got out to open the gate to the driveway. I bounced out behind him. The driver pulled up to the villa. Bolingbroke and I came after the car on foot. Hahnemann lingered in the taxi to haggle. Fern climbed out and stood beside me.

"Are you okay?" I asked her. She nodded. We looked at a sprawling rectangular palazzo with square columns and a massive carved *portone*—door—from the early nineteenth century. A patio wrapped around one entire side of the building, outside a huge ballroom with twenty-foot-high ceilings. A balcony looked out from elegant curving arches on the second floor. There was another arched balcony on the third floor. Mostly the place was dark, though wisps of lemony lucence shone out from a few windows on the second floor, and one on the third.

A spotlight went on over the *portone*, revealing that the exterior of the villa was painted yellow. The *portone* swung open. A willowy dark-haired woman wearing a dress out of the Victorian era stood in the threshold. "Ciao, Nonni!" she called. "Come in, *per favore*! Did you bring some chickens?"

"Emilie Bouchard," I said. I was happy to see her, despite the obvious ravages to her once mighty intellect. As a child, I'd spent many happy weeks with Aunt Emilie. It was heart-wrenching to see Emilie reduced this way.

"Sooey, sooey, bawk bawk bawk, come in, Nonni!" Emilie chittered.

"She's daft," Bolingbroke said.

"Oh, my, yes," I said. I would have said more but a tall, stocky figure lumbered up behind Emilie, and my eyes filled with tears. My throat closed up. Everything in me was overwhelmed with love and joy. All the intervening years collapsed like a worm-hole through time and space, and I was a little girl again. I couldn't speak, so I just hurtled myself toward the door like a projectile. He leapt out in front of Emilie with his arms outstretched, and the next moment, Daddy held me in his arms.

Chapter 21

"COME IN, COME IN, NONNI, IT'S SO nice to see you! How was the drive in from Orvieto?" Emilie was saying. I was burrowed inside my father's warm embrace and could barely hear her. Daddy's cheek rested on the top of my head and I thought I felt a splash of wetness on my scalp. Was he crying? How could my big, strong daddy cry? I stepped back to look.

"Daddy! I missed you so much! Are you okay? Daddy!" Now I was the one crying, and I was almost as incoherent as Emilie, who had struck up a conversation with Hahnemann about different kinds of hens. Then grown-up Laila weighed in, pushing little Laila aside, and a wave of fury flashed through me. "Daddy, damn it, you really hurt us! Me and Brad and Mama! We're a mess because you disappeared that way."

"Come inside. We'll talk," Daddy said. His blue eyes were watery. Other than that, he looked like himself. He was a big-boned bear of a man, with the broad face of his Swedish mother. There were subtle changes from the last time I'd seen him: his red hair was more shot through with white, and he had more crow's feet and laugh lines than I remembered. They were deeper, too, and there were lines cut into his cheeks, as if he'd been as scored by the years apart from us as we, his family, had been. The merriment that used to characterize him was tempered now with something else, something weighty and painful, some anguish which he hadn't had to carry before he vanished.

Life had always come easily to my father. He was a vibrant physical specimen, an intellectual giant, and a charismatic people-person. Those gifts had brought him ease. But I sensed that the ease was gone, and that he'd passed through a crucible. He had suffered. It softened me and made me want to forgive him. He was perusing me as carefully as I was him, and he took me by the hand and led me inside. He ushered the others in, stopping only to stoop and kiss Fern's cheek. Once inside, he closed the door firmly and threw the giant deadbolt.

"John Bolingbroke," Daddy said with affection, and shook Bolingbroke's hand. So they knew each other well. Interesting.

"Good to see you again, Robert," Bolingbroke said. Pleasure lit his angular face.

"You brought reinforcements," Daddy said, throwing his arm around me and hugging me to his chest.

"You were incommunicado. I feared the worst." Bolingbroke frowned. "Do you know Kristofer Hahnemann?"

"Only by reputation," my dad said. His eyes darkened, which I knew to be a sign of disapproval. No one else would know that, though, since he was always so urbane. He asked, "You collect my daughter's work, don't you?"

Hahnemann sort of pliéed out of courtesy. He was on his best behavior. He said brightly, "Yes, she is most talented. I prize her work, when I can find it."

"He used his own daughter as vampire bait," I said, with a gesture of disgust. Daddy and Bolingbroke exchanged a grim look over my head. Then we were in it. Into the discussion, into the heart of the matter, into the lost painting and the danger.

"So I looked for the painting for a few years in a casual way, but it became clear that it was a full-time search," my father said. "And a dangerous search."

"We got here in a few days," I said. We sat in a grouping of chairs at one end of the giant ballroom, a kind of makeshift parlor, with Fern and me on either side of Daddy on a dusty, sagging old sofa, Bolingbroke and Hahnemann in carved wooden chairs, and Emilie wringing her hands and hopping around like a stork. The huge room, with its twenty-foot ceilings, smelled faintly of long-ago cigarette smoke; more recent scents of roasting chicken and sautéed onions and Emilie's lavender perfume layered the air. Dusk pressed against the old lead-glass windows that stretched nearly from the ceiling to the floor. None of it could distract me from the length of time it had taken Daddy to arrive at this villa. How long had it taken me—a little over a week? I couldn't suppress another shudder of anger. Had he needed to keep us in the dark for so long, not knowing if he was alive or dead? "It took you all these years to get to the same place I arrived at in a week?" I demanded.

"Let me serve us all some wine," Emilie sang, clapping her hands. She was Mama's age, but her face hadn't aged in the same way, or maybe the dementia had taken away the time line of anguish and replaced it with the zero placeholder of youth. Her extreme slenderness and delicacy of feature made her look like a sculpted figurine, a look which was enhanced by her long, chestnut-colored banana curls and the cameo brooch at her throat. She danced out of the parlor with a swish of her long skirts. I almost envied her child-like innocence.

"I haven't your contacts." Daddy reached out and pinched my nose as if I were a little girl and he were teasing me. I batted his hand away; I was no longer a little girl, and he couldn't assuage my anger with some easy jocularity. He shrugged. "I spent the first few years lying low. I wanted the vampires to forget me, and my affiliation."

"With the Illuminati," I clarified.

He nodded. "Vampires have always tracked anyone who makes inquiries about *Coming Forth by Day*. They also track the Illuminati. I didn't want them to know what I was up to, or that I had a family. It was too dangerous for you and your brother and mother." He paused, staring quizzically at me. "How did you arrive here so quickly?"

"Belzoni said the painting was here. He'd seen it here with Mama and Aunt Emilie."

"Your mother?" Daddy looked startled and confused. "*Eleanor* knows about the painting? She knows where the painting is? Does she know what it shows?"

"She knows," I said.

"She saw it? When? Must have been when she was a girl. . . . I only discovered that it was here when I spoke to an old nun who came here to have trysts with a priest who'd brought it from Amsterdam. What else does Eleanor know about it? Does she know about, well, did anything lead her to suspect the reality of vampires? Did she make the connection between the painting and vampires?"

The shoe was on the other foot now, and Daddy was the one brimming with questions and confused surprise. Served him right, for disappearing and leaving us to worry and suffer. I slid into a reverie full of anger and wistfulness. All the years we hadn't gotten to share with him, all the time we would never get back. Most of it was picayune stuff, like the crappy boyfriends I hadn't been able to complain to him about, and the snarky comments from my thesis adviser that I hadn't been able to repeat to him, and my grumbling about how bad the wine was at the art history department cocktail party—we got wine in a box, for chrissakes! But it was my life, and he was my dad, and it had mattered to me. I wanted tell him something every day, no matter how quotidian. Some infantile part of me still wanted him to look at the snot on the tissue when I blew my nose.

Fern picked up the slack in the conversation. "Eleanor said that after you left, she found a notebook where you'd written a couple of lines about vampires, and she put it all together. About the Egyptian *Book of the Dead*, and about the Illuminati's mission."

"She didn't tell me she'd seen the painting, either," I said, softly. "Belzoni told me that."

"Eleanor, she was always so brilliant and curious and talented," Daddy murmured. His eyes veiled over with tears. "My beautiful, delicate Eleanor. How I've missed her!"

"You were divorced!" I snapped. Daddy's expression drooped.

"I have a nice Barolo, twenty years old," Emilie said, pattering back into the room. She carried a tray with eight brandy glasses and a carafe filled with murky brown liquid. "Everyone must have a nice glass of wine." She reached for the carafe, but Bolingbroke gripped it first.

"Allow me to do the honors, Signora Bouchard," he said, in his most courtly voice. He gave her a smile, and she wasn't so *pazzo* that she didn't instantly blush and simper and sink down onto the sofa next to Fern.

"Oh, my, aren't you the gentleman," Emilie giggled, covering her cheeks with her hands. "Are you single, sir?"

"No," Bolingbroke said. He raised an eyebrow at me, and, just for a split second, we smiled at each other. Then he was sniffing the contents of the carafe. "Mud," he mouthed. He pretended to pour the liquid into the brandy glasses, handed us each an empty glass. "*In boca al lupo*," he said, raising his glass.

"To Eleanor," Daddy said, reverently, under his breath.

"If you cared so much, you could have let her know you were alive," I said, not restraining the ferocity I felt.

"Laila," Bolingbroke reproved, mildly. He lifted his glass again. We all simulated drinking our pretend Barolo, twenty years old.

"What beautiful wine," Emilie tinkled. "I'll bake us a cake to go with it!" She hopped up and skittered out.

"Where in the house is the painting?" Bolingbroke said. "There'll be time later to autopsy the last few years. I'd like to retrieve the painting and get it out of here this minute. Before the vampires arrive. We used a commercial airline to come to Rome, but I can arrange to transport the painting privately so it can be studied and safeguarded."

"Where are you going to put it?" Hahnemann spoke up for the first time. "You have no secure location. Give it to me—I can protect it!"

"The Illuminati have strongholds all over the world," Bolingbroke said.

"Our security is better than the United States Bullion Depository," Daddy added.

"Strongholds? Security? Bah! The lodges in Paris, London, and Vienna were penetrated more than a century ago. Frankfurt and Venice, fifty years ago. Johannesburg and Kolkata were never safe. Colorado and Tokyo were breached twenty years ago. Seattle, Virginia, Cardiff, and Kuala Lumpur, with all their modernization, were infiltrated within the last two years. Those are considered the great strongholds. I haven't mentioned the smaller lodges, which have only minimal security, garlic and sprouting seeds and an arsenal of stakes."

"You know an awful lot about the Illuminati," Daddy said softly.

Hahnemann pulled his jacket straight with a quick, concerted jerk downward of both wrists. "The Illuminati know an awful lot about me. You've been spying on me for decades."

"The plan is to take the painting under armed guard to Kuala Lumpur," Bolingbroke said. "They've restructured and upgraded the premises."

"Vampires eat armed guards for hors d'oeuvres. Laser security systems were outdated in the 1980s," Hahnemann sneered. "An old vampire can fly almost at the speed of light and can easily fool a computer. Take the painting to my home. I have the only vampire-proof fortress in the world. I should have; I paid the ultimate price for it!"

The room fell quiet as everyone thought of Kadja. Bolingbroke broke the stillness, asking: "So, where is the painting?"

"I can't find it," Daddy said, sounding frustrated. He squeezed my hand again and shrugged. "I've looked all over. I've been here for two weeks, searching. I've looked in every closet, cabinet, attic, basement, drawer, and chest in this villa. Twice. There isn't a sign of *Coming Forth by Day!*"

"Mama mentioned a secret room," I said.

"*Ecco*, tiramisu!" Emilie tiptoed in, bearing a plate piled high with gray Roman stones and fragrant green basil leaves. She straightened and giggled. "Nonni, are you talking about the painting Ellie and I saw the other day?" She looked around with an insouciant grin. The room strained with an awkward silence. I could feel Daddy's breath catch in his chest. Emilie giggled again. "Why didn't you tell me you were looking for it? Ellie and Giovanni and I thought ghosts were after us, so we ran out! Giovanni ran fast. But I can find the secret passageway. I was just there a few days ago."

Bolingbroke stood and took Emilie's fragile white hand in his large one. "Bellissima, show us the secret passageway."

An hour later, we were still looking. Emilie had led us all through the rambling old villa, to no avail. Every time she pointed out a location, Bolingbroke and Daddy knelt and tapped on the walls. Hahnemann produced a stethoscope from his Gucci bag, and Bolingbroke listened with physician-like intensity at every likely location. Twice Bolingbroke used a trowel to dig out wallpaper and plaster and a few bricks, but had found nothing. The secret room seemed determined to elude us.

We regrouped for a few minutes in a second-floor parlor. I noticed a painting on the wall and went to examine it. It was a Madonna and child very much after Leonardo, reminiscent of the *Virgin of the Rocks*, except that the background landscape was more open, with cypress trees and a mountain and a distant city. The rhapsodic sweetness of the Madonna's face made me smile. What is it about great art that captures our hearts and minds and souls? Is it simply beauty, and the innate human response of joy in beholding beauty? Does beauty point to a higher order, a higher truth in our seemingly random cosmos filled with, well, forgers and liars and con artists, vampires and killers and secret histories hidden from the masses? I fingered the painting and felt the scratchy gloss of the craquelure. It was maybe from the eighteenth century, a fine copy by a consummate painter who adored the Renaissance Masters.

"I remember, this way, come with me!" trilled Emilie, tapping her forehead. She grabbed Daddy's hand and darted out, so we all filed out after them. I was beginning to doubt that she'd ever remember anything.

This time she trekked us up to a low-ceilinged fourth floor and waved her hand at an eave leading to an attic. Everyone oohed and aahed, and she was rosy and flustered with the attention, like a teenager. Daddy and Bolingbroke got out their trowel and stethoscope. Fern and Hahnemann crowded behind them. But I knew the painting wasn't here on this high floor. It was speaking to me again. It was calling me. It was below us.

I wandered back down to the second floor, thought about the da Vinci copy, and traipsed over to it. The unknown artist had a gift for the Leonardoesque that I admired and envied: the *sfumato*, da Vinci's masterful and subtle shading from light to dark which gives his paintings an illusionistic atmosphere, was perfection. If I'd thought the painting was older than the eighteenth century, I'd have been telephoning my mother and every other Leonardo scholar in the world! The hands of the Madonna were particularly lovely. I myself would have given one ovary to paint them. Maybe not an ovary, because there was a possibility that Bolingbroke would be human again and we could together create four red-haired, agate-eyed munchkins. I'd always wanted a big family. But I'd certainly give a canine tooth to have accomplished those hands....

Not just her hands, but her face and the drapery, the whole complex of psychological unfolding in which Leonardo excelled. Yes, this Madonna was a vision of supreme, beatific grace. What had Vasari, that rascally publicist and spin doctor for the great masters, called Leonardo? "An artist of outstanding physical beauty who displayed infinite grace in everything he did...." There is a way that all artists paint themselves over and over again, and Leonardo painted beauty in part because he himself was a divinely handsome man. The unknown forger had captured it all masterfully. I didn't know whether I could have done as well. I suddenly felt competitive.

"You like that painting, Laila? You can have it." It was Emilie Bouchard, standing behind me, smoking a cigarette. Her voice had dropped an octave in pitch. One look at her face, now graven with the stately intelligence of a beautiful and mature woman, told me that she was sane, and present.

"Aunt Emilie!" I cried, and we hugged. "How are you?"

"This might be one of my better days, I don't know. What was I doing?" she muttered. She clasped her arms around her midriff and took a deep drag on her cigarette.

"Showing us around the villa," I said. I watched as she digested that piece of information.

"*Dio mio*, I hate this perfume," she said, making a wry face. Her lively eyes scanned my face. "Who is 'us'?"

"Daddy, my roommate Fern whom you met at my graduation, John Bolingbroke, and Kristofer Hahnemann."

"Don't know John Bolingbroke. Kristofer Hahnemann, the Nazi?" She made a moue of distaste. "My parents hated him!"

"He gets that a lot," I said. I glanced back at the painting. "This is lovely."

"It's a Leonardo." She smiled.

"Almost," I smiled back.

Emilie looked merry. "What tipped you off, the frame?"

"And the craquelure. But whoever did it was an extraordinary mimic. Gifted." And I would know, because I was the greatest forger of them all. But this unknown artist could give me a run for my money. I thought maybe I'd try my hand at a Leonardo, when all this was over. Then I squelched the thought. The Vermeer was a once off. No more.

Emilie shrugged and went to an end-table for an ashtray, which she brought back with her. "What are you all doing here?"

"We're looking for something. A painting."

"There is only one painting that you can mean." Emilie handed me the ashtray with its smoldering cigarette while she popped off her cameo brooch and loosened her antiquated collar. "The painting from the secret room. The lost Botticelli that has caused generations of art lovers and historians and dealers to whisper and search. There's a kind of madness it brings on people. There were those who thought the hunt for lost Caravaggios was terrible, but this is a thousand times worse, and it has gone on for centuries. I have had colleagues, esteemed professors, dedicate decades of their lives to a quest for its whereabouts. *Coming Forth by Day.*"

"You remember it?" I asked, cautiously. Was she clued into its secrets about vampires and cures and secret societies? I was afraid to ask, in case the question jarred her back to the no-man's land where she spent most of her time. Poor Aunt Emilie. She had always been so bright and bubbly when I was a kid. She'd had a distinguished career as a history professor before the dementia set in. She'd written a few books, been loved by her students. As Italian women increasingly did, she'd gotten engaged late in life. But the guy had taken off when it became clear that there was no cure for her illness. I hoped she didn't dwell on what she had lost when she snapped back into consensual reality.

"*Cara mia*, I know all about that painting. I know about the secrets behind it." She let gray smoke trickle out of the side of her mouth. "My family has known about vampires since we moved to Rome two hundred years ago."

"You have? How did you know?" I was intrigued.

"My great ancestor, Captain Pierre-Francois Bouchard, who found the Rosetta Stone, also found another stone. Another stele in three languages."

"I've never heard of such a thing," I said, wonderingly. "There's no mention of that in any history books!"

"Of course not; it was kept secret. It was given to the church for safe-keeping. In my family it is called the stone of death and horrors. It talks about vampires."

"So your family has a connection to vampires. Is that why the painting was brought here, during the world war?"

"Yes. My papa was on the front line of the Illuminati's war against vampires." She smiled fondly at some memory that was playing out in her mind. I thought it must be a great pleasure for her to have memories, since most of the time her brain was scrubbed clean of its past. Or was that a blessing? Would I really be missing anything if I lost my memory of all my worry and anxiety and grief over my missing father? But this was an unanswerable question, and Emilie was talking, explaining. "We were close friends with a priest who helped Jews escape. This villa was a part of the underground railroad, hiding Jews and transporting them out of Europe. My papa told me that the priest fell in love with a nun who was also helping Jews. They met here. My family passed no judgments."

"Love has no boundaries," I said softly. I thought of Bolingbroke, and how I didn't care that he was a sinister creature out of a legend. Certainly he had killed legions of people before he had been given half his soul back; that's what vampires did—they killed indiscriminately. It didn't matter to me. And not only was love boundary-less, it was also timeless. It could spring forth fully formed in the smallest quantum of time, and then last forever. Two weeks ago, I didn't know Bolingbroke. Now I didn't want to think of my life without him.

Emilie blew out another plume of smoke. "Come. To the first floor. I feel the tickle in my brain, I don't know how long I will be here." She took a last deep, deep drag on her cigarette and then stubbed it out in the ashtray. She set the ashtray down and walked stiffly to the door, as if her age, when she recovered it along with her clarity, dried out her joints. She threw a grin over her shoulder. "How old is it?" Her eyes, as they flicked to the Madonna, effervesced with a wonderful wickedness that I recalled from years ago.

"Eighteenth century." I was certain. This was one of my specialties.

"It was painted in the early nineteen-seventies. By your mother. She had a run of forging, did pretty well at it." Emilie belly-laughed at the shock my face registered. "This was her best effort."

"How…how did you come by it?" I whispered. I could barely speak, the shock gripped my throat so tightly.

"Your mother gave up forging when her landscapes were critically acclaimed. She brought me some suitcases to store, said they were her old tools. Gave me the Leonardo as a gift. Told me it contained the secrets of our adventure."

"Why didn't she just throw out her tools?"

"She always thought that one day she would forge again. Until she saw your forgeries. Actually, she saw two: a Van Gogh and a Corot. Two such different hands, so perfectly, consummately achieved. She realized that she would never be as good a forger as you. She gave it up for good." Emilie laughed again. Then she was gone from the room. I was left stunned, staring at my mother's handiwork. I felt like I'd been kicked in the gut. All the times Mama had scolded me for forging, all the times she'd made me feel "less than." *And she'd done it herself.* I didn't know how to feel.

"Laila, no luck upstairs," Fern called to me. Her words didn't compute. I was still grappling with the concept of my mother painting forgeries.

"Laila, where is Signora Bouchard going?" Bolingbroke asked, from beside Fern.

"Um, the uh, what, uh, wh-what did you say?" I stuttered stupidly.

Fern and Bolingbroke looked at each other. They rushed over and stood by me, one on each side. I stared at the painting. Fern asked, "Laila, are you all right? You're pale. What happened?"

Mama forged. Suddenly I was pissed. *Really pissed*, almost as pissed with her as I was with Dad. Did Mama need to make me feel so guilty all the time, when she'd done it, too? Anger brought focus. "Aunt Emilie was lucid. She said the secret room is on the first floor." I squared my shoulders and marched out. I found Aunt Emilie on the first floor landing. Daddy trotted down from the fourth floor.

"No sign of the room on the fourth floor." He smiled at me, but I scowled.

"Did you know what Mama was up to? How many lies can you guys tell, how many hurtful secrets do you keep?" I shouted. "You think you can do whatever you want with impunity, and Mama can make me feel bad for something she's done, too?"

Daddy looked taken aback. "What? What are you talking about? Laila, everything I've done, I've done to protect you and Brad and Eleanor! I couldn't turn my back on the work the Illuminati are doing to keep humanity safe. We're at war! But I did everything in your best interests!"

"Nonni, Nonni, don't fret, I'll make toilette water out of the roses in the garden!" Emilie interjected. Daddy and I turned toward her. Her face had youthened, smoothing out as if scrubbed and ironed. It was like watching a different personality take over a multiple. She broke out into a girlish song about butterflies and rainbows.

"She was lucid?" Daddy asked. He stroked his face in confusion.

I nodded. "She said the secret room was off the first floor."

"We'll search there again," Bolingbroke said, as he and Fern and Hahnemann joined us on the landing.

"And bluebirds twinkle in the night sky," lilted Emilie, to the tune of Tarantella.

Chapter 22

IT WAS CLOSE TO MIDNIGHT WHEN BOLINGBROKE felt the vampires approach. Then he smelled them. Four vampires, two males and two females, gathered outside the house. They lounged and waited. Others would join them. Then they'd strike. Bolingbroke felt his blood speed up its rhythm through his veins. He sharpened his acute senses even further, so he could hear a mouse scuffling in the walls of the house down the block, and scent the chamomile in the lotion the lady of that house massaged into her hands. The hue of every color was intensified. Events became hyper-real, and slower. The world was a richer, more fascinating place. There would be a battle soon, which prompted riffs of joy in Bolingbroke, in the part of him that was still a vampire and still relished all forms of violence and bloodletting. Besides, he now had feral powers that vampires lacked. He would enjoy the battle.

But the humans felt otherwise, particularly the one that mattered most to him. Mattered more than anyone had in centuries. Laila stood leaning into a wallpapered wall, her face hidden, her arms hugging her chest. Her usual buoyance and sass had evaporated, dispersed like air let out of a tire. Something the Bouchard woman had said during her bout of lucidity had upset Laila. Bolingbroke felt a pang. Laila was emotionally distraught; she would soon be in grave physical danger. Could he protect her? Could he keep her alive? He would give his life to save hers. Would that be enough, even with all his powers?

He drew her off the wall into a loose embrace. "Do you have the mala?"

She snuggled into him and lifted her pretty, drawn face. "In my pocket."

"Put it on. It protects you around vampires. They can't see you when you're wearing it." He kissed her forehead gently, then released her. He watched as she pulled out the beads, ran them through her hands with an expression of appreciation. She could feel the mala's muted transcendence. That pleased Bolingbroke. For all Laila's brash outward energy, she was also sensitive and perceptive. He admired that in her.

"Wearing this necklace makes me invisible to vampires? How?" Her usual curiosity ebbed back into her face, which relieved Bolingbroke.

"I don't know how it works. I chanted mantram on this mala for hundreds of years. Mantras have power, and that power was invested in the beads. Somehow." Bolingbroke shrugged, wishing in passing that he did know, and smoothed the beads around her long neck. The corners of her pink lips turned up in her usual impish smile. He ran his thumb across her lips, and she puckered in a half-kiss that made his spine reverberate like a plucked guitar string. He felt someone's gaze on him, and turned to find Robert scrutinizing them. Emilie waltzed by, swishing her skirts to the tune of a song she was humming. The *Blue Danube*.

"It's not here," Hahnemann said. The old German looked disgruntled. "Maybe it's not even still in Rome. Whatever this crazy woman remembered when she was in her right mind, it's another red herring."

"Not necessarily," Laila said. Bolingbroke noticed an odd, internalized air about her. She raced past him and charged up the stairs. They all followed. She was poised like a bird taking flight in front of the painting of the Madonna and child that had caught her eye earlier. "Do you see anything in this painting that would speak to the secret room?" she asked.

"Of course not. Why would it?" Robert asked, puzzled. He ran a hand through his short red-and-silver hair. Bolingbroke noted how tired and dispirited Robert looked, and hoped Laila didn't notice. She didn't need any more stress.

Laila was studying the painting. "Because Mama painted it. It was one of her forgeries."

"Your mother didn't forge!" Robert bristled. "Laila, I know you have issues with your mother because of the fame Eleanor achieved as an artist, but really, this is too much. You're letting your jealousy run away with you!"

"Daddy, Aunt Emilie just told me that Mama had a run at forging, and this was her best effort."

"Emilie is completely out of her mind!" Robert shouted. "I've been here two weeks and she's not had one lucid moment!"

"She was lucid when she told me," Laila insisted. "She said Mama sent it with a note saying the painting was about their secret adventure."

"No one except you saw Emilie lucid," Robert said.

"Well, excuse *me!*" Laila shouted.

Fern, whom Bolingbroke liked for her pleasant lack of drama, laid her hand on Robert's arm. "Robert, we will take Laila at her word." Fern patted Laila. "What are you thinking, Gonzo? How does this relate?"

"It's nothing obvious," Laila said. But her eyes snapped, and Bolingbroke knew she was prowling down the trail to something. "Look carefully!"

The rest of them crowded in to peruse the painting. "There's nothing there to indicate a secret room, nothing at all," Hahnemann grumbled.

"Kristofer, I'm disappointed in you—you, of all people, who should know how to look with eyes that see," Laila said, with mock disapproval. She winked at Bolingbroke. "It's a Leonardo."

"Not a real one. Your mother loved Leonardo; is that why you think it's her forgery?" Robert said doubtfully.

"My mother knows everything about Leonardo, everything that would make a painting a real Leonardo," Laila said. She reached up and snatched the painting off its hook. She flipped the painting over. "Look!"

A few lines of tiny, indecipherable writing were scrawled across the back of the canvas. "Leonardo!" Hahnemann exclaimed. He grabbed the painting from Laila's hands.

"No, Eleanor Sidwell Cambridge," Laila said dryly.

"It's backwards, the writing," Hahnemann said.

"Of course. Mama was practicing."

"I can read it, but I'll need a mirror to do so," Hahnemann announced.

"I won't," Robert said, quietly. He took the painting from Hahnemann, studied the back for a moment. He lifted his head, looking contrite. "Laila, I—"

"Forget it, Daddy. You have so much else to apologize for. Besides, I'm just so happy to see you again." She waved at him. "Read the inscription."

Robert took a deep breath and lowered his brows in concentration. "To Emilie, my dearest of all dears, to commemorate our adventure. All my love, Eleanor."

"Good for Mama," Laila said brightly.

"That doesn't tell us where the room is," Hahnemann said.

"Daddy," Laila said, smiling. A lock of her red hair hung in her face. Bolingbroke restrained himself from smoothing it back and kissing her.

"I don't understand. What are you getting at?" Robert puzzled.

Laila sighed. "Didn't you live with her for twenty years? What was Leonardo's hallmark? What authenticates a Leonardo painting?"

"An expensive expert with expensive equipment," Hahnemann growled.

But Robert was smiling, his gaze not leaving Laila's. "Underpainting," Robert said. "Leonardo painted slowly and got new ideas, and he'd just paint over what he was doing. There's always underpainting in a Leonardo masterpiece."

"Where does Aunt Emilie keep the acetone?" Laila asked.

Now Bolingbroke had reason to smile. "There's no need to ruin a perfectly lovely piece of art. My vision can resolve to any depth." He took the painting from Robert and walked to stand by a lamp, then let his eyes gauge the paint thickness. It took a few moments. Then, there it was, under the Madonna: another painting. Three small figures, a villa, rooms in it like an elegant architectural rendering, one room with a tiny painting of a god and goddess standing over a bleeding youth.

Past the mantle in the parlor, there was an old closet. It was now covered over with fading twenty-year-old peacock wallpaper, but the outlines of the door were easy to feel. Bolingbroke handed me the trowel, and I cut loose the wallpaper. He pulled open the closet door.

The interior was filled with torn strips of moldy forty-year-old wallpaper hanging down off the walls. On the left side, near the bottom, was a patch of bricks.

"Fire in the hole," Bolingbroke said. We all stepped back, and he plunged his fist into the bricks. An explosion rang out. Shards of brick shot out into the parlor. Fern exclaimed and held her hand to her head.

"Fern! Are you hurt?" I cried. I lifted her hand. A piece of flying brick had caught her in her head, and blood oozed from a gash in her scalp above her right temple.

"It's nothing, just a flesh wound," Fern said. "Is the passageway there?"

"Yes, it is," Daddy said. He scrambled in after Bolingbroke. I tore a piece of fabric off my shirt and wiped Fern's head. Hahnemann went in after the other men. What was wrong with them, Fern was way more important than a secret passageway and a lost Botticelli! Okay, I understood their eagerness— but still.

"So your mother did some forging," Fern said. She raised her eyebrows at me, then winced. "Ouch!"

"When I get home, I'm going to confront her." I dabbed at the wound on Fern's head, which was a mess of black hair, torn flesh, and sticky blood. I didn't like the looks of it. "Does this hurt?"

"How did you know there was writing on the painting?" Fern asked. She didn't seem to be in pain or dizzy. Her pupils matched in size.

"The painting I saw under her bed, it was a study for a Leonardo. With Leonardo's backward handwriting on it."

"That's why you got so freaked out and we had to leave," Fern said, in a voice of dawning comprehension.

"You seem okay, but we should have a doctor look at this cut," I muttered.

"Not tonight," Fern said. "Chop-chop, round eye, get in tunnel!" She pushed me away and clambered into the closet.

"Wait!" I said. I took off the mala and draped it over Fern's head. "Wear this. Don't take it off. It makes you invisible to vampires."

"You'll need it," Fern argued.

"I've got Bolingbroke!" I leered suggestively and Fern giggled, and then we were both scrambling through the tunnel. I felt relieved that she was protected.

The passageway slanted downward. Then, once again, I found myself breathing dank, musty air in the resonant dark. The room was much smaller than the warehouse in Jersey, but it felt just as creepy. I wondered if we'd find bodies down here, and I felt a little sick at the notion. Bolingbroke and Daddy held flashlights whose beams of yellow light criss-crossed the walls. They both froze at the same moment, on a face: the commanding face of the god Osiris.

"I've found a lantern, and I have some matches," Hahnemann called out. "Who knows—maybe it will work." A few moments later, a soft radiance spilled out, illuminating a small room. The ceiling was low, not even seven feet up from the floor. Three wooden chairs, a small, neatly-made bed, and a table furnished the room.

Coming Forth by Day hung on one wall.

Hahnemann set the lantern on the table, and its glow reached the painting.

"The cellar is laid out around and under this, to hide the room architecturally," Daddy said. I wasn't listening. I was drinking in the most beautiful painting I'd ever seen.

Isis and Osiris stood beside a wounded youth who was stretched out on a pallet. The youth was a sort of stock figure in Botticelli's work, a lad with curly auburn hair and chiseled features—not dissimilar from the Mercury, whose model stood here with us. Isis, too, was clearly Botticelli's invention. Her face had the heart-rending beauty of his Venus standing in a clam shell in *The Birth of Venus*, but Isis' flowing hair was raven black, and her skin was the rich color of coffee splashed with milk. Her body was lissome and feminine. She had the balletic grace of all of Sandro Filipepi's women, but she stood with none of the modest diffidence of Botticelli's other female figures. I understood exactly why she had struck and shattered Belzoni and Emilie and my mother. Isis' unparalleled beauty was married to a wellspring of female power. Isis was the pure principle of female divinity.

Isis gazed toward her husband with love and longing that did not diminish her in any way. She radiated love with her puissance. Osiris smiled back at her. He had pale green skin and a crown, and his face, while handsome, was as striking as any of the grotesqueries that fill Leonardo's notebooks, because it was full of psychological complexity. Osiris was knowing and sad, jubilant and heavy-hearted, wise and suffering all at once. He was incorruptible. Clearly a king of kings. His eyes intimated that they'd seen everything between hell and heaven. His features were slightly androgynous-looking, like a modern teen heart-throb, and his lips wore an enigmatic smile. I was dazzled. I was struck to my core.

"Wow," Fern breathed. "So this is the painting that Botticelli and Leonardo da Vinci collaborated on!"

"Botticelli painted Isis and the youth, but Leonardo produced the Osiris," Bolingbroke observed. "There is no mistaking his hand."

I gave Bolingbroke a sidelong glance. "You knew them."

"Sandro better," Bolingbroke said, with a small quirky smile. I opened my mouth to ask him a million questions, despite the wondrous painting, but Daddy was speaking.

"Leonardo and Botticelli working together," Daddy mused. "There's so much to say about it, about them."

"No time for that; the vampires are here," Hahnemann said, from the other side of Daddy. We knew we should be moving, but such was the power of this painting that we all stood in a line, awestruck by *Coming Forth by Day*. It wrung every emotion from the viewer's heart: tenderness, love, pity, envy of the love shared by Isis and Osiris, sorrow, fear, anger, rapture, exaltation. It was a miracle of beauty, a wonder, a force of nature like the Grand Canyon or Mount Everest. I didn't know whether to weep or to break into an alleluia chorus. As close as I got to prayer, this was it, this reverence I felt for the stunning work of art that hung before me.

"Why is the boy's chest open?" Fern asked. "It's gross, the way the skin and ribs are flayed open. I've never seen anything like that in Botticelli's work."

Bolingbroke uttered a small sound. "Of course! They're planting the germinated seed in the boy's heart! That's the cure! Look, there's a spindle with thread and needle by the boy's foot. He's to be sutured back together!"

"This painting is an encyclopedia of Illuminati iconography," Daddy said, his voice sounding scared. I noted the symbols on Osiris' belt, and another one on Isis' necklace. Both Isis and Osiris made subtle gestures with their hands, and for sure each of the plants and animals in the painting had complex meanings. The pallet on which the bloody boy lay also showed signs that were disguised as decorative medallions.

"A vampire heart is dead but earthy, and the germinated seed would bring it to life," Bolingbroke was saying to himself. "Only Leonardo would have had the surgical skill, after the autopsies he'd performed, to repair the chest cavity. That's how he helped Sandro's brother."

"I hate to interrupt your party," called a voice from the sloping passageway. Aunt Emilie entered the secret room. Her voice was steady and mature, her movements creaking out from middle-aged joints. "There are a dozen vampires outside the house, more are coming, and I think they're all getting ready to come in. Whatever you're going to do, do it now." She walked to the painting and fingered it with a smile. "All these years, I always wanted to see it again. Sometimes I could feel it, like an ache or an itch. But I never knew where in the house it was."

"We've found the painting, but there's no way to get it out without a fight," Daddy said. He and Bolingbroke looked hard at each other.

"It's after one; can't we just hold them off until dawn?" Hahnemann asked. "They have to sleep during daylight. If we can hold them off, we can get away."

"I've got a supply of holy water, but that won't hold them off for long," Emilie said. She went to my dad and hugged him. "Good to see you, Robert, though I wish it were under different circumstances."

"Me, too," he said. "I've missed you. Eleanor has, too."

Hahnemann said, "Very touching, but right now we need a strategy."

Something was forming in my head. A question, a notion. Was it the painting speaking to me again, in its magical way? I said slowly, "Okay, say we fight and we win and we get the painting out."

"Big if," Daddy said, bitterness edging his voice. "I wish you'd stayed home."

"I couldn't, not if you're in danger." I shook my head. "You can run away from us, but you can't keep us from running to you!"

"I wasn't running away, I was trying to protect you. Wouldn't you do that for someone you loved?" He turned his face away from me but his eyes were still fixed on me. "Wouldn't you do anything to protect your loved ones, even if it meant hurting them?"

"Probably," I allowed. Some of my anger drained away like dead leaves into a rain gutter. I said, "We can discuss it later. For now, just say, for argument's sake, the fight goes well for us. We have Hahnemann's guns for wooden stakes and silver nanoparticle spray and Emilie's holy water. We have Bolingbroke with his superpowers. Then what?"

"I take it to my home, where it will be safe from vampires. The Illuminati can come to study it," Hahnemann said. But a sly expression slicked down his even Teutonic features. I wondered how much access the Illuminati would actually be granted.

"Won't vampires always try to get it, forever?" I asked. "They won't stop until they find a way to take possession of it."

"What are you driving at, Laila?" Fern asked. "I just want to get out of here with my blood still circulating in my body!" But Bolingbroke was watching me from under hooded eyes.

"Laila wants to copy the painting and give them a forgery," Bolingbroke said. He lifted one side of his mouth in his usual ironic half-smile. "Clever. Devious. Thoroughly Lailaesque. I like it."

"I do, too." Hahnemann looked cheerful. "It'll get them off our backs!"

"I don't understand," Fern said.

"I'll make a copy. It will be similar but different. It won't have the same iconography or show the real cure. We'll fight to make the scam look good, then surrender the forgery, so they'll think they have the masterpiece."

"Two artists worked on this painting," Daddy said. "Will you be able to handle the two different hands?"

I grinned. "Daddy, please. I'm the Michael Jordan, the Tiger Woods of the faux-art demimonde. Rain Man with a paintbrush." In truth, the challenge was exciting. A three-way, me and *il Maestro* and Botticelli!

"You look entirely pleased about it," Bolingbroke observed.

I smiled and paced around the room. "We need things. A wood panel and primer and paints. A way to dry it and make it look authentic, with craquelure. Most of all, time." I shrugged. "I guess it's a bad idea. I'd need several days to do this right."

"It took you only a few hours to do Belzoni's Vermeer," Bolingbroke noted.

"That was mostly finished. I was cleaning up after Belzoni's incompetence, not starting something from scratch." I felt a flicker of pride at my skill, couldn't help it. But why should I help it? Forgery wasn't the greatest evil on earth. My mother had forged. I had forged. I was good at forging. A genius. I loved doing it. It made the myriad humdrum moments of my life worth it. It filled my life with fun, with meaning. It inspired me. I was sorry about Vivian Goran and would spend the rest of my life regretting her fate. But she had chosen to fight for her painting. I had never asked her to do so. I'd have told her to chuck the thing! Ultimately, I couldn't be held responsible for what she had done. Vivian Goran had died because of her own choices.

"Wait a minute. Is this dangerous for Laila?" Fern demanded. No one in the room answered.

"Laila, I told you about your mother's suitcases," Aunt Emilie said, brushing her hair back from her shoulders. Her fingers combed through her curls, trying to flatten them. She had a faraway look in her eyes.

"Stay with us, Aunt Emilie," I said, grabbing her arm.

"I'm not leaving. Not yet. I'm trying to remember something. Sometimes my memories are scrambled even when I'm really here." She laughed shortly, sadly. "That's the worst of it. What's eroded when I'm back to know it's gone." Her eyes seared into mine. "I told you that your mother stored her forgery tools here."

I looked over and met Daddy's eyes. He didn't flinch, just gave me a compassionate look. He was sorry for doubting me. He was sorry for hurting me. I wasn't going to stay mad at him forever; what would be the point? He did what he felt he had to do, the best he could at the moment. Maybe I would have done the same thing. Maybe not. No way to know. I nodded. "Yep, you said that. Mama forged." Saying the words aloud made me grin suddenly, although I couldn't say why. Vice loves company?

Emilie nodded. "One of the suitcases has pigments and brushes."

"What about the other suitcase?" Daddy asked.

Emilie took a cigarette from her pocket and stuck it between her lips without lighting it. It seemed to steady her. "I opened it and looked. It held a half-painted canvas." Emilie inclined her head toward *Coming Forth by Day*. "It wasn't finished, but there was no mistaking what she was up to. She was trying to recreate that from memory."

Chapter 23

I WAS WELL INTO COMMUNION WITH BOTTICELLI, and enjoying Leonardo's presence at my shoulder, when the vampires broke through the ballroom windows upstairs.

Aunt Emilie had taken me to a guest room on the third floor. We pulled out old boots and shoes in boxes and found matching suitcases, vintage Royal Traveller soft-sided orange pieces. One was larger than the other. We didn't open them, but raced with them back to the secret room. I paused to glance out a window at the circle of shadowy figures ringing the house. They stood unmoving as statues. A shiver shook my whole body. I spent a moment in terror then forced myself into calmness.

"There have to be a hundred vampires outside," I told Bolingbroke, when we made it back to the secret room. He was loading one of Hahnemann's hawthorn stake guns and demonstrating its action for Fern.

"Fifty-three of them," he said to me. "What did you find?"

"The suitcases. Her suitcases." I knelt and unzipped the first piece of luggage, the smaller one. I sat back on my heels. There before me lay the mother lode of antique paintbrushes and jars of crumbling pigment. "Holy Toledo!" I cried. "This is a dream come true!"

"Not with fifty-three vampires about to break in and kill us," Fern said. Her voice sounded strained. She'd come too close to death at Kadja's hands to feel as cool and collected on the inside as she looked on the outside. She held the gun, tested its weight in her hand, practiced sighting along its barrel.

"That's been specially designed for the hawthorn arrows," Hahnemann told her. "Note that there are no arrowheads on the stakes. The ends have been sharpened, that's all."

"I prefer cedar," Bolingbroke added. "Fern, center on the chest when you shoot."

"The silver tubes have a simple pump action for spraying," Hahnemann said, demonstrating.

"When we run out of ammunition, we'll have stakes for hand-to-hand," Bolingbroke said.

I ignored their preparations for battle. I lifted out jar after jar of dried pigments, marveling at how clean they'd been kept. There was even a jar of oil and a small hand grinder for making the paints. "Sweet lord of mercy and all things holy, terra verte," I said, clutching it reverently to my chest.

"All as clean and tidy as your mother always leaves things." Daddy sighed. He stood over me with his arms crossed. He shook his head. "Oh, Eleanor."

"God bless Eleanor, she's going to save our bacon this time!" I cried. "If she hadn't had a pass at forging, I don't know what we'd do!"

"*Ecco*," Emily said. She lifted a canvas from the other suitcase. I rocked back on my heels. The others crowded around. It was an unfinished painting, with the outlines of the gods. The wounded boy on the pallet had been largely completed. The background was a typical Botticelli landscape. It held the figures, wasn't a character in its own right. I understood the choices my mother had made with the landscape, and it was proficient. But I would have done it a little differently and made it sublime. Was I a better forger than Mama, as Mama had told Aunt Emilie?

Upstairs, a rock went through a window. The tinkling of broken glass sounded on the floor above us. We all exchanged glances. "Now is a good time to get to work," Bolingbroke said. I set the painting on the table and examined it, which was necessary even with vampires about to burst in. There was a process. The process had to be respected. The process could not be short-circuited.

"Look, Mama's not so great. Look how thick the impasto is here," I muttered happily. The ugly smattering of impasto made me impossibly, wildly out-of-context, snidely happy. The old exalted feeling warmed my veins. "Come on, Eleanor, is this the best you could do?" I looked at the others. Who could help me?

"Kristofer, you grind the pigments for me. I bet you know how to do it," I said. "Give the weapons to the others. You're my assistant. I'll work faster." Hahnemann toddled over, and despite the severity of the situation, the gleam in his canny blue eyes told me that I'd chosen wisely. He was happy to be a part of my work. My wonderful, unique work, at which I was the best in the world—I, Laila Cambridge, who could not sing, dance, multiply, or conduct myself in a scholarly fashion. But I could wield a paintbrush, oh yes, and that was going to redeem us this night.

"We hold them off until Laila finishes the painting, and then we surrender it, reluctantly," Bolingbroke said, tersely. His fangs were long and sharp, muscles stood out on his arms, and his chest looked beefier.

"If I get bitten, will I die?" Fern asked, looking pale.

"Not necessarily," Bolingbroke said. "Only if you're drained."

"Turned into a vampire?" she asked.

Bolingbroke shook his head. "That takes…intention." He looked around the room. "Emilie, hide the other painting where it can't be found," he went on tensely. "Robert, Fern, you're with me. We'll make a stand on the first floor, in the ballroom, keep the vampires away from Laila and the forgery for as long as possible so she can finish the painting."

"I don't know what we'll do about drying the painting," Daddy muttered.

"I have an idea about that," I said.

Emilie bolted up the tunnel with the real *Coming Forth by Day*. Fern and Daddy scrambled up after her. Bolingbroke lingered for a moment. He lifted my face with a finger under my chin.

"You understand what this means, having found the painting," he said. His voice was husky and replete with ache. Real hope twinkled in his eyes.

I smiled back. "We found the cure. You can take it. We can be together!" With that he kissed me, fiercely. It was brief but I tingled all the way into the core of my being. I was going to forge, my forgeries were superior to my famous mother's, and the man I'd fallen in love with had figured out how to be with me. It was a sweet moment.

Then he was gone, and I set the terra verte in front of Hahnemann.

So, finally, I understood Sandro Filipepi, also known as Botticelli. He was far more humorous than his delicacy of figures and grasp of female beauty would have suggested. Vasari wrote of Sandro's fondness for jokes; I had read that.

It was another thing entirely to experience it for myself: the play of ribaldry in the man's consciousness, his restless imagination that seemed satisfied only with painting and drawing and laughing. He was shrewd and easily moved to admiration. He loved and hated with depth, and experienced the greatest range of feelings of any artist I had ever forged. He experienced light as a form of delight. I could have fallen in love with him, had he not been long gone, and I not already in love with Bolingbroke.

Then there was Leonardo. At a certain point, Sandro moved aside, and Leonardo slipped into my consciousness. I was not prepared for the level of thought, the complex and entirely graceful integration of consciousness and creativity, that characterized *il Maestro*. I could only witness in awe. But he was gentle and kind and encouraging, and I understood why his peers had loved him.

The fugue state waned as the painting neared completion. I became aware of glass shattering, of furniture falling and breaking, of screams and shouts and growls from upstairs. The sounds were frightening, alternately thunderous and soft, full of threat.

"I go," Hahnemann said softly. "They need me."

"I'm done," I said. I sat back and rubbed my eyes. "Send Bolingbroke down." Hahnemann nodded and left at a trot. I was groggy and exhausted but I noticed that he pulled something out of his jacket—a gun. Would it be effective in this battle?

The table was littered with brushes and pigments and I put them away hurriedly. I didn't stop to clean anything, I just screwed lids on jars and bundled brushes together. I filled the suitcase and zipped it shut, wiped off the table with my shirt sleeve. My mother would have been appalled, but what did I care? Her impasto was nowhere near as good as Botticelli's—or mine. I had just proved something to myself that I'd always needed to know. I felt resolved in a new way. It felt good.

More glass shattered upstairs.

"You sent for me?" Bolingbroke said. He was panting, and his eyes glowed with orange-red light. Veins had risen on his neck and swollen arms, and his fangs were fully extended. Splotches of a black substance, like tar, covered his shirt and pants.

"That energy column thing you do, I need you to do it."

"Now?" Bolingbroke shouted. "Right now? I've been holding off to conserve my strength. This battle will go the whole night! Why do you want me to do it?"

"The painting must be dried. Mama didn't pack a laser in her bag. Lasers weren't even being used when she was in the game." I stood back from the table and indicated the painting. "I noticed that your energy column radiates intense light and heat—Kadja was badly burned. That ought to do the trick."

Bolingbroke gasped. "It's beautiful! It's perfect!"

"Yes, it is," I agreed, accepting his verdict with well-earned pride. No other artist had the skill to do what I had done: finish the forgery so that it was indistinguishable from the real painting—except in a few details. They were important details. The boy's throat was open, not his chest. Osiris proffered a sharpened piece of wood that stuck up out of a loaf of bread covered with garlic, not a germinated seed. The symbols on belt and necklace and medallions, the flora, and the hand gestures had all been subtly altered. My real genius showed itself in keeping the figures the same. Osiris exhibited the same intensity and complexity with which Leonardo had painted him— because Leonardo had actually painted him. And Isis was Sandro's, her face so ravishing that I wept while recreating it. My mother would have been envious.

Another crash sounded upstairs. Fern cried out. "Dry it!" I said urgently. Bolingbroke dropped three stakes into my hand. Then a tornado hovered in front of me. It moved toward the painting. I watched for a moment as the tornado radiated itself close to the painting's surface. The wet oils hardened and cracked, with little popping noises and the acrid smell of burning minerals. No point in waiting for Bolingbroke to finish, no time to congratulate myself further. The pride of accomplishment, knowing that I was finally as good as my mother, would suffice. My family and friends were fighting for their lives. They needed every hand.

I ran up through the tunnel.

A pitched battle was in full heat. Vampires in the form of huge predatory birds flew in through the ballroom's oversized windows. Most then changed into human form but some flew around the ceiling, shrieking. Some vampires leapt through the windows already in human form. Fern and Emilie were shooting both vampires and birds with hawthorn guns, and Daddy was spraying silver. Hahnemann fired silver bullets out of the gun I'd seen in his hand; with his other hand, he sprayed the silver nanoparticles. Those who'd been hit fell, writhed, shrieked, and bled the tarry black stuff I'd seen on Bolingbroke's clothes. Several lay howling on the ground, staked somewhere not quite close enough to the heart. When they died, the staked ones either imploded into a running gutter of inky goo, or they exploded, spewing body parts all over the giant room. Emilie, Daddy, and Hahnemann all bled from fang marks. Fern was unscathed.

Vampires screamed and fell, but more kept coming. There seemed to be an inexhaustible supply of the undead. Our biggest advantage was that the vampires could not see Fern. Every time one eluded a hawthorn arrow or a spritz of silver, Fern sidled up and shot it through the chest with a hawthorn bolt.

"Laila, here!" Hahnemann tossed me a vial of silver spray just as a giant raptor dove in through the window at me. Its beak swiped my shoulder, tore open my shirt, and left my blood streaking my flesh. I fumbled with the cap on the vial, and the bird changed into a male vampire who lunged at me, fangs leading the way. He got me in the upper arm and dragged me hard onto the floor before I managed to squirt him. A fine, fragrant mist sprayed out on him, wafted over his mouth and eyes. The effect was immediate: he howled and rolled over, convulsing. He screamed, and his body contorted into the fetal position. Then a stake stuck out of his chest.

"Got him." Fern smiled. She ran toward Daddy, who was battling two vampires at the same time. I didn't have time to act on my terror—I just lurched toward Hahnemann. Another ghastly black bird attacked me, and I sprayed it before it shifted its shape. The bird dropped out of the air, screeching, but not before it had gashed open my other arm with its scalpel-sharp talons.

"We're running out," Hahnemann said, when I stood next to him.

"Goody! I came for the fun part, hand-to-hand," I said. A tremor went through me. I knew what hand-to-hand combat with a vampire meant: certain death. Only Fern, with the mala, or Bolingbroke, with his superpowers, could stake a vampire before being killed. Two more birds came at me; I got one with the silver spray but the other turned human and dropped to his knees, sinking his fangs into my waist. I couldn't help but scream with fear and pain. Then I dosed him with the silver spray.

"Last vial. Spray conservatively!" Hahnemann said.

"I'll remember that the next time one has its teeth in my intestines," I hollered. A concerted scream from many dying vampire throats made it hard to hear anything. But the stream of incoming birds, and vampires in human form clambering through the windows, was dwindling.

"I'm out!" Fern shouted. I waved at her to get away from the action. She couldn't be seen, so she could bide her time safely. Then a pair of female vampires who'd been crawling along the floor toward me leapt up, unscathed. They launched themselves at my arms and I fell backward, pinned. Fangs entered my neck from both sides. *This is it*, I thought. But Hahnemann yelped, and the two ladies screeched. As their bodies flopped with seizures, I scrambled out from underneath them. I got whacked by flailing limbs, but the bruises and fang marks meant nothing. I was still alive.

"I'm out," Hahnemann said, from behind a mound of vampire bodies. He stuck his snub-nosed gun into his pocket and clenched a stake.

"I'm out," Emilie said. "And the tickle is coming to my brain."

"I'm out," Daddy called, from the corner of the room. He pulled two of Bolingbroke's stakes from his belt. A giant vampire bird flew toward him, and Emilie threw her gun away and grabbed a large flask that was tied to her belt. She poured some water into her hand and tossed it at the incoming bird. Where the droplets landed on its back and wings, steam rose. It rolled over in flight like a glider performing a loop-de-loop, and smashed into the wall.

"Laila," gasped a voice from the closet. I glimpsed Bolingbroke on his knees, but I didn't have time to attend to him. A staked bird had fallen on Fern, and its talon had snapped the string of the mala. Beads rolled everywhere. Fern stood in the middle of the room, defenseless and suddenly visible to the vampires. Several birds and two humanoid vampires rushed at her.

"Fern!" I yelled. Her terrified face turned toward me. I threw the vial at her. She missed it and dove to the floor after it. I threw myself after it, too, scrabbled on my hands and knees, grabbed it and slapped it into her hand. She was spraying as the first vampire closed on her throat. It fell away in agony. A thrill of relief went through me.

Then I realized that I was defenseless.

"Now you're mine," came a purring voice. A bird had dropped from the ceiling and transformed into Kadja. She stood before me in a slinky red satin dress, her black hair hissing around her shoulders. She glanced over at Hahnemann. "Daddy dearest, you're next."

"Kadja, *mein Gott*, sweetheart, no," Hahnemann yelled back. "Please, child, leave this place without hurting anyone. I beg you!"

"But, Daddy, this is a party! Just the kind of party you dressed me up for, that night when you put me out on the lawn with the special lilies you said would call angels to me." She smirked and fixed her eyes on me, on my neck. "I knew I'd enjoy this moment." Her mouth yawned open, white fangs glistening, and she aimed herself at me. I closed my eyes. I didn't want to watch Kadja close on me. Sharp regret, sharper than fangs or talons, sliced through me. Now I'd never find out if Bolingbroke could be cured and we could be together. I'd never get to tell Mama that I'd seen her forgery—that I'd finished her copy of *Coming Forth*. I'd never get to share the art history department gossip with Daddy, now that I'd found him. A million stupid thoughts went through my head. It was amazing how silly the mind could be in its final seconds. At least I'd saved Fern's life.

A shudder of surrender went through me. I felt oddly relaxed. But there was a thud: someone leapt in front of me and took the blow meant for me.

Daddy.

My father is a big man and he swung his fists like hammers. Daddy held a stake stake in each fist, but he hadn't managed to land one, and Kadja wasn't fazed. She struck him back, sent him flying through the room. He crashed into a wall and moaned. Emilie was dousing everything that moved with holy water, and she was trying to make her way over toward Kadja, but Kadja was too fast. Kadja leapt toward my father and pummeled him. It was horrible to watch, his teeth splattering out of his head, welts rising up all over his body, blood streaming from his broken nose and dozens of cuts. I screamed and ran toward them. Hahnemann tackled me.

"No, Laila, *Zaubermaus*, he means to save your life," Kristofer said, urgently. I fought him, tried to shake him off, but the old German was stronger than he looked. He clung to me, held me down. I glanced around at the dozens of dead and dying vampires. Kadja was the last one standing.

Bleeding horribly, my father stumbled to his feet. He hit back. He sailed through the room again, thrown by Kadja. She was on him in a flash, throwing him again and again. I couldn't bear to watch. I couldn't bear to let this happen.

"Leave him alone!" I screamed. "Come here, you bitch, come get me!"

Furiously I wrestled with Hahnemann. I couldn't let Kristofer hold me down. I had to help Daddy. I'd just found him, after all the years of worrying about him and missing him, and I couldn't lose him again. I would not let this happen. I had to have my time with Daddy. I had to get back those missing years. Mama and Brad needed him, too. I would not lose my father now!

"Let go of him, Kadja, you bitch!" I screamed. "I'm the one you want!" With a mighty heave, I flung Hahnemann off me. I raced toward my father, stood over him and looked around for a stake or splinter of wood from the broken furniture. If nothing else, I had my bare fists. Panting, I faced off with Kadja.

"I'll kill you while your father watches, then I'll finish him," Kadja gloated, laughing. She lunged toward me, but now Hahnemann hurtled toward her, his hand raised. He got her in the arm with one of Bolingbroke's little stakes. "Aaaah!" she screamed and dropped to her knees. Hahnemann's hands seemed to sparkle, and then he threw a glistening silver net, finely spun as spider webs, over Kadja.

Of course, Hahnemann had come prepared.

"Now, Kadja, *mein liebes Kind*, you are mine," Hahnemann said. He knelt and pulled the netting taut around her body, securing her. He stroked her face as she writhed.

"Daddy!" I cried. I dropped to my knees beside him. "Daddy, oh, Daddy." He was shattered, broken bones sticking out of his arm and thighs, blood soaking his shirt and pants. He was panting and groaning. I knew at a glance that he was wounded unto death. Everything inside me went still and cold and hard and scared. It felt like a band of steel had wrapped itself around my chest, and I couldn't breathe.

"At least she didn't get to drain me, right, Little Goofy Bird?" Daddy was trying to smile. He couldn't because he was in such terrible pain. Arterial blood pumped up from his thigh in rhythmic pulses. I tried to apply pressure, but he shook his head. "Just hold me."

"Bolingbroke! You can save him. You can turn him!" I turned toward Bolingbroke, who still lay on the floor, half in and half out of the secret closet. I was desperate for a way to save my father. I cried, "Like that woman you almost killed, who you turned to save her. You can do that to my daddy. He'll be a vampire and he'll keep going, and then we'll use the cure on him."

"I haven't the strength," Bolingbroke said weakly. "I can't move right now. And there's no certainty that the cure will work for Robert. He could be condemned to eternity as a vampire."

"That's an eternity he won't have if you don't save him!" I begged.

"No, Laila. No. I don't want to be one of those things, not even for ten minutes," my dad said. He smiled a little. "Not after being Eleanor's husband and your father and Brad's father. That's what I'm proud of. That's how I want to go."

"No, Daddy, please! I don't want you to die!" I wrapped my arms around him and cradled his head, putting my cheek next to his. His skin was cold, and brought a flood of tears to my face. "Daddy, I'm so sorry. I love you. Please, Daddy, I'm so sorry."

"Me, too," he croaked. "I didn't mean to hurt you and your brother and mother."

"I know," I said, and the knowledge that ached through me was worse than anything I'd ever felt. Would I ever be whole again, knowing that he'd given his life to save mine?

He gripped my arm. "Promise me...."

"What?" I was crying incoherently. "Anything!" I meant it. Anything he asked me for, I'd do. I owed him that.

"Take the painting to the Illuminati. The real one. They need it. Don't let Hahnemann hoard it." Blood tricked down from one eye that had turned into pink jelly.

"I won't let him. I'll make sure they get it!" I kissed his cheek and forehead, which just smeared his blood around his face. I hugged him close. "Don't worry, Big Goofy Bird, I'll see that the Illuminati get that painting!"

He tried to smile. "I love you. Tell Eleanor and Brad I love them, too." He twitched. "It's all been worth it," he murmured. Then his silvery red-haired head rolled to the side. He was gone.

I cried in deep, unhinged gulps and sobs. I couldn't move or let go of him. Fern and Aunt Emilie dragged Bolingbroke out of the closet toward us, then Fern sat next to me with her arm around me. We sat together, shell-shocked, bleeding from multiple wounds. Hahnemann was bent over Kadja, murmuring to her. Emilie put her arm around me on my other side, though her face had lost its maturity and she was telling her *nonni* that crows had invaded the attic.

"They'll be back. We don't have long," Bolingbroke said. "I can't get up. I spent all my energy on the painting."

Who cared? Let them come back. All that was left was grief.

"There's got to be something we can do to restore you," Fern said. Fern. Her soft voice reminded me that I wasn't the only one here. I had to rouse myself to help Fern. Daddy would want me to save her. And myself.

"He needs some of your holy water, Emilie," I hiccupped. "It restores him."

"We have to go to church for holy water, *Nonni*," Emilie said, in a simpering little-girl voice. She wiggled, and the bodice of her gown gaped open, revealing that she was losing blood from a long gash that started on her clavicle and went down almost to her nipple. Fern let go of me and crawled over to tend to her. Fern left a trail of blood, too. She also needed tending. We all needed serious medical attention.

I sat, crying silently and hiccupping, staring at the grotesque heaps of dead vampires, at my father. My sweet, strong, loving father, who had sacrificed himself for me. Was I going to make his sacrifice meaningless? No. I was going to do what was necessary to save myself and the others. I let Daddy's body slide off me. It was the hardest thing I'd ever done. I crawled over to Bolingbroke. Our eyes met. He knew what I was going to do. His face shuttered over.

"No," he said. "I forbid it."

"You have to," I said. I smeared my hands at my face, wiping off the tears. "We need you to be strong. Or we all die. You're all we've got left."

"I won't be able to stop myself. And I may, I may turn you. Sexual intensity is part of the formula for that," he murmured. "You know how I feel about you!" His eyes blazed, briefly, before dulling.

"We'll pull you off her," Hahnemann offered. He'd caught on, shark that he was. "So much depends on this, Herr Bolingbroke. Everything. You must save us and the painting. I must save my daughter; it is what I have lived for, these last two decades. She has been staked, and I can handle her while she is weak. But I must remove the stake soon, else she dies."

"You're our last hope," I said. I pushed what was left of my paint-spattered sleeve off my arm, extended my wrist to Bolingbroke's mouth. He closed his eyes. Then he growled, caught my arm in his hands, and lunged. The last thing I saw, before delirium, was his fangs flashing.

I don't know how to describe the next few minutes. My father's death, the vampire battle, forging Botticelli—it was all forgotten as bliss coursed through my veins. Every muscle, every particle of fascia, trembled with pleasure. It was orgasmic, but deeper than any climax I'd ever experienced, and I'm no slouch in that department! Nothing remained except the fire of pleasure burning me up from the inside out. I moaned and writhed in ecstasy.

"Enough, Bolingbroke, enough!" Hahnemann was shouting. I parted my lids to see Fern and Emilie beating Bolingbroke. Hahnemann was slapping him, too.

I didn't want Bolingbroke to stop.

"*Basta, basta*, Nonni, you're done!" Emilie jumped on Bolingbroke's back. She tried to strangle him, but he paid no attention at all.

"John, stop! You're killing her!" Fern shrieked.

And all it once, it ended. I fell backward, more fatigued than I'd ever been in my life. Of course, a lot of my blood was now missing, so that was a factor.

"What have I done? I'm sorry! Laila, Laila, speak to me!" Bolingbroke grabbed my shoulders. I felt too drowsy to answer and just let him shake me. "Laila, I mean it, answer me! *Now!*"

"Holy cow," I murmured. "Do that again!"

A quarter of an hour later, the vampires returned. Before that, barely conscious, I had been propped up against the wall where I could see everything— when I was awake. It was a kind of grace to be semi-conscious, because while I still felt the pain in my heart over my father's death even when I drifted off, I didn't relive the beating he'd taken. When I was awake, I kept seeing it in my mind's eye, over and over again: the blood, the jellied eye, the bones protruding through his skin. Fern covered me with a blanket. Emilie was singing Italian nursery rhymes, but she brought me a little glass of fortified red wine—real wine, not mud—which made my dream state very soft indeed. Bolingbroke, who seemed keyed up and full of fire and fettle, knelt next to me and kissed me, deeply, lingeringly.

"Carissima, your sweet, sweet blood was amazing. It has given me the strength of a hundred vampires," he whispered.

"You already had that," I murmured. *Kadja was beating my father, he was sailing through the air and crashing into the wall....* Even Bolingbroke's kiss couldn't stop the images from rolling past. I turned my head to see Kadja. Kadja moaned and thrashed her head from side to side. I hoped she was suffering. With what little vitality was left in me, I wanted to behead her. Stake her, burn her. Watch her suffer and die. *Let me have vengeance,* I prayed.

"I am even stronger now." Bolingbroke smiled. "I can finish what we started, see it through to the end. When this is over, I'll undergo the cure, and we will be together!"

"Something to look forward to," I said, trying to keep my eyelids up. When you're almost out of blood, it's hard to stay alert. *My father was smiling at me as blood geysered up out of his thigh....* It was much better to be unconscious. Bolingbroke kissed my forehead and went to stand in the center of the room.

Fern and Hahnemann stood next to Bolingbroke. Emilie meandered off somewhere. I wasn't sure how much time passed, because I was in and out of consciousness. But I saw it when a dozen black birds dive-bombed through the windows simultaneously.

Bolingbroke was ready. He spun into the whirling energy column and tore through the first six, chopping them into feather and meat confetti that littered the grotesquely stained floor. Then he transformed back into himself.

The other six birds transformed into a line of vampires who neither advanced nor retreated, but just posed by the windows, a line of soldiers at attention. Then a last giant bird sailed in, unfolded into the stately Native American man.

"Intihuaca," Bolingbroke greeted him.

"John Bolingbroke," Intihuaca said. "My old coven mate."

"It has been more than a century," Bolingbroke said, impassively.

Intihuaca shook his head once, slowly, his red eyes fixed on Bolingbroke. "It is true, what Kadja told us. You are not as you were. You are not one of us."

"I am not." Bolingbroke indicated the shredded vampires. "Do you wish to take me on?"

"No," Intihuaca said. "Nor do you wish to take us on." Bolingbroke inclined his head, acknowledging the truth of Intihuaca's words.

"We are at a stalemate," Bolingbroke said. "Dawn arrives, the sky lightens. I suggest you leave. There will be another night for us to meet."

"I will not leave without what we came for," Intihuaca said.

"We wait," Bolingbroke said. He stared out the broken windows. Pink streaks lit up the horizon.

"If we leave now, we will hunt you forever," Intihuaca said. "Let us negotiate."

"No!" Kadja screamed. "Kill them! Do not deal with them!"

"What do you propose?" Bolingbroke said. His voice was cold.

"We have come for the painting," Intihuaca said. "We will take it. In return, you and your..." he gazed around, his eerie eyes lighting on Fern, Hahnemann, me, and Aunt Emilie, who was dancing, "your domestic pets will not be hunted or harmed."

Bolingbroke appeared to reflect. "This is the bond of your great age?"

"Yes. My years hold the truth of this."

Bolingbroke gestured to Hahnemann, who grabbed my *Coming Forth by Day* and carried it toward Intihuaca. Hahnemann set the painting down in front of the Indian. Intihuaca gestured at one of the vampires in his line. The man came forward, knelt, and examined the painting. He looked familiar. With a jolt of surprise, I recognized him as an art history professor from Harvard who was rumored to have died ten years ago. The professor ran his fingers over the surface of the painting. He leaned close and sniffed. He examined it as carefully as could be done without equipment. Then he rocked back on his heels and nodded at Intihuaca.

Intihuaca snapped his fingers, and another one of his minions took up the painting, turned into a giant bird, and flew out with my masterpiece clutched in its talons.

"Free the wounded one. We will take her," Intihuaca said, looking at Kadja. "That is part of the bargain."

"No! She is my daughter, my child!" Hahnemann shouted. "You may not have her!"

"She is one of us now," Intihuaca said. "She is my daughter now." He gestured, and two of his vampires went toward Kadja. They reached toward her, and then paused. They straightened and glared at Hahnemann.

"Release her," Intihuaca ordered.

"No! Kadja is mine," Hahnemann said. The next moment, quicker than a heartbeat or a blink, Intihuaca held Hahnemann in the air, by his throat.

"I have no fondness for you, Nazi," Bolingbroke said, in a steely voice. Intihuaca threw Hahnemann to the ground.

"I always liked Nazis," Intihuaca said, with a smile that made me shiver. "I give you one last warning. Unbind the wounded one."

Hahnemann gasped and rubbed his throat. Tears rolled down his face as he crawled over to Kadja. "*Mein Liebling*," he whispered. His hands shook as he unwrapped the netting from her. She hissed at him. Hahnemann pulled the netting and she rolled, unsteadily, to her feet. She was covered with black tar, and cradled her arm as she limped toward Intihuaca.

Intihuaca gestured again. The other vampires turned into birds. Kadja shot a scorching look at me. I met her gaze evenly. It was not over between her and me, no matter what Intihuaca had promised. Kadja knelt at Intihuaca's feet.

"Lilith will not be pleased," Intihuaca said to Bolingbroke.

"I no longer answer to Lilith," Bolingbroke replied. Intihuaca nodded, and turned with no preamble into a giant bird. The bird hovered in the air, its rapacious avian glance sweeping around the room, taking us all in. It grabbed Kadja in its talons. Then it was gone.

I was left with an old memory: my father visiting me at boarding school, taking me skiing for the weekend. He loved to ski, and was good at it. I insisted on snow-boarding, which he found to be *brutta figura*—bad form. But, true to his nature, he tolerated my antics with good humor. Another boarder nearly ran me off a trail, and when we rode up the lift to the next peak, I complained about it. "I could have gone off the side of the mountain," I said to him.

"Boarders—you know, they're immature. But, Laila, I would never let you go off the side of a mountain. I'm right here for you, always," he'd said, and smiled.

And now he'd gone off the mountain instead, and left me alone on the trail.

Chapter 24

I WAS IN MY OWN BED, SLEEPING. Sunlight fell on my face, and I stretched luxuriantly. Sunlight! I sat upright. My room! In New York!

I rose, and found myself wearing Curious George and a pair of boxers left over from Fern's last boyfriend, the druggie bum. I pattered over to my window and looked out. There were the familiar brick backs of the townhouses on the street that ran parallel to ours. Disjointed images trickled in: a plane ride. Hahnemann holding *Coming Forth by Day*. Bolingbroke carrying me up the stairs to our apartment. Fern covering me with my quilt. A coffin loaded into the bay of the airplane. Someone in a white coat standing over me, putting in an IV—yikes! There was a bandage and a purple bruise where it had been removed.

"You're awake. How do you feel?" Bolingbroke said, from my doorway. He looked tall and scrumptious, as always, in a white shirt and black pants. He held a steaming mug. "For you. Tea."

I accepted the mug gratefully, took a deep swallow. Wakefulness seeped into my brain. Caffeine, my favorite. "A doctor came and gave me a transfusion?"

"The Illuminati sent one," Bolingbroke responded. "You were nearly out of blood. You were transfused on the plane."

"I feel better," I said. My memory seemed foggy, but I felt physically whole. Something in the back of my mind tugged at me.

"Good to hear. I have a gift for you. Two, really." He smiled, and went back out of the room. I sipped my tea. Steaming Earl Grey with lots of milk and sugar, exactly the way I like it.

Bolingbroke returned with two packages covered in shiny, expensive blue and green wrapping paper, the high-end kind you buy at specialized stores. The packages were rectangular and flat. Paintings.

"A bread basket," I sang. He lifted up one corner of his mouth in his ironic half-grin. He sat down on the edge of my bed and handed me the larger gift first. It was good-sized, three feet by four feet, a substantial piece. I could have opened the wrapping delicately, paying attention to the tape and keeping the paper intact. But where was the fun in that? I tore through the wrapping with glee. One look at the painting: richly hued, the abstract black form of a woman bounded by a shocking, aggressive explosion of color—"De Kooning? Is this a joke?"

Bolingbroke was laughing at my indignation. "You once told me you approved of primal energy and sexual compulsion...."

"You unloaded millions of dollars on this piece of crap? Wait, is this a forgery?"

"No, of course not! Only one person in the world could forge this well." Bolingbroke was still laughing to himself. Good that I could entertain him so well with my outrage. He asked, "You didn't do this one, did you?"

"Please, no. Look at the borders here. I would have chosen—"

"Sweetheart, that is an actual Willem de Kooning piece. Those are the actual choices he made."

"Hmph. Well. Every artist has off days. I can't believe you got this for me."

Bolingbroke raised his eyebrows. "Would you like me to take it home?"

An actual de Kooning, huh? "No, no." I waved with noblesse oblige. "Since it's a gift and all. I'll hang it my bathroom or something." I rested the painting against the wall and hopped over to settle on Bolingbroke's lap. I kissed his cheek and his forehead, and squirmed so he could feel my bottom in his lap.

"Yes, that's what everyone should do, hang a twelve million dollar painting above the toilet," Bolingbroke agreed, dryly.

"Glad you think so," I said. I kissed him for real. He reciprocated, with enthusiasm.

"Here, open the other one," he said, a little hoarsely. He scooted me off his lap and laid the smaller package in my hands. Again, I tore through the wrap. The Leonardoesque Madonna and child. Mama's Leonardo forgery. Aunt Emilie had given it to me. Before the vampires came.

Before my father's death. "Daddy," I whispered. My throat closed up. My heart burned like old leaves drying into dust. I was alive now because my father had saved me. He had given his life for mine. The images from the battle, unrecalled until this moment, tumbled back into my memory, stark and unrelieved and as bruising as the tools of an Inquisitor. My father thrown through the air by Kadja. My father's eye beaten into pulp, his bones smashed out through the skin. My father broken and bleeding in my arms, apologizing, telling me he loved me and my brother and mother.

Daddy's really gone now, forever. Just when I found him. I cried and cried. My tears dripped onto the painting. I'd cherished so many plans, during the years of my father's absence, plans of what we'd do together once he was back. Plans I'd barely acknowledged to myself, though they lived fervently in secret inside me. And then I found him. We were supposed to have time together, time to make up for what we'd lost. No sooner had I found him than I'd lost him. He'd left me alone again. This time, it was for good. I'd never felt so alone and so empty.

Bolingbroke laid his hand on my cheek and turned my face toward his. He kissed my eyes and the paths of my tears. "I'm sorry," he said. He turned my face to look into my eyes. I remembered that I wasn't alone anymore. I had Bolingbroke. Bolingbroke whom my father had asked to protect me. It was almost more than I could bear.

"I'm sorry, too," I said. My heart was swollen with love and loss and hope and closure. "I have to see my mother today. She has to know," I whispered. I rose and went to the window. "Give me some good news. Tell me when you're doing the cure."

Bolingbroke's eyes dropped to the floor. "Laila, I love you. I will always love you."

There was bad news. My heart, already full like a river bursting its boundaries, nearly drowned me in the unbearable sadness emanating from Bolingbroke. My voice broke. "Say it, half-soul."

"The Illuminati doctor. He examined the painting, and he examined me.

He says my heart's not like a typical vampire heart; it won't withstand the procedure."

"Won't withstand it?"

"Won't survive," he clarified.

"You'll die if you take the cure?" I said, not quite comprehending. "You can't take it, then."

"I will if you ask me to," he murmured, with a look of tenderness so profound that it shattered what was left of my composure. I ran back to his sheltering arms.

"Of course you won't take it, you fool," I said. "I can't let you risk your life. I can't lose someone else I love!" Then he held me while I sobbed. Fern heard me from the living room and came in and sobbed with me, curled into Bolingbroke's chest beside me.

An hour later, I was showered and dressed and semi-coherent. I was full of ache that felt like it had no beginning and no ending. But I had to hold myself together for the task ahead of me. Besides, there'd be a tiny mote of pleasure in the day, when I showed my mother her old forgery. Then she'd fall apart at the news of my father's death, and I'd have to hold her. I dreaded that, but I had to do it.

Bolingbroke and I went into the living room, where Fern sat on the couch, holding a box of tissues. She had cried for almost as long as I had, then showered and painted her toenails seashell pink. Now she had her feet up on the coffee table, with tissues separating her toes, and other tissues in her hands to dab at her swollen eyes. She never cried, my stoic roommate. It was going to be a while before we were both back to normal. If ever.

"'My neighbors mocked me while they saw me pass, so empty handed back,'" Bolingbroke said to her. His voice was sad, and I sensed that he was telling Fern how it went with me by means of poetry I could not identify.

But I would try. Isn't that what I do, who I am? I always try. That's what Daddy would have wanted me to do: to keep on trying. "Elizabeth Barrett Browning?" I asked hopefully.

"Christina Rossetti, *An Apple Gathering*," Fern said. She threw down the wadded paper and came to hug me. She didn't even stop to pull the tissues from her toes. I wish she had; it would have meant that she was healing. She whispered, "Are you okay, Laila?"

"No, but I need to borrow Dex's car," I said. I started to sniffle again, and it made Fern's eyes run with tears.

"We're going to see your mother," Fern said. She gave me a serious, approving look. "I'll get my purse. And shoes."

I slipped my arm around her slim, dear shoulders. I wasn't as alone as I felt, when the tidal waves of grief over my father's death swelled up over me. I had Fern. I had Bolingbroke, even though he had to remain at a distance, for now. They both loved me. I was lucky. My dad would have wanted me to dwell on their love, not on the unbearable loss. He had wanted me to live. He'd proved his desire with his life. I intended to live, to honor him.

I pushed Fern away, gently. She couldn't help me with what I had to do. It was my burden alone.

I said, "Not this time, Fern. I'm going alone. Brad is meeting us up there." I smiled. "Besides, I have this painting to show her." I indicated the Madonna and child in my tote bag.

"Call me if you need me. I'll be waiting," Fern said.

"So will I," Bolingbroke said. "And take my car."

"Not if it still smells," I said. "Whew—Fern and I made a stinky mess of that Bentley." We all laughed a little, which was a pretty good start to my journey. Both of them were holding me, and I could take that affection with me, too.

ACKNOWLEDGEMENTS

I must thank Lori Handelman, whose wonderful editing skills helped shape this novel.

I always thank Gerda Swearengen for her loving support and wisdom.

Stuart Gartner has been a source of humor and sage advice, and I am grateful. 1-800-STU-KNOWS-BEST.

I am grateful to Lane Shefter Bishop for her ongoing support and encouragement, especially regarding IMMORTAL.

I would like to thank Mary T. Browne for her warm support and good advice. I am also very grateful to Komilla Sutton for her support and belief in me. Dr. Daniel Booth Cohen has been of profound help and encouragement.

Victoria Wells Arms has copy-edited and cheered my writing: thank you! You have beautiful children!

Rachel Leheny is the best drinking buddy in the whole world, and one of the smartest people.

I am grateful to Kirstin Peterson for her copy-editing. Charlie Robb read an early draft: thanks!

I am most grateful to everyone at Telemachus Press and to genius Joe Mills at Black Sheep Design.

I send love and gratitude to: Caitlin Alexander, Dani Antman, Thomas Ayers, Barbara and Stephen Baldwin, Ali Baldwin, Matthew Baldwin and Dana Harlan, Timothy Baldwin and Megan Adams, Lori Belilove and John Link, Paul Brodeur, Michelle Czernin von Chudenitz, James Cooper, Kristin Gamble and Charlie Flood, Tommaso Gobbi, Elizabeth Haase and Andrew Meyers, Debra Jaliman, Alain Kattnig, Sue Perillo, Stephanie Kip Rostan, Geoffrey Knauth, Marcia and Howard Levy, Jennifer Weis Monsky, John Morehouse and the Salmagundi Club, Frederick Morton, Margery Newman, Sarah Novotny, Rusty Shelton, Don Steelman, Peter Thall.

A special thank you to Steven Beer, who always rocks.

I am grateful to my four daughters for their constant inspiration: Julia Howard, Jessica Hendel, Naomi Hendel, and Madeleine Howard. You are the reason for everything; you are all wonderfully imperfect, and so lovable.

Finally, to Sabin Howard, thank you most of all.

ABOUT THE AUTHOR

Traci L. Slatton is a graduate of Yale and Columbia. She lives in Manhattan and travels regularly to Italy, which inspired her historical novel *Immortal* and her contemporary art history mystery *The Botticelli Affair*. Her romantic dystopian After Trilogy is made up of *Fallen*, *Cold Light*, and *Far Shore*. *The Love of My (Other) Life* is a bittersweet romantic comedy. *The Art of Life* is a photo essay about figurative sculpture, and *Dancing In the Tabernacle* is her first book of poetry.

www.ingramcontent.com/pod-product-compliance
Lightning Source LLC
Chambersburg PA
CBHW070102260626
47160CB00004B/1287